DEITY

CREATION

PAUL MEE

Published by Tribes Press 2020.

This paperback edition first published in September, 2020.

Tribes Press policy is to use papers that are sustainably sourced from manufacturers with EU Ecolabel certification and FSC® and PEFC™ chain of custody certification.

ISBN 978-1-912441-24-2

www.tribespress.com

To my wife Sheena and my daughter Charlotte

Part I

Genesis of Creation

Chapter 1

Extract from Progress Report 30.153 – Section 15 'Deity Creation'

As has been referenced in prior reports, the enthusiasm for belief in a divine power remains steadfast. This unique factor was the catalyst for the recommendation in Progress Report 23.134 that an experiment be instigated to create a single deity to replace the multiplicity of deities that were developing. The results from that attempt, despite the investment of significant resources, have been far from impressive, notwithstanding initial encouraging results.

The single deity has only been accepted by a small percentage of the population with the majority unwilling to change their beliefs. Most extraordinary is the fact that those who have accepted the single deity, are the subject of widespread religious intolerance. The experiment is at a point where it requires further resources to allow it the chance of achieving its objective, otherwise the experiment will stagnate and ultimately fail.

On balance, the objective of creating a single deity on Earth remains a worthwhile pursuit in the context of the wider plan, so it is recommended that a team be set up to re-energise the project. The team will need members with a proven history of adaptability, a wide range of skills, and the attributes of creativity and ingenuity. The team will have to be led by an individual with actual experience in the area. Our suggestion for team leader is Professor Yiler, head of the theology department of the arts university in the central capital on Deusi Prime.

****

Yiler was not happy. He was commuting to work on a Monday morning, squashed into a crowded and stuffy Undertram, with a couple of hundred other glum looking middle-aged commuters. The windows were wet with condensation due to the air conditioning malfunctioning again. He placed his hand on the collar of his shirt and pulled it away from his neck to allow some air to circulate to his chest, which was damp with sweat. He was still suffering the after-effects from his going away party at the university, which didn't help with his perspiration. He had at least had the sense to have it on a Saturday night, but his legendary inability to consume even a moderate quantity of alcohol had doomed him to a ferocious forty-eight-hour hangover that kicked in early on the Sunday morning and was only now beginning to dissipate. If asked how he was feeling by any of his fellow passengers, which would have been unprecedented, he would have replied 'barely tolerable'. However, the main reason for his unhappiness was where the Undertram was taking him and why.

He sighed loudly, a common occurrence during the three days since he had received the 'e-mail of doom', as he referred to it. He had been comparing the religious belief on a recently discovered planet with those he had already researched, when his computer had alerted him to an incoming e-mail. He had opened it and was horrified when he saw its contents. It was a letter informing him that he had been reassigned. He was to be transferred to the Sub-department for Administrative Affairs within the Department of Labour, with only three days allowed for a handover. He had sat there rereading the letter, hoping that it was a mistake or a practical joke. When he realised that it wasn't, he had tried and failed to think of any justification for him being transferred to a role not relevant to his skillset.

Yiler had never left a task uncompleted; the idea was alien to him, so he wasn't going to depart from his theology department without a fight. He had immediately contacted the dean of the university and reminded the dean that, for ten years, he had devoted his life to the formation of the department of theology. Every obstacle he had encountered, and there were many, had been successfully overcome. It would be ludicrous to transfer him just as the department was beginning to gain acceptance within the academic community. He had argued that it was only he who would have the commitment to secure its long-term future. The dean had agreed and suggested that Yiler should put in a written request that the transfer be reviewed. His staff member and students sent supporting e-mails. There were only five. He only had one assistant and four students. As well as forwarding Yiler's letter of protest, the dean had made representations on his behalf. She had assured Yiler that she would get it resolved, so he was devastated when the answer came back that there would be no change.

A despondent Yiler had spent his last three days in the theology department handing over his work in progress. He was bemused that his replacement was coming from the accounting and finance department. Perhaps the love of money and the love of a deity were one and the same. Neither he nor his replacement were sure about that.

He sighed again when the intercom blared. "Parkland Station, next stop." Either the automatic announcements were not working that morning, or the driver was keeping himself amused by making personal announcements. He groaned and stood up along with about half of the commuters on the Undertram. The Undertram usually ran on time, so he left the station on schedule which pleased him because he hated being late for anything. He looked around when he walked off the escalator and saw a forest of homogenous grey office blocks. He thought that whoever named the Undertram station 'Parkland' had an ironic sense of humour. He started to compare what he saw now to the tree-lined thoroughfares and manicured lawns of the university but stopped himself. It was pointless. This grey mess of office blocks was his new home for the foreseeable future, and he just had to accept it. He headed over to the office block where the Subdepartment of Administrative Affairs was located and arrived on schedule at nine o'clock.

The building where the subdepartment was located had no signage on it. Yiler surmised that this was in keeping with its low profile. Yiler hadn't known there was such a subdepartment within the Deusi Civil Administration until he received his letter. He entered the building and walked over to the security desk, where he spotted a very small sign indicating the tenant of the building. Even to his untrained eye, it was obvious that a substantial amount of money had been spent on the security system, as he observed top of the range equipment everywhere. The security guard looked up. She eyed him up and down suspiciously. "Can I help you?"

"I'm sure you can. My name is Professor Yiler. I am starting a new job with the subdepartment today. Here is my work assignment letter."

The security guard took his letter and placed it over a scanner. A green light flashed on her computer. She sniffed audibly. "You are on the visitor list. Please place your hand on the scanner." Yiler did as he was ordered. "Your supervisor will meet you shortly. Here is a temporary badge. Do not lose it. Your permanent one will be ready when you leave later. Don't forget to pick it up. Take a seat over there." She indicated where he should go with a nod of her head to the right.

Yiler had been in a bad mood when he came in, and the abrupt attitude of the security guard nearly pushed him over the edge. He was biting his lip as he sat down in the waiting area. It was a small space, bordered by a veritable jungle of plants with a couple of seats arranged around a small table. He took out his e-reader. He was about to turn it on when the intercom barked.

"No electronic devices are permitted in reception."

Yiler looked up to see the security guard glaring at him from her security station. "Did you not see the sign?" She helpfully pointed toward a sign on the wall.

"Sorry, I didn't see it because of the hedge." Yiler put away his e-reader, but he couldn't contain himself any longer. "You could have just told me without the dramatics of the intercom. I'm only a few metres away." Yiler grinned as the security guard gave him a withering look before turning back to the flickering security monitors.

****

General Lateel was reading the latest meeting minutes of the board of Special Operations Executive, or SOE for short, when she received an e-mail from security that Yiler was waiting for her downstairs. She was delighted with the interruption, as the minutes were unbelievably dull. She decided to leave him there for a short while to increase his anxiety in the hope that it might make him more amenable to what she planned to propose to him.

While she sat there, she ran through the approach she would use to persuade Yiler to lead an experiment on Earth. She was looking forward to his reaction when she revealed the fact that it was fifteen hundred years since the initiation of the experiments. It had all started with the discovery of Earth by an SOE ship and the imagination of the infamous Commander Gerton. While the news of finding a planet with a sentient species should have been immediately passed to the civilian administration, Commander Gerton perceived a unique opportunity for the SOE and decided not to do so. Since Earth was a planet that only the SOE knew about and its remote location made its discovery by anyone else unlikely, the SOE could do whatever it wanted with Earth. Commander Gerton had proposed targeted societal and behavioural engineering on Earth's sentient species. The SOE board had initially been less than impressed and concerned about the legal ramifications, but Commander Gerton carried on pursuing his idea regardless. He had argued that since the species on Earth was physically like the Deusi, it made successful societal and behavioural engineering a real possibility. Commander Gerton eventually presented his idea to the full SOE board and it was approved by a small majority. Commander Gerton had been proven right, as all the experiments had been successful, apart from one which had stagnated, with a considerable amount of useful knowledge gained.

Lateel stood up and stretched her head to the side with an audible click. She took a deep breath as she entered the lift and focused herself on the task of convincing Yiler to become a key part of reenergising that stalled experiment.

****

Yiler was starting to become annoyed at having been left waiting and had just begun to inspect one of the plants encroaching on the tiny seating area, when he heard a lift opening in the lobby. A female leaned part way out of the lift. "Professor Yiler?" she called, as if she was trying to find one person in a large crowd.

Yiler stood up and made a point of looking around to make sure that other people had not entered reception without him noticing. "I am Professor Yiler."

"Excellent. If you'd please join me." Yiler walked over and stepped into the lift. "I am Lateel," said the female. She took her hand away from the lift door and offered it to Yiler who shook it briefly as the door closed. "I will be your supervisor."

"Best wishes to you," said Yiler politely.

"And best wishes to you also."

Lateel looked at Yiler closely. "Are you alright? You look pale."

Yiler groaned. "Leaving party at the university."

"Why on Deusi did you have it last night?"

Yiler looked offended. "I didn't, it was Saturday."

"That must have been some party."

Yiler considered telling Lateel about his chequered history with alcohol but instead decided to change the subject. "Can you tell me what my new job actually entails? The letter was less than illuminating. I take it that you are in some way responsible for my being here."

"If you don't mind, I will explain when we get to my office." Lateel stood ramrod straight with her hands clasped behind her back, staring at the lift doors to avoid eye contact. Yiler took the hint, and they lapsed into silence. He glanced over at Lateel for a second. His first impression was that she was unlike any civil servant he had ever met. He would guess military if he didn't know any better. She was about ten centimetres taller than he was and much broader. Her tight fitted uniform emphasised her toned and well-muscled body. His 'I should really work out more' flabbiness did not compare well. His eyes were fixed on the lift door when he decided to break the silence with some small talk.

"Is Lateel a created or inherited name?"

"Inherited. I got it from my great grandmother on my father's side. You?"

"Inherited as well. I got it from my grandfather on my mother's side."

"He must have died young."

"He did. It was a gravflyer accident."

"They were unpredictable when they were first introduced. Much more reliable now."

The conversation ceased when the lift pinged, and the doors opened. A second security station awaited them. After placing their hands on the scanner, they were cleared to pass by the security guard. Yiler couldn't fathom why such tight security was required in a civil administrative department. They entered a long, well-lit corridor that contained a lot of doors with names on them. Lateel's office was the second on the right, so they reached it after a few seconds and went in. Yiler had always prided himself on keeping a tidy office, but Lateel's office was a class above his. There was no paper or clutter anywhere.

"Please sit down." Lateel offered him one of the two seats in front of her desk while she sat behind it. Yiler sat and watched Lateel as she looked in one of the desk drawers and fished out a couple of documents. "Before I explain your new role, you need to sign these." Lateel pushed the papers over to Yiler who picked them up and read them.

"Why do I have to sign two non-disclosure agreements. What could I possibly be doing that requires me to sign these?"

"You need to sign first, and then I can tell you. If I tell you and then you refuse to sign, I will have to kill you." Lateel did not laugh when she said that. Yiler picked up a pen and passed the signed pages over to Lateel.

"I have signed them on the basis that I am still not legally bound to take this job assignment."

Lateel ignored him. "Welcome to the Special Operations Executive. I am General Lateel. Your rank is colonel, so you can address me as general or sir. I don't mind which. I hate madam though."

Yiler sat there with his mouth open. It was thirty seconds before he spoke. "This is crazy. There must be some mistake. What use would I be to the military? You do know that I am a professor of theology, don't you?"

"Yes, I am aware of that. The SOE is not a branch of the military. We are independent of them. Membership of the SOE board is hereditary, and everyone on the board is a lineal descendant of a founder. No one applies to join us. If we have a project that requires exceptional people, we have them reassigned to us. You should congratulate yourself that you are one of those people."

It suddenly occurred to Yiler that his right of privacy might have been infringed. "Did you have me under observation? You must have, to make a statement like that."

"Of course, we did. You had the required expertise to work on a key project, so we assigned an operative to you. We have been observing you for three months and have been very impressed. I note that you never spotted our operative. We have superb people."

"Self-praise is no praise. Are you newly formed? I don't have any recollection of hearing the SOE name previously."

"Don't let the fact that you haven't heard of us fool you. The SOE has been in existence for a long time. Our current location is just part of our strategy to keep the SOE under the radar."

"What exactly does the SOE do?"

"Our role is to guide and shape current events to fit the long-term policies of the Deusi government."

"What is the long-term strategy of the government? Like many others, I've always wanted to know." Yiler's tone was dripping with cynicism, which Lateel chose to ignore.

"Let me answer a question with a question, which I know is rude. What is the thing that irritates you most at present?"

Yiler thought for a moment. "Apart from being here in this office with you?"

General Lateel frowned. "You are aware of the concept of insubordination, aren't you?"

"Please accept my apology. Apart from being here in this office with you, sir?"

"Adding sir at the end doesn't change anything. In answer to your question, yes apart from that, what irritates you most?"

"Then, with that exclusion, the answer is the Santu."

Lateel was not surprised by his answer because the Santu were extremely unpopular with the Deusi. Shortly after the Santu had successfully tested and produced the first Faster Than Light, or FTL drive, 1,750 years ago, they had commenced the exploration of surrounding star systems. It didn't take them long to encounter another race, the Flambi, who were also experimenting with FTL technology. The Santu and Flambi founded the Federation and started a joint exploration programme seeking more first contacts. The Federation was now comprised of twenty-eight races, twenty-five of which were full members, with another three on the pending list.

The Deusi has developed FTL technology and formed a loose alliance with five other star systems sixty years before first contact with the Federation took place. The Deusi had not reacted positively to the Federation and disagreements with the Santu surfaced immediately, and those arguments had worsened in recent years. The Federation portrayed itself as a benign entity that promoted mutually beneficial contact with any race that it encountered. However, the Deusi and their allies were not convinced about joining. They perceived it as a significant threat to their way of life, because only races that adopted Federation economic principles were admitted.

The Deusi alliance had a monetary economic model. The Santu had developed the same model but subsequently abandoned it for a civic model after they concluded that a monetary economy had several structural and unsolvable problems. The Santu's primary argument was that the prosperity of any society and the well-being of its citizens should not and could not be determined by a monetary economy. Monetary based economies have peaks and troughs, impossible to forecast or determine in advance. In addition, the triggers for economic downturns could not be discerned in time to stop them happening. It was illogical to have the quality of people's lives, both on an individual and planetary level, determined by an uncontrollable monetary economy.

The Santu also concluded that, in a monetary economy, consumerism takes over, and the gathering of material possessions becomes the prime objective. The Santu determined that the gap between those who succeed in a monetary economy and those who don't becomes wider and ultimately unsustainable. The inevitable creation of a class of permanently unemployed, underutilised young adults and their alienation from society could be avoided in a civic model.

When first contact took place with the Deusi, the Santu, in order to encourage the adoption of their civic model, issued documents demonstrating that there were no economic troughs or peaks or excessive consumption within the Federation. They promoted the fact that Federation citizens contribute freely to bettering society and are not concerned with gaining material wealth. Every Federation member had accepted those arguments and adopted the civic economic model. The Deusi and their allies had not agreed. They decided to retain their monetary based economy, a decision that barred them from joining. As the Federation expanded and colonised more planets, tensions with the Deusi alliance increased as it also expanded and colonised but without any prior agreement or discussion with the Federation.

"What specifically about the Santu?" asked Lateel.

"The fact that they frustrate every attempt by us to involve ourselves into the Federation without us agreeing in advance to their impossible list of conditions, which is clearly never going to happen. Not being a member makes it impossible for us to colonise planets and expand."

Lateel nodded in assent. "I agree wholeheartedly. Every time we discover a habitable planet, the Federation arrives with excuses as to why we cannot colonise it, and we don't have the military muscle to start a fight with them. We can't carry on like this much longer. Our home worlds and existing colonies are close to their population limits. Having our excess population as workers on Federation space facilities is not sustainable or desirable."

"The tension between us and the Federation is getting worse day by day, and it has the potential to spill over into armed conflict," said Yiler. "I don't believe what the media tell us."

Lateel was very pleased with how the conversation was progressing. "Nor should you. I knew that I was right about your potential. I fully concur with your analysis. The long-term policy that you enquired about, is to reduce the influence of the Santu over the Federation. We can only do that by joining the Federation and eventually usurping them as the leading member."

Yiler leaned back in his chair and folded his arms. "That's an ambitious long-term goal. Before we go any further, I must emphasise again that I haven't said that I would join yet. I just signed the non-disclosure agreements. You still haven't told me exactly what I would be doing?"

"Have you ever heard of a planet called Earth?"

"No, I have not."

"Well, that's good. It shows our security protocols are solid. Earth was discovered by us about fifteen hundred years ago. The planet is populated by a sentient race which we called the humans. We have been carrying out some societal and behavioural engineering experiments on Earth since then."

"I'm far from an expert in the area, but isn't that illegal?"

"It's a grey area. Anyway, we have become fascinated by the fact that the humans have an unprecedented level of belief in divine powers. They have a multiplicity of gods. The human ethnic groups, of which there are many, believe in different gods. We want to attempt to create a single deity that all humans will believe in."

Yiler was stunned. "Why would you want to attempt to do something like that? What could you possibly gain scientifically?"

"We want to see if we can create a single deity religion and then control the civilian population through the hierarchy and structure of that religion. There is no permanent central government on Earth and no prospect of one in the medium to long term. We think that a religious administration can operate as effectively as a civilian administration. With your background in theology, we think that you are the right person to lead this project."

"This is completely crazy. The concept is ludicrous. Most importantly, I have absolutely no idea how to do this. How can I go to an alien planet and create a deity for them to believe in?"

"We are not expecting you to do this on your own. We will provide the resources you need."

"I don't know what resources I will need to achieve the impossible."

"Maybe a computer, a pen and some paper." Lateel laughed at her own joke. "Don't worry. I have assembled a very strong team for you. You will have a sufficient budget, and your own ship for the duration."

"How long is the duration likely to be?"

"Barring unforeseen circumstances, you will have an unfettered run on Earth for fifty years. No other experiments will commence in that period. Any ongoing experiments are in their second stage and will just run their course while you are there."

Not for the first time, Yiler was rendered speechless, and there was a long uncomfortable silence as Lateel's comment sunk in. "Fifty years is a lifetime."

"Yes, I'm aware this is a major commitment on your behalf."

"I guess the facts that I live alone, my parents have deceased, and I have no procreations had a bearing on me being nominated for this. No one will miss me."

"Yes, plus the fact that you had no pets." Lateel laughed again, but Yiler didn't.

He took a deep breath. "Hold on a second. I just want to go back to what you said about the SOE and government policy. Are you telling me that creating a divine power on this planet is part of the long-term strategy?"

"The short answer is no. The elongated answer is that it couldn't be government policy because the civil administration does not know about the existence of the planet. Earth was discovered by an SOE scout ship, and it was decided to keep the discovery within the confines of the SOE. That is about to change though, as the president will be informed shortly about Earth."

"This gets worse and worse. It's an SOE solo run." Yiler sat there with his hands on either side of his face, moving them slowly up and down. "Let me think about this." Lateel sat waiting silently for his response. After three minutes, Yiler turned to her and said, "Okay, I can hardly believe that I am saying this, but I'm interested. I still don't see how this can be achieved, no matter what you give me."

"Let's head down to a conference room to meet your medical advisor and assistant programme chief, Dr Nowlett. When you have seen and heard her presentation, you might feel more optimistic." General Lateel left her office with Professor Yiler following.

"Dr Nowlett?" said Yiler as he hastened to keep up with her long stride.

"Affirmative. It seems that you have heard of her."

Yiler looked surprised. "Of course, she is the leading medical device innovator of our generation. I am a great admirer of hers."

"Really, an admirer. Have you met her in person?"

"I wish. I just follow her on some of the professional social media platforms."

"That explains it then."

"That explains what?"

Lateel said nothing and just smiled. Since no response was forthcoming, Yiler carried on talking. "I have tracked her career through the many research papers that she has published on the data place. I am surprised that you managed to persuade a female of the quality of Dr Nowlett to join this madcap venture."

"I'm not really comfortable with the use of "madcap" as an adjective for this project. Once Dr Nowlett understood the extent of the challenge, she was hooked. You'll see why."

****

Dr Nowlett sat in the conference room waiting for Lateel and Yiler. She was working on her computer, updating the graphic capability to keep herself amused. General Lateel had asked Dr Nowlett to prepare a presentation on the biology of the humans to help convince Yiler that creating a deity could be done. She was one hundred percent confident that she could convince Yiler but was not looking forward to having to do it.

Dr Nowlett was not generally comfortable with social interaction, especially with males. She knew from prior experience that she could create a bad first impression, General Lateel being the latest unfortunate example. She tended to say the first thing that came into her head. In the "General Lateel incident", she had just advised that, in her opinion, a career in the military was a life with long periods of boredom, punctuated by brief moments of sheer terror with nothing to show for it at the end. Unsurprisingly, Lateel wasn't fully in agreement and a lengthy, and somewhat heated, debate ensued.

Her comments were frequently perceived as being sharp or blunt. People formed the impression that she either lacked empathy for the person she was addressing or was simply rude. She felt that impatient was a fairer description. All she wanted to do was to get to the conclusion of a discussion as quickly as possible and move onto other matters, and the best way to do this was to get straight to the truth.

The HR director in Biotech Inc, where Dr Nowlett worked previously, had tried to help. She had advised Nowlett to pause before she spoke to assess what the other person might be feeling, use humour, and not to take everything literally. On her problems with males, the HR director assured her that they were nothing to do with her and were probably due to most males having incurable genetic idiocy. Dr Nowlett had immediately explained to the HR director why idiocy could not be a genetic trait, at which point the HR counsellor had given up.

Surprisingly, Dr Nowlett was not fazed by large group presentations. She had given hundreds of them in her time in Biotech Inc, the larger the group the better, as far as she was concerned. She felt as if the end of the stage was an invisible barrier between her and her audience, and that she could set the terms of any interaction with the audience, which relaxed her. Her favourite ones were where she presented to a group of her peers. The question and answer sessions were invigorating, requiring her to fend off the barbs and bat back the curve balls, some subtle some not, contained within her colleague's questions. She heard the conference room door open and stood up as Lateel and Yiler walked in.

"Professor Yiler, may I introduce you to Dr Nowlett and vice versa," said Lateel.

"Best wishes to you." Nowlett put out her hand and Yiler shook it.

"And to you."

In his excitement of meeting Nowlett, Yiler forgot to let go of her hand. "Dr Nowlett, I am thrilled to meet you. I am an avid reader of every research paper you publish."

Nowlett was not accustomed to protracted male handshakes, so she removed her hand politely from Yiler's grasp. She remained motionless apart from gently rubbing her hands together. Yiler just stood there with his hands by his sides. Lateel was confused. Yiler had barely glanced at her, but his reaction to Dr Nowlett was the response that Lateel generally received from males. Somewhat arrogantly, she had assumed that Yiler was not interested in females, but it seemed that she was wrong. Lateel was primarily attracted by physical beauty, so she couldn't understand what Yiler saw in Dr Nowlett, who in her view was a diminutive, plain looking female.

Yiler had developed a bad case of dry mouth and swallowed to clear it. "I have tracked your career from your earliest research papers. Everything you write is both innovative and thought provoking. I also enjoy your posts on professional social media."

"Thank you very much. I wish I could reciprocate your kind comments, but I hadn't heard of you until a few days ago when General Lateel announced that you were to lead the Deity Creation Group. Your department of theology doesn't have a high profile because it is so new, which is probably why your name is unfamiliar." Lateel put her elbows on the table, rested her chin on the tips of her fingers and shook her head slowly from side to side.

Yiler ploughed on bravely. "I suppose that I could take offence at that but, to be fair, you are not the first to say that, and what you say is after all true."

Nowlett smiled grimly. "If everyone had such a reasonable attitude to hearing the truth, my life would be far less complicated. I'm sure I would have heard of you in time."

"You probably would have. I had great plans for the department. Remember that big trees can grow from small seeds."

"Growing it would have been challenging. You were studying something that doesn't exist. What is the point of that?"

"You really do get to the point, don't you? I was studying why some races are predisposed to believe in something that doesn't exist. That is the purpose of the department. I am not trying to prove that a deity exists. That would be pointless."

Dr Nowlett scratched her chin. "An interesting view, Yiler."

Both Yiler and Nowlett lapsed into silence. Lateel was surprised by the exchange and congratulated herself on finding two people who already looked like they had the makings of a solid leadership team. Lateel decided that she better end the awkwardness. "Dr Nowlett, I am sure that you want to get down to business, so without further ado, let's start your presentation." Dr Nowlett did as requested, and her first graphic was a picture of a ship. "This the *Nubla*."

She was surprised by the blank look from Yiler who decided he better say something. "It looks old."

Lateel laughed. "Yiler, you need to get out more. Seriously, you must have heard of the *Nubla*. The big marble monument in City Park is dedicated to it."

"To be fair, it was lost circa forty thousand years ago," said Dr Nowlett. "And he works in the arts university, which is a long way from the city centre, so I am sure that he doesn't get to the central park much."

"Oh, that ship," said Yiler. "As I recollect, it had dozens of scientists on board at the time, hence the erection of the memorial."

Dr Nowlett smiled. "Correct. An SOE scout ship found a probe that came from the *Nubla*. Isn't that amazing? The chances of that happening were astronomical. I have done some calculations on it and…"

General Lateel shifted in her chair. She was already aware of Dr Nowlett's tendency to go off track. "Dr Nowlett, time is short. Could you keep to the point?"

"Did the probe shed any light on what happened to the *Nubla*?" said Yiler.

"It did. The *Nubla* was lost because its FTL drive had a malfunction that sent it off course. The probe gave us the location where the crew regained control of the FTL drive. Do you want to see a star chart that shows how far the ship went off course?" Yiler nodded, and Dr Nowlett's hands flew over her keyboard until a hologram hovered over the table.

Lateel looked surprised. "I didn't know we had holographic technology in this room."

"You didn't. I upgraded it while I was waiting for you." Lateel looked even more surprised.

"That was a major malfunction," said Yiler when he saw the distance between the flashing blue light that was Deusi Prime, and the flashing red light that marked the *Nubla*. "Not surprising that the ship wasn't found. Did we have to do a lot of searching to locate the wreckage?"

"No, the probe gave us the location of a planet that the *Nubla* was attempting to reach after the accident. They placed all their hopes on it being life bearing. The odds were in their favour because the planet was in the middle of the temperate zone. When the scout ship got there, the crew discovered sentient life on the planet. Here is what the planet looks like."

Yiler saw a blue planet shrouded in places with white cloud. "I presume that this is Earth?"

"Correct again," said Nowlett.

"Well, that is really interesting. You and General Lateel both mentioned sentient life. Doesn't that mean that we were, and are, prohibited from landing on the planet. Maybe the strict rules in force now didn't apply back then."

Nowlett glanced at Yiler. "That's a very interesting question. My interpretation of the legal situation is that..."

Lateel decided to interrupt swiftly. "Dr Nowlett, could you move on please?"

"Maybe we could discuss that later," said Yiler.

"Apologies and yes, Yiler, that would work for me," said Nowlett first with a grimace and then a smile. "General Lateel had a concern that you might not sign up because you thought that creating a deity was not feasible. She wanted me to allay those concerns. This should do it."

A picture of an alien standing upright popped on the screen, and Yiler leaned forward. "Amazing. I take it that this is a human."

"Right again. As you can see, Professor Yiler, the humans are very similar to us physically. You will observe two arms, two legs, one head. However, there is much more to the similarity than that. The humans are a carbon-based life form with varying proportions of oxygen, hydrogen, nitrogen and phosphorous within their cell structure. They breath oxygen and exhale carbon dioxide. The amount of oxygen required is very similar to the mix on Deusi Prime. They have a skeletal system, a muscular system and an integumentary system."

"What is the last item?" asked Yiler.

"The integumentary system is the largest organ," answered Nowlett. "It consists of their outer skin, plus their hair and nails. Their skin regulates temperature, keeps water and salts in balance, protects from the environment and contains the receptors for pain, heat and cold. They are covered in hair which traps warm air close to the body, assisting in regulating temperature. We have much less hair, but what we have performs almost as efficiently.

They have a circulatory system consisting of a centrally located heart and a blood system that transports respiratory gases, waste products, digested products, hormones and immune cells. The blood system also regulates heat. Their lungs are located close to the heart and intersect with the blood system to supply oxygen and remove carbon dioxide. Their cerebral organ is contained in their skulls."

"Okay, Dr Nowlett, I get it," said Yiler. "They are very similar which will pique the interest of the anthropologists, but you haven't dealt with my point that we can't interfere with the humans. Surely, even the SOE has to adhere to the Sentient Species Directive."

"The directive does not apply if the humans are a Deusi hybrid," said Lateel.

Yiler gasped and put his hand over his mouth. He rubbed his upper lip before taking his hand away. When he spoke, his voice had dropped an octave. "Are you telling me we created the humans?"

"That's what we believe," said Lateel. "The crew of the *Nubla* did it."

"And I have been considering how they did it," said Dr Nowlett. "Now, let me open up my research. It all comes back to Dr Teclo, who was on the *Nubla*. She was a genetics expert. Now, I think that…"

Lateel tapped the table sharply. "Dr Nowlett, please stop. You can discuss this theory along with your other one with Professor Yiler later. Can you give us your conclusion?"

Dr Nowlett paused for dramatic effect. "Professor Yiler, I am confident that, with only a few minor tweaks, Deusi can look like humans. The ability to have our team members interacting with humans will be a key factor in our ability to carry out our mission."

Lateel frowned. "I wouldn't necessarily agree with Dr Nowlett's definition of minor."

"If what Dr Nowlett has postulated is possible, then that would remove some of my doubt," said Yiler. "But with all due respect, Dr Nowlett, you have never tried something like this before."

"I have a prior precedent to rely upon."

"What precedent?"

"Professor Yiler, we have tried to create a single deity before, during which experiment, we successfully placed Deusi on Earth."

Lateel decided that it was time to dismiss Dr Nowlett to keep the rest of the meeting tightly focused. "Now might be the time for me to tell Professor Yiler about the enigma that is Moses. Thanks for the presentation, Dr Nowlett. You can go now."

"I'd rather stay. I enjoy talking to Professor Yiler."

Yiler and Lateel both looked dubious. "You do?" they said in unison.

"Of course. It is my first experience of intellectual equality since being harangued into the SOE."

****

When Lateel had finished running through the 'Moses Experiment', it was nearly lunchtime. Lateel declined Yiler's offer to go to lunch, having considered it for a microsecond, so Yiler and Nowlett headed off to the staff canteen on their own. When they arrived there, Yiler spotted the security guard he had met earlier on that morning. Nowlett looked surprised when he went over to her.

"How is your lunch?"

The security guard looked up in surprise. "What?"

"How is your lunch? Any recommendations for us newbies?"

"It's all okay, I guess."

"Good to know. Will I be seeing you every morning?"

"Probably. My shift is 7 am to 4 pm."

"Fantastic, I shall have a spring in my step every morning with the mere prospect of seeing your smiling happy face."

The security guard looked uneasy. "Umm… okay."

"Anyway, you enjoy your lunch. See you tomorrow."

Yiler walked back to a puzzled Nowlett. "What was that all about?"

Yiler started laughing. "She annoyed me this morning, so I thought that I would interrupt her lunch and wind her up a bit."

Nowlett nodded. "Perhaps a little petty, but understandable given her brusque personality. I've already had a run in with her. She is very insistent on ID being shown to her every morning. I made the mistake of forgetting mine once, and she gave me a hard time about issuing a temporary one for one day. Every morning she acts as if she has never met me before. It's very annoying, and I told her so when she was issuing my temporary ID. Anyway, enough about her, let's get our food and then onto the *Nubla* theories that Lateel would not let me talk about."

Yiler grinned broadly. "I can't think of a better way to spend my lunchtime. I have one major question for you. I don't believe Lateel's explanation as to why we are being asked to do this. If the creation of a single deity was that important, why wait until now to reenergise the experiment. It should have been done immediately after the Moses experiment stalled.

"I agree completely. There is more to this than Lateel is letting on, and I intend to find out what is really going on here. Yiler, I have a question for you. Are you fully committed to this?"

"I am sufficiently intrigued to invest some time into this. I will make my final decision just before our ship has to leave for Earth. Is that fair enough?"

"Yes, that is entirely reasonable. I hope you decide to go to Earth. I believe that the two of us could lead the team to successfully complete the experiment."

Chapter 2

Yiler and Nowlett had spent the four weeks since they had been introduced reviewing the profiles of team members, splitting them into two-person teams, preparing a briefing document and outlining a plan for the course of the experiment. The selection of team members had been easy thanks to Lateel. The general had given them a list of eight SOE operatives that recently had been initiated into the organisation, like Yiler and Nowlett. Yiler had pointed out that it was unlikely that he would need less than eight, so this didn't allow them any input in the team selection. He asked for more names. Lateel countered that she did not have an unlimited supply of SOE personnel available, so their choice of taking all eight was technically still a choice. Yiler and Nowlett had protested, but Lateel refused to budge.

During those four weeks, Yiler and Nowlett had spent every minute they were awake, apart from when they parted at the Central Undertram station to go to their separate homes, in each other's company. Yiler had fallen completely and utterly for Nowlett. His feelings for Dr Nowlett had come as a shock to him. He had never felt this way before about a female. He had been blown away by her intellect. He had yearned for lunchtimes and their journeys on the Undertram, where they had time to discuss diverse topics not connected with the Deity Creation experiment.

Despite all this time together, he still had no idea how Nowlett felt about him. She was very hard to read. Although he wouldn't admit it to anyone, his growing infatuation with Dr Nowlett was the reason why he had pushed aside his nagging concerns about the purpose, result and probability of success of the Deity Creation experiment. He had decided to board the ship to Earth, commit fifty years of his life to the experiment and hope that Dr Nowlett would eventually reciprocate his feelings. He was optimistic that he hadn't made the wrong decision on all counts.

Despite the prospect of losing his exclusive access rights to Nowlett, both he and Nowlett were delighted when their team was assembled for the first time on the Deusi ship *Tesfa* for their forty-day journey to Earth. The ship had just left the civilian space station at Deusi Prime. They were on the observation deck, which was located on top of the bridge, which in turn was situated above the living quarters and cargo hold. This segment was oval shaped with a short thin tube connecting it with the box shaped section containing the shuttle bay and FTL engine room.

The team was watching the ship moving to the Faster Than Light jump point. As the ship jumped to FTL, the view screen became a kaleidoscope of colour as they moved into FTL space. When the spectacle was over, they made their way back to the office accommodation which had been built in the cargo hold. Five cubicles, with two workstations per cubicle, had been constructed evenly around the exterior of the room. The workstations were small, equipped with a desk, computer, chair and either one or two pot plants beside the desks. The centre of the hold contained a large table surrounded by a low wall around which the eight other new SOE operatives were seated along with Yiler and Nowlett.

Yiler got to his feet. "Ladies and gentlemen, welcome to the first meeting of the Deity Creation Group. I am Professor Yiler, the programme chief, formerly head of the theology department in the arts university. Beside me is Dr Nowlett, head of medical affairs and assistant programme chief, formerly head of research at Biotech Inc. Both of us are looking forward to working with you. I hope this accommodation, which will be our base throughout the experiment, is to your liking." Yiler took a sip of water. "Maybe you could also introduce yourselves, starting to my right."

"I'm Captain Denned, Deusi Marine Corps, mechanical engineering specialist."

"My name is Hyet. I used to work as the IT director for an advertising company."

"My name is Sidion. I am a behavioural analyst, and I used to work in the Department of Business Enterprise. Hopefully, you will remember my name since I am the only female apart from Nowlett." There was an uncomfortable silence after that.

"I am Uhet. Prior to joining, I was a nutritionist, so I guess my job is to find food sources on Earth."

"My name is Fawter, and I used to be a private security consultant before being recruited into the SOE."

"I am Konacht, and I was Fawter's partner, in business just to be clear."

"You two are the biggest males I have ever met," said Hyet.

Fawter laughed loudly. "The benefits of personal training in the gym, Hyet. There is one on the ship so maybe you could have a go."

"If we could move on please," said Yiler who pointed at the next person.

"I'm called Cannet. I used to be a fitness trainer, so you might be seeing a lot of me in the gym as well over the next few weeks."

"I'm Commander Hennegy, Deusi Navy, last posting as executive officer of the Battlecruiser *Raker*. I'm not a fan of the gym."

"Thank you for sharing, especially your views on exercise regimes," said Yiler. "Now the team allocations. Team 1 will be Hyet and Sidion who will look after our technology needs. Team 2 will be Denned and Hennegy. You will oversee all operations on Earth. Team 3 will be Uhet and Cannet, who, as well as advising on diet and nutrition, will provide personal security. Team 4 will be Fawter and Konacht, who will also provide personal security and will be Dr Nowlett's medical assistants on Earth. Fawter and Konacht will be scheduling close combat instruction in the evenings for all team members, especially Hyet. Denned will give us the benefit of his marine training in small arms in later sessions."

"Now, with the introductions out of the way, let's discuss why we are here. The first deity creation experiment has stagnated. We have been given fifty years to re-energise and complete the project. I see that you all have a copy of the briefing document prepared by Dr Nowlett and me. I think that the document is all encompassing; it should be, given its length. If any of you have queries, feel free to come and talk to either myself or Dr Nowlett. Open door policy for both of us. Dr Nowlett will now brief you on your first assignment. Dr Nowlett, if you'd please..."

Nowlett looked surprised. "Thank you, Professor Yiler, even though I thought that we had agreed that you would do the briefing."

"Did we? I don't recollect."

"I assure you we did." Nowlett took out some written notes. "You have been organised into two-person teams, each with carefully selected complementary skill sets. The first task for each team is to document what you think we should do when we get to Earth. We want those suggestions within two weeks. Yiler and I have already done the same. We will draw from all these papers to create a final blueprint. You can now go to your workstations and start work. I hope that you get on well with your partner. No reallocations are permitted... well, at least for the first week, I suppose." Hyet laughed at her joke. Nowlett was pleasantly surprised at the response, notwithstanding that the humour wasn't intentional. "Oh sorry, one final thing to mention. Don't be constrained by what you think can and can't be done. If you have a good idea, include it, and then it will be our job to find a way to implement it. All we want from you is creativity."

Yiler stood up and started speaking again. "I want to talk about the gender imbalance since there are only two females. This is deliberate. Earth is a male dominated society, by far the most imbalanced that we have come across. In human society, females have no leadership role and are not involved in making important decisions. They are second class citizens. Because each two-person team may be on Earth for long periods, we needed to have a disproportionate number of males on the team."

"Why is their society so male dominated?" said Sidion. "No other race is like that. Not even the Santu."

Dr Nowlett took a deep breath. "I have some thoughts on that..."

"In order not to lose half a day, I'm going to interject here." Yiler smiled at Dr Nowlett, who rolled her eyes and waved her hand in acknowledgement. "Dr Nowlett surmised that the creation of a male dominated society was another SOE experiment. She pressured General Lateel on the topic and the general eventually confirmed that she was right."

"Why would we do that?" The question came from Hyet.

Dr Nowlett leant forward and placed her elbows on the table. "The SOE are implementing a series of micro experiments that have the macro objective of creating a human society that differs from normal standards."

"Again, why would we do that?" asked Sidion.

Dr Nowlett shrugged her shoulders. "I hate to disappoint, but in this case, I have no idea. I do think that General Lateel knows more than she is letting on. She won't budge though. No matter what I tried, she wouldn't give me any information. I might have annoyed her with all the questions."

Yiler nudged her arm. "We know that you have a theory, so you might as well enlighten us."

Dr Nowlett grinned. "This is pure speculation, but I think that Earth is not the only planet that we have colonised without Federation permission. I am convinced that the SOE have other secret Deusi colonies. At some point in the future, the existence of one or more of them will be discovered by the Federation. It is impossible to predict how the Federation will react. I believe that Earth is being prepared as a test case, and it will be disclosed to the Federation at a time of our choosing."

Yiler looked surprised. "Why would we ever deliberately disclose a colony to the Federation? They could resort to extreme measures when they find out."

"The SOE will be testing the reaction of the Federation to a planet that we can legitimately argue evolved naturally and is not a Deusi colony. The further human society can be removed from Federation and Deusi societal norms, the more likely the Federation will accept Earth as a natural phenomenon. We do not believe in a higher divinity, therefore, the entire human species believing in the one god with this belief as the foundation of their society, is one way of demonstrating that. If the Federation's reaction to Earth is positive, it might act as the catalyst for the disclosure of other Deusi colonies to the Federation. If the Federation resorts to the extreme measures referred to by Yiler to deal with Earth, then we will know that we have to keep the others a secret."

"So, you think we are just one small part of a large scheme to create the most abnormal society ever discovered by the Federation," said Yiler.

Dr Nowlett perceived a general feeling of incredulity as she gathered up her notes from the table. "It's logical when you consider the unique features of Earth. There are the multiplicity of languages, hereditary dictatorships, slavery, human sacrifice, xenophobia, widespread acceptance of currency and casual brutality to other species to which features will now be added a single deity. I also think that the DNA evidence might be of help in us arguing the natural evolution point, but that requires more research before I postulate a theory. Now, before Professor Yiler complains about me wasting any more of your time, let's create a deity."

The team members, apart from Yiler and Nowlett, left their seats and walked over to their workstations. "Good speech," said Yiler.

"Thanks, but you know damn well that we agreed that you would do it."

"Yes, but it was a perfect opportunity for you to break the ice with the rest of the team, and I couldn't let you miss the opportunity. Please don't thank me, I'll only get embarrassed." Yiler turned with a broad smile and walked out before Nowlett had a chance to reply.

****

Hyet smiled at Sidion as she sat down beside him. "Welcome to Team 1."

"Thank you, Hyet." She shook his hand. "Should we start by exchanging some personal details?"

"Good idea. I am thirty-five, no procreations, that I know of anyway."

"I am thirty-two, also with no procreations. I am sure about the procreation bit."

Hyet grinned. "I imagine you would have noticed having a procreation. I see that you have adopted the current trend for shaved heads. I have adopted the same style, but mine wasn't a choice."

Sidion smiled broadly. "Premature baldness, I presume. Well, at least you don't have to shave your head every couple of days to keep the look."

"There is always a bright side, I suppose. Pity that everyone else has a full head of hair. I fear our team will soon be named 'Team Eggheads'."

Sidion sighed. "I wouldn't be happy with that."

"Me neither. What do you think of Nowlett and Yiler?"

Sidion scratched her gleaming head. "I haven't decided yet. I'm leaning towards weird."

Hyet grinned. "They have an odd chemistry. I am sure that you spotted that little bit of sniping and griping during the introduction. I don't have a view yet as to how effectively they will lead the group."

"They did a good job on our team. Our professional skills certainly suit each other."

"Indeed, but that means we have no excuse for not coming up with some brilliant ideas," said Sidion. "Did you see that we are being asked to act as the group's communications and technology experts."

"I did," said Hyet. "I would not consider myself an expert in the area. You?"

"Not really. When we finished our work on the blueprint, we won't be bored anyway. A lot of manuals to be read and digested."

"I perceive one positive in our assigned specialism."

"What is that?" said Sidion.

"Very few trips to Earth, if any. We won't be able to bring a lot of technology down to avoid raising suspicion among the natives, so we will spend most of our time on the ship. Have you ever travelled in a drop pod?"

Sidion grimaced. "Once, it was horrendous."

"Same here. I hated it."

Sidion laughed. "Well, in order to make sure that we don't get transferred from our technology role, we better get started on the blueprint and leave enough time for the manuals."

Hyet suspected that Sidion might have been more diligent than he on reading the material provided by Yiler and Nowlett, so he decided to start posing questions to disguise the fact. "Having read the briefing document, what is your assessment of religious belief on Earth?"

"Well, let's start with the Roman Empire, which is the largest and most civilised political area on Earth."

Hyet laughed. "The competition isn't very high for that title."

"True. Can you remember how many gods they have? It was in the document."

Hyet looked blank. "Not exactly sure. Ten... twelve?"

"A lot more than that. There are Jupiter the King of Gods, Juno the Goddess of Marriage, Neptune the God of the Sea, Saturn the youngest son of Uranus, father of Zeus, Venus the Goddess of Love, Pluto the God of the Underworld, Vulcan the God of the Forge, Ceres the Goddess of the Harvest, Apollo the God of Music and Medicine, Minerva the Goddess of Wisdom, Diana the Goddess of the Hunt, Mars the God of War, Mercury the Messenger of the Gods, Bacchus the God of Wine, Proserpine the Goddess of the Underworld, Cupid the God of Love and Gaea the Goddess of Earth."

"That is a lot of gods."

"And that excludes minor gods and house spirits."

"And the fact is that many other human groups and associations also have their own gods," said Hyet. "It is incredible. What is it about the humans?"

Sidion shrugged her shoulders. "I don't know. Honestly, the humans would worship anything. Some human cultures believe that there are spirits in the air, water and trees. This intense belief is why we instigated the Moses experiment. Dr Nowlett explained our objective of trying to prove that if you create one religion, then you will be able to exert control over the planet. Based on an analysis of the few races with religious belief, we concluded that religion is often the mechanism that is used to introduce civil law into societies, where civil authorities do not exist."

"Can religion really regulate a society?" said Hyet.

"It should be possible. Fear of incurring the wrath of your ancestors or a powerful deity encourages compliance with the rules of that religion. If the rules of the religion are accepted widely and mirror the rules of a civic society then you will have a stable society. Religion can give meaning to the lives of those who are at the bottom of a monetary based society like ours, something the Santu don't have to worry about with their civic based economic model. If you believe that this life is just a path to a greater afterlife, then you will be prepared to accept what you believe is only a temporary low quality of life. If you are a slave, as many humans are, with no quality of life and no hope of it getting better, then your religion and the hope of an afterlife are the only positives."

Hyet decided to change the topic. "So, what do you think of Moses?"

Sidion smiled. "I think that Moses was an amazing leader of the original experiment. He suggested the Hebrews, who were slaves of the Egyptians, as the group to experiment on. He devised a plan whereby, through divine influence, he would lead the Hebrews out of slavery into a promised land. There they would be free to worship Moses' god. He planned the ten plagues that afflicted the Egyptians but did not affect the Hebrews. The first nine plagues were water turned into blood, frogs, gnats, flies, disease to their cattle, boils, hail, locusts, and darkness. Each of them had a major impact on the Egyptians, but the tenth plague of killing the firstborn sons of the Egyptians was the one that broke them. That was a work of genius."

"I think that the tenth one was over the top," said Hyet. "Didn't Moses have to face an internal inquiry into that one?"

"Well, the Egyptians were killing off all newborn Hebrew males, so you could argue that they deserved it. The enquiry concluded that since Moses had been given no restrictions by the SOE as to what he could or couldn't do, he didn't have any case to answer."

"I think that the most impressive manoeuvre was the escape of the Hebrews from the Egyptian army. Using the thrusters of three military grade shuttles to part the Red Sea to let the Hebrews escape and then crashing it down on the Egyptian pursuers was incredible. I've seen the recording of that a few times."

"You can just about make out the shuttles if you enlarge the picture and look carefully," said Sidion. "The chameleon camouflage was amazing, even back then."

"So why didn't the plan work? Moses had demonstrated the power of his god convincingly to the Egyptians and Hebrews. Why didn't other humans convert to this god? Their gods had never done anything to prove their existence, so belief was just based on obscure legends with no physical proof."

"Hard to say," said Sidion. "The Hebrews were convinced that they were God's chosen people. They were given the Ten Commandments on which their lives were to be based. It was a simple and uncomplicated message that they had to spread. They should have been evangelist missionaries spreading the word of their god. It just didn't happen. They didn't spread the message vociferously, so their religion got lost in the multitude of religious beliefs. That's why we need to come up with something revolutionary."

"It will be difficult to come up with something bigger than what Moses tried," said Hyet. "Even if we do, what is different now compared to then? Let's say we fake a meteor crashing onto Earth and then have the son of God step out of it. Only a few people will witness the event unless we crash it into the middle of a city – just to be clear, I am not suggesting that as an option. Even then you might have only a few thousand who witness it. So, what is the crucial difference that will enable the Hebrews to better spread the message of God this time?"

Sidion paused. "Rome. The crucial difference is Rome. In Moses' time, there was no large, stable and functioning political entity. There were just competing tribes, city states and smaller geographical areas. None were large enough to allow extensive safe travel. However, now the Roman Empire ticks all the required boxes. It is large and stable with strong civic principles, relatively speaking. This time the Hebrews can safely move through the Roman Empire and spread the word of God."

****

Hennegy sat on his seat with his legs stretched out in front of him and his hands behind his head. He watched as Denned walked over and saluted. Hennegy stood and saluted back. They shook hands and sat down.

"Have you seen any action?" said Hennegy.

Captain Denned leaned forward with his elbows on his knees. "Unfortunately, sir, the answer is yes. I was based on three different planets where colonisation disputes with the Santu arose. What about you, sir?"

"Please drop the 'sir'. I was on convoy duty protecting ships probably on route to some of the places where you were stationed."

"Have you procreations at home?"

"No, have you?"

"No." Denned rubbed his head. "I don't think that a fifty-year posting like this and procreations would be a good mix."

"True. I doubt that anyone on this ship has procreated, probably a prerequisite to being selected. I'm thirty. How many years have you?"

"Thirty-one. Does it reflect badly on the imagination of the programme chief that two military personnel are put on the same team?"

"Maybe, but it is a logical choice. Our team is no doubt destined to do the grunt work on Earth, keeping the rest of the team safe. Plenty of drop pod trips."

Denned scratched his nose. "Fawter and Konacht would have been perfect for the marines. I haven't seen physiques like that since the end of basic training."

Hennegy leaned back and rubbed his stomach. "You have kept yourself in shape. It is a while since my midriff has experienced planks or sit-ups. I hope those two go easy on us in the close combat sessions."

"You haven't piled on the weight. A couple of weeks of workouts and you will be back at your peak. Have you family, Hennegy?"

"Just one sister but we are not close. You?"

Denned looked sad for a moment. "Two sisters whom I am very fond of, even if we don't get to see each other that much. I'll get to see them even less now."

"More than you expect, hopefully. Right, we better start coming up with some ideas."

"You will be delighted to know that I already have an idea." Hennegy said this with a serious face and Denned couldn't tell if he was joking or not.

"That quickly? Go on then, enlighten me," said Denned in the tone of voice that implied he anticipated a fairly poor suggestion.

"When you read your briefing, you will have seen references to a series of writings by the humans called the Old Testament. The Old Testament, which includes a lot of the details of the first experiment, was attached as an appendix to the briefing document. Did you read it?"

Denned picked up the briefing document and flicked to the appendix containing the Old Testament. "I remember that bit now. I sort of skimmed it. It is turgid stuff."

"I agree, but I still read it fully to see if I could glean anything useful from it. The hands of the legendary Moses are all over it. What I learned was that Moses had already laid the groundwork for the introduction of a messiah, the son of his God. This was his backup plan in case his attempt failed. Look at these extracts from the Old Testament, which outline what he wanted to happen in the next attempt. 'Isaiah 7:14: 'Therefore the Lord himself will give you a sign: The virgin will be with child and will give birth to a son and will call him Immanuel.' 'Isaiah 9:6: For to us a child is born, to us a son is given, and the government will be on his shoulders. And he will be called Wonderful Counsellor, Mighty God, Everlasting Father, and Prince of Peace.' 'Micah 5:2: But you, Bethlehem Ephrata, though you are small among the clans of Judah, out of you will come for me one who will be ruler over Israel, whose origins are from of old, from ancient times.' There are loads more."

"That's amazing," said Denned. "It sets out exactly what Moses wanted done."

"True, and the Old Testament tracks out the plan for the whole life of this son of God, not just the birth. It also deals with his life and death. Moses was so keen on detail that he gave a name for the new religion. Christ is the son of God, so the new religion should be called Christianity. The whole plan is there in the Old Testament."

"So, the starting point is engineering the birth of the Messiah in accordance with the Old Testament?" said Denned.

"Exactly. By adhering to the Old Testament, it will prove that what we are doing now is part of God's plan."

Denned was impressed by Hennegy's unexpected scholarly genius. "So, how should we progress this?"

"We have to read through the Old Testament again and pick out every reference to the Messiah. I haven't found them all. Then we sketch out a life plan starting with the virgin birth all the way to his death, highlighting the key waypoints. The intellectuals can work out how to do it."

"Honestly, I am not being condescending when I say this, but that is a really good idea, just one slight problem. How could we possibly engineer a virgin birth?"

Hennegy started to laugh. "That, as I said before, is where the intellectuals come in, especially Dr Nowlett."

"From what Dr Nowlett said, this is exactly the sort of challenge that she is expecting from us."

****

Yiler stretched his hands above his head and groaned loudly. "I need to take a break."

Nowlett closed her laptop. "Good idea. My eyes are getting tired. As a distraction, can I ask you a few theology questions?"

"Of course. It's my favourite subject."

"Great, but before I do, I want to make something clear to you. I am asking you because I am interested. I'm not trying to massage your ego or ingratiate myself with you. I say what I mean as succinctly as possible. There is never any double meaning or hidden agenda with me."

"I appreciate your candour, but after five weeks of working with you, I had already come to that conclusion myself. What do you want to know?"

"You were studying why deity belief exists on some planets yet is non-existent on other planets. What did you conclude?"

"My work was incomplete, but I believe that the strength of belief in a species is linked to evolution. Species disposed to religious belief generally congregated into groups of likeminded individuals. These groups were better able to withstand environmental variations and so, flourished. Those who weren't as disposed did not readily form such groups. Atheism, the lack of a belief in a divine power, was not enough to bind them together. These individuals or smaller groups were not able to withstand the environmental challenges and either died off or joined the larger groups."

"They pretended to believe in order to survive."

"Exactly. The capacity or willingness to believe became a trait that was passed on and strengthened from generation to generation. The groups got bigger and bigger."

"So why don't we have religion?"

"I don't know. It could be that the need or desire to believe or belong in such a community never existed within the Deusi. Alternatively, it is possible that it existed, but the groups that formed were weaker than the groups that had no belief. Maybe atheism became the inherited trait for the Deusi."

"That's a fascinating theory. It's a shame that you didn't get to finish your work."

"When I get back home, I hope that it will be written up and published by the theology department."

Nowlett patted him on the shoulder. "I am sure that it will be."

****

Yiler and Dr Nowlett were delighted by the quality of the proposals they received and the fact that they had all been received within the requested fourteen-day period. The four teams had produced a broad range of ideas. Some ideas were brilliant, some were strange, some were both.

Yiler's favourite of the bizarre ideas came from Team 3, Fawter and Konacht, who had displayed far more imagination than what he had expected from private security consultants. Their plan was to hover the *Tesfa* over Rome at night and illuminate the city. A cable would be used to slowly lower Yiler until he hovered two hundred meters above the city; they speculated that this distance would be out of the range of primitive human missile fire, probably. He would then announce the arrival of the one true god on Earth. The ship would then destroy the ten largest temples in Rome to demonstrate God's displeasure with the worshipping of false gods. The ship would repeat the process in the next three largest cities on Earth, Alexandria, Antioch and Ephseus. The idea lacked subtlety, but Dr Nowlett thought that it was technically possible. Although Yiler found the idea amusing, he wasn't convinced. He felt that Moses had made a mistake by opting for a god of punishment and that Team 3's idea was replicating it.

Team 4, with Uhet and Cannet, had suggested replacing the Roman Emperor with one of the team. Coincidentally, they also felt that Yiler was best qualified for the job but would have to be surgically altered. The new emperor would announce that he was the son of God and insist that all Romans convert to the new religion. The first to refuse to convert would have to be sacrificed. Thereafter, the incentive of staying alive would give the necessary encouragement. Dr Nowlett advised that the surgical element was no more than a minor tweak and could easily be done. Yiler felt that this was also creating a god of punishment and this was not what he wanted to do.

Team 2, Denned and Hennegy, had searched through the Old Testament to look for a plan left by Moses. Yiler was amazed when the team extracted a roadmap from birth to death. Team 2 suggested that, by following this roadmap exactly, they would show that the Old Testament had predicted the coming of the Messiah. They believed that following this preordained plan should convince the Hebrews that the son of God had come to Earth. This in turn would be the catalyst for the Hebrews to enthusiastically commence missionary work. Team 2 neglected to include any practical suggestions as to how to implement any of the steps.

Team 1, Sidion and Hyett, had also plumped for the idea of the son of God with a link to the God created by Moses. Otherwise, there was a risk that the new religion could grow in tandem with the Hebrew religion. Neither religion would reach the critical mass required to supplant the multitude of gods of the Roman Empire. Even if the Roman gods could be supplanted, they speculated that there was a risk that the two competing religions would eventually lead to conflict. There was no evidence to support this theory because no race with religious belief had been observed with two competing deities. However, Yiler agreed that conflict was a very real possibility if two opposing religions emerged from the experiment, so it was best avoided.

He groaned and stretched his hands above his head and brought them down onto his computer keyboard. "Okay, Dr Nowlett, let's start writing this up."

"That habit of groaning while stretching is intensely irritating. I thought that you needed to know."

"Thanks. I'll bear that in mind."

****

Fawter clapped his hands gleefully. "With the academic work out of the way, it's time for personal combat followed by weapons training." There were a few audible groans from group members, who were all well-padded. "It's great to feel energy and enthusiasm in a room. We are going to split up into groups. I will take the eggheads and Yiler." Hyet's fears had been well founded.

"Konacht will take Uhet, Cannet and Dr Nowlett. Denned will initially work with Hennegy one to one, and when Hennegy is ready, Denned will help train my group and Hennegy will work with Konacht. We will do an hour each of personal and weapons practice. Today's lesson is basic personal protection. While we will have side arms and other weaponry on Earth, we will not be carrying them regularly. Therefore, you must be able to defend yourself if you are accosted. Now to start, I need to pick a victim. Sidion, you're up."

Sidion stood in the middle of the gym on a soft matt a couple of metres away from Fawter. "Ok, I am going to approach you from behind and attempt to pin you to the ground." Sidion turned around as he moved towards her, bending down from the waist to shift her weight forward. She twisted into Fawter and pushed her elbow into his neck. This gave her the room to turn fully and drive her knee into his groin. Despite the padding, Fawter still crumpled to the floor.

Konacht nearly collapsed laughing. "Not a complete novice then, Sidion."

"Should have asked me before you started," said Sidion as she helped Fawter up.

.

****

Nowlett was reading over the final draft of the plan which had taken herself and Yiler a further ten days to complete after the teams had delivered their papers. With fourteen days left on the *Tesfa* until reaching Earth, they still had adequate time to complete their work. Across the office, Yiler slumped on a reclining chair with his eyes closed. Every now and again, Nowlett would sigh and change a word or two.

Yiler opened one eye. "You must be finished by now."

"If I am still editing, how can I be finished? Also, I will never be finished if you keep asking me if I am finished."

"Sorry."

"Your interruption is well timed though. Unfortunately, there is a major flaw in the document."

Yiler opened both eyes and spoke slowly. "What do you mean there is a flaw?"

"No need to raise your voice. My hearing works fine. There is no insurance, no plan B."

"Again, what do you mean?"

"What happens if the child Messiah dies before we are ready to move on to the final phase?"

"The experiment ends."

"Your ability to point out the stunningly obvious is extraordinary."

"As is your ability to ask obvious questions."

"It was a rhetorical question actually. Anyway, that is the risk that we must protect against. I can't envisage proceeding with that risk hanging over us. We must have another option."

"You seem to have something in mind, so can you just tell me?"

"We need someone to shadow the child and replace him if required."

Yiler looked at her incredulously. "Do you mean like an insurance baby? That only works if the second baby is born at the same time as the first one, but that's impossible. The chosen mother cannot have twins. It's not in the Old Testament."

"Yiler, that is, once again, stunningly obvious. There is another way though. I can easily fertilise a second egg at the time of the child's conception and bring it back to the ship. The children will be fraternal twins and not identical twins."

"But for what purpose? What are you going to do with it then?" Yiler's eyes widened. "Are you going to be a surrogate mother? Have you asked Sidion to do it?"

"Both are options but somewhat of an imposition on our personal lives. I have another alternative in mind. During my last few months in Biotech Inc, I designed a prototype artificial womb. I called it a uterine replicator. From the array of equipment and parts that I have brought on board, financed by General Lateel's generosity, I can build one."

"A *uterine replicator!* If that is a proven concept, surely Biotech Inc would have commercialised it? Does it really work?"

Nowlett glared at Yiler. "Of course, it does. I wouldn't release anything unless it was proven."

"Do Biotech Inc think that it won't attract customers?"

"Let me think about that one. The agony of expanding a gap, normally two centimetres in diameter, to squeeze out a three to four kilogramme baby, versus a machine doing all the painful work for you. That's a hard one. Of course, it will be a sought-after service. The issue is cost. It will be very expensive to set up and run a uterine replicator clinic, so only the rich would be able to afford it. Biotech Inc are already being accused of making products only accessible to those with premium level healthcare plans. That is why they are unsure of what to do with it."

"So, we have the technology to do it, but have you thought about the practicalities of raising a child? Presumably, the child will be held in a nursery on the ship after being born."

Nowlett rolled her eyes. "Let's consider chapter three of the parenting skills book "How Not to Raise a Disturbed Child". This states that raising a child in an environment with no family structure and no contact with children of its own age is a sure-fire way of ending up with a catastrophically neurotic child. Yiler, come on. Think!"

"You want us two to raise the child? As if it were our own?"

"So close."

"You want *us* to adopt the child."

"Exactly. I knew that you would get there in the end."

"Why do you keep springing things like this on me? It would have been much better to gradually introduce the idea to me."

"Well, you can hardly talk. You didn't give me any warning when you made me do that introductory speech."

"I don't think making you do an introductory speech is comparable to me being asked to adopt the twin brother of the infant son of a god!" Yiler exhaled slowly. "What else is there to consider?"

"We will have to bring the child home with us to Deusi Prime to allow him to go to school there. This will be facilitated by the hiatus in the plan from when the child is born until he reaches twelve or thirteen, and we insert his implant. There will be a further hiatus until we decide the time is right to go to the final phase. One or both of us will be back on Deusi Prime for long periods, and when we aren't, he can spend time with us on the ship. He will have to spend time on the ship anyway to shadow what his brother is doing on Earth."

"It won't be easy for him to blend in on Deusi Prime."

"We can just say that he has a mild genetic disorder. That will adequately explain the physical differences."

"To the adults yes, but to his classmates no. He will have a difficult time in school. Adopting a child is a big step, but we will be adopting a child with a predetermined destiny. What happens when he finds out that he is part of an experiment? He is unlikely to be happy about it. What about our emotional attachment to the child? I need to think about this."

"That's reasonable. However, I think if you are as fully committed to the task as I am, you know it is the right thing to do."

Yiler resigned himself to succumbing to the will of Nowlett. "Okay, you win. Anything else?"

"Oh yes, one thing. We will need to cohabit to raise the child properly."

Yiler sat up. "Cohabiting?"

"Of course, unless you don't want to."

"Oh, I want to. I really want to."

"Excellent, that's all settled then."

"Should we start when the child is born?"

Nowlett looked quizzically at Yiler. "Well, we could, but I was getting the clear impression from you that you wanted to move our relationship on. Did I pick you up wrong?"

"No, it's just that I never knew that you were thinking this way. I didn't want to appear pushy."

"I have decided that we should cohabit now, so no further discussion required. Will you help me move some of my things from my cabin? I will keep my cabin for when I need peace and quiet for research projects."

Yiler stood up. "It would be my pleasure. Shall we go now?"

****

The team members were seated around the table in the conference room, all expectantly waiting for the results of their work. Nowlett handed a pile of manuscripts to Hyet, who was the closet person to her, and asked him to pass them around. The title on the first page was "Deity Creation – Blueprint." Yiler waited until everyone had a manuscript and started talking.

"Thank you for the papers you submitted. These were exactly what we wanted. The difficult part was selecting the best suggestions from all the proposals, but we have now done that. The teams that contributed most to the plan were Team 1, Sidion and Hyet, and Team 2, Hennegy and Denned, but all of you had great ideas. You deserve a lot of credit."

"Unfortunately, there are no prizes," said Dr Nowlett, which incited a laugh from the table.

Hyet leaned towards Nowlett. "Very funny," he said in a low voice.

Nowlett looked bemused. "Oh, thank you Hyet. I appreciate that, but I was only stating a fact. We don't have prizes."

Yiler tapped the table loudly. "The key to the plan is adhering to the steps set out by Moses in the Old Testament. By doing this, we will prove that God has had his son, the Messiah, born on Earth exactly as he had planned. The challenge now is deciding how to implement each of those steps.

"Putting meat on the bones, so to speak," said Nowlett. "Speaking of bones, the fact that you all are stronger, taller and larger than the humans with much less body hair will make it difficult to blend in when you go down to Earth in stage one of the plan. You will all need plastic surgery to make your facial features more human. I can assure you that it is reversible. There is also the possibility of leg shortening surgery. An extracted bone can be frozen and stored safely for years before being reinserted. There are two solutions to the lack of body hair. You can apply a follicle stimulating cream, but it must be applied daily. The other possibility is semi-permanent implants. You need to schedule appointments with me so we can agree specific treatments."

Yiler saw some horrified looks. "Hyet and Sidion, as our technology and communications team, along with me, will primarily be based on the ship, so we are exempt from these procedures unless and until we have to spend an extended period on Earth." Hyet and Sidion exhaled in relief.

"So, no drop pods?" said Hyet clenching his fists.

"Correct, unless and until you have to go to Earth."

"I must work on the drop pod issue," said Nowlett.

Yiler tapped the table gently. "The rest of you will be based on Earth, so the alterations must be done before you go down, apart from the leg surgery which is optional." The rest of the team looked slightly less uncomfortable after the threat of major surgery had been removed. "Now, can you all please turn to paragraph one on page four, headed 'Stage 1 – The Virgin Birth'."

****

The president's aide heard the raised voices as he walked down the main corridor of the private area of the residence of the Deusi President, pushing the refreshment trolley. He didn't remember President Flanstid ever sounding as angry as this. She never lost her temper, well, hardly ever. Normally, he would enter the president's office without seeking permission, but this time he knocked loudly at the door. The room went silent, and President Flanstid told him that he could enter. He pushed the trolley into the room and closed the door behind him. He didn't say anything as he served, carefully avoiding eye contact. He did notice that the president was seated at her work desk, leaving General Lateel in an uncomfortable position facing her. The back of the desk was solid wood and immovable, so General Lateel was leaning forward awkwardly. The president could have chosen to use the large meeting table with six chairs near the window. Neither President Flanstid nor General Lateel said a single word while he was there.

President Flanstid started speaking as soon as the aide had left. "Well, give me your opinion of what happened yesterday, since I am clearly wrong." She almost snarled the words.

"The advisory council voted to select one option from the alternatives presented," said General Lateel calmly. "Our objective is to achieve a military stalemate with the Santu and agree an accommodation with the Federation that doesn't require us ripping our society apart and adopting their civic economic model. The alternative is acceding to the economic preconditions. That would be unacceptable. Selecting the option of a strategic withdrawal back to Deusi Prime was the correct decision. I don't know why you left the advisory council meeting with the impression that success was guaranteed. The general rule is that no plan ever survives contact with the enemy. In this case, even small deviations could cause the strategic withdrawal to fail. Everything, and I mean everything, must fall in our favour. That could happen, but there is a high probability that it won't."

"You didn't make that clear when you spoke during the meeting," said the president who was calming down a little.

"With all due respect, I did. You and the advisory council heard what you wanted to hear."

"You and the military representatives were hiding the possible failure of the armed forces to secure a definitive victory over the Santu despite all the resources that will be given to them."

"Again, with all due respect, the failure, if it happens, cannot be attributed solely to the military," said General Lateel. "It was the failure of diplomatic efforts that caused most of our allies to move from being positive, to being neutral about us joining the Federation. Worse still, most of those who held a neutral position moved to the side of the Santu, allowing them to impose strict conditions. Our negotiating position is weak. Madam President, it is pointless discussing this further. The decision has been made, correctly in my view, and you can't go back and change that. In the meantime, we should plan for the worst-case scenario, instead of just waiting for it to happen. Let me ask you a question. If our strategy fails, and we enter surrender discussions, what do you think the worst-case scenario will be?"

"Losing our colonies and being left only with Deusi Prime and D2, maybe D3," said the president. "What do you think might happen?"

"I agree with you," said General Lateel. "The Santu will permit us to spread into the Federation as second-class citizens. Our future population expansion will be in off-planet facilities in Federation space. We will not get new colonies. By dispersing us throughout the Federation in small numbers, the Santu will feel that they can control us. Our position will only ever change if the Santu become less influential in the Federation. The Santu losing their dominant position in the Federation will be a long time coming though, if it ever happens. I know for certain that none of us will be alive to see it."

"You said that you have a proposal for dealing with a Santu victory and the aftermath. Since this meeting is off the record, I fear that your proposal will have no legal basis."

"You know me too well. My proposal is that we will work against the Santu through a covert organisation separate from the military and the legislature, answerable only to the office of the president and the board of the SOE. It could be vital if, as I suspect, Santu intelligence already knows about the SOE."

The president shook her head. "As I suspected, illegal. You are proposing to set it up under the control of the SOE, whose own constitutionality is debateable."

General Lateel handed over a file to the president. "Legal or not, I have a list of people who are currently working in the organisation."

"Working in it?" said the president in surprise. "I thought that we were considering a proposal?"

"We may spend thirty to forty years building towards one final, hopefully successful, battle. If we lose, then our ability to create this organisation after signing the treaty disappears. Scrutiny by the Santu will ensure that. So, I created it six months ago. It will be well established and fully functional even if the Santu win."

"You should become president since you are now making the key decisions." The president started reading the list. "You do realise that what you have done has broken so many laws that you could spend the rest of your life in prison." General Lateel just smiled and nodded. "These names are all unfamiliar."

"I assure you that these people have exceptional skills. I spent a year identifying them with the help of a couple of trusted SOE operatives."

"What are they doing?"

"I think it is better that you have no knowledge of what the organisation is doing. At least then you can plausibly deny all knowledge of it. I guarantee that they will not have the resources to undertake any form of military action against the Santu."

"What have you called this organisation?"

"They are just a section within the Department of Labour called 'The Subdepartment for Administrative Affairs'.

"With a name like that, no one will ever want to see what they are up to." General Lateel was relieved that the president's humour had improved.

"I sourced space in the Department of Labour on two unused underground floors. They moved there a month ago. Everyone will be recorded as being Department of Labour employees with no mention of the SOE of course."

"An ever-expanding Department of Labour. A place for the mundane, the dull, and now the covert too." The president let out a brief snort in amusement. Shaking her head, she asked, "Anything useful produced so far?"

"Yes, Madam President. We already have one very promising project that the team has taken over from the SOE."

"What is it?"

"The SOE discovered a planet fifteen hundred years ago with sentient life. We have called it Earth."

"Fifteen hundred years ago. Impossible. I've never heard of it."

"You wouldn't have. It is only known within the SOE."

"Are you seriously telling me that the SOE kept this a secret for fifteen hundred years?"

"There are matters that are best kept within the SOE, as opposed to being disclosed to the civilian administration."

"Since when does the SOE make decisions like that without the knowledge of the civilian administration?"

"We did what we felt was right."

"This is unbelievable. The SOE usurped the government by taking control of a newly discovered planet."

"I wouldn't quite put it like that."

"I would. This is something that we need to come back to later. I mean that. I can't let this slide. For the moment, let's go back to this planet, Earth. What have we been doing with it for the last fifteen hundred years? Why disclose it now? What are we going to use it for?"

Lateel sighed. "In order to answer all of your questions, you will have to cancel your meetings for the morning."

"Fine." President Flanstid pressed her intercom. "Itelle, please cancel all my morning meetings. Rearrange them for later this week. Right, General Lateel, start talking."

Lateel shifted in her seat uncomfortably. "Can we move to the meeting table?"

The president stared at her and said, "No."

"The SOE has colonised five planets of which Earth is one. The board had come to the conclusion that the Federation were never going to allot planets to us, so we took unilateral action. The Deusi planets are close to being overpopulated, so something had to be done."

The president went white in the face. "What? How do you manage that without the Federation finding out and blocking you?"

"That would take a long time to explain, so I will skip that for the moment. Four of the planets are modelled on Deusi Prime. Earth, however, is a different story. We are making Earth as divergent from us as possible through a range of experiments, some of which are completed, others are ongoing."

"Why would you do that?"

"In the future, it may suit us to allow the Federation to discover Earth. We hope that the Federation will accept that it has evolved naturally. If they don't, then the secondary benefit is that we will be able to gauge their reaction to what they believe is a Deusi colony. A reasonably positive reaction would allow us to consider commencing a staggered revelation of the other four colonised planets. If the response is negative, which could even entail the eradication of Earth, then we will know for certain that the existence of the other four colonies must be kept a secret."

"You might be prepared to sacrifice Earth?"

"If necessary, yes. Anyway, the humans are not pure Deusi. They are a hybrid between Deusi DNA and the race that was discovered when we first found Earth."

The president sighed. "I see now why I had to cancel the morning for you. Go on, how did you create a hybrid species?"

Chapter 3

Hennegy was currently sitting in the middle of a copse of trees near Nazareth in Galilee, sweating profusely. For the umpteenth time, he mentally cursed Yiler for banning unnecessary technology, which in Yiler's opinion included temperature-controlled skinsuits.

It had been four weeks since the *Tesfa* arrived at Earth. The first week was spent confirming the location of all the places that Moses had referred to in his plan in the Old Testament. When that had been done, the next step was to identify suitable targets for selection. Consequently, Hennegy was monitoring a female called Mary of approximately fourteen years of age to assess her suitability for the experiment.

He felt a slight vibration as his implant indicated that another team member was contacting him. He accessed the implant and discovered that it was Denned.

"Are you awake?"

All the members of the Deity Creation Group had received military standard upgrades to their civilian implants, which had been inserted in their early teens. The upgrade allowed for communication to be made by internal vocalisation which took some getting used to. You had to be very careful to make sure you designated who you wanted to contact. Commander Yiler was less than amused when he heard some of the references to him by the team members. Dr Nowlett on the other hand, was pleasantly surprised.

The implants were much safer than using earpieces and verbal communication. These ran the risk of the team being observed talking to themselves, which would arise suspicion among the humans.

"It's the middle of the day. What do you want?"

"No need to get angry. You do sleep a lot. Anyway, I have news from Fawter and Konacht on the number one prospect."

"Which is?"

"She's no longer our number one."

"Are they sure she has copulated?"

"Oh yeah. Fawter was watching her and a man's heat signatures, and it was clear what was going one. That's one month of Team 3's time wasted."

"Well, that makes Mary number one then."

He linked Fawter, Konacht, Uhet and Cannet to the conversation. *"Well, what do the rest of you think?"*

"Mary is the best prospect by far," said Uhet.

"We agree," said Fawter.

"I will send an update to the people on the ship and let them make the final call," said Hennegy.

****

"We need to make a decision," said Yiler to Nowlett, Sidion and Hyet as they had lunch in the ship's observation deck, watching Earth pass by underneath them. "Target number one is now Mary, daughter of Eli. She is fourteen years old."

"Before you say anything else, I have to say again that I am not comfortable with her age," said Sidion. "I am struggling to reconcile with it."

"I have the same problem," said Nowlett. "However, you have to view this in the context that the human life expectancy is only thirty-five years, and because of that, the custom is that girls marry young to ensure that they can raise their own children to maturity before they die. You cannot consider it in Deusi terms. Our average life expectancy is one hundred and fifty years."

Yiler smiled grimly. "Dr Nowlett is correct in her analysis. Mary has been under close observation by Hennegy's team for two months. They have assessed Mary as being reasonably intelligent, healthy and fertile. They have observed regular ovulation. She is a virgin, as far as we can tell. Mary is betrothed to Joseph, son of Jacob. Joseph is also assessed as being reasonably intelligent, circa twenty-two years old. No reason to speculate on his fertility because that isn't crucial. They are betrothed and soon to be married. We don't know if it is an arranged marriage, but even if it is, they do seem to have formed a real bond. Both are deeply religious. Both seem quite pliable, but that is a difficult one to make a call on."

Nowlett was tapping her fingers on the table. "Don't ignore the fact that Joseph believes that he is related to the famous King David and, if so, that fulfils another of Moses prophecies."

Hyet groaned audibly. "Remind me who he was?"

"David, one of our early projects, was the first king to be based in Jerusalem. His reign is looked back on with great fondness. His reputation as a great fighter who slayed the giant Goliath is legendary. David became king about one thousand years ago because the lawlessness of the period created a popular desire to have a king to exert control. The benefit of a king with strong leadership outweighed the risk of the king exploiting the people's wealth and resources to promote and expand his own power. There was a prior king called Saul, Israel's first king, but he had to be removed due to continual disobedience. We appointed David as his successor, maintaining that this was done at God's direction. David was hugely successful, and his reign was one of peace and prosperity."

Yiler frowned as a point occurred to him. "That is an accurate summary of what we discussed at another meeting, but we didn't attach much value to it. Joseph is related to David, and Joseph is not going to be the father of the child."

"I think that we discounted this prematurely. That nuance might well be overlooked in the future, with Joseph being his father legally."

"You two are going off point again," said Sidion. "We can't second guess the team on Earth from up here in orbit. We have to go with their recommendation."

"I agree," said Hyet. "When is Mary's next ovulation?"

Nowlett looked down at her notes. "Three weeks' time."

"Three weeks to set up the virgin birth," said Hyet. "I think I should work with Dr Nowlett to get everything ready. You two work with the Earth based teams." Hyet had decided to make a play for Nowlett at the first meeting of the Deity Creation Group. He was not particularly attracted to Nowlett physically, but she was the only available female on the ship. There was no way he would get involved with Sidion because they worked so closely together. He had reckoned that he had the edge on Yiler, so it was worth a try. He wasn't happy when his chance to do so disappeared when the final plan included Nowlett and Yiler adopting the second child. He decided to extract a little revenge by attempting to get Yiler convinced that he was still interested in Nowlett.

"I think that it would be better if I worked with Dr Nowlett on this," said Yiler immediately.

Sidion sighed. Males, she thought to herself. "I will liaise with the Earth-based teams. I think that the two of you are required to help Dr Nowlett."

Nowlett smiled happily. "It's great to have you both. We will have a great time working together."

Hyet grinned broadly.

****

Yiler and Hyet sat across from Dr Nowlett in the medical room. Hyet knew that Dr Nowlett enjoyed theorising on everything, so he decided to throw a difficult question at her to encourage her to talk. "The briefing document gives no guidance as to what the crew of the *Nubla* did when they reached Earth. Have you an opinion?" Nowlett smiled at Hyet, and he settled back for a long answer.

"What do you know about natural history and genetics?"

"I never worked on anything related to either area, so my knowledge is limited," answered Hyet.

"I will keep it simple then." Yiler sniggered but stopped when Hyet scowled at him. "The humans are an experiment in genetic engineering, specifically gene therapy, which commenced when the *Nubla* discovered Earth. The experiment probably commenced by default rather than design."

"Why do you say that?" said Hyet.

"Earth was populated by a first stage sentient race when we found it. Our regulations at the time, like the existing Federation ones, were not to colonise such planets. Nevertheless, the crew of the *Nubla* decided to commence the experiment. Why remains unclear. How, is something that I intend to investigate during visits to Earth when time permits, and when my excursions are authorised by someone." She frowned at Yiler. Hyet smirked this time.

Yiler decided that a question was the best way to deflect Nowlett away from the ongoing row over his order, blocking her exploratory trips. "Dr Nowlett, I am aware of the term gene therapy, but I don't really know what it means."

"Not part of the theology syllabus then," said Hyet.

Dr Nowlett carried on oblivious to the tension between Hyet and Yiler. "Gene therapy is where the DNA sequence of a gene is altered by an insertion that changes the number of DNA bases in a gene by adding a piece of DNA. It is normally used to treat or prevent disease by replacing a mutated gene that causes disease with a healthy copy of the gene. However, it can also introduce completely new genes.

A gene that is inserted directly into a cell usually does not function. Instead, a carrier called a vector is genetically engineered to deliver the gene. Certain viruses are often used as vectors because they can deliver the new gene by infecting the cell. The viruses are modified, so they can't cause disease in the general population. Some types of virus, such as retroviruses, integrate their genetic material, including the new gene, into a chromosome of the target cell. Other viruses, such as adenoviruses, introduce their DNA into the nucleus of the cell, but the DNA is not integrated into a chromosome.

The vector can be injected or given intravenously directly into a specific tissue in the body, where it is taken up by individual cells. Alternately, a sample of the patient's cells can be removed and exposed to the vector in a laboratory setting. The cells containing the vector are then returned to the patient. If the process is successful, the new gene delivered by the vector will make a functioning protein. We make extensive use of the second method.

The assimilation of viral sequences into the host genome is a process referred to as endogenization. This occurs when viral DNA integrates into a chromosome of reproductive cells and is subsequently passed from parent to offspring. Retroviruses can generate such endogenous copies in vertebrates." Nowlett laughed. "You are probably sorry that you asked the question. Now that you understand gene therapy, you will be able to understand how it was used to create humans."

"It is hard to believe that we actually created a new race," observed Hyet.

"It's not exactly a new race," stated Dr Nowlett. "You see…"

Yiler was confident that Nowlett had forgotten about being annoyed with him, so he decided to interrupt. "Dr Nowlett, I would love to hear more, but we should focus on the matter of the impregnation of Mary. How are you going to do it?"

"All I have to do is jump from the ship in a drop pod, meet with Hennegy, Denned, Fawter and Konacht, get to Nazareth, insert some nanobots, impregnate a human with Deusi sperm, collect some viable eggs and get back into the drop pod for extraction. Should be easy enough."

"Easy?" said a surprised Hyet.

Dr Nowlett looked at him quizzically. "Of course. The risk created, due to me having no experience of any of this, can be eliminated through proper planning."

"I can't tell whether you are joking or not," said Hyet.

Yiler laughed softly. "I can assure you that she isn't. "Fail to plan, plan to fail" is one of her favourite mantras."

Nowlett coughed and picked up a plastic cup and shook it in the air. The two males shifted uneasily in their chairs. "Which of you will provide the sperm? Now, before either of you say anything, I want to make two points. The first is that I am not going to have any hand… sorry, bad choice of words… any part in obtaining a sperm donation. The second is that it must be Deusi sperm. The second stage of the plan requires the insertion of an implant into the procreation. The chances of a successful implant are enhanced if the offspring has fifty percent Deusi DNA, so it cannot be a human sperm. So, who is it to be?" She sat back and folded her arms.

"As programme chief, I should do it," said Yiler glumly.

"Good for you." Dr Nowlett handed him a plastic cup. "Look at it this way. You are about to become the father of a God."

"Marvellous," responded Yiler. "Now?"

"Yes, but you can start after we leave. Hyet, don't look so chuffed, you are not off the hook. I must test Yiler's fertility. If it is not okay, then you will have to step in."

"Does being out of shape affect fertility?" Hyet struggled to keep a straight face as Yiler's face went red.

"Possibly, but he looks healthy enough. When I have a viable sample, I will isolate the Y chromosome sperms and freeze the sample. Then, I get to visit Earth."

"You have no doubt that you will succeed," said Hyet.

"None at all. My part is based on proven science. Denned and Hennegy must convince Mary that she has been impregnated by a God that never touched her. That is going to be far more challenging. One last question. I need constant data from Mary post impregnation, so will I have access to a permanent satellite link?"

"Yes," said Yiler. "It's a military grade satellite at low orbit. We can keep her under observation at all times."

"Isn't a low orbit satellite visible to the naked eye?"

"Not military grade," said Yiler. "A civilian grade satellite would look like a bright star at that altitude, but the military grade has chameleon light deflecting plating."

Sidion scratched her chin. "Dr Nowlett, how are you going to carry out the procedure on Mary?"

"Keyhole surgery, with an incision at her navel. The incision will allow me to insert a micro camera and light, nanobots and Yiler's sperm. The nanobots will spread out into the fallopian tubes to search for the egg, and I will see a soft red light when they find it. I will check the viability of the egg and if everything is in order, I will order the nanobots to surround the egg, leaving just a small opening. I will then release Yiler's sperm and it should all happen naturally from there. This isn't the simplest way to do this, but it is the least invasive from Mary's perspective. Mary will notice the scab from the incision, but she will assume that it was an insect bite during the night."

"Have you spoken to Hennegy yet about stepping into the role of the angel to break the news to Mary?" said Hyet. "He doesn't strike me as someone comfortable with subterfuge."

Yiler nodded. "Nowlett and I did. He wasn't very happy about it even after I told him that his military background made him perfect for the role. He exudes confidence and authority, so he is the natural choice. He argued that his acting as the angel would compromise his future interaction with the family. He was worried that they might recognise him."

"I dissuaded him of that," said Nowlett. "Firstly, Mary will barely be conscious, having just come out of sedation and secondly, the angel outfit that he will be wearing will disguise his features."

"Does it do that?" asked Hyett.

"Not yet," said Nowlett. "I will have that resolved before I bring it down with me in the drop pod."

****

Hennegy and Denned stood close together with their faces turned towards the sky. "There it is," said Denned, pointing towards what looked like a shooting star. "I wonder how Dr Nowlett is feeling."

Denned thought back to the first time he had used a drop pod. He had been deployed to D9 when the colonists had rebelled against a federal tax to cover central government costs on Deusi Prime. Neither the practice nor the simulations had come close to the real thing. He had vomited almost from start to finish despite the anti-nausea injection. He had thought that towards the end of the drop, he had nothing left in his stomach. He had been wrong. When the parachute had deployed at the minimum height of five hundred metres from the ground, he had felt his stomach heading towards his mouth, and he had managed to throw up again. When the thrusters had kicked in two hundred and fifty metres from ground, the same had occurred. He was never as glad again to breath in fresh air as when the door on the pod opened. Seasoned soldiers had jumped out from other pods and moved to cover. His squad, all novices, had crawled dejectedly out of theirs. Some had even forgotten their armaments and had to go back for them. It had taken thirty minutes for the squad to function as a collective again, at which point they had been informed by their sergeant that they would have all been dead if some of the angry colonists had turned up unexpectantly. He had done ten jumps since then and had thrown up every time but was now able to walk out of the pod in a functional state. "This is her first drop after minimum practice and simulation. I expect that we will be carrying her out."

The drop pod parachute deployed, and the thrusters kicked in to slow the descent. Denned turned to Hennegy. "They could have set the parachute to deploy at a higher altitude. That was unnecessary. It's not as if she is landing in a hot zone. If a few Roman soldiers turned up to investigate, I think that we could handle them."

The drop pod landed gently, and the door opened. They walked over to extract the unfortunate Dr Nowlett. They were more than a little surprised when Dr Nowlett walked out without any help from either of them. She flicked the catch on her helmet, took it off and took a deep breath of air. She then roared, "I'm on Earth!" at the top of her voice. "Denned and Hennegy, it's a pleasure to see your happy faces. This place smells very strange, but I suppose I will get used to it. I have two medicinal bags in the drop pod. Don't damage them. Where's the transport?"

Denned and Hennegy were speechless and stood motionless. "Don't just stand there gaping. Go on and get them. Mary's ovulating and her egg is not going to hang around forever in her fallopian tube, you know."

"Yes, doctor," was all Hennegy could manage. They retrieved a bag each from the drop pod. "How did you find the trip down?"

"Absolute blast." Dr Nowlett remained eerily cheerful. "Better than the fastest entertainment park rides and beats a shuttle any day. I loved it. I better do this a lot more during this mission. What are those again?" she asked, pointing at the three animals tied to a tree. Her enthusiasm was beginning to unnerve Hennegy and Denned.

"The locals call them camels," replied Denned. "They might account for the smell you mentioned. We will be using them to get into Nazareth. Not as fast as a gravcar but less likely to be spotted than a chunk of metal travelling at one hundred kilometres per hour."

"Brilliant… absolutely brilliant… a ride on a native animal."

"The camels look slow, but we will make it in an hour or so. The egg will still be there, won't it?"

"Oh, definitely. It doesn't move that quickly," Nowlett said while moving to inspect the animal.

Denned caught Hennegy's eye who nodded before he spoke. "Excuse me, Dr Nowlett, but what did you take before you got into the drop pod?"

"I don't suffer from travel sickness, but I took an anti-nausea concoction that I developed in the lab just in case. It did the trick, but a side effect seems to be a touch of over enthusiasm. Might have overdone the stimulants a little."

"You should give General Lateel the formula of whatever you took," said Hennegy. "She will be very interested."

"Yes, I'll tell her next time I see her, but I will reduce the number of amphetamines. Why are looking at me like that? Do these animals have any peculiar habits I should know about before I get on?" Dr Nowlett eyed Denned and Hennegy suspiciously.

"They do tend to spit at their riders… and make a lot of noise," said Denned.

"I'll take the last camel then; they probably can't spit backwards. I don't want camel saliva in my face. Come on, help me up."

Denned and Hennegy handed Dr Nowlett some native clothes which she placed over her skin suit. Hennegy noted that Yiler had allowed Nowlett to wear a skinsuit unlike the rest of the Earth-based team. They hoisted Dr Nowlett onto her camel and mounted their own. Denned and Hennegy soon discovered that Dr Nowlett's enthusiasm was not dissipating. She asked a never-ending stream of questions about everything she saw and expected Denned and Hennegy to know the answers. By the time Nazareth came into view, the males were mentally exhausted.

"Nazareth, I presume," said Nowlett. "Wow, I can smell it from here. How are we to get to Mary's house without being discovered? Will we have night suits and goggles?"

"Not necessary," said Denned. "We are only securing one house, so it's not a combat zone. We have a tent at the edge of the village where we can get ready and move in on foot from there. It's nearly midnight, so we are unlikely to meet anyone, but just in case, Fawter and Konacht are already in Nazareth and Uhet and Cannet will be coming with us. They have neural stunners to deal with anyone they might meet. Hopefully, there won't be anyone waking up in the middle of the street tomorrow morning wondering what happened to them. You will be the only one wearing a skin suit under your clothes, but keep it powered down. You will create havoc if it senses a threat and takes off on its own."

Nowlett opened one of the equipment bags and took out a package and handed it to Hennegy. "Here is your angel suit." She could see by the expression on his face that he wasn't happy. "I promise you that the lighting effect that I have installed will disguise your facial features adequately, so your future role in the experiment will not be compromised."

Hennegy smiled weakly. "Great, thanks for that. I'll check on the progress in Nazareth."

"Fawter and Konacht, is Mary's house ready?"

"All the family are sedated," replied Fawter.

"Okay, copy that. ETA ten minutes."

"That quickly?"

"Dr Nowlett did not need to clean up first."

"You can't be serious."

"Yes, I'm serious. See you in a few minutes."

Denned faced Dr Nowlett. "We have the house secured with Mary and her family sedated".

They arrived at the tent on the outskirts of Nazareth and secured their animals to a nearby palm tree. Denned brought the camels food and water while Hennegy brought Dr Nowlett into the tent. The tent was a mess. Sleeping mats and blankets were strewn everywhere. Nowlett held her nose. "Do you people ever wash?"

Hennegy started laughing. "How can we when nobody else does? Us smelling well would be a giveaway. Do you need both of your bags for the operation?"

"Yes. I have doubles of everything. I know that it weighs a lot, but I couldn't run the risk of a crucial instrument not functioning. I only want to have to do this once. I have Yiler and his arm to think of."

With that unpleasant image in their minds, Denned and Hennegy each picked up a bag and headed out of the tent with Dr Nowlett.

"It is only a few minutes," said Denned.

They walked slowly and silently to Mary's house with any conversation taking place through their implants. Fawter and Konacht were standing beside the covering that acted as a door for the house. Dr Nowlett entered and moved through the kitchen with the other two following.

"Where are the parents?" asked Dr Nowlett. "I want to check on them." Denned pointed towards an internal door with no covering. Dr Nowlett walked in and turned on her small headlamp. She scanned the two of them and then administered some more sedative. "That should keep them sedated for another two hours." She pointed to another door. "I presume that Mary is in there."

"Yes," said Denned.

Dr Nowlett walked in and scanned Mary. "I am going to inject some more sedative. Slightly less for Mary because we will need to wake her up before the rest. Put the bags beside Mary, and I will set up." Denned and Hennegy placed the bags carefully beside Mary's bed and then moved to stand at the door.

"I would like to preserve Mary's dignity as much as I can, so you two can go," said Dr Nowlett. Denned and Hennegy shuffled through the door and stood outside with Fawter and Konacht patrolling the street. Dr Nowlett set up two portable lights over Mary's bed, attached goggles to the camera and carried out the procedure exactly as explained to Sidion earlier. With the goggles pulled over her eyes, she watched as the released sperm swarmed around the egg. She thought that it looked like a pack of Deusi males fighting during one of the numerous ridiculous sports that they insisted on playing. After about thirty seconds, one sperm cell managed to adhere to and enter the thick protective shell-like layer surrounding the ovum. The sperm produced enzymes, which allowed it to burrow through the outer jelly coat of the egg. The fertilization process continued as the sperm plasma fused with the egg's plasma membrane, and the sperm head disconnected from its body. The egg then polarized, repelling any additional sperm, which the nanobots helped to push away as well. She knew that the zygote was male because the egg had been fertilized by a sperm that carried a Y chromosome. She was tempted to use sperm with the X chromosome, why couldn't God have a daughter after all? But she knew that they had to adhere exactly to Moses plan. She ordered the nanobots to form a protective screen as the zygote began its five-day journey down the fallopian tube.

With this stage complete, she moved on to the creation of the insurance baby. She had initially decided upon a clone, but because that technology was unproven, she eventually opted for a fraternal twin brother. Yiler had agreed with her despite the increased risk. A clone would be an exact copy, but a fraternal twin would create two brothers, with the possibility that their resemblance might not be sufficiently convincing to avoid suspicion if the second child had to be utilised.

She removed the plastic tubes with the empty vials. She took out a new tube and vial and navigated through the fallopian tube and arrived at the ovaries. She looked for a mature follicle about fifteen to twenty millimetres in diameter. When she found one, she carried out an egg aspiration procedure to retrieve some eggs. The fluid in the follicles was aspirated through the tube, and when the eggs detached from the follicle, they were sucked out of the ovary and into the vial. She sealed the vial and then placed it into a well-padded and insulated cold box to be brought back to the ship where she would fertilise the egg later.

She started withdrawing her equipment but stopped the camera when she reached the egg. It had only moved a small way down the fallopian tube which was normal. The ovum was no longer a single cell. It had divided several times to form a ball of cells; the cell division was proceeding within normal parameters. She ordered the nanobots to make sure that the ovum moved through the fallopian tube and safely embedded in the wall of the uterus. This wouldn't happen for five or six days. The last thing she wanted to happen was an ectopic pregnancy. She extracted the camera, cleaned her equipment and carefully packed it away. She double-checked to make sure that every piece was accounted for. It would be a disaster if Mary found some Deusi technology in her bedroom.

"Denned and Hennegy, you can come in now."

Denned was first in. "All went to plan?"

"Mary is pregnant. No doubt about it. The egg is viable and cell division is normal. The nanobots will help to get it embedded in a few days. All indications are that we should have a normal pregnancy."

Hennegy had followed Denned. "So, I can go ahead with the big announcement then," he said unenthusiastically.

"Absolutely. Let's get the bags out, and then it's over to you." Dr Nowlett and Denned carried out the bags while the somewhat reluctant Hennegy prepared himself. He was not happy, but orders were orders. He put on the white luminous clothing and turned on the lighting effects, so that Mary would be able to see the outline of his face but not discern any features. Dr Nowlett walked back in and administered an injection to counter the sedative. She gave Hennegy a small square piece of material. "When you finish, make sure that you place your hands close to her face and squeeze this. It will provide enough sedative to knock her out again while we make our exit." Mary began to stir, and Dr Nowlett left the room.

Mary moaned softly. "Ohh…"

"Mary do not be afraid. I am an angel of the lord bringing you happy tidings and wondrous news."

Mary's eyes opened wide and she sat up slowly. As her eyes accustomed to the light, she saw a tall figure in front of her surrounded by shimmering white light. "Is that you, Joseph? Are you crazy? My parents will kill you for being in my room." She evidently hadn't comprehended what Hennegy had said, so he tried again.

"I am an angel, Mary. The lord has chosen you for a wondrous task. He has decided to give his only son to you to nurture and raise until he reaches adulthood."

"Where is this child?" Mary looked around the room. "Is he outside?"

"I am not making myself clear. You are to be the mother of this child." Mary looked puzzled. "Tonight, the Lord has given you his child to carry." Mary still looked puzzled. "You are with child." Mary still wasn't getting it. "You are pregnant."

Mary put both hands to her cheeks and gasped. "How can that be? I am a virgin."

"The Lord works in mysterious ways. I can assure you that you are with child as we speak. In nine months, you will be the mother of the son of God."

"Why me? What have I done to deserve this?"

Hennegy was beginning to think that Mary was never going to be able to grasp what he was saying. "You were chosen to be the blessed one many years ago. Your kindness and devotion are like a shining light among all humans."

"I meant, why am I being punished in this way? I was due to marry Joseph in a few months. How am I going to tell him that I was made with child by the hand of God? He won't believe me. He might think that I am covering up that I have lain with another man and am having his baby. My life is ruined. What have you done to me?" Mary started to sob.

Hennegy was starting to sweat. "Mary do not be afraid. The Lord will help you with Joseph if required." Mary cried for a few more minutes and then stopped and wiped her eyes.

"When can I tell Joseph about this?"

"You can tell him after five weeks have passed. You cannot tell anyone else that the child is not Joseph's. You and Joseph must get married immediately. You must raise the child as your own and love and nurture him. In the future, when the time is right, the Lord will reveal the truth to his son and set him on his path to greatness."

"What should we call the child?"

"Jesus is the name that you should give him."

"We will do that then. Are you going to appear regularly?"

"I don't think that you will see me again until the child is born, unless you really need me. Until then you must just trust in God. He will be watching over you constantly."

Mary looked down at her stomach sadly. "I will do what God wants," she said after a few moments. "What choice do I have?"

Hennegy moved towards Mary. He placed his hands on either side of Mary's face. "Mary, you are very brave and courageous. Place your trust in God and remember, he is watching over you always."

"I suppose I have no other option other than to trust you." Mary closed her eyes and Hennegy laid her down carefully onto her bed. Hennegy covered her up and placed his hand on her forehead. Mary reached up and placed her hand gently over his. In a few moments she was asleep again, and Hennegy moved her hand to her stomach.

Hennegy walked out of the house and picked up one of the bags that had been left outside. He walked back to their tent without saying a word to Dr Nowlett or Denned. He didn't speak on the way back to the drop pod either. Even Dr Nowlett gave up on trying to get him to speak and concentrated on Denned, who did his best to keep Dr Nowlett entertained. When they reached the landing site, they carefully loaded Dr Nowlett and her gear into the drop pod and shut the door. Even when they exchanged goodbyes, Hennegy didn't say a lot. He barely thanked Dr Nowlett when, after she had dosed herself, she gave him her extra anti-nausea supply just in case.

"What's up with you?" asked Denned as they watched the drop pod shoot into the sky.

"Mary, that's what. It's easy to plan to do this on paper, but when faced with another sentient being, who you are cajoling to your will for the purpose of a societal engineering experiment, it isn't so easy. Especially when Mary is just a kid. A nice one at that. We have just impregnated her against her will. Yiler and Nowlett are blinded by achieving what they were tasked to do. They are not thinking about the ethical and moral issues of what we have done. I am though."

Denned didn't know how to respond. "I hadn't thought about it until now, but you have a valid point."

"Perhaps I don't care as much as they do about creating a deity. If the experiment fails, we will go home and both of us would be assigned a new task without any further comment. Yiler and Nowlett have their professional pride to think about if they went back. Maybe that is the difference between them and us."

****

Yiler was waiting expectantly beside the docking bay for the drop pod to finish the post landing check. He watched as the light of Dr Nowlett's pod moved from red to green. The door opened with a swish, and Dr Nowlett walked out clutching her two medical bags. Yiler took one from her.

"Congratulations," said Yiler. "An outstanding job."

"Thank you, but it's only half done." They walked the short distance to Nowlett's lab in silence. Yiler could tell that Dr Nowlett was deep in thought, so he left her alone. When they arrived at the lab, Dr Nowlett opened one of the medical bags and took out the metal case containing the harvested eggs.

Yiler placed his hand on Nowlett's to prevent her opening the case. "Are you absolutely certain that you want to do this?"

"Yes. We have discussed this at length. It is necessary to have a backup plan if anything happens to Jesus."

"I didn't mean that. As far as anyone is concerned, we will be the parents, so it will be our job to look after him. I am the biological father, so I have a moral obligation to do that. You don't."

"I know what I am getting into. It will be difficult, but I haven't yet shirked a challenge, and I am not going to start now. We will be fine."

Yiler took his hand away. "Then please proceed."

Dr Nowlett opened the metal case, extracted an egg and placed it under a microscope. When she was happy that the egg was perfect, she took another vial of Yiler's sperm from the fridge and commenced to fertilize the egg.

After a few minutes, she looked up at Yiler. "Your sperms are very active. Happy to tell you that we have another successful fertilization."

Yiler grinned broadly. "So, Hyet's input won't be needed then. I will make sure to tell him personally."

Nowlett looked at him quizzically. "I was going to do that myself, but you go ahead." Yiler bounded out of the room to find Hyet.

Nowlett picked up the dish with the fertilized egg and went over to the door to a small room adjoining the lab. The uterine replicator was humming quietly, and the artificial amniotic fluid bubbled gently. She opened the seal on the side and implanted the egg into the wall of the replicator. "No going back now. The day Jesus is born, we will become parents too."

Hyet feigned excitement when Yiler gleefully informed him of his proven fertility. After that, Hyet decided that he had better desist his attempts to wind up Yiler because he never wanted a conversation like that ever again.

****

Mary was sitting beside the River Arnon with Joseph. They had walked to their favourite spot, as they did most evenings, to sit and talk. It was under a large tree, about five meters from the riverbank.

The tree was very old with a wide canopy, giving shade during most of the day, hence its popularity. Denned and Hennegy were observing from a camouflaged hide that had been set up previously.

"Is it really necessary to have a plasma rifle aimed at Joseph's head?" said Denned.

"Considering five weeks have passed since the night of the impregnation, I think Mary is about to break the news, and I am concerned about how Joseph might react. We have both witnessed males assaulting females for perceived slights to their male pride. I hope that we do not have to intervene, but there is no way that I am going to permit Joseph to rough Mary up. Before you ask, the rifle is set at stun, so he should live."

"Joseph would be the first human to be hit with a plasma rifle, so let's hope you are right. Yiler would be furious if he knew you had the plasma rifle with you."

"I couldn't care less."

They lapsed into silence as Mary and Joseph sat down. As soon as they did, Joseph asked her what was wrong. Joseph had noticed that Mary had not been her usual happy and carefree self for the last few weeks.

"Everything is wrong," said Mary. She started crying.

Joseph took her hands into his. "Mary, please tell me, so I can help."

"Joseph, I am with child."

Joseph dropped Mary's hands. "*What!* Mary, how could you have lain with another man. We are betrothed. Who was it? I have seen the way the son of the wine merchant looks at you. Was it him? I will bloody kill him."

"Joseph, please calm down and listen. What I am about to tell is going to be difficult for you to believe. Firstly, I am still a virgin. You must believe me."

"Mary, how can you possibly be with child and still be a virgin? Talk sense. Have you been drinking wine or something? That might explain the nonsense coming out of you."

"It is not nonsense. A few weeks ago, I was visited by an angel of the Lord. He told me that I was with child, and the child was the only son of the Lord. He told me we must raise the child as our own. You must come with me and tell my parents that the child is yours and we are to be married immediately."

"Mary, I don't know which is worse, being with child or covering it up by using our Lord's name in vain with this ridiculous story?"

"It is not a ridiculous story. It happened. The angel was standing at the end of my bed in shimmering white clothes. He told me that God sent him."

"Mary, you ought to be ashamed of yourself. Please, say no more. I cannot meet with your parents today because I am too angry. I will come to your house in the morning at first light to break the news to them. Your poor parents. The shame you will bring onto their house." Joseph stood up. "I will walk you back to your parents' house, so they do not get suspicious. Speak nothing to them of this son of God foolishness until tomorrow morning. It is madness. Hopefully in the morning, you will be willing to tell them the truth of how you have become pregnant."

Hennegy looked at Denned and shook his head. "Joseph is clearly not as pliable as we hoped. Damn it, another night for me as an angel. I had hoped that my first time would be my last."

****

Joseph woke up with a start. He tried to get out of bed but couldn't get his limbs to work, so he lay there looking at the tall white figure at the end of his bed.

"Joseph be not afraid. I am an angel of the Lord."

"I had a suspicion that you were going to say that. What do you want?"

"The Lord has asked me to assure you that what Mary said to you today is true."

"How do you know what passed between us?"

"God is close to her at all times. She is, after all, carrying the son of God. Please do not be angry with her or cast her out. The Lord wants you to marry her and raise his son as if he were your own. Only you and Mary can know the truth. Your reward will be that your name will be revered by all men in the future, and your place in heaven is assured. Will you do this for the Lord?"

"I don't care about any of that. My only concern is Mary. What choice do I have if I want to stay with her?"

"You can do as you want. This is your decision. However, whatever path you choose, you must remain fully committed to it."

Joseph didn't say anything for a few minutes. "I will do it. However, the only reason I am doing this, is because I love Mary and want to be with her. She is innocent in all of this, and I am not going to cause her any more suffering. You have inflicted enough of that already."

"Thank you, Joseph." Hennegy placed his hands on Joseph's head. "Now, go back to sleep, and when you wake up, go to Mary straight away. She is in great pain after your conversation earlier."

****

Mary was lying in her bed. She had slept very little and her eyes were red from crying. She was dreading telling her parents that she was with child and no longer betrothed to Joseph. She could not tell them that God was the father of her child. She had promised not to. Her father might even throw her out of the house. When the first light of dawn crept slowly into her room, she resigned herself to her fate. She dressed quietly and sat at the end of her bed. When she heard voices from the kitchen, she realized that it was Ruth and Eli welcoming Joseph, so she got up, sighed deeply and left her room. As soon as she entered the kitchen, Joseph walked over and placed his arm around Mary. He edged her over to the bench in the kitchen and they sat down together.

"Joseph, please don't," she whispered in his ear. He squeezed her shoulder.

"Eli and Ruth, please sit down. We have something to tell you." He waited until they sat down before continuing. Both looked at him, Eli suspiciously and Ruth anxiously. "Mary is with child. We are to be married immediately." Everyone gasped with surprise at Josephs' news. Eli looked furious. Ruth started to sob. Mary however looked relieved and started to cry in unison with her mother.

"Mary, I am very disappointed in you," said Eli. He then pointed at Joseph. "You on the other hand, I want to kill. How could you take advantage of our daughter before you are married? You are a mature man who should have known better. Mary is not much more than a child."

"Eli, I am sorry. We were sitting by the river in our usual spot and we lost control. Well, I lost control. I couldn't stop. It is shameful, I know. Mary is blameless. I instigated it. It is entirely my fault."

"Eli, at least they were betrothed, and they are getting married," said Ruth.

"Damn right, they are," said Eli fiercely. "The whole of Nazareth will know why they are getting married though because of the rush."

"So what?" said Ruth. "It will be news for a day or two, and then the villagers will move onto gossip about something else." Ruth ushered the young couple out of the kitchen. "You two go out for a walk now. I need to talk to Eli about the arrangements which should calm him down. You know how he is about money." Joseph took Mary by the hand as they left the house. They walked down the street and exchanged good mornings with the early risers. When they reached the outskirts of the village, they stopped.

"I love you, Joseph."

"I love you too."

"Why did you change your mind?"

"Very hard to resist when an angel is standing at the end of your bed."

"You got a visit too."

"Oh, I did." Joseph put his arms around Mary and kissed her.

Hennegy put down his binoculars and looked at Denned. "All back on track, it seems. That's another human being that I have duped."

"Hennegy, I think you just have to accept this as part of the job. I understand your qualms, but you have to move on."

Hennegy started disassembling the plasma rifle. "I'll try."

Chapter 4

Quirinius, Roman governor of Syria, looked up from his desk as his chief aide, Mettellus Bantius entered. "Is this important? I am in the middle of planning my next campaign against the nomads."

"It is an urgent message from Rome," said Mettellus. "Shall I open it?" Quirinius nodded assent, and Mettellus read the note. "Caesar Augustus has ordered a census. Each family must register at their familial city of origin at a date within six weeks from now." Closing the note, Mettellus looked at the governor with a tired expression. "Our province is unfortunately included."

"It must be wonderful to have the time to come up with ideas like that and have somebody else implement them," said Quirinius. "Please issue orders to all of the regional sub governors and make sure they know that the census is compulsory. I will select the latest possible date to give us as much time as possible, so the census will start exactly five weeks from today, allowing one week in which to register. Add whatever punishment you want for not registering to the end of the order." Quirinus pursed his lips. "Crucifixion excluded."

****

"I don't believe it!" said Nowlett as she thumped Yiler's office desk. "A census around the time that Mary will be giving birth. It would be a logistical nightmare if Mary gives birth kilometres away from the base and medical support. Why are you looking so pleased about this?"

"Emperor of Rome, Caesar Augustus, has done us a big favour. Where does Joseph have to register for the census?"

Nowlett started tapping on the icons on her tablet. "Hold on and let me check the dataplace to see where he was born. Oh, wait, there isn't a planetary dataplace yet."

Yiler stared at Nowlett. "No need to be cranky. We already know where Joseph has to go to register, so we can plan accordingly." Yiler contacted Denned and Hennegy through his implant, updated them about the census and asked for their opinion.

"We read some texts other than the Old Testament from the time of Moses when we were preparing our paper," said Denned. *"We found this prophecy from Micah, one of the twelve minor prophets of the Hebrew Bible. 'But you, Bethlehem Ephrathah, though you are little among the thousands of Judah, yet out of you shall come forth to Me the One to be Ruler in Israel.' It is Bethlehem where Joseph has to register."*

"Yes, but we hadn't taken the quotation literally," said Yiler. *"We had interpreted it as a broad reference to a link to the house of David, satisfied by Joseph, and thus planned to have the birth in Nazareth. If we can induce labour while Mary is in Bethlehem, we will have the place of birth exactly as predicted by Moses. Nowlett, can you induce labour by using nanobots?"*

"I believe I can, but I can't control the exact time the baby will be born. I can only start the process."

"So long as it happens sometime during the time they are in Bethlehem, it will be fine."

****

Mary sat on the end of her bed rubbing her very large belly. "Joseph, I can't go to Bethlehem. I am close to giving birth. Look at the size of me. I feel like a cow. I can't walk all that way."

Joseph rubbed her arm gently. "I am aware of all of that, but we have no choice. We'll be fined if we don't register, and since we have very little money, we can't afford a fine."

Joseph hurried about the room, preparing a bag for himself and Mary. "It will take about five days to get to Bethlehem at a moderate pace. I know that you can't walk, so I asked Eli if I can borrow his donkey and he has no problem with that. It is a bit on the small side, but it will be able to get you to Bethlehem and back. If all goes well, you will be back here before the baby is born."

"I hope so. I will need my mother to help me. I am very scared about the birth. Nothing can happen to the baby or else we will face the wrath of the Lord."

****

"They have nearly made it," said Hennegy as he looked through his vision enhancer. "One more night in the open and then Bethlehem."

"They only made it because Fawter and Konacht took out that band of robbers that were moving in on them," said Denned. "They would have murdered them last night for sure."

"Mary looks really uncomfortable," said Hennegy as he watched Mary cradle her swollen stomach. Joseph was nearby, setting up their small tent in an olive grove.

Denned took the vision enhancer from Hennegy. "So would you if you were stuck on a donkey for four days."

"I know that, but she looks more than just uncomfortable," said Hennegy. "She really does not look well. I will get in contact with Dr Nowlett to get an update."

They had been following Mary and Joseph on their very slow journey. Compared to Mary and Joseph, and the borrowed donkey, the two Deusi had travelled in the lap of luxury. They had camels, a portable tent, comfortable bedding plus food for the journey. Mary and Joseph had to find lodgings on the way which had proven difficult, and they had to buy food with their very limited resources. The camels could carry Hennegy and Denned and their provisions, including portable communications and medical supplies, with ease. The donkey could just about manage Mary if she walked for thirty minutes every couple of hours. Joseph had to carry all the other essentials.

Denned looked worried. "I can't get hold of Dr Nowlett. The link seems to be down, which means trouble."

****

Yiler had asked Nowlett, Sidion and Hyet to go to the conference room as soon as the problem with the satellite came apparent.

"I thought that a military satellite was impregnable," said Sidion.

"Apparently not," said Hyet. "It is not responding at all. Not even to a reboot signal."

Dr Nowlett was very unhappy. "I need real time data; I have just induced labour and the baby will be born soon."

"Soon?" said Hyet.

"The timing of birth with humans is far from exact," said Nowlett in an icy tone. "Labour in humans is very unpredictable."

Yiler rubbed his hands over his head. "Hyet, get a shuttle out to the disabled satellite and get it repaired. Sidion, get the backup satellite online in the meantime to provide information to Dr Nowlett."

"One problem," said Sidion. "If the backup satellite is to give real time data to Dr Nowlett, it will have to go into an even lower orbit. To power the thrusters, it will have to deploy all its solar panels. It'll be the brightest thing in the sky."

"No choice," said Yiler. "It won't make any difference anyway."

****

Gaspar, Balthasar, and Melchior, renowned astrologers and honoured Magi, were seated around a small table arguing. Last night, a mysterious light appeared in the sky which became a luminous star that persisted in the western heavens. The three Magi had immediately gone to their library to study the ancient sacred scrolls. As usual, they had argued the meaning and counter meaning for a long time. In fact, they spent most days arguing over star charts and ancient scrolls.

"The star is clearly visible in the sky over Israel," said Gasper. "The prophecy of Balaam in the Old Testament has come true 'A

Star shall come out of Jacob; a Sceptre shall rise out of Israel'." He pointed out the relevant paragraph to the other two.

"For once, I agree with you wholeheartedly," said Balthasar. "The prophecy of Micah is even clearer "But you, Bethlehem Ephrathah, though you are little among the thousands of Judah, yet out of you shall come forth to Me the One to be Ruler in Israel." The only conclusion is that his coming is near." He put his finger on the paragraph he was quoting from.

"I'm still not convinced," said Melchior. "The references are very vague and open to interpretation." He was always the last of the three to reach a position on anything. The exact meaning of the sacred writings was often open to a few interpretations, and Melchior seemed to be able to see interpretations that occurred to no one else.

The other two worked on convincing Melchior. Eventually, they collectively determined that the scrolls indicated that the Messiah had been or was about to be born, and they should go in search of him. Melchior argued that they did not know the exact location, but the other two convinced him that the guiding star would lead them on their way.

"We cannot arrive empty handed to the Messiah," said Melchior. "We must have gifts that will not perish on the way. What could we bring?"

"The traditional gifts for a noble newborn are gold, frankincense and myrrh, so why not go for that," said Balthasar. "They would be simple gifts, and each of us can carry one."

"Agreed," said Melchior. "That seems a very satisfactory idea for presents. Let's start the journey before we change our minds. I know what you two are like for changing your mind after we have made a decision." Gaspar glanced at Balthasar, who just rolled his eyes.

****

"All done," said Joseph as he walked out of the administrative building for census registration. "Now the difficult part. We need to find somewhere to stay." On the way into Bethlehem, they had asked at every inn if there was a bed to rent. Because of the census, everywhere was full. Joseph was pinning his hopes on an inn on the far side of Bethlehem that was not on a main road and so should be a little quieter.

"I really need a bed," said Mary. "I feel awful."

****

Nowlett and Yiler were alone in the conference room, as Hyet and Sidion worked on the satellites. Sidion had the backup satellite working within an hour of the issue on the main satellite arising and was now helping Hyet.

"Mary's going into labour," said Dr Nowlett.

"The timing is perfect," said Yiler. "When will the baby be born?"

"Sometime in the next twelve hours. I can't be more exact than that. Can't I go down?" said Nowlett hopefully.

"I'm sorry, but the geographical location means that it's not possible," said Yiler.

"Well in that case, who should we use to intervene if there are complications."

"It can't be Denned and Hennegy. They cannot break their cover. It will have to be Fawter and Konacht, since they have already received rudimentary medical training from you after being designated as your medical assistants. I will let them know."

"What cover story will they use if I need them?"

"I don't know. I will leave that up to them. They're an inventive bunch."

****

Joseph looked desperate as he pleaded with the innkeeper. "Are you sure that you don't have a room? You are our last hope. My wife is with child, and our baby is due very shortly. The sun is about to set, and I don't want to be looking for shelter in the dark."

"I wish I could help, but the place is full because of the census."

"Is there anywhere else we could go?"

"I don't think so. All of the inns in town have been full for the last few days." Mary groaned loudly. The innkeeper eyed Mary warily before turning back to Joseph. "Your wife does not look well. You might need shelter sooner than you think." The innkeeper scratched his head in thought. "Alright, I'll help. If you go behind the inn, you will see my stables. The roof and the walls are solid. You can place your sleeping mats and blankets on the fresh straw. It is better than nothing."

"Thank you for your kindness. How much do you want for the lodging?"

The innkeeper laughed. "No charge for sleeping in the stables. I will get my wife to bring dinner over to you. You can pay for that and the feed for the donkey. Is that fair?"

"Yes, it is. I can't thank you enough. My name is Joseph, by the way. My wife is Mary."

"Jacob is mine, and Ruth is my wife."

Joseph led the exhausted donkey, with the even more exhausted Mary perched on its back, behind the inn to the stables. He helped Mary off, and she sank onto a stone seat. He tied the animal to one of the stalls beside a large brown horse. He laid out a large pile of fresh straw and placed their sleeping mats and blankets on top of it. He helped Mary over and made her as comfortable as possible. She lay down and continued groaning.

"Are you feeling any better?"

"A little, but the pain comes and goes. Lying down helps."

"Do you think the baby is coming?"

"How would I know? I haven't done this before."

Joseph was about to say that there was no need to snap at him, when luckily for him, there was a soft knock at the door. It was pushed open by a kind-faced woman holding a tray. "Joseph and Mary, my name is Ruth. I'm pleased to meet you. I have brought you some food. Bread, steamed fish and fresh fruit. I don't have a lot left. I had a lot of hungry travellers dining tonight."

"Thank you very much. What do I owe you? I agreed with Jacob that I would pay for the food."

"Don't worry about what he said. It is only a small amount of food. Is Mary alright?"

"I hope so. She is just over eight months with child, so the baby should not be coming tonight. It is probably stomach cramps."

"Maybe she ate some food that was off. I will get some towels and some fresh water just in case. Oh, and some more feed for the donkey."

Ruth was back quickly with everything she promised. "Joseph, please come over to the inn if you need help. I would stay with you, but I have a full house tonight, and my husband can't manage it on his own."

"Thank you again for your kindness. I'll come over if anything happens."

Mary ate some of the bread and fruit before falling asleep. Joseph fed and watered the donkey, ate the rest of the food and lay down beside her. He fell asleep as well. It was dark when Joseph woke up to find Mary sitting up grimacing in pain. "Joseph, I think that the baby is coming now," she said through gritted teeth, and with that, her waters broke.

"Oh, for the love of God," said Joseph. "Surely, he could have waited until we got back home before starting the arrival of his son. Why does he want his son to be born in a stable?"

****

"I need to send in Fawter and Konacht now," said Dr Nowlett. "Both Mary and the baby are in distress. Unfortunately, the baby is in a breech position with no sign of turning, so I am going to have to turn the baby. I will need good light in the stable when I do this."

"We can't bring in portable lamps," said Yiler. "Mary and Joseph would notice them, even with all the commotion of a birth."

"What then?"

"The satellite can deflect light from its solar panels. Fawter and Konacht can break off some of the stable roof to let the light in. We can tell Mary and Joseph that it is the light of God shining on them."

"The light beam will be obvious to everyone who is up at this hour."

"Hopefully not too many are awake. Denned and Hennegy can deal with anyone that gets too interested in what is happening in the stable."

****

Gaspar, Balthasar and Melchior were seated around a fire eating their supper. Gaspar jumped up. "Look, the star has changed. It seems to be illuminating a specific spot. It will guide us to see the Messiah."

"It must be Bethlehem as was foretold," said Balthasar. "The light is in that general direction."

"I admit that you were right," said Melchior grudgingly. "This proves that our journey will not be a wasted one. We interpreted the stars and ancient scrolls correctly; the Son of God is probably being born now under that light, and we might be the only people in the world who know it."

****

Joseph was about to go and fetch Ruth when there was another knock at the stable door. He was expecting Ruth again, but instead, two very tall shepherds entered carrying two lambs. "Are you Mary and Joseph?" one of them asked.

"Yes," said Joseph suspiciously. "How did you know our names?"

"We are Benjamin and Thomas," said Konacht. "We were minding our flocks when an angel of the Lord appeared. He told us that a miracle was taking place tonight, and that we were to come

86

here and help. He told us a light would guide us, and it led us here. It is still shining on the stable. We'll show you." Benjamin and Thomas stood up and removed large pieces of wood from the roof. The stable flooded with a bright light.

"Well, I would have believed you without you having to take the bloody roof off the stable to prove it." Joseph said, annoyed by their intrusion. "The innkeeper won't appreciate that when he sees it in the morning... As a matter of interest, was the angel wearing white?"

"Yes, he was."

"That figures. He is probably the same one that visited us."

"What did the angel look like?" said Mary.

"He was tall and thin," replied Fawter. "Gangly, really."

"Thanks, Fawter," said Hennegy. *"I'll remember that."*

Fawter suppressed a grin. "He was surrounded by white light. It seemed that his body glowed. His voice was soft and clear. Very calming."

"It is definitely the same angel who visited us. It is clearly God's will that you help us," said Mary.

Joseph shook his head. "I would have preferred the help of your wives, if I am honest."

"We all must do God's bidding," said Fawter. "He can work in mysterious ways."

"Mary, do you mind if we have a look and see how the baby is doing?" said Konacht. Mary looked dubious. "I have helped lots of lambs into the world. The principle is the same."

"Aw, come on," said Joseph. "You can't compare a lamb with a baby."

"Joseph, the angel appeared to them and asked to help us. It is his will." Mary pulled up her skirt to her hips and Fawter and Konacht examined her gently.

"I think your baby will be arriving pretty soon," said Konacht confidently. "However, there is a problem. The baby is in a bad position, it will come out feet first. This is very dangerous for both you and the baby. We will see what we can do to help this baby into the world safely."

"Konacht, the baby is in distress," said Dr Nowlett. *"Unfortunately, you are going to have to perform an ECV."*

"Dr Nowlett, I have no idea what that is."

"ECV is one way to turn a baby from breech position to head down position while it's still in the uterus. You must apply pressure to Mary's uterus to turn the baby from the outside. Place your hands on her stomach. After locating the baby's head, you will gently try to turn the baby to the headfirst position."

"Dr Nowlett, seriously! You have only given us very basic medical skills."

"Aw, for goodness sake, Konacht. Would you prefer if I took over for the procedure?"

"I hate when my implant is used that way, but damn right I do!"

"You will need to retain your ability to talk to Mary and Joseph though, so I will leave you vocal access," said Dr Nowlett.

"Okay, that's fine. You can link your implant to mine now."

"Okay, that's done. Konacht, you need to explain what is about to happen."

Konacht took a deep breath. "Mary, I am not sure you are going to be able to push the baby out on your own safely. I am going to try to turn the baby into a headfirst position." Mary and Joseph looked very doubtful, so Konacht decided to improvise. "I had to do it for one of my kids because the village midwife was helping another woman. It won't hurt too much, I promise. I am going to rub in some rosemary oil first which helps with the pain. Benjamin, could you get what I need from the bag I left outside."

"We are placing the life of our baby in your hands," said Mary, staring intently at Konacht.

"I didn't know that rosemary oil did that," said Joseph. "Remarkable."

"We will not fail you," said Konacht, ignoring Joseph. "I promise, we won't." Fawter came back in and handed Konacht the oil, who rubbed it in gently.

"Well done, Konacht. The local anaesthetic only takes a few seconds to take effect, so I am taking over now."

"Dr Nowlett, I can't adequately describe how happy that makes me feel."

Joseph watched as Nowlett placed Konacht's hands on Mary's stomach and started pressing gently. Nowlett found the head and started to turn the baby. Mary moaned slightly, but the powerful local anaesthetic did its job.

"That rosemary oil is amazing," said Joseph. "I can't believe that the village elders have never mentioned it. It would have been very handy over the years."

Mary grabbed his hand and squeezed it tightly. "Will you please shut up?"

After about five minutes of massaging, Nowlett moved Konacht's hands away. *"Konacht, all done. Told you that it was easy. Tell Mary to start pushing. I'll decouple from your implant now."*

Konacht was happy to be back in full physical control, now that Dr Nowlett had done her part. "Mary, the baby is in the right position so the next time you feel the urge to push, push as hard as you can." Mary groaned loudly and pushed with all her strength. The baby's head appeared.

"One more push should do it, Mary." She waited for the next contraction and pushed again. The baby came out fully. Konacht held the baby in his hands and Fawter cut the cord. He slapped the baby gently, and the baby started crying.

"Congratulations, it is a boy. Looks just like his mother, I think."

"No surprise there on either count," said Joseph. Konacht passed the baby over to Joseph, and he wrapped the baby in a towel and handed it to Mary.

"He looks perfect... thank God for that," said Mary, cuddling the baby.

"Amen to that... he did have a big part in this." Joseph placed his arm around Mary and put his finger into the baby's fist, who grasped it enthusiastically. "He is a very big baby. It is no wonder that you had problems in pushing him out."

The placenta was ejected almost immediately, and Fawter wrapped it in a towel and placed it by the door.

"Thank you, Benjamin and Thomas," said Mary, beaming at them. "The Lord was right to send you to help us. I couldn't have done this without you."

"I didn't realise that shepherds were that knowledgeable about birthing babies," added Joseph. "What you did there was incredible."

"We are pleased to have witnessed the birth and done the Lord's will," replied Fawter. "We will leave you alone now. We promise to speak of this to no one, as instructed by the Lord."

"He does seem to be quite keen on the secrecy alright," said Joseph." He told us the same thing. Thanks for all your help."

Konacht and Fawter left the stable. Joseph was getting Mary comfortable when the stable door opened. Joseph looked up and saw Konacht and Fawter returning. "I didn't expect to see you so soon."

"Sorry," said Konacht. "We forgot our lambs."

****

Yiler, Hyet and Sidion were standing watching Dr Nowlett. She was bristling with nervous energy as she flew around the laboratory, double and then triple checking everything.

"Dr Nowlett, I think that we are as ready as we can ever be," said Yiler softly.

Dr Nowlett nodded. She walked into the darkened side room where the uterine replicator was located. She removed it from the permanent power supply and checked that the short life battery had kicked in. When she was happy, she wheeled the uterine replicator into the main lab. Nowlett was hopping from foot to foot. She looked at Hyet and Sidion. "Are you sure I have explained what to do clearly?"

"Yes," said Sidion patiently. "We are so familiar with this technology, we could do this with our eyes closed. I don't know how many times we have practiced this, after you told us that you just wanted to be an observer at the first birth from a uterine replicator. Just sit down and let us get on with it."

Yiler and Nowlett did what they were told and sat down. Hyet slid the uterine replicator onto an examination table and turned it on its side. It rested solidly on its four plastic legs, but Hyet kept a strong

Paul Mee

grip on it anyway. Sidion placed her hands on the two seals at the bottom. She took a deep breath and broke the seals. The green amniotic fluid gushed out and down the drain on the examination table. Sidion reached in and extracted the baby. She cleared the nasal passages with cotton buds. She was about to administer a sharp smack when the baby let out a load wail of complaint. She wrapped the baby in a blanket and handed him to Nowlett. "Congratulations. It looks like you have a healthy baby boy."

"Hello, Jestoo," said Nowlett and Yiler in unison.

Chapter 5

The three Magi sat at a table in a bustling tavern near the temple in Jerusalem having food and wine. After travelling for two weeks, they were exhausted. They had decided to rest and recuperate in Jerusalem for a few days before making the final push to Bethlehem. Because these men were distinguished travellers, they had received a lot of attention. Initially, they had told people about their quest to see if the Son of God had been born. The reaction from those that they had told ranged from scepticism to cynicism. They had grown tired of being ridiculed, so now they just kept to themselves. They had always kept their exact destination a secret though. They didn't want anyone to get there before them.

The noise in the tavern died down as three members of the king's guard entered. A captain and two soldiers walked slowly through the tavern and stopped at the table where the Magi were sitting.

"Can we help you?" said Balthasar.

"Honoured Magi," said the captain politely. "King Herod has heard of your quest to find the Son of God and wishes to find out more. He has invited you to his palace for an audience at your convenience."

"Would tomorrow suffice?" said Gaspar.

The captain placed his hand on Gaspar's shoulder and clasped it roughly. "I suggest you might find this evening more convenient when you think about it."

Gaspar winced as the pressure was applied. "You are right. Having thought about it, tonight would be fine for us." The captain removed his hand.

"Can we finish our meal?" asked Melchior, who at times could best be described as clueless. "It would be a shame to waste it."

The captain had been warned to be friendly to the Magi. He had a reputation for heavy handedness, and his instinctive reaction was to drag all three of them from their chairs and march them out of the tavern. He clenched his fists. "Of course, it would be fine for you to finish your meal. We will wait at the door." The captain attempted a warm and friendly smile, but it came across as a tight-lipped grimace. He walked to the door, with the two soldiers following, and stood there impatiently. The three Magi stayed silent until the soldiers were out of earshot.

"If that captain's attitude is anything to go by, I think that we are in trouble," said Balthasar.

"We have to keep an open mind about whether this invite from King Herod is or isn't for a benign purpose," said Gaspar.

"What I have heard about Herod in not very positive," said Melchior. "This request to meet us can't be taken at face value. We will have to be very careful in what we say. We can't appear evasive, but equally we can't risk telling King Herod all that we know. We don't know what he would do with the information. We can tell him that we think that the Son of God has been or will shortly be born, and that we are on a quest to find him. We must be vague about when and where. I suggest that I speak for the three of us to keep the story consistent. You two only answer direct questions if any are asked."

"I agree, but if you are starting to stray from the story, we will interrupt," said Gaspar. "We were very stupid. We should have kept quiet about the purpose of our journey. Someone we spoke to must have been in the pay of King Herod and told him what we were doing. We better go. The captain is getting red in the face." The three Magi paid for their meal and walked over to the soldiers.

"We have King Herod's personal carriage outside. Your camels can remain where they are. We will have you back within a couple of hours in time to go to bed, so you can be rested in the morning to continue your journey."

"Thank you," the Magi said in unison, before climbing into the carriage for the brief trip to King Herod's palace. A short time later, the three Magi lay prostrated in front of King Herod's magnificent gold and jewel encrusted throne with their eyes focused on the king's feet. King Herod gazed down at them for a few moments, drumming his fingers on the arms of his chair and then spoke. "Honoured Magi, please stand. Welcome to my court. It is wonderful to have such renowned and learned scholars in the palace." The three Magi stood and bowed to the king.

"We are honoured, your exalted highness," said Melchior.

Herod waved his hand in acknowledgement. "I asked you to come here because I heard about your quest. You are looking for a baby that has recently been born, a Messiah that will eventually become the king of the Jews. It is just and right that the Messiah assumes this position, and we must make sure this happens."

"That is generally correct, your highness. However, we don't know if the baby has been born yet. The baby is or will be the Son of God, so therefore he will be the religious head of the Jews. A religious king, if you like, more than a political one, like your good self."

"That subtle difference will be lost on many. The Messiah will yield immense power. You believe that the scriptures foretold this?"

"Yes, we saw a bright star in the sky a few weeks ago, much brighter than the other stars. We consulted the holy texts, and we concluded that the miraculous event was soon to take place."

"I would like to pay homage to this child myself. The king of the Jews holds a much higher status than I, and it is only right and fitting that I do this. Also, if the child has not been born to a noble family, he will need security and protection. Where is the child located?"

"As I said, your highness, we don't know if the child has actually been born yet. Also, I am afraid to say, we only have a general idea of his location from the holy scrolls. We think the baby will be in a village close to Jerusalem."

"In what direction, north, south, east or west?"

"As I said already, we do not know. We plan to start with villages south of Jerusalem and then work our way east."

"It could be a long search then, but I am sure that you will be successful. You are being guided by the scrolls. When you have completed your task, I want you to come back here and tell me where I can find the new king of the Jews. I will go there and offer the parents of the child the security and protection of my palace."

"Rest assured, your highness, that the first person we shall come to is you on our way home. I am sure that the parents of the child would be delighted to be under your protection."

"Excellent, that is settled then. The captain of my personal guard will escort you back to your accommodation. Are you planning to leave in the morning?"

"Yes, your highness. We are rested and ready to start on what hopefully will be the last part of our quest."

Herod again waved his hand dismissively. "I wish you the best. You may go now."

The three Magi walked backwards out of the throne room and when they turned around, they found the captain waiting. He escorted them to the same carriage, and he watched it leave the palace with two of his men following on horseback. He walked back to the throne room. King Herod had remained seated in his throne with his head resting on his hand. He beckoned for the captain to come over.

"Captain, I don't trust them. I suspect that they know where the child is, and there is a good chance that it has already been born."

"I can get the information out of them."

"No torture. My court magus would not tolerate it."

The captain looked disappointed. "Pity."

"Have one of your people follow them. As soon as he suspects that they have found the child, he must get back here as quickly as possible. Give him one of my best horses. You can lead a patrol of the king's guard to take the family into my care."

"I will put my best man onto it."

****

The three Magi stood on the street outside the tavern watching the carriage leave. There had been very little conversation on the way back.

"He is a poisonous snake," said Melchior. "I don't trust him."

"I agree," said Balthasar. "I am certain that if King Herod finds the child, he will kill him. All he cares about is preserving the power and control that he has in this area, nothing more. We have poked a stick into a bag of black adders. Now, we have to make sure that we are not bitten."

The three Magi did not sleep well and left the inn early, as soon as the sun had risen. They had suspected that King Herod was going to provide them with an armed escort for "protection". They were relieved to find none when they went to the stables and retrieved their camels. From the moment they left, they kept watch to see if they were being followed. Confident that they had escaped unobserved, they proceeded to Bethlehem and arrived there mid-morning.

The men had decided to adopt a subtle approach in Bethlehem and not to mention their quest. Melchior had suggested a cover story about trying to return property to a couple who they had met in Jerusalem. They believed the couple had gone to Bethlehem, and they might recently have had a baby. With a cover story in place, the Magi decided to stop in the inns and taverns and have a glass of wine or some other refreshments to see if they could pick up some useful information. At the fifth inn, during the fifth glass of wine, they finally found a good lead. The innkeeper was talking to a customer who was telling him a story about two other innkeepers, Jacob and Ruth. This innkeeper had told the customer about a couple, whose first child had been born in a stable during the middle of the night, and who were still staying at Jacob and Ruth's inn while the wife recovered. The Magi finished their wine and left. They asked a passer-by for directions to Jacob and Ruth's inn and were helpfully pointed in the right direction. After a short camel ride, they arrived at the inn, nervous but excited. They walked in and were met by Ruth. They ordered food and water with no wine because they were already well on the way to being inebriated. When Ruth brought the food over, they used their cover story. At first, Ruth was suspicious, but as they talked to her, she became more comfortable that they were not lying.

"Two weeks ago, a couple called Mary and Joseph came here on the night of the census. I could only give them the stable to stay in. Mary ended up giving birth in the stable. Can you believe it? They didn't even call me to help. They managed it themselves, even though it was a difficult birth. Mary wasn't able to travel home, so they are still here."

Gaspar could barely contain his excitement. "Where are they now?"

"Upstairs. You can go on up if you want to."

Konacht was in a camouflaged observation point on a small hill overlooking the inn. *"Denned, three men have just arrived at the inn. Well dressed and in a style not from this area. You should get close to the inn, just in case."*

Denned and Hennegy both moaned. They had just prepared lunch and were about to start eating it. They took a couple of quick bites and put down their food. They were using a cover of being transient traders from Carthage, so it took them a couple of minutes to dress appropriately. Their tent was located on the edge of Bethlehem, about five hundred meters from the inn, so they got there quickly.

Konacht was getting nervous. *"The men have entered the inn and are asking Ruth about a couple that they are looking for who might recently have had a baby. They want to return some property to them. It sounds like complete bullshit to me, but she's falling for it big time. Damn it, she's sending them upstairs. I think that you need to run."* Denned and Hennegy started to run which was difficult in the ankle length robes they were wearing.

Konacht was struggling to stay calm. *"They are outside the room… hurry."*

The three Magi thanked Ruth and they went up the stairs. Gaspar knocked at the door gently.

"Come on in, Ruth," shouted Mary.

"We are not Ruth," said Melchior.

"Who are you then?" asked Joseph.

"We are three Magi on a long quest to find the newborn Son of God," said Melchior. "I am Melchior, and my companions are Gaspar and Balthasar."

Joseph leaned over to Mary and whispered in her ear. "I don't believe it. I thought that no one else was supposed to know about this."

"They must have been sent by God like the shepherds. Open the door."

Joseph opened the door slightly. "Did an angel send you by any chance?"

Melchior was perplexed. "No, it was not an angel that sent us. "

"If no angel sent you, then how exactly did you find us."

"A few weeks ago, we saw a bright star in the sky, and we consulted the scriptures as to its meaning. The holy text indicated that the Son of God was to be born and pointed us towards Bethlehem as the birthplace of the Son of God."

Joseph started laughing. "No angel was involved then." The three Magi all looked at each other with confused expressions. "Long story. You will be glad to know that you have come to the right place. I am Joseph, son of Jacob. Come on in and behold the Son of God in the arms of my wife Mary, daughter of Eli." The three Magi walked into the room and kneeled by the side of the bed.

"I don't believe it," said Konacht. *"It's impossible."*

"What's impossible?" said a breathless Hennegy.

"These guys are telling Mary and Joseph that God gave them a sign in the ancient scrolls to come here and see the Son of God. Is this something that was planned by us?" It was fortunate that Konacht spoke when he did because Denned was about to burst through the door of the inn. He skidded to a halt instead, and Hennegy ran into the back of him.

"Who are these guys?" said Denned as he rubbed his back.

"May we hold the child?" asked Gaspar.

"Of course, Gaspar," said Mary. "His name is Jesus. You have travelled a long way to see him, so your quest should end with you holding him." The three Magi placed their hands in turn on the baby.

They then took off the bags that they were carrying on their backs. Each of them pulled out a carefully wrapped package.

"We have brought you gifts of gold, frankincense and myrrh to honour your son," said Balthazar.

Joseph wasn't impressed. "Myrrh, you brought Myrrh."

"You are very generous," said Mary glaring at Joseph. "Thank you so much for your kindness."

"You are welcome," said Melchior. "However, along with our gifts, we are giving you a warning."

"Konacht, what are they doing now?" said Denned.

"They are taking turns to hold the baby. It is very touching. They are so reverential." Konacht was silent for a short time. *"Have either of you ever heard of King Herod?"*

"Local monarch," said Denned. *"Bit of an idiot. Why?"*

"Apparently, there is a very good chance that Herod wants to murder Jesus."

****

"Your Highness, my spy has returned," said the captain. "The three Magi found the baby, but they have betrayed you. They are returning home on a different route and are not coming back here."

"Well done, captain. What about the parents and the baby? Are they on the move?" said King Herod.

"The family is still staying at an inn in Bethlehem."

"Send two patrols. The first, to secure the family and bring them back here. The second, to hunt down and kill the Magi for betraying me."

"I will issue the orders, your highness."

****

Mary and Joseph were standing with Jacob and Ruth outside the inn. Jacob and Ruth were passing Jesus between them for one last cuddle. "Thank you for all of your kindness," said Joseph. "You will be in our thoughts and prayers forever. Are you sure that you won't take anything in return for the food and lodging?"

"Won't hear of it," replied Jacob, handing Jesus back to Mary. "We just want you to get safely back to Nazareth." Mary placed Jesus into his carrycot on the back of the now fully refreshed donkey. They exchanged final goodbyes, and then the family set off on the road back to Nazareth. Jacob and Ruth couldn't understand why they were insisting in taking the longer route home, when the shortest route was through Jerusalem.

They had only walked a short distance when Mary turned around and cupped her hands around her mouth. "Make sure you look under the bed in our room. You might find a surprise."

****

Jacob and Ruth were sitting at the kitchen table in the inn. They had just finished getting the breakfast for their guests. Jacob was passing one of the gold coins that Mary and Joseph had left them yesterday through his fingers. "They really didn't need to do this. They paid us nearly two month's income." They looked up when there was a knock on the front door. Jacob walked over to open it and was surprised to see a captain from King Herod's personal guard standing there. Jacob peered around him and saw eleven other soldiers on horseback, one of who was holding the captain's horse.

"Can I help you?" said Jacob suspiciously, as he hadn't had any previous positive experience with King Herod's soldiers.

The captain smiled broadly. "I hope that you can. I am looking for a married couple who have just had a baby. King Herod is concerned for their safety and wants us to escort them back to Jerusalem. We had a visit from three Magi who explained to us that the baby could be a very important child."

Ruth moved to stand beside her husband. "Important how?"

The captain smiled again, which was proving a challenge to him. "The Magi were a little vague on that, but it must be important if they decided to travel such a long way to visit the child. Is the family still here?"

"No," answered Jacob. "They are on their way back to Nazareth."

"That's not possible. We have come from Jerusalem, and we checked all the families we met on the way."

"They didn't take the Jerusalem route," said Ruth. "They took the longer route."

"How long since they left?"

"Yesterday," said Jacob. "You should catch up with them no problem. They are moving at donkey pace. When you do, pass on our best wishes and thank them for the gift they left us."

The captain bowed. "I certainly will. Thank you for your help." The captain walked over to his horse and mounted it. The patrol cantered slowly out of the village, and when out of sight, the captain turned to his patrol commander. "Those Magi warned them not to come back through Jerusalem, so they must have suspected Herod's intentions. No point spinning them a story when we get to the family. They won't believe it. We will just take them prisoner." The captain galloped off, followed by the rest of the patrol.

****

The captain spotted the two men from about a kilometre away. They were standing at a point where the road ran through a ravine with sheer rock walls about ten meters high on either side. The patrol was galloping at full speed, so they quickly came upon the men. The captain pulled up his horse and shouted.

"Get out of the way, now!"

Denned and Hennegy just stood there staring at the captain, who tried again. "You have ten seconds until I order my men to move you. There are eleven of them with very sharp swords. You have nothing. Now move before we have to kill you."

"Would you actually kill a newborn baby and his parents?" said Denned.

The captain was startled. "Who are you people?"

"That doesn't really matter, but for your information, we are angels of the Lord, protecting his son from harm."

"And I am King Herod's father," laughed the captain.

"Really. You don't look old enough. You never answered my question. Would you?"

"Would I what?"

"Would you really kill a newborn baby and his parents?"

"We are acting under orders from King Herod, and if that is what he wants, then that is what we will do."

"And that makes it okay? Someone in higher authority gives you an order to commit a terrible act, and you think that frees you from any responsibility."

"I have to obey his orders."

"No, you don't. You have a choice. You can turn around and go back and say you didn't find them."

"I have had enough of this," said the captain. "Draw your swords." The soldiers took their swords from their scabbards. The beautifully polished swords glistened in the sun. The captain was getting nervous about the attitude of these men. "You have your last warning."

"And you have your last warning. By the way, if you look around, you will see that your escape route is now closed."

The captain turned around to see two other men, dressed similarly to the two in front of him, standing at the other end of the ravine where the patrol had entered. "Four Carthaginian traders against twelve of King Herod's personal guard, not great odds for you."

"You will be surprised at what we can do, trust me. I will ask you again to turn around and go home."

"I've had enough of this. Okay men, dismount and clear the road."

"*You are cleared to engage with maximum force,*" said Yiler.

"Bad choice," said Hennegy as he pulled a plasma pistol from his coat. Thirty seconds later, the twelve soldiers from King Herod's personal guard were lying dead on the road. Eight had died where they had dismounted, and the other four, who had mounted their horses and galloped in the opposite direction, met the same fate at the hands of Fawter and Konacht.

"Yiler, shall we bury them?" asked Konacht, who had walked up the road after taking out the soldiers that had tried to escape.

"No," said Yiler. *"Leave them where they are. It might dissuade Herod from taking any other action against Jesus, Mary and Joseph."*

"Uhet and Cannet, have you taken out the other patrol that was pursuing the Magi?" said Denned.

"We had the same satisfactory result as you," said Uhet.

"We can't take the risk of Herod not getting the message," said Yiler. *"We need an angel to give directions to Mary and Joseph to get out of the area until the coast is clear. Egypt should be safe."*

Hennegy groaned loudly. *"Not again."*

"Sorry, but we need the family out of the country until Herod is satisfied that the child is not a threat," said Nowlett.

"Or King Herod dies," said Fawter helpfully. *"We can easily arrange that."*

Yiler had had a few problems with team members attempting to disobey the minimum interference principle which General Lateel had drilled into him, so he decided that an unequivocal response was required. *"Our orders are clear. We are not allowed to assassinate King Herod. He is not directly linked to or part of our experiment. Another concern is that Herod might be part of another team's experiment. We cannot touch him."*

"With all due respect, Herod is linked," said Fawter. *"He is aggressively pursuing Jesus."*

"Yes, but we can resolve that by relocating the family to Egypt. We do not have to assassinate him. Hennegy, let's get the angel visit done tonight."

Hennegy looked like he was about to explode. Denned grabbed his arm, placed a finger over his lips and shook his head. Hennegy took a deep breath and remained silent.

****

The Deity Creation Group, except for Denned, Hennegy, Uhet and Cannet, who were on Jesus watch, were all gathered around the large meeting table. The teams on Earth were patched in on their implants. Jestoo was sleeping in a cot beside Nowlett being rocked gently by her. Professor Yiler stood up.

"Congratulations to you all on the successful conclusion of the first stage. Your dedication to the mission has been exemplary. Because stage two is not scheduled until year twelve, possibly thirteen, there is no point in us all hanging around here twiddling our thumbs. I have sent you a roster for team rotation. There will be six of us here at all time, sometimes seven if you include Jestoo. There will be two on the ship and four stationed on the ground. The supply ship will come from Deusi Prime at a minimum once every two months to resupply and change teams. We will still see a lot of each other, but I look forward to the full team gathering again in twelve years. Enjoy your time back home."

Dr Nowlett perused the roster. "I think that I might extend the length and number of my shifts. Apart from having to mind Jestoo, I want to do some more research to understand how the crew of the *Nubla* used gene therapy to create humans. Yiler will be doing the same as me, won't you?"

"Apparently so," said Yiler, just as Jestoo woke up with a loud and elongated grunting sound.

"I think Jestoo just exploded," said Hyet, holding his nose and backing away.

Yiler grinned as he picked up Jestoo and carefully carried him over to Nowlett. "Your turn."

Nowlett grimaced. "Damn it."

Part II

Creation Implementation

Chapter 6

Deity Creation – Update Report – Stage 2 Commencement

Mary, Joseph and Jesus were happy to follow Hennegy's instruction to stay in Egypt until Herod's death. This proved to be a prudent decision. When Herod discovered the bodies of his patrols, he went apoplectic with rage. His fixation on preserving power for him and his prodigy remained absolute. Herod concluded that his only option was to murder all children aged below one year in the area under his authority. Despite further requests from all the team members to intercede, Yiler made the decision to allow Herod to proceed, because Herod's action kept him from looking further afield for Jesus. The appalling bloodshed that followed removed any lingering doubts that Mary and Joseph had about the safety of returning while Herod was alive. It is open to debate as to whether Yiler was correct in his decision not to intercede.

Joseph found enough work to provide for his family. He began to build a reputation as a skilled carpenter and began to get commissions to make special pieces for wealthy merchants. Mary proved to be an exemplary mother to Jesus, always patient and kind, allied with the sense of knowing when to say no to Jesus. He was one of the better-behaved boys in the area, but he still got into plenty of trouble.

By the time the news came that Herod was dead, they were very comfortable financially. As soon as they heard the news, Joseph abandoned his thriving business and brought the family back to Galilee from Egypt. They settled back into the town of Nazareth. The only person unhappy with this decision was Jesus who was very aggrieved about having to leave his friends.

Jesus is now twelve years old. Like most boys his age, he has an uncanny knack for discovering innovative ways to injure himself. Thus far we have been able to intercede in time to avoid permanent damage. Mary has become skilled at repairing the minor damage with Dr Nowlett aiding her infrequently.

Dr Nowlett has confirmed that she is content with Jesus' physical and mental state. Therefore, she is now preparing for the implant procedure.

****

Jestoo was standing on the *Tesfa* beside Dr Nowlett bouncing from foot to foot. "Come on. Come on."

Dr Nowlett smiled. "Jestoo, the supply ship has docked. It will only take a moment to confirm that the docking tube is airtight, and the airlock will open. Try to stay calm."

"I know Mum. It's just that I haven't seen Dad for six months. It's the longest time he has ever been away."

"He wasn't very happy about being forced to stay that long. It wasn't his choice. Travel has become more difficult due to the Santu attempting to block some routes from Deusi space."

The lights on the airlock changed from red to green and the airlock opened. "Finally," said Jestoo as he ran up the docking tube. Yiler was carrying his luggage and dropped the cases as Jestoo hurtled towards him. He braced himself as forty kilograms of a twelve-year-old adolescent crashed into him at speed.

Jestoo hugged Yiler as tightly as he could. "Dad!"

Yiler hugged him back and then pushed him back with his two hands on his shoulders. "Let me have a look at you. Jestoo, you have grown. Let me guess, one centimetre and one kilogram."

Jestoo laughed. "Wrong. Two centimetres and one and a half kilos in six months."

"So close. Since you are so big and strong, you can grab one of these." He pushed a metal case towards Jestoo who picked it up. "Come on, son, I want to go and say hello to your mother." Yiler walked up to Nowlett and gently took both of her hands in his. He leant forward and kissed her.

Jestoo grimaced. "Sick."

Yiler ignored him. "I missed you. Sorry about how long I was away."

"I know that it wasn't your choice. I missed you too. How is everything at home?"

Yiler shrugged his shoulders. "Not too bad, considering. The Santu arrived in force at our most distant colony system, and after a long struggle, we were forced to withdraw. However, if you believe the media reports, we have only withdrawn after inflicting heavy damage on the Santu fleet. People are not happy about the loss of a colony. We can't keep withdrawing from colonies because if we do, we will eventually have the Santu at Deusi Prime."

Jestoo bent over and started to try to open the case he was carrying. "Are these the implants for Jesus and me?"

Dr Nowlett retrieved the case from his grasp. "Yes, so not something for you to take apart and investigate."

Yiler put his arm around Jestoo. "So, what have you been doing while I was away."

"We made loads of trips to Earth to keep an eye on my brother. When we weren't doing that, we went on expeditions and made some amazing discoveries. Well, Mum did. I just helped."

"Did she indeed? Lots of trips despite the risk."

Dr Nowlett pushed Jestoo gently in the back. "Did you forget about our little secret?"

"Oh yeah, sorry. Mum told me not to tell you. Don't be angry."

"I have learnt that being angry with your mother is pointless. Have you a slideshow ready with your discoveries?"

Dr Nowlett laughed. "You already know the answer to that, but it will have to wait."

They reached their cabin and sent Jestoo into his, which was next door. Yiler hugged Nowlett again when the door closed. "Are you ready to go down to Earth?"

"I'm looking forward to seeing him again," said Nowlett.

Yiler scratched his chin. "The drop pod is scheduled for one hour's time. What could we do in an hour I wonder?"

Dr Nowlett opened the top button of her tunic. "What indeed."

****

General Lateel was waiting in President Flanstid's office in the presidential residence as she returned from the parliament building. She had watched the emergency session from the president's office, during which it was agreed to suspend elections until the Santu crisis was over. She looked up as the president came in.

"Congratulations on being elected president for the duration of the crisis."

"Lateel, do not provoke me. I'm not in the mood. I am not happy about lying in parliament."

"You didn't lie; you just withheld sensitive information."

"The members think that this crisis might last two or three years and so suspended elections for that period. If they knew that your plan is for this withdrawal from the colonies to go on for eighteen more years at least, they would never have made me president for that long."

"You couldn't disclose that in parliament, so what else could you do other than accept the decision?"

"That doesn't make me feel any better. Did the occupation of D15 by the Santu go to plan?"

"Yes. We repatriated key personnel and technology. The navy and orbital platforms inflicted severe damage on the Santu before the navy withdrew, and the orbital platforms self-destructed."

"Eighteen years more of this. Is it worth it?"

"Of course, it is. We have to stand up to the Santu and preserve what we believe in."

****

Mary was baking bread for dinner and looked up when she heard Jesus coming in. He was holding his head and moaning. She could see some blood coming from underneath his hand. She exhaled deeply and went outside to clean the flour and bits of dough from her hands. Mary picked up a damp cloth and went over to him. "What happened this time?"

Jesus looked down at his feet. "I don't know. I was playing down at the river and must have slipped or something. I woke up lying by a rock. I guess that I must have fallen and hit my head. It really hurts."

She removed his hand, cleaned the blood away, and examined the wound. "Hmm... the damage isn't too bad. There is only a small cut on your head. Your clothes are soaking though, so it was lucky that you didn't drown after you fell. Do you want to go to bed and rest for a while?"

"I think I will. I feel really tired."

Mary helped Jesus out of his wet clothes and over to his bed, and he got into it without any complaint. Much to her surprise, when she went back to check on him ten minutes later, he was fast asleep. Mary went back to the kitchen and finished baking the bread. Joseph came in about one hour later. He was making furniture for the house of the town elder and had been putting in long hours. He walked over to Mary and kissed the back of her head.

"You're home early."

"I'm tired and we have a long day tomorrow. Where is Jesus?"

"In bed. He fell over and hit his head today."

"That boy is unbelievable. How bad is the damage?"

"No dents, just a small cut. He has a very hard head."

"Must have been serious enough if he went to bed. Will he be okay to go on our pilgrimage to Jerusalem tomorrow?"

"I think so. He's had worse than this and been fine the next day. Anyway, he is really looking forward to it. You know he's stubborn as an ox. If he wants to do something, then there's no stopping him."

****

Sidion, Hyet and Yiler had met Dr Nowlett when the drop pod returned from Earth and were now standing behind her as she worked at her desk in her laboratory.

"Any signal from the implant yet?" said Yiler.

"No," replied Nowlett. "Could you stop asking me? It is becoming irritating. I will let you know as soon as I get a link to the implant. It does take a while for the nanobots to complete the neural pathways after they are injected."

"Are you sure they are doing it correctly?" asked Sidion.

Dr Nowlett shrugged her shoulders. "As sure as I can be. The use of nanobots to create a neural implant is proven technology for all Deusi. We have never tried it in a human/Deusi hybrid. The fact that Jesus has gone to bed to sleep is a good sign. The nanobots have triggered an impulse to sleep while they work. You can't create a neural implant when someone is conscious."

"The fact that this is untried…" started Hyet, but Dr Nowlett interrupted him when her console binged.

"I have contact from the neural implant," she shouted excitedly. "I will run a diagnostic on it." The other three stayed silent while she did it. Dr Nowlett did a fist pump. "The neural implant is fully functioning."

"And Jesus?" asked Yiler.

"Jesus is still asleep which is exactly what I would expect. I won't fully activate the implant until the morning."

"So, we still don't know for certain."

"Step by step, Yiler, but it's looking good." Nowlett stood up. "Now, time to go to find my next victim." She grabbed her medical case and walked to the medical room with Yiler following her. Jestoo was sitting on a medipod reading, and he put his book down when they walked in.

"How did it go with Jesus?"

Dr Nowlett rubbed Jestoo's head. "Very well. Now it's your turn."

Jestoo didn't look even slightly nervous. "I'm so excited. I'll finally be part of the team."

****

The next morning, Jesus, Mary and Joseph were walking to Jerusalem. They were all carrying small packs, but most of what they needed was loaded onto their donkey. Jesus was walking with Joseph a few metres ahead of Mary, who was leading the donkey.

"What do you think the stars in the sky are, father?"

Joseph glanced at his son curiously. "I haven't really thought about it. They are just lights, I suppose."

"Why do they disappear during the day?"

"I don't know why we can only see them in the dark."

"I think that they are suns like our one but very far away."

"That's an interesting thought."

"If I am right then there is a good chance that there is somewhere like here beside those suns. That would be very interesting."

"That's possible, I suppose. You think that there are people like us out there?"

"Maybe, but it is equally likely that whatever life is out there is very different from us. Maybe some suns have things like frogs. The frogs might talk to each other like we do. They already croak here."

"That seems unlikely."

"Why should we all be the same?" Jesus scratched his chin. "Although the lack of an opposable thumb could be a problem for the frogs."

"Jesus, will you go back and lead the donkey now? I need to talk to your mother."

"Yes father." Jesus walked back to Mary, told his mother that Joseph wanted him, and took the halter. Mary walked up to Joseph and as soon as she reached him, he picked up the pace, so they were walking quicker than the donkey.

"Why are you walking so fast?" asked Mary.

"Shh, wait until we get further ahead." Joseph waited until he felt Jesus couldn't hear him. "I think that we need to keep an eye on Jesus."

"Why?"

"That knock on the head might have affected him more than we thought. He is babbling on about frogs with opposable thumbs living beside suns."

"What other suns?"

"The stars in the sky are all suns apparently. Has he acted like this before?"

"No. This is the first time." Mary gasped. "We could have a philosopher as a son."

Joseph started laughing. "Over my dead body. He can be a carpenter who thinks while he is working."

"I don't think that it is fair that you two are laughing at me," shouted Jesus who was nearly twenty meters behind. Mary and Joseph both jumped and stared at each other.

Mary leaned over and whispered in Joseph's ear. "Can a bump on your head improve your hearing?"

"I heard that too," shouted Jesus.

"Apparently, it can," said Joseph.

****

"Where is Jestoo?" said Yiler as he worked at his desk in his cabin on the *Tesfa*.

Nowlett closed her computer. "He is in the engine room. Remember, he has implant now, so you can check him yourself."

"The engine room, has he ever gone there before?"

"Not that I recollect. Let's find out what he is up to. *Chief Gurun, is Jestoo with you?*"

"He is indeed, Dr Nowlett. I am explaining the science of FTL travel to him. He has a surprising level of knowledge on the subject."

"If he is bothering you, will you send him back immediately?"

"Don't worry, I enjoy having him here. Hold on a second. Jestoo, don't press that! Sorry, got to go." The chief cut the link.

"What are these implants doing to Jesus and Jestoo?" said Yiler.

Nowlett shook her head. "I don't know. This was not anticipated."

****

After they had visited the main temple to pray, Joseph had taken Jesus to the furniture making district to see what the current trends and fashions were, so he could bring them back to Nazareth. Mary decided that a much more productive use of her time would be to go to the market and look for cloth for clothes. Joseph had been doing very well recently in Nazareth and was getting lots of orders from the richer merchants. He had given money to Mary for the market but hadn't suggested a use of it, which was his subtle way of giving her a gift.

She spent a very enjoyable couple of hours in the market, wandering from stall to stall looking at cloth and bargaining a good price before moving onto to the next unsuspecting vendor. She eventually went back to the original stall and bought the cloth that she had tried in the first place. She just had to be sure that she had the best value. When she had completed her purchases, she had enough left for some food, so she went to one of the food stalls and bought some pitta bread, dried fish and olives. She sat down by a nearby fountain and ate her food slowly. She watched the hustle and bustle of the market for a while and then made her way back to the inn where they were staying. She made sure that she had plenty of time because she didn't want to be walking through Jerusalem when it was getting dark. She didn't know Jerusalem very well and was relying on memorised landmarks to get back. The innkeeper waved at her when she entered and pointed towards the corner furthest away from the door. She spotted Joseph sitting at a table with a jug of wine. He pulled out a seat for Mary and poured her a cup of wine.

"Jesus must be upstairs then," said Mary. "Is he asleep?"

Joseph looked up with a startled expression. "No, I thought that he was with you."

"No. I haven't seen him since I left you at the temple. Why do you think that he would be with me?"

"He got bored looking at furniture, so I agreed to let him go to the market to find you." Joseph jumped up. "I watched him go, he was on the road to the market."

Mary looked alarmed and started out of her chair. "We need to go find him, Joseph. He is still young, and Jerusalem is a dangerous place for a boy his age."

Only a half-step behind his wife, Joseph said, "Let's go out and check the route from furniture district to the market. He must have got lost along the way." Joseph put his arm around Mary because she looked about to cry. "Don't worry, we will find him. You know what he is like; he is even worse since that bump on the head."

Mary and Joseph left the inn and retraced their route back to the market. They asked a lot of people if they had seen Jesus, but notwithstanding that he was a tall, good-looking lad, nobody remembered seeing him. They spent a few hours looking for him, and it was dark by the time they got back to the inn. When they asked the innkeeper if Jesus had come back and he replied that he hadn't, Mary burst into tears. Joseph put his arm around her and led her to a table in the corner where she continued sobbing. Neither of them had eaten for hours, but they didn't feel like eating, their stomachs were in knots with worry. They discussed what they might be able to do to find Jesus. Joseph heard the door of the inn opening and looked up expectantly. A priest from the temple had entered and was talking to the innkeeper. The innkeeper pointed towards Mary and Joseph, and the priest walked over.

Mary was white as a dove. "Something has happened to him. The priest is here to break the bad news to us."

"Are you Joseph and Mary from Nazareth, parents of Jesus?" said the Priest.

Joseph went paler than Mary. "Jesus, has something happened to him? Is he alive?"

The priest laughed softly. "Don't worry, Jesus is alive and well. We are having a very interesting theological debate with him at the temple, and we all lost track of time. I was sent to ask you would it be all right if we gave him lodgings and breakfast at the temple. I think that our discussions might stretch into the morning."

Mary and Joseph sat in stunned silence. "What exactly is a theological debate?" was the first question that popped into Joseph's head.

"Theology is the study of the nature of God and religious belief," answered the priest. "Don't you have these discussions with Jesus at home?"

"Not on a regular basis," said Joseph.

"Not ever," added Mary.

"Remarkable. His views on theology are very interesting, but to consider that his ideas are self-taught... truly remarkable."

"So just to be clear, you are telling us that our son Jesus is debating theology with the high priests of the temple, and you find what he says stimulating," said Mary.

"Absolutely. He has the potential to become one of us."

"Two days ago, he was throwing rocks over a tree to his friend on the far side, and he decided to see if he could catch one with his toes," said Mary. "That didn't end well. Today he is a learned scholar."

"Every child has hidden talents."

"Very well hidden in my son's case," said Joseph. "Anyway, to answer your question, I am not entirely comfortable that he lodges with you. He is only twelve."

"Joseph, if we can't trust the priests in the temple, who can we trust?"

"Mary, I've heard stories." Joseph moved towards the priest leaving only a small gap between them. "I am giving you the responsibility for looking after my son, so nothing better happen to him." The Priest gulped. "Also, we need to be on the road home by lunchtime because I have work to do in the afternoon, so you can only have him for the morning."

"Thank you. I will come to collect you in the mid-morning and bring you to the temple." The priest stood up and left the inn. On the way out, he dropped some coins into the innkeeper's hand and told him to give his finest dinner to Mary and Joseph.

Mary shook her head. "Jesus... theology... the temple. I can't take it in."

****

The next day, the same priest arrived on schedule and walked with Mary, Joseph and their donkey to the temple. He led them to the stables where they left their donkey and waited until their belongings were stored and locked into a room. When they entered the temple, they saw a group of priests around Jesus in a semi-circle. Denned and Hennegy were part of the crowd, standing behind the priests, listening. The priest beckoned to Mary and Joseph to follow him, and he led them to a place where they could hear the debate, but Jesus could not see them. They listened as Jesus and the high priest carried on their discussion.

"While our debate on the nature and existence of God has been thought provoking, may I respectfully point out that there is one obvious fact that we have ignored," said Jesus.

"Which is?"

"The existence of God is irrelevant at this point." There were audible gasps from the group. "We have all agreed that we have a belief-based God. None of us have seen him or will ever see him until we pass into heaven. God will not engage in acts to demonstrate his existence just to copper-fasten our belief in him. We either believe, or we don't. It is our free will. However, God's influence on us through our traditions is now so entrenched in Hebrew society that it doesn't matter if God exists. Our culture, our way of life, our daily routine, our laws and the key events in our lives are linked to and regulated by our faith. It doesn't matter anymore if God exists or not."

The high priest nodded in agreement. "That is a very fair point. Personally, I would be very annoyed to find out that he didn't exist because his existence justifies my life choice. There is another point that I would like to get your view on. Why is it that God has only selected the Hebrews as the chosen people? We are a small tribe, at the far reaches of the Roman Empire. Surely, God wants to have all people on Earth as believers in the one true faith? Why did he spend all that time and effort to free us from the Egyptians if we are to be the only believers?"

"The answer is obvious. We failed God. I believe that God wanted us to be his missionaries and spread the word of God. We didn't do that. We settled down and created a comfortable life for ourselves. We were cowards. We were afraid of what might happen if we took an aggressive stance and tried to spread the word of God far and wide. We feared a backlash from those in power. The fact that this fear was justified, should not have deterred us from carrying out God's will. The more time elapsed, the more contented we became in our lives. We were satisfied that we believed in the one true God, and if other people wanted to join us, they were more than welcome to, but we were not going out to persuade them. So, we failed God."

"So, you are calling us cowards and failures." The high priest was getting red in the face, and the veins on his head were getting prominent.

Joseph decided that it might be advisable to stop the debate. He walked forward to Jesus and placed his hand on his shoulder. "Time to go home now, Jesus. We have work to do."

"Father, I did not know you were here. Did you listen to some of the discussion?"

"A short part, but it was enough. Let's go, now!"

The high priest moved to stand beside Joseph. "That is one interesting son that you have. I am sure we will hear a lot more about him in the future."

"Hopefully not. He will be concentrating on my furniture business and won't have time for this sort of stuff." Joseph placed a protective arm around Jesus as they exited the temple, collecting Mary on the way. As they exited, they brushed by a couple standing with their adolescent son at the back of the group, who had been listening to the debate.

"Now I know what I want to do with my life," said the young man. His father, Zachariah and mother, Elizabeth, had been trying to get him to focus on one trade or business for years, but nothing had really interested him. His parents looked at him with a surprised expression.

"John, I don't understand," said Zachariah. "How can you suddenly decide just like that? Yesterday, we argued about this at length, and today, you know what you want. Bizarre. Anyway, you might as well tell me what this miraculous decision is."

"I am going to do as Jesus asked and spread the word of God."

"Are you trying to annoy me, because if you are, it is working," said Elizabeth.

"I am serious. Jesus is right. The Hebrews are God's chosen people, yet all we do is cower here. We were chosen for a reason. We should have been brave enough to spread the word of God. Well, that is what I am going to do. I will go far and wide and preach the word of God and baptise as many as possible into his faith."

His mother was stunned. "You have never taken our advice, but you are happy to follow the advice of a young boy you have just listened to. I think that you have had too much sun."

"I assure you that I am fine. There is something about Jesus. He is different to everybody I have ever met. He is special in some way that I can't explain."

Zachariah grabbed his arm. "Enough of this. I am not going to get stressed, because I know that you will change your mind again, as you always do."

Elizabeth's eyes were brimming with tears. "It will be so embarrassing when people ask me what you are doing. "John is a preacher, or John is a baptiser" is not the answer that I thought I would be giving."

"Well you better get used to the idea. I am not changing my mind."

The family left the temple in silence. Zachariah gave John a handful of coins. "We should get some food for the journey home. Will you run over to the market and get some dried fruit and bread?"

"Yes, father," replied John. He ran off to the market with the enthusiasm that all teenagers displayed when the prospect of food was dangled in front of them.

Zachariah watched him disappear into the market as he stood beside Elizabeth. "Well, Elizabeth, what do you think?"

"Incredible. Let's hope he comes to his senses soon."

****

Jesus had gone to bed, and when Mary checked on him after half an hour, he was fast asleep. Mary sat down close to Joseph, so they could keep their voices low.

"Do you think that this is the start of it? Is he beginning to understand who he really is?" said Mary.

"I don't think so. If something major was happening, we would have had a visit from the angel. That hasn't happened. Also, Jesus has not mentioned anything to us about being the Son of God. I think when he finds out, we will know in advance. It might just be that he is very intelligent."

"It is impossible to become that intelligent in a couple of days. He was barely an average boy, and now look at him. Maybe God decided to give him intelligence beyond his years."

Joseph nodded in agreement. "If he did, then it wasn't a very smart move. I thought that he was supposed to keep a low profile until the right time. I don't think making him this intelligent will help do that. Look at the reaction from the priests in the temple. We are going to have to shield him from any interest these theologists may show in him."

Mary sighed. "I think I prefer him as he was."

****

Yiler, Dr Nowlett, Hyet and Sidion sat around the conference room on the *Tesfa* in the dark, reviewing the recording of Jesus' conversation with the high priest. When it finished, Yiler turned on the lights.

"On the positive side, we can safely conclude that the implant worked," said Dr Nowlett.

"That's the understatement of the year," said Yiler. "Are there recorded cases of implants increasing intelligence that dramatically?"

"No. Implants might make you appear more intelligent but that is because they allow you to access the dataplace. You can seem to be an expert on anything by accessing the right information. Jesus was accessing nothing. He just became more intelligent as the

121

implant accessed his neural pathways. It really is very exciting. I am looking forward to studying this unexpected development further."

"Sorry to break the bad news, but the implant has to be turned off," said Sidion. "Even after a couple of days, he is displaying signs of becoming a genius. He is thinking about astrophysics and theology. What will happen if he keeps getting more intelligent? He is only aged twelve. What if the implant hasn't reached its full potential? At this rate, he might be inventing powered flight next week."

"We don't know what level of intelligence the implant will bring him too," said Yiler. "I agree that the implant has to be turned off tonight before he wakes up. The timeline for our plan requires Jesus to be an adult male before we tell him who he is. It simply won't work with a twelve-year-old child genius. He lacks the gravitas of a grey-haired adult. The plan requires that we start with a fifty-year-old male, and that is the timeline that we must adhere to. Since human life expectancy is thirty-five years, a male of that age will have the advantage of been perceived in the locality as an exceptional person."

Dr Nowlett looked a little glum as she nodded her assent. "I know you are right, but it would have been fascinating. I will go back to my office and shut down the implant."

Yiler touched her arm gently. "At least, we will have Jestoo to observe. There is no need to turn off his implant."

****

Yiler and Nowlett were sitting in Yiler's cabin, reading. "Yiler, do you think that what happened today will have an impact on the plan?" said Nowlett as she put her reader down.

Yiler looked up from his reader. "After Jesus returns to normal, people will begin to forget about him. The high priests will remember though, but they will not repeat what he said because who likes to pass on the criticism of a child. I am confident that no harm has been done."

They lapsed into silence, and Nowlett decided to change the subject. "School term starts in two weeks. It will be nice to go home as a family for a few months. It has been a long time since we were together on Deusi Prime."

"Is your enthusiasm for going home linked to further analysis of your research on Earth?"

"It is." Nowlett jumped out of bed and retrieved her laptop. Yiler moaned loudly, so when she got back to the bed, she picked up her pillow and hit him with it. "It's your fault for asking, so brace yourself. Jestoo needs to be here for this. I'll summon him." She activated her implant and asked him to drop in. Less than a minute later, Jestoo chimed to gain entry. Yiler walked over to the door. "Who is it?"

"Still not funny, Dad! Let me in."

"What's the password?" said Yiler, grinning at his wife. Nowlett decided that Jestoo had been tortured enough, so she allowed him in. Jestoo bounded over with a memory stick in his hand.

"I've something to show you before Mum does her presentation."

He plugged it into Yiler's computer and opened a file.

"What are you showing us?" said Nowlett.

"I've made a CGI film."

"What about?"

"The *Nubla*. I've made a film about what happened to the crew of the *Nubla* after their FTL drive went down. It sets the scene for Mum's research. Do you want to see it?"

Yiler sat down on the bed beside Nowlett. "Of course, we do."

"Yes," said Jestoo as he pressed play.

The Nubla by Jestoo
Episode 1

The female woke up abruptly as she took a deep breath that finished in a snort. The bright light in the room hurt her eyes, so she immediately shut them again. She wriggled around on the bed to stretch her limbs. She concluded that although it was a comfortable bed, it wasn't the bed in her apartment at the university. As she breathed deeply, she smelled a slight antiseptic aroma. Her intuition was that she was in a medical facility of some sort, unless someone had thoroughly cleaned her apartment and put in a new bed without telling her.

If it was a medical facility, she wasn't sure why she was in one. She didn't remember being sick or having an accident. It was as if recent memories were hidden in a dense fog that drifted away at the last moment. It was incredibly frustrating. She knew who she was though, which she guessed was a good sign. Maybe it was only her short-term memory that was affected by whatever happened.

She half opened her eyes and looked around her. Even through squinted eyes, she knew that it was a medical facility. The room held ten sickbay beds which appeared to be brand new. Hers was the only one occupied.

She heard the click clack of footsteps approaching, so she opened her eyes to see who was coming over to her. She winced at the bright lights, but this time she got used to the glare. She turned her head and watched the male who was wearing a doctor's uniform walking over with a beaming smile. She didn't even vaguely recognise him.

"Professor Teclo," said the man. "You have woken up, I see."

Professor Teclo tried to speak but only a croak came out. Her mouth felt like it was full of sand. "Water," was all she managed to say.

The male picked up a container with a straw and brought it up to her mouth. He pressed a button on the control panel to raise the bed to a comfortable angle. "Just take a couple of brief sips, otherwise you will have a coughing fit." Professor Teclo did exactly as she was told. The water washed away the sandy dry feeling, and she cleared her throat.

"Who are you?"

"I am Dr Meyer, the medical chief on this ship."

"What ship is this?"

"We are on the passenger liner *Nubla*."

Professor Teclo dug deep in her memory and after a few seconds, it came to her out of the fog. "We are on the maiden voyage. The first Faster Than Light ship to carry passengers."

"Correct. What else do you remember? Do you know who you are?"

"I am Professor Teclo, head of the Genetics Department of the Deusi Technical University and chairperson of the Deusi Science Institute. I was supposed to make a speech to the other scientists after we got back from the test run. Did I? It's all so hazy. What's wrong with me? Why can't I remember? Am I concussed?"

"No, you are not concussed. The loss of memory is common to everyone who didn't wake up immediately after the incident. It will improve quickly, you will be glad to know."

"What incident?"

"I asked Captain Certrul to come down from the bridge as soon as the Medipod instruments indicated that you were regaining consciousness. She can explain. She will be much better with the technical details than I am."

"You're avoiding my question. How long have I been in sickbay?"

"Well... sixty days."

"What? Sixty days! Why haven't I been moved to Deusi Prime while I was unconscious instead of being treated here? No disrespect intended." Dr Teclo tried to sit up but fell back into the bed.

"None taken, and please don't try to get up straight away. You have been on the flat of your back, so your muscles will require some work before you can start moving on your own. In answer to your question, moving you to Deusi Prime would have presented certain logistical difficulties."

"What is that supposed to mean? You have shuttles on board. I remember seeing them when I arrived on the ship. One of those could have been used. Surely, I should have been in a hospital if I have been unconscious that long. Again, no disrespect intended to your medical skills."

Dr Meyer was beginning to look a little agitated with beads of sweat on his forehead despite the cold air conditioning in the sickbay. He dabbed a handkerchief against his head. "Captain Certrul will be here in a few seconds. Really, you should talk to her."

Professor Teclo was about to question Dr Meyer further when the sickbay door opened and a tall female walked in, wearing a blue civilian ship captain's uniform. Dr Meyer looked visibly relieved.

"Professor Teclo," Captain Certrul began. "I can't tell you how pleased I am to see that you are awake. You had us worried, you know."

"What was this incident?" said Teclo impatiently.

"The FTL drive had a catastrophic failure when engaged. Everyone on board was rendered unconscious for a time, some for longer than others. As the crew woke up, they tried to shut down the drive, but nothing worked. Eventually, the scientists on board who had technical FTL expertise, worked out a solution and successfully disengaged the FTL drive. That was five days ago."

"Where did we end up? Forty days in FTL drive would have sent us an extraordinary distance."

"We don't know. The available star charts are only able to tell us that we are not currently anywhere in the mapped universe."

"Are we on the way home then?"

"No. When we disengaged the FTL drive, it began to overheat uncontrollably. We had to jettison it before it blew up which it did most spectacularly. We only have ordinary propulsion engines to get us home."

"So how long will it take using ordinary engines?"

"We don't know that either. We have a general idea where Deusi Prime might be, and if we are right, we think that it would take around twenty thousand years, give or take a thousand years. Even that would require us burning the engines to maximum thrust to create as much velocity as possible, leaving us with very little manoeuvring capability in the future. Unfortunately, this ship was not designed to carry passengers for an extended period. For example, the hydroponics facility is not up to the task. The ship would suffer multiple breakdowns in a period of that length which could not be repaired."

"So, we would probably crash into a sun, planet or comet, or whatever else gets in our way, or the ship would fall to bits. Not forgetting starvation of course."

"That's pretty much it."

"Is there anything positive about our situation?"

"Hopefully. Our long-range scanners have picked up a solar system where the sun is a yellow dwarf star. There are four outer planets and four small inner planets. We think that the four inner planets are primarily composed of rock and metal. The outer four are gas giants, which are substantially larger than the inner planets. The larger of the four are composed mainly of hydrogen and helium. The two smaller gas giants are composed largely of ices, probably ammonia and methane, so they are more accurately described as ice giants."

"Why are you telling me about gas giants, ice giants and yellow dwarf stars? What is positive about that?"

"Because the third planet from the sun may be capable of supporting life. We have the option of moving the ship to that planet."

"To what end? Do you think that we might discover an FTL capable race who could help us repair the ship and send us home?"

"The odds against that are astronomical. I'm more hoping to find it uninhabited. Maybe we can establish ourselves there, and perhaps, I don't know... build a colony; something that will thrive and prosper long after we have gone."

"Even if we could do that, how will that colony ever be found?"

"We will send all of our probes back towards Deusi Prime with details of what happened and what we plan to do. Hopefully, one of them will be picked up and a ship sent to find us. No hope of discovery in our lifetimes of course. It will be thousands of years before our descendants are found."

"How many people are on the ship?"

"There are sixty people. Twenty-five crew and thirty-five passengers."

"That might not be enough to establish a viable colony due to an insufficient genetic pool. I need to think about that. How long until we get to the planet?"

"It will take fifty days to get there." Professor Teclo folded her arms across her chest and closed her eyes.

"Good idea," said Dr Meyer. "You could do with the rest."

"I'm not resting," she replied. "I am thinking." She opened her eyes again. "Why were you so pleased that I have woken up?"

"We checked the database to confirm who should be in charge. Your position as head of the Science Council, which is a principal officer appointment in the civil service, makes you the leading member of the Deusi Civilian Administration on this ship. You outrank me." Captain Certrul seemed to be very pleased to relay this piece of news.

"So, I am the de facto president of this merry band sailing into the unknown with all our hopes hinging on whether a planet in the middle of nowhere might support life."

"I suppose you could put it that way."

"Then we are in deep... you know what. You have my authorisation to proceed though if you need it. Now, go away the two of you, I'm going back to sleep. My head is beginning to hurt."

Episode 2

Elder Son watched as his father, Clan Leader, moved cautiously to the side of the clearing closest to the tusked 'rough-fur' and its calf. The tusked 'rough-fur' was trying to move the terrified calf out of the forest. The calf had strayed while its mother was drinking at the water pool. Clan Leader was trying to attract the mother's attention away from the calf to allow Elder Son and Youngest Son to move in to kill it. Elder Son and his brother had armed themselves with sharp throwing rocks and were hiding in some bushes to the opposite side of the clearing from where his father was standing.

They began to push branches aside and move out of their hiding place.

The tusked 'rough-fur' looked like it was falling for the move as it began to turn towards Clan Leader. At the worst moment, Youngest Son stood on a branch which cracked loudly. The tusked 'rough-fur' span around and charged. Luckily for the children, they were still well hidden behind trees. They moved further back into the undergrowth to avoid the attack. The frustrated tusked 'rough-fur' stopped short of the foliage and looked around to see what had made the noise.

Clan Leader took the opportunity to move closer and threw another rock at the calf. The large rock hit the calf on the side of the head, and it staggered to one side. It had been hit by three heavy rocks and was bleeding badly. It cried out plaintively. The enraged mother spun around again, and this time she spotted the danger, Clan Leader. He realised that the tusked 'rough-fur' was about to charge, and he sprinted towards the nearest strong tree and climbed up it. He secured a firm grip on a branch midway up the tree, just as the mother hit it with a resounding thud. The tree was strong, but even so, the roots on one side appeared above the earth with the force of the impact. Clan Leader was left hanging with one arm, but he manged the scramble to safety. He peered out from between the leaves and saw the tusked 'rough-fur' moving back for another charge.

Elder Son decided that since his father was out of the fight, he would take the lead. Elder Son knew that the hunt would not go on much longer, and that his clan would be eating well tonight if he could score a few more hits. He took careful aim and threw another rock that unfortunately hit the calf in its rump. The terrified calf cried out in pain. The mother turned away from the tree where Clan Leader was hiding. She stamped on the ground in frustration because she could not see where the danger was coming from.

All the clan members, and the tusked 'rough-furs', looked up when they heard a deafening sound. The sky was clear, so Elder Son could not understand why this had happened. Normally, the sky was wet when they heard noise from it.

Youngest Son pointed upwards and grunted. He gestured fear. Elder Son gestured calm, but as he looked up, he also became terrified. A bird unlike anything he had ever seen was swooping down on them. It was huge, and its wings did not move as it dived. Elder Son grunted loudly to attract his father's attention and gestured question. Clan Leader gestured hide, but the two boys stayed where they were, mesmerised by the sight of the swooping bird.

The bird levelled off and turned in the direction of the clan caves. By the time Clan Leader had remembered the hunt, the tusked 'rough-fur' and calf had taken the opportunity to escape and were now on open grassland and out of danger. Clan Leader climbed down from the tree and grunted to attract his sons' attention. He gestured "follow and run" and headed toward the clan caves. The two children followed him. They were barely able to keep up, as Clan Leader was running as fast as he could.

As they approached the clan caves, they began to hear grunts of fear and panic and squeals of pain from the female and younger clan members. At the crest of the last hill, overlooking the clan caves, Clan Leader stopped to pick up throwing rocks and his sons did the same. They crawled forward, and hidden behind a large rock, looked over the hill. Clan Leader grunted in surprise. The bird had landed beside their clan caves. Smaller creatures were moving around the bird. They were all the same grass colour, and had no fur covering, apart from some on the top of their heads.

Elder Son grunted and gestured to his father to look to the right side of the camp. The clan females and babies had been captured as prey. Many had been killed and were lying still on the grass, ready to be eaten. Clan leader screamed in anger and ran towards the bird followed by his sons.

A couple of the creatures spotted them and brandished small sticks. The three of them stopped and braced to throw stones. Youngest Son screamed in pain. He looked down at his leg where he saw a large thorn with a feather sticking out of it. He pulled it out with his hand and fell slowly onto his knees before toppling over. Clan Leader and Elder Son charged onwards and threw more rocks. The creatures managed to dodge most of them, but one creature was hit in the head with a glancing blow and staggered backward. Clan Leader and Eldest Son screamed in pain as the feathered thorns also hit their legs. They staggered forward for a few more paces and collapsed on the ground. Elder Son lay on his back and watched the creatures move forward to kill him. He could see but he could not move any of his limbs to protect himself or his father. He could only snarl.

"I am getting sick of rounding up these animals," said Technician Greult. Elder Son watched as it got down into the position for releasing dung and put its hand onto his chest. "Good strong heartbeat. He is still conscious despite the drugs."

"You know why we are doing this," said Technician Hasfi, who prodded Eldest Son with his foot before securing his ankles and wrists. "Professor Teclo was very clear."

Technician Greult stood up. "Never believe anything that a superior tells you. I was told that this was a no risk trip when I agreed to join the crew."

"I was told the same when I signed my contract," said Technician Hasfi. "Anyway, nothing to be gained dwelling on that. Let's get these three onto the shuttle and up to Professor Tello."

Elder Son heard them making noises to each other, but he had no idea what the noises meant. His last conscious thought before closing his eyes was that he now knew how the calf must have felt when they were trying to kill it.

The screen went blank momentarily when the film ended. "Well, what do you think?" said Jestoo.

"You did all of that in a couple of days?" said Yiler.

Jestoo was beaming. "Yes, all on my own." His lower lip quivered slightly. "Do you not like it?"

Yiler pulled Jestoo towards him. "Not like it, you must be joking. It is amazing."

Jestoo's beaming smile returned. "Thanks, Dad. Mum, your turn to impress now."

Nowlett cleared her throat. "Jestoo and I have called the animals in the film the Neanderthals. On our trips to Earth, Jestoo and I found and analysed fossils that laid out the evolutionary path from the Neanderthals to the humans. When the *Nubla* arrived at Earth forty thousand years ago, the Neanderthals were the dominant species. They were widely dispersed, and they would have evolved into the dominant species except for one small problem. They were wiped out by a cataclysmic event. The event was the emergence of a forebear species of the humans, whom I have called Homo sapiens. The Homo sapiens DNA was a mix of Deusi and Neanderthal. This sharing of genetic material ensured that the race that evolved from this process had the capability to usurp the Neanderthals."

Yiler could not believe what he was hearing. "If we created a hybrid Deusi race on Earth then that makes it an undisclosed and illegal colony. If the Santu discover this, we can forget about joining the Federation. There is no telling what the Santu might do if they find out."

"Thankfully, we were very careful circulating information about Earth after we discovered it. Also, bear in mind that Earth is far from inhabited space."

"So, no one knows about it," said Yiler.

"Exactly. An added protection is that once we discovered Earth officially fifteen hundred years ago, extensive societal and political engineering commenced. The results have been spectacular. The belief in a divine power is but one of numerous human traits that distinguish them from every other race. Notwithstanding the superficial physical resemblance, these traits will adequately distinguish us from the humans. I understand from General Lateel that there are more experiments in the pipeline that will further distinguish us from humans. If the planet is ever discovered, we can plausibly deny any connection to us."

"How exactly did we create the humans?"

"The Neanderthals lived in sparse and small populations across Europe. They were fundamentally ill-equipped to deal with any advanced newcomers. They didn't have the numbers to challenge the Homo sapiens if we created enough of them. The crew of the *Nubla* captured some male and female Neanderthals from Europe and relocated them to Africa. They used RNA viruses to introduce Deusi DNA into the Neanderthal DNA, and by endogenization, the inserted DNA was passed down to the offspring of the Neanderthals infected by the RNA viruses. They must have contained this new group within a small geographical area. The Deusi DNA was introduced over several generations by a chain of RNA viruses. When the Homo sapiens with the altered DNA were sufficiently advanced and numerous to guarantee that they could replace the Neanderthals, they were released from their containment. Homo sapiens spread into Europe replacing the Neanderthals. This process was replicated in a few other locations.

Once the Neanderthals became extinct, the descendants of the crew must have released further RNA viruses to adjust the DNA of the Homo sapiens gradually evolving them into humans. Descendants of the crew are probably still on Earth albeit now fully integrated into human society."

"Let's assume that the Santu will discover Earth. Surely, if you reached this conclusion, so can they after they arrive."

"They will know nothing about the *Nubla*. Without that knowledge, there is adequate evidence of the evolution of the human species alongside the evidence of the evolution of other species. Jestoo and I found the fossilised remains of Neanderthals, Homo sapiens and the various stages that led to the humans in several locations. They are ready to be discovered by human anthropologists and archaeologists in the future."

Yiler looked stunned. "So, what you are telling me is that, if the Santu do get suspicious, we have two defences. The first is that the human species, while similar physically to the Deusi, is still radically different in all other areas. The second is that the human DNA retains a substantial amount of Neanderthal DNA."

"Correct," said Nowlett.

"Well, that was truly fascinating," said Yiler, who then yawned loudly. "Jestoo, back to your own room please, so we can turn the light off and get to bed. I'm very tired."

"Hopefully not that tired," said Nowlett.

Jestoo ran out of the room. "Yuck. Too much information."

****

Jesus walked over to the breakfast table where Mary and Joseph were seated eating some bread and fresh fruit. He yawned loudly and stretched himself before sitting down. His mother winced as he cracked the bones in his hands.

"Good morning, mother and father."

"Good morning, Jesus," said Mary. "What did I tell you about cracking the bones in your hands."

"Sorry. I have a question for you." Mary and Joseph looked worried. "It is something that I have been thinking about for a while." Mary and Joseph looked even more worried. "Can I please get a pony? Almost everyone else in the village has one."

Joseph suppressed a smile. "We don't have room in the stable."

"We could get rid of the donkey to make room," said Jesus helpfully. "What does a donkey taste like?"

Mary was quite obviously stifling a laugh. "You are seriously suggesting that we slaughter our donkey to make room for your new pony. On the question of the taste of donkey meat, I suggest that the clue is in the fact that no one eats it. Of course, we are not killing the poor donkey and getting a pony."

"My son is back," said Joseph, ruffling Jesus' hair. "Come on, let's get to the workshop."

Part III

Deity Acceleration

Extract from personal notes of programme chief Yiler 'Integration and Status of Jestoo within the Group'

The future role of Jestoo within the Deity Creation Group has been the subject of much discussion. The current proposal from Dr Nowlett and I is that Jestoo takes on the role of God and thus the key interface with Jesus. To consider this proposal properly, it is necessary to examine the context in which it is made. i.e. the type of person that Jestoo has become.

Dr Nowlett has had the most significant influence on his development. I, despite being his biological father, wasn't initially as committed to parenthood. I took the view that my role had only been to supply the sperm as part of the experiment. Dr Nowlett quickly persuaded me otherwise with the threat of cessation of our co-habitation, the key driver to my change of mind. Dr Nowlett divided Jestoo's childhood between Deusi Prime and the Tesfa. When he reached school age, he spent school holidays on the Tesfa with both of us.

Dr Nowlett's careful nurturing has resulted in her core principles being adopted by Jestoo. Dr Nowlett's "never give up" attitude is mirrored in Jestoo. He approaches problems on the basis that a solution can always be found if you look hard enough. He believes that no technology is perfect, and there is always a better way to achieve the same result.

His charm, sense of humour and keen eye for spotting an opportunity for a good practical joke ensured that Jestoo was popular among his classmates and the Tesfa crew. His spare time was spent among the crew, all of whom were happy to spend an hour or two entertaining him, or more often, being entertained by him. He especially enjoyed any new crew member, spending time getting to know him or her. Because Jestoo did not know any better, he had assumed that a life with adults on a small spaceship orbiting a planet was normal. He was twelve when he discovered that this was not in fact the case.

His implant was installed at the same time as Jesus'. Before it was installed, Nowlett and I explained the experiment to him, at least the parts we felt he would understand. He was only twelve years old, so some of the finer points went over his head. What he understood was that he had a brother on Earth, who he was going to have to shadow, and if anything happened to his brother, he would have to replace him. From the day that Jesus' implant was installed, Jestoo's implant has been permanently linked to it.

Jesus' implant had to be adjusted after the dramatic increase in his intelligence culminating in the debate in the temple in Jerusalem. The implant was switched to dormant mode, which restricted it to sending data to Jestoo and the rest of the team.

The implant to implant connection works in three ways. The first is a first-person virtual reality connection. Jestoo learnt to lie prostrate when he used it. The need to lie down was learnt from bitter experience and quite a few bruises caused by reacting to what he saw while located in a different physical environment. The second is a third-person connection where images are portrayed like a scene from a film in his mind; sometimes he had them displayed on a large screen in his room. The third is audio only. The importance of an event dictated which of the three he utilises, but his preference is always the first-person virtual reality. When not on the ship, he receives data dumps that he must trawl through, which he loathes.

Nowlett and I decided to leave Jestoo's implant fully active to study the effect of an implant on the intellect of a Deusi/human hybrid. His intelligence level quickly went off the scale, which resulted in him becoming bored of being Jesus' shadow. Jesus' life was mundane and ordinary. Nothing exciting ever happened.

Because he only had to devote a small part of his time to studying Jesus, he was able to transition smoothly from first school to second school. He successfully sat the second school graduation exam with excellent grades which allowed him to go to university. He wasn't interested in pursuing a university course because his career choices were limited due to his obligation to monitor Jesus. From the limited choices available, he decided to join the Deusi Military as a cadet engineer to combine an engineering career on the Tesfa with a role within the Deity Creation Group. He was delighted when we agreed to his proposal and sent the application to Deusi Prime. He was not enamoured with the negative reply which referred to the blanket prohibition on aliens joining the Deusi military. He appealed, arguing that there was no bar to a Deusi/human hybrid joining the military. After a protracted and lengthy exchange of correspondence, the response from Deusi Prime was positive, and he was appointed an engineering cadet on the Tesfa and on its supply ship. The person he was dealing with in the Deusi Navy Personnel Section admitted later that he wore them into submission.

When on the Tesfa, he spends every available moment in engineering with the chief and assistant engineer. Because the Tesfa hardly ever moves, the engineering crew deal with minor issues and have a lot of spare time. The tsunami of enthusiasm that Jestoo brought to bear on the engineering team was infectious.

Within a few days, he had the engineering crew stripping down and reassembling parts to fully comprehend how they worked. The more he did this, the more he began to make suggestions for improvements, which the engineering chief tested to validate that they worked, and generally they did. Specifications for improvements began to flow back to Deusi Prime, and by being accredited with them, Jestoo gained a reputation for being an engineering genius. He was twenty-three when his engineering lieutenant's uniform arrived on the Tesfa. He told us that this was the proudest day of his life. Little did they know that he saw it as a steppingstone to what he really wanted to do.

The engineering chief was appalled when the newly qualified engineering officer suggested taking apart the FTL apart. None of them realised that Jestoo was manipulating them because he knew he would not be allowed near the FTL drive with his limited experience. His actual objective was to spend more time on Earth to experience it for himself, without his mother. He suggested this as a compromise, which I fell for. I approved Jestoo's regular trips to Earth in the hope that it would deflect him from the examination of the FTL drive.

Jestoo took his first solo trip to Earth a few weeks later. He enjoyed the drop pod thanks to Dr Nowlett's anti-nausea injection, which is now used extensively by the Deusi military. Earth's gravity was another matter. After he was used to the effects of real gravity, he started to help in the base camp, manned by Fawter and Konacht or Uhet and Cannet. He wanted to be allowed to visit some towns and villages, so he adopted his normal tactic of pestering until his victim succumbed. At first, he found Fawter and Konacht unmoving. My order of not allowing Jestoo past the perimeter of the base camp was adhered to. Jestoo focused his attention on persuading me, and when that didn't work, he expressed a wish to return to the ship to start on improving the FTL drive. The tactic worked, as I was appalled by the idea of Jestoo working on the FTL drive. I altered my orders, subject to the caveat that under no circumstances was he to go close to any town where Jesus was, with a total exclusion from Nazareth. I was fearful of Jestoo bumping into one of the extended family, who would notice Jesus' doppelganger.

His first trip was into the town of Galilee, accompanied by Fawter and Konacht. He found the experience fascinating especially when he managed to escape the clutches of Fawter and Konacht by pushing Fawter into the woman in front of him who had then accused Fawter of accosting her. Fawter and Konacht *were trying to convince the irate husband that nothing untoward had occurred, when Jestoo made a break for it. He didn't get very far since Fawter and Konacht could track his implant. He did have enough time for a jug of wine and was making his way upstairs in a brothel, when Fawter and Konacht intervened. He did the honourable thing and paid, notwithstanding that the service had not been delivered. Since then he has made regular trips to Earth with no negative results, albeit that there were several further successful escapes after he learnt to switch off tracking on his implant.*

Taking the above into account, our conclusions on Jestoo are that he is supremely intelligent, but he disguises that fact to remain popular and to ensure that people let their guard down when dealing with him. He is an arch manipulator, and when he doesn't get his own way, he devises schemes to achieve what he wants. When he wants something, he is relentless. Most of the time, he is successful on the first attempt. His ability to proactively and speedily alter his plans as circumstances dictate is incredible.

Therefore, we decided that Jestoo be utilised as the interface with Jesus and take on the role of 'God the Father' when the experiment goes live as planned when Jesus reaches the age of fifty.

Chapter 7

The *Tesfa* was very quiet. There were eleven people on board, and since the ship was built for carrying thirty people, there was plenty of space. Eight of the eleven were crew, Hyet and Sidion were the ship-based team, and Jestoo was dividing his time between the ship's crew and the Deity Creation team. Uhet and Cannet were on Earth which made Hyet and Sidion surprisingly jealous. They were doing very little on the ship and were thoroughly bored. Jestoo was in the engine room tinkering with the FTL drive. Yiler and the engineering chief had given up trying to stop him.

With twenty years remaining until Jesus began the final phase of the experiment, the teams on the ship and Earth focussed on keeping him healthy. Due to their dedication, Jesus was in amazing health compared to his neighbours of the same age, who could best be described as decrepit. Jesus' comparative youth and vigour had, as Yiler and Nowlett had expected, marked him as someone exceptional. Nowlett had been confident that the combination of Deusi and human DNA would extend Jesus' life expectancy well beyond an average human. The implant maintained his health by sending nanobots to deal with any issues that cropped up. The nanobots cleared veins and arteries blocked by cholesterol. Jesus' diet was unhealthy with too much meat and not enough vegetables. There was the occasional emergency; the nanobots had recently completed the repair of a weak artery in the brain that could have caused an aneurism.

Hyet and Sidion's only regular task was turning on Jesus' implant after he went to sleep and turning it off again when he woke up. As the implant was deactivated while Jesus was conscious, it slowed the increase in his intelligence thus reducing the risk of another incident like the one in the temple in Jerusalem. Even so, there were signs of Jesus' level of intelligence gradually improving.

Hyet received the signal that Jesus was waking up. Hyet leant forward and hit an icon on his screen. "Implant turned off. Sidion, please confirm."

Sidion leant forward and pressed the same icon on her screen. "Confirmed."

Hyet smiled. "That's it for the day then. I'm exhausted."

"I will do the first couple of hours of monitoring. You can go off and amuse yourself."

"Did I mention to you that I like the new look? Hair really suits you."

Sidion brushed back her long blonde, curly hair from her face. "Thanks, Hyet. Washing it is a bit of a pain, but I am really happy with it. Are you sticking with your look?"

"Well, unlike you, I don't really have a choice."

"You could buy a wig."

"Thanks for that, Sidion. I might go and see what the technicians are up to. They might need a hand."

"More accurately, you hope to find a certain female technician needing help."

"Hopefully. I think we are close to deciding about a procreation. Give me a call if anything happens."

"I will call you if I need you, but I am sure that I won't."

****

Jesus was widely respected by the other men and thoroughly adored by the women of the village. He was a head taller than the next tallest man, darker skinned and the strongest man in the area. He was the first port of call when there was some heavy lifting to be done. He was universally popular with the village children. He spent a lot of time with the youngsters and organised games almost every night. Every child tried to impress him during the games, and a word of praise from Jesus was worth like being given a bar of gold.

This morning, he jumped out of bed with more vigour than usual. He had decided to take a day off from making furniture and wanted to make the most of it. He had heard villagers and customers talking about a local preacher called John the Baptist, who was preaching the word of God and baptising those who listened. His message was that the Messiah was coming soon, and that only those baptised in the name of God would be worthy of his grace. Jesus had found out that John the Baptist was preaching in Bethany, which was close to Nazareth, and had decided to go and see him.

When he left his bedroom, he walked over to Mary and Joseph who were having breakfast by the newly installed stove. Jesus' prowess for making furniture had gained him a reputation for quality and a large following of repeat customers. He had spent most of his profits on improving his parents' house. Joseph was quite old now and needed a lot of care and attention. He was getting forgetful at times and tended to lose track of conversations or worse, ramble on uncontrollably. Because Mary was younger, she was able to look after him, but Jesus was getting concerned about the future of his parents.

"Good morning, Father, Mother. No furniture making for me today. I am going to see John the Baptist in Bethany. I might even get baptised by him, it's the fashionable thing to do."

Joseph looked at Jesus. "No need for you to be baptised. You were born baptised."

"Hush, Joseph. Ignore your father. He is having one of his off days."

"No, I am not. He needs to know the truth. He deserves to hear who he really is. It has been thirty years since we last had a visit from… you know who. It could not have been intended that it should be this long before he found out. Maybe we were supposed to tell him."

"What is my father talking about? Tell me what?"

"Nothing child. You go along now and enjoy your day with John the Baptist. We will see you this evening when hopefully your father will be more lucid."

Joseph stood up from his chair and shoved it back angrily before he grabbed both of Jesus' hands into his own. "I am in control of all of my senses," he said slowly and deliberately. "You need to know. I am not your father. You are the Son of God."

"Father, please sit down. You are not well."

Mary grabbed Joseph's sleeve. "Yes, Joseph, please sit down."

****

Uhet and Cannet were sitting in their tent monitoring Jesus' house. To say that they were currently in a state of panic, was somewhat of an understatement. "Oh no, oh no," said Uhet. "Joseph is going to tell him. It's twenty years before the time set out in the plan."

"Relax, there is no way Jesus will believe him. He will think that it is just the rambling of a senile old man."

"Even so, I am going to alert Hyet and Sidion. Get our gear ready, we might have to move on short notice."

****

"Jesus, I am not delusional," said Joseph. "What I am telling you is the truth."

"How could I possibly be the son of God?"

"There have been so many signs if you knew to look for them. You have never been sick. You have the eyesight of a hawk. You are an amazing man physically and mentally. Everyone you know admires and respects you. You are becoming more intelligent by the week. You remember the day when you were twelve and visited the temple? You amazed the high priests that day. In one day, you become a theologian able to debate with the high priests and hold your own. Your true potential was revealed to us that day by God to show us what you will achieve when you undertake your task on Earth. One day later, you lost it all and went back to normal."

"Father..."

"We were visited by angels who told us the future, and it all unfolded exactly as they predicted. That is why we ended up living in Egypt. The angels warned us that we had to protect you from Herod. The murder of those innocent children was all about Herod trying to find you. If you still don't believe me, ask your mother?"

Joseph turned to look at Mary. "You have a choice now. You can tell him the truth, or you can let Jesus think that his father is a babbling fool. It's your decision."

Mary looked down at her feet. "I cannot lie. I think Joseph was wrong to tell you, but what he said is true. All of it."

Jesus went silent and then paled visibly. "Did you... you know... with God?"

"No, it was an immaculate conception. He never touched me."

"Dad, did you actually believe that?"

"Not initially, but when an angel arrives during the night and tells you it is true, it is very convincing."

Jesus stood up abruptly. "Aw, come on, seriously. Immaculate conceptions and angels of the Lord. I am going to visit John the Baptist. I will talk to you tonight when, all being well, you will have come to your senses."

****

Hyet and Sidion were very stressed by the time Jestoo arrived in the conference room. The possibility of being in charge when Jesus commenced life as the Son of God, twenty years ahead of the scheduled time, was something that had not occurred to them.

"Should we notify Yiler and Nowlett?" said Hyet to Jestoo.

"We have two options. We could wait and see what happens after Jesus processes the information." Jestoo sat down. "The other is to be proactive. My brother will get baptised by John the Baptist. That baptism is a major milestone, so it must be marked with a sign from God. We cannot waste the opportunity to convince Jesus that Mary and Joseph were telling the truth even if it upsets the timing in the plan."

"How?" said Sidion.

"I don't know. We are going to have to improvise."

"Let's assume that whatever we do persuades Jesus that he is the Son of God," said Hyet. "What do we bloody do then?"

"We make sure that Jesus does nothing more until the full team gets here," said Jestoo.

Hyet rubbed his face. "How exactly do we do that?"

Jestoo shook his head. "All I know is that it will take a team effort."

Sidion grinned. "Couldn't we just order Uhet and Cannet to take whatever action they deem necessary. They are closer to the action."

Jestoo laughed at the suggestion. "Tempting, but that might open us up to the accusation of blatantly abdicating our responsibility to Uhet and Cannet. I suggest we turn on Jesus' implant permanently, so we can follow what he says and does, and I can talk to him when the time is right."

****

Jesus thought about what his parents said as he walked to the river Jordan. He would have dismissed it as nonsense, but the look on his mother's face had convinced him that it wasn't. The more he thought about it, the more incidents he remembered that individually seemed innocuous, but collectively formed a pattern. The time he had fallen from a tree and woken up with just a few cuts and no broken bones. The friend with him had broken his arm. The time he was surrounded by eight robbers on the way back from delivering furniture to a merchant in a neighbouring town. The robbers were after his payment of gold coins. He fought them off and managed to knock them all out. He didn't remember landing a solid punch, yet all eight were lying on the ground unconscious at the end of the fight. The time he stood between Matthew and his wife Matilda when they were having an argument. Matthew had lost all reason and was about to throw a knife at his wife. Jesus stood in the way, but Matthew drew his arm back to throw the knife. Inexplicably, Matthew had lost control and only managed to hurl the knife sideways. It had shot out of his hand. The time he fell into the river and nearly drowned. He remembered going under the water and thinking that this was it, he was never going to see his parents again. He managed to get to the bank somehow but didn't remember doing it. The incidents piled up in his head, one after the other. It wasn't luck. Had someone been protecting him and keeping him safe the whole way throughout his life? But how could he be the Son of God? His thought process was interrupted when he approached Bethany and heard noises from a crowd gathered by the river Jordan. Jesus headed towards the noise and joined the queue for baptism.

Uhet and Cannet had been following Jesus with their two camels loaded with as much equipment as they could carry. The camels were complaining loudly about the weight. When Uhet and Cannet saw Jesus walking towards the riverbank, they moved into an olive grove where they could observe him. Uhet and Cannet assembled a drone, which they camouflaged as a dove. When Jesus moved to the top of the queue the whole team was listening. There, at the edge of the water, Jesus stood face to face with John the Baptist.

"And who are you, my son?" said John.

"I am Jesus of Nazareth, son of Mary and Joseph."

"I thought you looked familiar. We have met before, you know."

Jesus was shocked. "You have the advantage on me, I'm afraid. I don't remember you."

"It was a long time ago. Eighteen years to be exact. It was the temple in Jerusalem when you were a young boy discussing theology with the high priests. What you said that day, about why we were chosen and what we should have done, is the reason I am here. I listened to your words and started to preach the word of God. I have converted many in your name over the last eighteen years."

Jesus was stunned. "In my name? Why?"

"Because, from the first time I saw you in the temple, I knew that you were the Messiah, the Son of God. I wondered how long it would be before you came to find me."

Jesus was struggling to take this all in. "The Messiah? Really? My parents first and now you, both completely out of the blue. I have just come here to be baptised by you. I'm not the Messiah."

"I am your disciple. You are not one of mine. I cannot baptise you. You should baptise me."

The man behind Jesus was getting impatient as Jesus talked to John. "Could you hurry up please?"

"Shh, Brian," said his mother who was standing behind him.

Jesus looked back and saw disgruntled faces. "John, there is a queue building up and some of them are getting angry as I stand here talking to you. I don't like pulling rank, but since you are working for God, and I am the Son of God, well you sort of have to do what I say."

"Could someone just baptise someone?" said Brian. "I have a lovely bit of halibut at home for dinner, good enough for Jehovah."

John laughed. "You have me there. Jesus, if that is what you want, then I will baptise you." John stood behind Jesus and caught him as he fell backward. He lowered him gently into the water and baptised him. "I am baptising the Messiah," he shouted. "The one that we have all been waiting for. Behold the Son of God."

The large crowd went silent and waited expectantly to see what happened. There were a few people who laughed, but the people beside glared at them and quietened them down.

Jestoo was arguing with Uhet and Cannet. "This is it. This is the big opportunity to convince Jesus that he is the Son of God. We have to do something."

"If you are wrong and we mess this up, Yiler will kill us," said Uhet. "Probably not literally, but you never know."

"The crowd is standing there waiting for God to do something. They have been told by John the Baptist that he has baptised the Messiah. By taking the correct action, we could have a thousand fully convinced converts to our new faith. If this goes badly, I will take the blame, I promise."

"Easy to say, with the comfort that you are Nowlett's son, and so she probably won't kill you," said Uhet.

"No, we are a team, so it is collective responsibility," said Cannet. "Let's get the dove drone in the air and fly it over the crowd. Let's hope we are good at improvising."

Uhet picked up the controls of the drone and switched it on. "Cannet, why a dove?" he asked.

"I don't know really," said Cannet. "I just like doves." The drone was about a metre wide with the main structure being the body of the dove, with the wings containing the rotors. Uhet flew it out of the olive grove and hovered it about a hundred metres above where John and Jesus were standing in the River.

"Shine the spotlight on them, please," asked Jestoo. Uhet turned on the powerful spotlight, and Jesus and John shielded their eyes as the light dazzled them. The crowd looked up as well and covered their eyes.

"Speakers and a loud noise now please," asked Jestoo. Uhet maximised the volume on the drone's speakers and nodded to Cannet. He played the sound of a violent thunderstorm, while Uhet used the spotlight to replicate lightning. It worked brilliantly, as the crowd began to look panicked and edged back up the riverbank.

Jestoo took a deep breath. "Be still. This is my son in whom I am well pleased. From this day forward, you must follow him. This is the word of God." After some more thunder and lightning, the drone was flown back to the olive grove.

The crowd had kneeled and were staring at John and Jesus who were standing together in the river. John kneeled in front of Jesus as well. "I am the Son of God," said Jesus under his breath. The crowd, which had been stunned into silence, reformed a queue and patiently waited their turn to be baptised by John and Jesus.

****

The team could scarcely believe what had happened. They had taken the tumultuous decision to put the last stage of the Deity Creation plan into effect. It had happened years before schedule with both Yiler and Nowlett absent.

"Well done, guys," said Hyet as he activated the speaker on the table in the conference room. "That was a brave call."

"I think it was the only call we could have made," said Cannet. "What are we bloody going to do now though?"

"I think that we have two immediate issues," said Jestoo. "The first is to send a message to Mum and Dad to update them. The second is what we do with Jesus before the full team gets here. We can't deal with the first issue until we decide on the second. They must know what will be happening while they are getting back here. They wouldn't relax for a minute otherwise, especially Dad."

"How long before we have the full team here?" said Uhet.

"Forty days is the best estimate to get all the team back here," said Hyet.

"We can't have Jesus doing his own thing for forty days," said Cannet. "Who knows what he will do? We have to contain him."

"I think that 'contain' is a polite term for kidnapping," said Uhet.

"We can't kidnap him," said Jestoo. "He has to go somewhere away from human contact."

"Turn on his implant and order him into the remotest part of desert for forty days," said Cannet.

"Where he will die, you idiot," said Hyet.

"We can keep him alive," said Uhet. "Cannet and I are nutrition and fitness experts, so he will remain fit and well."

"Assuming that we can do that, what possible reason could we give for sending him into the desert that would be convincing?" said Sidion. There was silence for a few minutes while they thought.

"Make it a test of his worthiness," said Jestoo. "God wants to know if his son is up to the task of leading his chosen people, so he has to test his mettle."

"I like it," said Cannet. "But it will have to be a test of his mental and physical worthiness for this to be convincing. I know exactly what we can use. The desert training programme for the Deusi Army is perfect, with as Nowlett would say, a few tweaks."

"Great idea," said Jestoo. "However, we also need to test his faith to fully convince him. We must put temptations in his way to see if he has the resolve to be the Son of God."

"How will we do that?" said Sidion.

"No idea," replied Uhet. "Unsurprisingly, testing of a recruit's faith is not an objective of the Desert Training Programme, so we will have to improvise as we go along. Jestoo, will you persuade him that heading out to the desert for forty nights is saner than it sounds? Jesus will recognize your voice from when he heard it earlier. The forty days can start tomorrow, so we can send him home to talk to Mary and Joseph. Cannet and I need to set up a base camp in the desert wilderness, and we need a little bit of time to do that. Jestoo, you can start when you are ready."

Jestoo considered what to say for a few minutes and then began speaking. *"Jesus, be not afraid. This is your father speaking."*

Jesus stopped baptising the crowd. "Forgive me friends, my father is talking to me and I must listen."

"I didn't hear anything," said Brian, who was still hanging around.

"Will you be quiet," said his mother, pulling her black head scarf around her neck. "You are so naughty sometimes."

Jesus stood still with his hands outstretched and eyes closed as Jestoo continued. *"The task I have for you is very difficult. I need to know if you are worthy of being my son and the Messiah. You must go into the desert for forty days. You will be faced with trials and tasks that will test not only your physical endurance, but your faith too. If you successfully complete them, then I will know that I have chosen well."*

Jesus opened his mouth to reply. Hyet grabbed Jestoo's arm. "Quick, tell him that he can just think his answers and you will hear them. The crowd might think that he is mad if they just hear one side of a conversation."

"And it's very irritating," said Sidion.

"Jesus, no need to speak, I can hear your thoughts, my son."

"I will do as you ask, father."

"Go home to Mary and Joseph and spend the night there. You have a lot to talk about. I will give you directions in the morning for your journey into the desert. You should tell the crowd what is happening, so they are not suspicious about your absence. Until tomorrow then, my son."

Jesus opened his eyes. "My friends, my father has asked me to go into the desert for forty days to prepare myself for the work that has to be done. I will finish baptising you all and then go home to say goodbye to my family. Do not be concerned. I will return." With that, he started the baptisms again.

"That went well, Jestoo," said Hyet. "He accepted your commands as his father."

"I think I know better than anyone how his mind works, which helped."

Cannet scratched his head. "Just forty days to go until help arrives. I hope we all survive, never mind Jesus."

Chapter 8

Everything moved quickly once the rest of the crew arrived on the supply ship, exactly forty days after the messages had been received by Yiler and Nowlett. Fawter and Konacht were immediately dispatched in a drop pod to Earth to take over Jesus' personal security. Thirty minutes after landing, the drop pod returned to the *Tesfa* with Uhet and Cannet on board.

Yiler and Nowlett went looking for Jestoo, who was conspicuous by his absence, when they had exited the docking tube from the supply ship. He managed to avoid meeting them until the arranged meeting with the full group commenced. Yiler, Dr Nowlett, Denned and Hennegy seated themselves on one side of the table, with Uhet, Cannet, Jestoo, Hyet and Sidion on the other side. Fawter and Konacht were linked in through their implants.

"Well, you five have been busy," started Yiler. "I got your reports, but please give me a verbal summary of what happened over the last forty days."

"You were given a challenging situation to deal with," said Nowlett. "We do appreciate that. Nevertheless, some of what you did was frankly bizarre." She looked at Jestoo when she said that, and he squirmed a little in his seat.

Uhet coughed. "We have agreed that I will be the spokesperson for the group, if that is acceptable."

Yiler nodded assent. "That might speed this up."

Uhet took a deep breath. "Okay, here it goes. We staged the divine presence at the baptism because we had no choice. I presume you accept that."

"We all agree, it was the right step," said Yiler.

"I am greatly relieved to hear that," said Uhet. "Jesus went home to visit Mary and Joseph and spent the night with them. That gave us one night to prepare for his trip into the Judean desert. In that brief time, we constructed a rudimentary shelter and left adequate survival food supplies for two days.

"Why two days?"

"That is what the Deusi Infantry Desert Warfare Manual suggested. I'll just call it the manual, otherwise it's a bit of mouthful. After two days, the manual requires the test subject to forage for food or be rewarded by being given food for completing physical and mental tasks. Uhet and Cannet worked out the minimum daily calorie intake required, so we could help him if the foraging wasn't successful."

"But you didn't always follow the manual, did you?"

"No. We needed tests that would prove the strength of his faith to his father. It wasn't enough to prove that he was physically and intellectually capable. His faith had to be proven to be absolute."

"So, you used the "devil"," said Nowlett, looking at Jestoo. "I wonder who came up with that gem."

"The notion was conceived by Moses," blurted out Jestoo, and Uhet glared at him. "Sorry."

"We orchestrated three temptations by the devil. We focused on the physical need for food first. We cut Jesus' rations even further, and then the devil tempted him to turn stone to bread. He refused. The second attempt was to ask for proof of God's existence. We tried to get him to cast himself off a mountain where angels would save him to prove that God existed. He refused to do that."

"What would have happened if he did jump?" asked Nowlett.

"We knew that he wouldn't jump."

Yiler shook his head disbelievingly. "Really. A man weakened by lack of food, possibly delirious, wouldn't jump? You didn't consider that, did you."

Uhet scratched his neck. "No, we didn't allow for that. If he jumped, then that would have been the end of the experiment. Anyway, he didn't jump because Uhet and Cannet had given him adequate nutrition, so moving on swiftly, the third was to see if he could be corrupted by power. The devil offered him all the kingdoms of the world if he would turn away from God. Again, Jesus rejected the devil's temptation and sent him on his way."

"Would you deem what you have done a success?" said Yiler.

"If by success, you mean that Jesus has proved his worth to God? Then yes. This guy is ready for the task. We should let him loose and start converting people."

Nowlett leaned forward. "How is he? How badly did your forty days of physical torture impact on him?"

"Apart from losing a small amount of weight and a few bad sunburns, he is fine physically. Being back home with Mary is getting him back to full fitness. She is feeding him up."

"And mentally?" said Nowlett.

"He had a few bad days, but overall, he handled it without any obvious side effects. He is well enough to carry on."

"So, in conclusion, because of what has happened in the last six weeks, we have no choice other than to proceed with the rest of the experiment twenty years ahead of schedule," said Yiler. "We will revise the dates in the plan, amend as necessary, and circulate version two to you within the next couple of days. I am confident that the team will be able to adapt to this new reality."

Jestoo perceived a chance to change the topic. "Great, that's all cleared up. Now, what about the Santu? Are they still winning the military struggle?"

Nowlett smiled. "Subtle as usual, Jestoo. The situation at home is worrying. The Santu keep taking over our colonised star systems despite the efforts of our military. It won't be long until they get to the home system."

Yiler nodded. "It could be six to twelve months before they force their way through to Deusi Prime. That will be the final stand for us because we can't withdraw any further."

"If that is so then why are we carrying on with the experiment?" asked Uhet.

"I posed the same question to General Lateel," said Yiler. "She told me that our orders remain as is until she tells us otherwise."

"Her answer confirms that what I told you about what this and the previous experiments are attempting to accomplish on Earth is correct," said Nowlett. "There is a bigger picture here on Earth, and

155

she is not willing to let us see it. She would be shocked if she knew we have worked it out for ourselves."

****

General Lateel was waiting for President Flanstid in her office in the presidential residence as she returned from the parliament building. Lateel had watched the latest emergency session from the president's office, during which Flanstid was castigated for her handling of the Santu crisis. She stood up as the president arrived.

"You are the last person I wanted to see. I have been criticized in both the parliament and the media for my leadership that has led to the Santu knocking on our front door, and it is all the fault of the SOE, despite what I said in my speech."

"I thought you deflected the blame onto the military quite eloquently during your speech. The military will not be happy."

"I don't care. Is this plan going to work?"

"All indications are that it will. I have been advised that we will have new weapons and tactics ready in a couple of months. The navy have been training with them day and night. Admiral Ydarb has been given overall command, and he is supremely confident that these innovations will allow him to take the maximum advantage from the logistical nightmare that the Santu are dealing with. Their supply lines back to Santu are extended beyond a point that anyone could maintain."

"So, it will be over soon."

"Yes, one way or another."

"How is the experiment on Earth proceeding? I have lots of other things to be concerned about, but I just can't get Earth out of my head."

"There is only one live experiment, the Deity Creation. I received news yesterday that they are much further along than was originally planned, twenty years to be exact."

"Impressive, but is that a good or a bad thing?"

"Time will tell, but I remain confident that the team will succeed."

"If we lose against the Santu, you still believe that Earth could become a very important part of our future strategy of dealing with the Santu."

"Yes, but hopefully that will never be the case. Don't worry, I will keep the team under pressure to get this experiment successfully completed."

****

"Breakfast is ready," called Mary. She had put enough food on the table for four people because Jesus was eating a phenomenal amount. Jesus came out of the bedroom and sat down in front of the piles of food.

"I still can't believe that God did this to you. Look at you. You are just skin and bone."

"Don't be too hard on my father. I have very difficult duties ahead of me, and he needed to be sure that I was able for them."

"Surely, there is a better way to find that out than torture. That's what it was, you know."

"What's done is done. No point is discussing it. He is omnipotent after all."

"I am not sure what that means."

"Sorry. All powerful."

"Being all powerful doesn't make it right."

"I don't want to think. I just want to eat breakfast and to go back to bed." Jesus proceeded to load up his plate with food. "You better make extra lunch."

****

Yiler, Dr Nowlett, Hyet, Sidion and Jestoo were in the conference room. Everyone else was providing protection for Jesus, who was currently preaching in Galilee. Jesus, after some prompting from Jestoo, had made visits to neighbouring villages, to make his first public statements. The trips had gone very well, with Jesus convincing several dozen people to become his disciples.

"He is amazing," said Yiler. "He has exceeded my highest expectations."

"He does have a talent for dealing with people," said Sidion. "They respond well to his calm demeanour."

"Also, he does not care what other people think," said Nowlett. "He says and does what he feels is right."

Yiler smiled. "Remind you of anyone?"

Nowlett ignored him. "That incident with that prostitute in the village of Bethany proves that. She wanted to talk to him, but some of the villagers tried to block her. Jesus moved them out of the way and sat down to talk to her. She told him all about her past life. That was not an easy thing for her to do. When she had finished, he placed his hand on her head and asked her if she repented her sins. She said she did, and he told her that she was as much a child of God as anyone else. He told her that she was welcome to join his group of disciples if that was what she wanted to do. Think about that. A reformed prostitute walking around Galilee with a group of unmarried men as one of Jesus' disciples. It was scandalous to the villagers, but he didn't care. He told them that belonging to God is not a club reserved for the perfect."

"Speaking of disciples, this is a great opportunity for Denned and Hennegy to get closer to Jesus as two of his disciples," observed Hyet. "Albeit quite tall ones."

"I agree," said Nowlett. "As the popularity of Jesus grows, the greater the risk of a violent incident. We need Denned and Hennegy close."

"We need them to develop quickly into his key aides," said Yiler. "That will ensure that they will be in the right place if needed. They better get used to their adopted names, Andrew and Peter. I think that they are going to be using them a lot more in the future."

****

158

Hennegy was not happy. "Us becoming Andrew and Peter, the designated next leaders, Yiler cannot be serious."

Denned supressed a laugh. "Hennegy, stop fighting this. I told you before that you must push your moral concerns to one side. To be fair, Yiler is correct in his decision. Our military background makes us the logical choice to lead the group after Jesus."

"I have duped Mary and Joseph intermittently. That was bad enough. Now I must convince Jesus that I am a loyal disciple and get him to announce me as his deputy. I will be acting as someone else for years. It's unbearable."

"Hennegy, I understand. I really do, but you must decide if you want to see this through or resign and ask to go home. The mission is at a critical point. We can't afford you vacillating."

"I'll think about it," said Hennegy. "If I decide to stay, I promise that I will commit myself fully, and I won't bring any of this up again."

Denned smiled. "Good. I am sure that you will make the right decision."

****

Mary was irritated. "Is that camp by our house going to be a permanent fixture? It is really beginning to upset your father. You know that he is too old for all of this upheaval."

"I know that he is not coping. I am sorry about that. I don't know about the permanence of the disciple camp, Mother. I hope that it is temporary, but I fear not. I can't stop people following me if they want to. It is my purpose in life after all."

"Well, permanent or not, I don't want them following us to Cana."

"When are we going to Cana?"

"Jesus, I told you this. Being the Son of God has not removed the male trait of being incapable of listening properly. We were invited to this wedding ages ago. How is it that men remember the unimportant things and forget the important ones?"

"It's a hereditary talent. Just for the record, I have no recollection of you mentioning this before. Who is getting married? Do I know them?"

"The couple getting married are Gideon, son of Andrew and Naomi, and Rachael, daughter of Lucas and Deborah. It is in three weeks' time."

"Who are they?"

"Jesus, you must remember Lucas and Deborah. They were in our house a few times with Rachael, when you were younger."

"Exactly how old was I when they were last in our house?"

"Let me think… you were five, I think."

"Well, that explains why I don't remember them. Like most kids, my earliest memories are not visiting strangers. Why have they invited us?"

"Well, I would like to say it was because of natural love and affection that has stood the test of time, but I think that it has probably more to do with you. Deborah likes to make an impression. To have the Messiah at your daughter's wedding would be ideal!"

"Why are we indulging her by going? It sounds like you don't like her."

"Well, I don't dislike her. I am going because I don't want to get a reputation for being elitist. You can imagine what she will say if we declined the invitation. The mother of the Son of God was too good to go to our daughter's wedding… she would make the most out of that."

"So, are we going?"

"Yes! Don't try to get out of it. I will not be happy going on my own. Joseph wouldn't be able for the journey, so I will be depending on you."

"I mightn't be able to go. I am still recovering from being in the desert for forty days and nights."

"Not a chance. I will have you back to your handsome and much fatter self in three weeks, no doubt about it."

****

Jesus and Mary walked the short distance to Cana on the morning of the wedding. As Mary predicted, Joseph was too frail to come along, so he stayed at home. Jesus suspected that Joseph might be overstating his health problems, because when Jesus turned around to wave goodbye, Joseph gave him a broad smile and wave, before bounding back into the house. They were followed by a group of twenty disciples including Denned, Hennegy and Mary Magdalene, the woman from Bethany. Denned and Hennegy, or the brothers Andrew and Peter as they were known to Jesus, had been readily accepted into the disciples and were establishing themselves as the leaders of the group. Jesus had tried to persuade the disciples not to come with him, but to no avail, even with Mary pleading with them. They walked a polite twenty metres behind Jesus and Mary, stopping whenever they halted which drew some very puzzled looks from passers-by. As they approached the wedding venue, they saw a small figure hurrying towards them. Deborah had been keeping an eye out for them and had walked down the road to greet them.

"Mary, thank you so much for coming," said a beaming Deborah. "Jesus, we are so honoured that you have come to my daughter's wedding."

"Thank you, Deborah, but I am honoured by an invite to the most important ceremony of your daughter's life."

"Thank you for your kind words." Deborah peered beyond Jesus and Mary at the dishevelled group in the background. "Who are those people?"

"They are my disciples. They took my words about God straight to their hearts, so they started following me around to listen to more of my preaching."

"Astonishing," said Deborah. "They won't need to be fed, will they?"

"Not at all, they are quite self-sufficient. They normally fend for themselves and only require water." Deborah looked a little nervous despite the words of assurance from Jesus. "I will go back and have a word with them if that makes you feel better."

"I would appreciate that. I have enough to worry about, organising the wedding without twenty extra mouths to feed. I will walk with Mary to the wedding venue while you talk to them." Jesus walked back to the disciples to explain while Deborah linked arms with Mary as they started to walk. "Mary, is it really true? Is Jesus the Son of God?"

"I know that it might sound crazy, but I believe that it is true."

"And that makes you the mother of the Son of God, a very important position." Deborah's tone implied that she believed the exact opposite.

"I am not important."

"How did… you… sort of… you know? If you see what I mean."

"I don't see what you mean."

Deborah blushed slightly. "How was Jesus conceived?"

Mary frowned. "There was no physical contact, if that is what you are thinking."

Deborah started laughing. "Since there was no physical contact, then it was a miraculous conception."

"That's a good way to describe it."

There was an uncomfortable silence as Deborah pondered her next comment. "Anyway, it is fortunate that we have the Son of God at the wedding. Not many wedding couples can claim that." Again, the tone implied she meant the opposite, and this time Mary could not suppress the urge to come out fighting.

"Deborah, why don't you come out and say what you really think? I am growing tired of your jibes and cynical tone."

"Fine, I will. It can't be true. There is no way that Jesus is the Son of God. It is a ridiculous story with absolutely no proof. Well, can you prove it?"

"It is up to you whether you believe it or not. Jesus will do what he must do, and people will either follow him or they won't. He isn't in the business of proving himself to everyone he meets, including you. Anyway, I have taken up far too much of your time. Surely, there must be other guests more deserving of your time and pearls of wisdom." Mary unhooked her arm from Deborah's and turned around. She walked back towards Jesus, who had delivered a lecture to his band of disciples on their behaviour during the wedding.

Jesus had never seen Mary looking so furious. "Everything okay, Mother?"

"All fine, thank you. Let's go to the wedding."

The wedding started on time and both Mary and Jesus enjoyed themselves enormously. Jesus had attracted a lot of attention, which he dealt with in his usual polite and friendly manner. Mary had come outside to get a bit of peace and quiet and was sitting on a bench close to the well, when she spotted Deborah coming towards her. Mary steeled herself for more irritating questions.

"Mary, I was hoping to get some quiet time with you. We didn't manage to finish our conversation earlier."

"I am pretty sure that we did."

"No, we definitely didn't. I have lots of questions about Jesus. You undoubtedly believe your story. The strength of that belief has been enough to allow you to convince Jesus that he is the Son of God. However, isn't there a chance that you are deluded, and so he is as well."

"I didn't do anything to convince him. He asked me if it was true after it had been revealed to him by Joseph, and I said yes. What might have convinced him was when he met John the Baptist, who also told him that he was the Son of God."

"I saw John the Baptist preach once. He didn't strike me as the sanest person that you could ever meet."

"He has to make an impression when he speaks, so he can be forgiven for being overenthusiastic about what he believes in."

"Overenthusiastic would be a polite way of putting it. Would it not be best for Jesus if you persuaded him that he was mistaken? He could settle down in the family carpentry business, start a family and live a normal life, much better than this madness." Mary, who was becoming increasingly exasperated with Deborah, opened her mouth to reply, but before she could do so, the owner of the inn came over.

"Deborah, can I have a word in private please?"

Deborah and the owner walked out of the earshot of Mary and the other wedding guests. Mary could tell that it wasn't a happy conversation because there was quite a lot of hand waving with Deborah's facial expression getting angrier and angrier. When the inn owner left, Deborah came back to Mary with tears in her eyes.

"Mary, I need your help. We have nearly run out of wine."

"I am very sorry to hear that, but I am not sure how I can help. I don't travel laden down with barrels of wine."

"Could you ask Jesus to turn some water into wine? After all, if God created Jesus through a miraculous conception, turning water into wine will be easy. Before you answer, bear in mind that this an opportunity to convince the wedding guests of the veracity of Jesus' claims."

Mary didn't think before replying because of her annoyance with Deborah.

"Of course, he can do it. I will go and ask him."

"Brilliant, you have saved the wedding." Deborah walked away smiling. Mary wasn't sure whether it was because Deborah was pleased that Mary had agreed to help, or because Mary had fallen into a carefully laid trap. Mary walked over to Jesus, took him by the arm and led him away from the group of men that he was talking to.

"Is this really important? I had a few of those guys on the edge of becoming disciples."

"Be prepared to be annoyed about what I am about to ask. However, just to give you some context, Deborah does not believe who you are. She pushed me on the topic until I reached a breaking point."

"You didn't hit her, did you? I've never tried to repair a broken nose."

"No, I did not hit her, though I was tempted. She told me a few minutes ago they were running out of wine."

"What point are you making?"

"I sort of committed you to help her."

"No. Please tell me you didn't."

"Jesus, I did. I've committed you to turn the water into wine."

****

Hyet and Sidion were monitoring Jesus with Jestoo. As soon as they heard what Mary had said, they called Yiler, Dr Nowlett, Fawter and Konacht into the room and linked in with Denned, Hennegy, Uhet and Cannet who were on Earth.

"What are we going to do?" said Hyet.

"What can we do?" said Jestoo. "We can't convert water into wine."

Yiler could not believe what had happened. Moses' plan had not provided for physical representations of divine power, so they had not included it in the Deity Creation blueprint. Instead, it planned for the religion to be spread by Jesus and his disciples first in verbal and then written form.

"Divine miracles are not supposed to happen," said Yiler, pointing out the obvious.

Nowlett nodded in agreement. "We considered but excluded them because the risk of failure was so significant."

"Well, we have to do something," said Denned. "Unfortunately, Deborah has announced to the wedding party that the wine is running out and that Jesus is going to solve the problem. The wedding guests nearly pissed themselves laughing at the idea. Deborah has set up Jesus for a major fall. The wedding guests are all locals. It will be a disaster if we can't do something. Jesus will be the talk of the area for weeks, not in a good way, and all the progress that has been made will be undone."

"Cannet and I have checked to see what we have in supplies," said Uhet. "We have pure alcohol, sugar and powdered red and white fruit juice. We can use the ingredients to create a liquid that looks like wine. We also have four large used plastic water containers in which we can store it. It is probably going to taste awful. Our dietary and nutrition supplies can only do so much."

"Pity wine making isn't part of the Deusi Desert Warfare Manual," said Yiler.

Uhet laughed. *"We can mix the ingredients in the containers and load them on the aircar. At full speed, we can get there is ten minutes. The journey might help mix the ingredients."*

"Mixed or not, as Uhet said, it is likely to be a horrendous concoction," said Yiler.

"Quite likely," replied Cannet. *"We will increase the alcohol percentage a little. Most of the wine drinkers are intoxicated already, so a stronger wine will push them quickly to full inebriation. When they wake up in the morning, they might think that it was great stuff."*

"Can you check one thing for me?" said Nowlett. "Do you have emergency rations in store?"

"Yes, I found some," said Cannet.

"Have a rummage and see if you can find some bags marked 'Military Rations Long Life Salt.' Cannet went off to have a look and came back after a minute.

"Yes, I found some."

"Divide the contents of the bags between the containers before you add the liquid."

Yiler looked dubious. "Nowlett, wine and salt are a very bad mix."

Nowlett sighed. "I know that. It isn't salt. It's a universal taste improver. The chemicals in the powder fools the taste buds, so emergency rations taste better. Seriously, have none of you ever wondered why emergency rations taste so good?"

Jestoo was again amazed by his mother. "How could you know that? Don't tell me you invented it." The look on Nowlett's face gave it away. "You did invent it."

Nowlett put her hands in the air. "Guilty as charged."

"Unbelievable," said Jestoo.

"Will it work on human taste buds?" said Sidion.

Nowlett shrugged her shoulders. "I don't know for sure. However, if what you produce is as awful as we expect it to be, it can't make it taste worse."

Yiler thought for a moment. "Okay, let's do it. Denned and Hennegy, discourage anyone from entering the area where the water containers are situated. Uhet and Cannet, get the mixture made up as quickly as possible and onto the aircar. Hyet, Sidion and Jestoo, keep Jesus debating on whether he should or shouldn't do this until the guys get there, but keep him on the positive side. Don't let him convince himself that he should not do this. It is difficult to get him to change his mind when he has decided. It's a family trait, isn't it, Jestoo?"

****

When asked by Mary, Jesus was not inclined to intervene. He didn't think he could ask God to help on such a trivial matter. The guests might think he was trying to prove who he was. He couldn't do that all the time; people just had to believe in his words. When he realized that Mary was getting upset, he agreed to take some time to think about it. In deep concentration, he started to slowly walk around in a circle. Mary knew by his body language that he was in discussion with God, and so she made sure that no one interrupted him. The debate was intense, and this was reflected in the expression on Jesus' face. The wedding guests who had gathered to watch, quickly lost interest as he walked around.

Uhet and Cannet arrived at a grove of trees about a kilometre from Cana. They unloaded the canisters with the artificial wine from the aircar onto an anti-gravity sled disguised as a timber cart. They had used these on numerous occasions to carry a large load quickly without attracting attention. Uhet and Cannet contacted Denned and Hennegy to let them know they were on the way, and Denned had given them directions to where the water canisters were stored at the inn. Hennegy had advised that they were preparing a distraction to allow Uhet and Cannet clear access to the water canisters. He didn't elaborate on what it was. He just asked for notice when they were one minute from the inn.

"One minute away," said Cannet. *"Holding here until you notify us the distraction has worked."*

"Noted," replied Hennegy.

Jesus came back over to Mary. "I have decided to do it. I felt that it was a trivial matter, but my father has convinced me otherwise. He thought that it was time we demonstrated my abilities."

Hennegy immediately activated the incendiary device he had placed in an empty, partially collapsed stable beside the larger, fully occupied stable. Within thirty seconds, there was smoke billowing from the stable.

Mary went looking for Deborah to tell her that Jesus would do as she wanted, but when she heard a commotion behind her, she turned around and saw a tall man waving his arms.

"Fire… fire!" shouted Hennegy. For the next fifteen minutes, everyone at the wedding, guests and staff, either formed a chain of buckets from the well or helped move the animals out of the way.

Jesus and Mary were walking back to the inn together, when Deborah came up to them brushing ash from her clothes. "Jesus, please can you help us? We have no wine left and the wedding is still in full flow."

"My mother already told me. I have considered your request, and I have decided to help you. Please bring me some water containers."

"Jesus, thank you so much," said Deborah, grinning broadly. She immediately jumped up on a stone bench and waved her hands in the air. "Good news, everyone. Jesus has agreed to turn some water into wine, so we can carry on with our festivities for a few more hours." There were a few ironic cheers and some nervous laughter. Deborah looked at Jesus with a look on her face that could best be described as triumphant.

"Jesus, are you sure that you can do this?" whispered Mary.

"I have faith in my father. He assured me that this can be done if I will it."

Deborah asked the innkeeper to bring the water jars, filled by Uhet and Cannet with the wine substitute, from the storage area. With some help, he brought over two of them. Jesus stood quietly as they were gently positioned in front of him. He placed his hands on each of the containers for about thirty seconds and prayed to his father. There was some more nervous laughter from the onlookers.

"The water is now wine," he announced suddenly. The guests moved closer expectantly. A servant scooped out some of the liquid with a wooden ladle and poured it into a cup for Deborah. Deborah was surprised to see what looked like wine in the cup. There was a hushed silence from the guests as she gingerly took a sip from the cup.

"Jesus, you bloody did it!" she cried out. "He made wine. It really is." All the guests crowded forward and held out their cups for a taste. Instead of laughter, there was now a hushed awe as the guests had a drink of the wine. They were amazed how good it tasted. They all had a cup of both wines, just to make sure that the red wine was as good as the white wine. Within a very short time, the wedding guests began to get quite raucous and an impromptu music session started with some wild dancing. The guests recollected afterwards, albeit somewhat hazily, that the wine was of a higher quality than the wine that had been served during the wedding.

Chapter 9

The day after the wedding, the whole team was jubilant. They had successfully achieved their first miracle with no advance planning. Nevertheless, Yiler and Nowlett had decided that divine interventions would remain excluded from the plan. The risk of failure and the stress in their execution weren't worth it.

Fawter, Konacht, Hyet and Sidion were monitoring Jesus from the *Tesfa's* conference room. Yiler and Dr Nowlett were in Yiler's cabin talking to Jestoo about the potential impact of the miracle but stopped suddenly. A well-dressed man came up and stood beside Jesus, who was talking to Mary and Deborah. He was bouncing from foot to foot, trying to get their attention. Mary finally turned around to talk to him. "Can we help you my friend?"

"My name is Abel, and I am a friend of the family. I am also a royal official in the court of Herod Antipas. I live in Capernaum with my wife and two sons. One of them, Luke, is very sick. I think that he is close to death. One of my friends heard you preaching that you were the Son of God. I didn't pay a lot of attention to him at the time, but what I saw yesterday convinced me that there is truth behind this. As you are the Son of God, I know that you have the power to heal him. I have come to beg you to heal my son before he dies. If you do this, then I will be your devoted follower for as long as I live."

"Oh, not again," said Yiler, who paled visibly. "Jestoo, tell Jesus to reply to Abel that he will consider the request."

"We need to set some ground rules for miracles," said Nowlett with a sigh. "Otherwise, we will be in a state of permanent chaos."

"My Son, we need to discuss this," said Jestoo. *"Can you move somewhere quiet where we can talk without being disturbed?"* Jesus walked away, and when he was a reasonable distance away, Jestoo spoke to him.

"Jesus, you cannot cure every ill in this world. Everyone cannot expect to see a miracle before they believe. It would be impossible. You should refuse this request. I can't countenance a situation developing whereby, unless people see signs and wonders, they will never believe. I am not persuading people to follow me with personalized miracles. However, if you are going to do this, then I don't

want it to be that easy for Abel. You must ask him to pray to me, to ask my forgiveness and then you might intercede. However, this is the last time I will perform a miracle unless I agree to it first. Is that clear?"

"*Fine,*" said Jesus grudgingly.

Jesus walked back to Abel. The royal official said, "Sir, please come down to my house in Capernaum before my child dies."

"If you pray to God and ask for his forgiveness," Jesus advised, "then your son will live."

The man took Jesus at his word and immediately prostrated himself on the ground and then looked up. "How will I know when to stop praying?"

"You will know."

During the six hours that Abel prayed, Uhet and Cannet managed to find the house, knock out Abel's wife with a sedative, scan the child, wait while Dr Nowlett downloaded the instructions to the nanobots, administer the nanobots, check that the heart defect had been fixed, administer the antidote to the mother, collect up the gear and get out of the house, all without being seen. They were justifiably pleased with themselves.

Abel was still prostrate on the ground, praying as hard as he could. He never wavered, so he had no idea how long he had spent praying. He didn't stop until he was distracted by a dove that landed on the water bucket in front of him and took a drink. The dove had been purchased by Hennegy from a street vendor and then released from behind the stable. Abel remembered that he had been told that God had been seen in the form of a dove, when Jesus was being baptised by John the Baptist. He decided that this was the sign. He stood up, dusted himself down and started on his journey back to Capernaum. It was late evening when he drew close to Capernaum, and when he entered the town, he spotted two of his servants running towards him. When they met him, they delivered the news that his son was sitting up in bed eating his supper. He fell to his knees. "When did my son get better?"

"It was in the early afternoon that he began to improve," answered one of the servants. Then the father realized that this was the exact time at which Jesus had said to him, "Your son will live."

"There is only one I can thank, Jesus. We have to tell everyone we meet about what he has done for my son."

****

Yiler and Nowlett were sitting with Jestoo in Yiler's cabin. "Jesus keeping a low profile with two successful miracles is going to prove difficult," said Jestoo.

"I had hoped that we could build momentum slowly," said Yiler. "The exponential acceleration in people converting to Christianity created by miracles is the reason why I never included them in the first place. My concern is that if we don't have enough support built up around Jesus, it will prove easy for someone to make a move against him. Moving slowly will create the required level of strong local support; miracles will only attract unwelcome attention."

"Do you have someone in mind who might make that move?" said Nowlett

"The Pharisees," said Jestoo.

"They are the most likely," said Yiler. "Jesus and our religion are a major threat to them, and the news of these miracles is going to reach them and attract their attention."

"The high priest would be another threat if we fail to get him on our side," said Nowlett. "Jesus must meet him before the rumours about his work spread to the temple in Jerusalem. That court official, whose child Jesus saved, must be well connected in the temple and might already be telling his story widely."

"It would be better if Jesus talked directly to the high priest to counter the rumours and half-baked truths that the high priest will hear," said Nowlett.

"Makes sense to me," said Yiler.

"I agree," said Jestoo. "Let's ask Jesus to make a visit to the temple, and we can see if he can get an audience with the high priest."

"Since there have now been two miracles, we are going to have to factor in more of them," said Yiler. "The people will be expecting them."

"I'll get working on that," said Nowlett. "If we plan them well in advance and keep them simple, we should be able to carry them out successfully with a minimum amount of stress."

"I'll let the team know," said Yiler. "We can send around the list of scheduled miracles when you have it ready in version three of the plan. Hopefully this will be the last revision."

****

Jesus, Mary, and the disciples travelled to Jerusalem for the feast of the Passover. Jesus was insistent on making the visit even though Mary wanted to go home and see how Joseph was doing. When they arrived in Jerusalem, Jesus decided to go straight to the temple. Jesus hadn't seen the temple since his last visit when he was twelve years old. He was keen to see it again.

When they arrived at the temple, they walked into the Court of the Gentiles. This was the space outside the holy inner chambers. These chambers were reserved for the Jews, but others still wished to pray to the God of the Jews, and they did so in the Court of the Gentiles.

Jesus was aghast as he looked at the spectacle within the temple. It was full of cages of live animals, mostly birds. "What is going on here?" Jesus asked Denned in a quiet voice.

Over time, the Court of the Gentiles had become the place where vendors sold live animals to those coming to offer sacrifices at the Temple. All Jewish males living outside Jerusalem were required by the Jewish law, inexplicably in Yiler's opinion, to make three annual pilgrimages to the temple to celebrate liturgical festivals. For them, being able to purchase animals there was a convenience;

they did not need to bring and keep live animals with them on what could be a long trip. Denned was sure that Jesus knew this, so he phrased his answer carefully.

"Well, I suppose it is difficult to bring live animals with you on a pilgrimage, so they have to be bought here before they are sacrificed."

"I know that," said Jesus sharply. "There is plenty of space outside where this can be done. By the way, remind me to refute the ludicrous idea of sacrificing God's creations to keep him happy in a future speech."

Jesus moved further into the temple and spotted people going to several tables where wealthy merchants were seated. He stood by a pillar watching what was going on. It soon dawned on him that these were money changers, who had set up in this area to exchange foreign currency from the visiting pilgrims. The pilgrims required coins to pay the annual temple tax and to buy the animals to be sacrificed. Only the Tyrian shekel was accepted. Jesus could see the opportunities for corruption and extortion that were being exploited widely. His face turned dark with his jaw clenched tight. Hennegy had joined Denned at this stage, and both were getting worried.

"I have never seen him like this," said Denned. "He looks like he is ready to take on the whole temple."

"I know," said Hennegy. "He was supposed to meet the high priest and reason with him. I don't think that he is in the right state of mind for that. What is he doing now?" They watched as Jesus collected some cords and began to twist them into a whip.

"We better go over and calm him down," said Denned. They walked over and stood on either side of him.

"I can see that you are angry," said Hennegy, "… before you do anything, can I remind you that both the selling of animals for sacrifices and the payment of the temple tax are activities required by Jewish law and are central to the temple's functions."

"Peter, I note what you say, but it does not have to be done within this place of worship." Jesus took one practice whack of his whip against one of the columns. It made a loud cracking noise when it impacted. "Excellent." He strode purposefully over to one of the moneylender's desks and stood there waiting his turn. When he reached the top of the queue, he just held the whip in his hand, tapping it gently on the table before looping it into the belt tied around his robe.

"Get on with it," said the moneylender. "I haven't got all day."

"Why do you steal, murder, commit adultery, swear falsely and then come and stand before my father in this house, only to go on doing all these abominations? Has this house become a den of robbers?"

"What the hell are you talking about?" said the startled moneylender. "Go away if you aren't doing any business here. There are people behind you."

"I have grown tired of the hypocrisy and presumption that by simply adhering to temple rituals, God would grant you grace. You have turned the Court of the Gentiles, which is supposed to be a place of prayer and contemplation, into a marketplace. This is yet another sign of the terrible spiritual desolation that afflicts the Hebrews." At this point, all business had ceased, and the other moneylenders and their customers were watching the scene unfold. Some were already laughing.

"You are a lunatic," snarled the moneylender. With that, Jesus put his two hands under the table and flipped it over into the lap of the moneylender before taking out the whip and giving him a few lashes. The moneylender shouted in pain and surprise.

"If you aren't here to worship, get out of the temple, now!" Jesus shouted at the top of his voice before moving to the next moneylender and doing the same thing as he had done to the first. He proceeded down the line of tables. Anyone who had tried to interfere found themselves in contact with the fists, foot, knee, elbow or head of either or both Denned and Hennegy, so Jesus had a free run down the line of tables. There was chaos as the moneylenders tried to gather up their money, either from the table, for those who had not yet encountered Jesus, or from the floor, for those who had. Their prospective customers had decided that this was a chance to make a bit of money for themselves. Most of them were helping to pick up the spilled money, but unfortunately for the moneylenders, were neglecting to pass it onto the rightful owner. The sellers of the live animals had seen what was coming and were frantically moving their half-full cages out of the temple, before they felt the impact of the whip.

It took about thirty minutes for the chaos to cease and the temple to become quiet. Jesus stood in the middle of the Court of the Gentiles perspiring heavily but looking quite pleased with himself.

"Much better," he announced to Denned and Hennegy. "Now, I'll go and introduce myself to the high priest."

Denned shook his head. "I am pretty sure that you have done that already."

"Definitely," said Hennegy. "I suggest that we get out of here before we are arrested." With that, and before Jesus could complain, they marched him out of the temple over to where the rest of the disciples were waiting.

"What happened?" asked Mary. "There was pandemonium outside the entrance with people running all over the place."

"We'll tell your later," said Denned. "We need to head to Bethlehem now."

No further questions were asked, and the group gathered themselves up and left the vicinity of the temple.

****

Three people stood on at the top of the tower overlooking the entrance gate. They had observed everything and were now watching Jesus and the disciples leave.

"Well, that was highly entertaining," observed Pontius Pilate, the Roman Governor. "Is the temple normally this lively?"

"Not normally," said Caiaphas, the high priest quietly.

"Not ever," said Annas, his father in law.

"So, the show is over then," said Pontius Pilate. "You asked me over here to discuss something important. What is it?"

"You have just seen it," said Annas. "That was Jesus."

"The so-called King of the Jews," added Caiaphas. "This is what I wanted to warn you about."

"He just strikes me as your typical religious zealot," said Pontius Pilate. "I don't see why you are so worried. There is no need to arrest him. He is harmless."

"I hope you are right, but I suspect that this is not the last time that any of us encounter Jesus of Nazareth," said Annas.

****

Yiler and Nowlett were beginning to relax, as they grew confident that version three of the plan was working. The incident at the Jerusalem temple had not caused any negative reaction. Jesus had been preaching for a few months and his area of influence was expanding gradually, which was exactly what Yiler had hoped for. Jesus was receiving requests from distant villages to come to preach to them. Even with just word of mouth, progress had been faster than expected. Yiler wanted to decide on new ways to substantially increase the size of the area under the influence of Jesus without risk to his person, so he had arranged to meet with Nowlett and Jestoo in the conference room on the *Tesfa* to discuss next steps.

"I understand your excitement about the pace at which the religion is spreading, but we need to be very careful about how quickly we do this," said Jestoo. "The Pharisees are already agitated and that could be dangerous."

Yiler nodded in agreement. "A clash is inevitable between them and Jesus. The Pharisees place great importance on temple worship, but they have no personal relationship with God. Their worship is merely formal religious observance of the written and oral. The motives of the person behind the public show of worship are considered irrelevant. There is widespread self-righteousness and hypocrisy among the Pharisees. Jesus is the exact opposite of everything that they adhere to. Continued verbal attacks on the Pharisees will be very popular. They are universally disliked."

"I agree that a clash is inevitable and speeches against the Pharisees would be popular," said Nowlett. "However, if we get Jesus to continually and deliberately target the Pharisees, then the clash will be earlier than we have allowed for. I agree with Jestoo that we must restrict him to responding only when they attack him."

****

The meeting at the Jerusalem meeting house of the Pharisees to discuss Jesus had been called at short notice, but the room was packed, with every seat taken and every aisle full.

"This Jesus of Nazareth is beginning to threaten our position in society," said the head Pharisee. "What he preaches to the people is utterly false. We are the keepers of the Mosaic law. This guardianship of the law is the proof that we are God's chosen people, so it is us to whom the Messiah will come. The Messiah will be an earthly king, a son of David, whom God would help to raise up. That king will establish an all-powerful earthly kingdom thus freeing us from Roman rule. He will be a ruler over Israel and the Jewish nation and most certainly not a friend of Gentiles and sinners. The Messiah is not Jesus. We know that to remain in favour with God, the keeping of the Mosaic words is essential. Our experts have adjusted the Mosaic law with precepts to make its violation almost impossible. Oral customs, which have been handed down through generations, and tie into Mosaic law, must be adhered to. The condition of a person's heart towards God is unimportant. Our strict adherence is what separates us from gentile sinners and keeps us from being defiled by them. Jesus threatens all that we believe in. We have been keeping him under observation for the last few months. I regret to say that Jesus constantly, and openly, violates many of our oral and written laws."

There were audible gasps of surprise and some angry voices from the gathering of Pharisees. The head Pharisee motioned silence

178

with his hands. "Jesus has mixed freely with tax collectors and sinners, including prostitutes, thus making him ceremonially unclean. He ate and drank with them and so he is a glutton and a drunkard. Jesus ate with ceremonially unclean hands. He broke our Sabbath laws by healing people and gathering corn to eat on the Sabbath. He forgave people's sins which is blasphemy, pure and simple. Finally, he has dared to freely criticise us for hypocrisy and self-righteousness."

More cries of outrage erupted from the audience. Again, the head Pharisee held up a hand to request silence. "Fear not my friends, we cannot, and will not, allow this situation to continue. I am sending a team of our most learned Pharisees to engage Jesus at tonight's gathering. His credibility will be undermined, and he will lose followers. We shall do that at every meeting until the threat posed by Jesus dissolves, and the man himself is forgotten." The crowd rose to their feet and started applauding.

****

"Biggest crowd yet in Nazareth," said Hennegy as he stuck his head into the tent where Jesus was resting.

"Don't worry, Peter," replied Jesus. "I will be ready."

"I don't want to be a doomsayer, but I am very worried about the Pharisees sitting in the front row," said Denned who was sitting with Jesus. "They are there to cause trouble."

"Thanks for the warning, but I'll be able to handle them. They are full of pomp and bluster, so let's not worry about them. The rest of the audience will listen to me, even if they won't." Jesus stood up and walked out of the tent with Denned and Hennegy. It was only a short distance to where the crowd was gathered, who grew quieter as they saw Jesus approaching. When he reached the stone podium at the front, they were completely silent and gazed at him with expectant faces. Jesus opened his mouth to speak, but before he could do so, one of the Pharisees stood up.

"Jesus of Nazareth, it has been observed that some of your disciples have been eating their bread without washing their hands. All Jews will not eat unless they wash their hands ritually in accordance with our traditions. I have a simple question. Why do your disciples eat bread with ritually unclean hands contrary to the rest of the Jews? Are you better than the rest of us? Do you know better than God?"

Jesus shook his head slowly. "I am continually stunned by the level of your hypocrisy. Perhaps I shouldn't be, because Isaiah prophesied correctly about you hypocrites, as it is written:

'The Pharisees honour Me with their lips, but their heart is far from Me. They worship Me in vain, teaching as doctrines the commands of men.'

You would do anything to maintain your traditions and most importantly your positions of power. Evil in the form of theft, murder, greed, deceit, blasphemy, pride and foolishness comes from people's hearts. Adherence to your ridiculous doctrines and customs will not change that. I care about the person within, not the cosmetic show of worship."

"Our traditions underpin our religion and were given to us by God, you can't pretend otherwise," countered the Pharisee.

"Actually, you wrote most of them yourselves to suit yourselves. Is there anything else you want to say before I start preaching?"

The Pharisee spokesman was looking uncomfortable. "There is another matter that I want to bring to your attention. We have observed that a demon-possessed man, who was blind and unable to speak, was brought to you. The man could both see and speak after you touched him. You can heal because you can drive out demons. That power has been given to you by Satan, the ruler of the demons. You are his servant."

Jesus had remained calm up to this point, but the Pharisee's comment pushed him over the edge. "You are seriously questioning my motives in curing a blind and mute man? Every kingdom divided against itself will self-destruct. If Satan drives out Satan, he is divided against himself. How then will his kingdom survive? I drive out demons by the spirit of God. My power comes from the kingdom of God."

The Pharisee started laughing. "If it is the spirit of God then show us a sign from heaven. God should bear witness that you have come from him. We would then of course believe in you as the Messiah and help you convert our people to your faith."

Jesus gave him a scathing look. "I am not going to give you a sign to help you believe. Either you do or you don't. Now, either be quiet or go away. I have wasted enough time talking to you, when I should have been talking to people who are prepared to listen and make their own judgements."

With that, the Pharisees stood up and left. The rest of the crowd booed them and called them some rather unpleasant names.

****

The head Pharisee walked around his office waiting for news from the meeting in Nazareth. He heard horses entering the courtyard beside the meeting house and rushed out.

"I bet Jesus is sorry he went to that meeting," said the head Pharisee.

"It was us who were sorry."

"He destroyed us."

"I would guess that anyone in the crowd who wasn't a follower of Jesus before, has become one now."

"I'm not doing that again… count me out of future meetings."

The head Pharisee could scarcely believe what he was hearing. "I better go and talk to the high priest in the temple. We may need to combine our efforts to counter Jesus."

Chapter 10

Nowlett, Yiler, Hyett, Sidion and Jestoo were sitting together on the *Tesfa* with the teams on Earth linked in. This would be a defining moment for the team, especially for Yiler. Aside from the overall command of the team, his key responsibility was to design a religion that could gain wide acceptance and become a unifying force. This would create the opportunity for its leader to set the civic rules for the areas that had accepted the religion. With thirty years of observing the humans and the knowledge gained from the reaction to Jesus' preaching, Yiler was satisfied that he had developed eight key points of a religion that would achieve this objective. It was finally ready to be revealed to and then preached by Jesus. Jestoo had informed Jesus three days earlier that the largest gathering yet was to take place at a hillside location on the north-western shore of the Sea of Galilee between Capernaum and Gennesaret. Jestoo had also told him that there would be eight fundamental points that he wanted Jesus to preach at the gathering. Fawter, Konacht, Uhet and Cannet had been busy installing a concealed audio system that would carry the sermon to the thousands that would gather on the hillside, but had halted temporarily to listen in.

Jestoo cleared his throat. It was going to be a long conversation.

"Jesus, are you ready to talk?"

"Yes, father. As agreed yesterday, I am alone in my tent. Peter and Andrew have orders to keep everyone away, so we can talk freely."

"Firstly, well done again on how you dealt with the Pharisees. However, I want to emphasise again that I don't want you to attack them in public. You can only respond when they attack you. If you provoke them, I fear that they will move against you."

"I don't agree."

"I acknowledge that, but I need you to follow my instructions on this with no deviation."

"As you wish," said Jesus grudgingly.

"The purpose of this conversation is to outline what I want you to preach tomorrow. This is the speech that will determine the success or failure of our religion, so you need time to absorb the details fully."

"I've decided that we need to have memorable titles for the speech and the meeting."

"What?" said a surprised Jestoo.

"We need something more notable than 'the eight points'. I was thinking about calling them 'The Beatitudes'. I think it is a word that has gravitas. Also, what about the 'Sermon on the Mount' for the gathering, since the location is on the side of a mountain?"

Jestoo looked at Yiler for guidance, who motioned to Jestoo to carry on. "It's not important, so I haven't given it any thought, therefore fine, whatever you think. Before I start with the key points... sorry 'Beatitudes', I need to go back to the time of Moses."

"Why so?"

"To explain the mistake that I made with Moses. I know now that the ten commandments were doomed to failure. Let us look at them again.

You shall have no other gods before me.

You shall not make for yourself an image in the form of anything in heaven above or on the earth

beneath or in the waters below.

You shall not bow down to them or worship them.

You shall not misuse the name of the Lord your God.

Remember the Sabbath day by keeping it holy.

Honour your father and your mother.

You shall not murder.

You shall not commit adultery.

You shall not steal.

You shall not give false testimony against your neighbour.

You shall not covet anything that belongs to your neighbour."

Jestoo turned the speaker on so Yiler could listen without his implant. He then cleared his throat with a soft cough. "Jesus, why did these commandments not work."

Jesus thought for a moment. "The commandments were too absolute and difficult to adhere to. I think that people decided that compliance was impossible and didn't bother trying, or else they tried, failed to obey one commandment, and then gave up. Even the Jews have found it impossible to follow the ten commandments absolutely."

"Exactly, which is why I want some vagueness and latitude in the new religion."

"Thus, making it easier to adhere to the rules," said Jesus. "That should assist in persuading people to convert."

"I am pleased that you agree because 'The Beatitudes' of the new religion are deliberately ambiguous. The first is 'blessed are the poor in spirit, for theirs is the kingdom of heaven.' I don't mean poor in terms of finances or possessions. I am referring to poverty of spirit. Never give the impression that you will enrich our followers in earthly possessions and power. All you can promise is to enrich them in spirit."

"Because the poor person and the rich person are treated the same, we will attract followers from the poorest echelons of society," said Jesus. "The Pharisees will not like that."

Jestoo started speaking again. "The next one is 'blessed are those who mourn, for they will be comforted.'"

"That seems an easy one to understand," said Jesus. "We will offer comfort for the pain and grief triggered by the loss of a loved one."

"We should also explain that grieving is only temporary. They must understand that death does not have the final victory over them." Jestoo turned over to the next page of his notes. "The next one is 'blessed are the meek, for they will inherit the earth.'"

"I don't understand that one. It doesn't make sense. Is this the vagueness and latitude that you want to introduce?"

Yiler leant over and pointed to a paragraph in the notes and Jestoo nodded to Yiler. "Maybe I should explain what I mean by 'meek'. The meek are those who are gentle, with self-control. They do not exploit and oppress anyone. They help the weak and the oppressed."

"So, if you adhere to our religion, you are meek by default," said Jesus.

Jestoo gave Yiler a thumbs up. "Exactly. The next one is 'blessed are those who hunger and thirst for righteousness, for they shall be satisfied.'"

"I have no idea what that means."

"I am describing people whose passion in life is to do the right thing for everyone and not just for themselves, in order to achieve social justice on Earth."

"So, the essential point is that those who adhere to our teachings will not tolerate injustice and will take action to right what is wrong."

"Correct. The next is 'blessed are the merciful, for they will be shown mercy.'"

"That seems easy. We show mercy to them through the forgiveness of sins, so they should show mercy to others. And if they show enough mercy to others, they shall obtain mercy from you in the form of you welcoming them into heaven."

"Close, but you can't store up good deeds. There isn't a quota system. Our followers cannot think that they have earned a place in heaven and then become intolerant of others. The good deeds must be continuous. The next one is 'blessed are the pure in heart, for they shall see God.'"

"Presumably, you are describing an inner purity."

"Yes, to be pure in heart means that every act you undertake has to be for a good reason, unlike our friends the Pharisees."

"So, the key point is that if they follow the word of God, this will change the way they think and purify their hearts."

Jestoo rubbed his arm across his forehead to remove the beads of sweat that were forming. "Now, the second last one, 'blessed are the peacemakers, for they will be called the sons of God.'"

"Is this the legitimisation of physical violence to achieve a righteous purpose? This would give a lot of latitude on the use of force."

Yiler pointed to another passage in the notes. Jestoo scanned it quickly. "I would like to be able to condemn all physical violence. However, there will always be strife and conflict. The peace that we offer should not be confused with a world with no hostilities. True peace needs a complete change of nature in humans. It begins with reconciliation with God and then extends to reconciliation with other people."

"So, the true peacemakers promote the kingdom of God through understanding and spiritual love," said Jesus. "I still think there is a risk that this will be manipulated by people to justify physical violence. They will say they are acting in your name."

"Possibly. To reduce this risk, our disciples should promote peace by spreading the gospel of peace and avoid physical violence if possible," Jestoo responded and took a deep breath. "And now, the last one 'blessed are those who are persecuted for the sake of justice, for theirs is the kingdom of heaven.'"

"This is letting our disciples know that they can expect a rough time when they are spreading the gospel, but that you will reward them with a place in heaven," said Jesus. "That is a lot to get through tomorrow, but I will do my best." Jesus sounded uncertain.

"The Beatitudes will underpin every speech from here on, so you must reference them at every opportunity. I am fully confident that you will succeed."

"I understand, and thank you for trusting me," said Jesus. "I will go and prepare for tomorrow."

"Call in Peter and Andrew and explain the Beatitudes to them as practice for later."

Jestoo broke the link with Jesus. He stretched his hands above his head. "Yiler, I'm exhausted. This is complicated stuff."

"Yiler, are you sure that the listeners will understand all this?" asked Nowlett. "Even if they do, isn't there a risk that the next day, they will only remember fragments? The message could get garbled."

"It could, but I am confident that the core elements will be retained," said Yiler.

Nowlett pursed her lips. "I hope that you are right, but I think that your optimism might be misplaced."

"With all due respect, Nowlett, I didn't interfere in your area of expertise, and maybe you should reciprocate by not interfering in mine."

"Is this a row?" said Jestoo.

"Be quiet," said his parents in unison.

****

A vast crowd had gathered on the low-lying mountain by the sea of Galilee. Far more than at any meeting before. Denned and Hennegy were trying to estimate the size of the crowd when Jesus walked up to them.

"Peter, how many do you think are here?" said Jesus.

"I would guess between ten and fifteen thousand people," said Hennegy.

"I hope that they will all be able to hear me. My father said they will be able to, no matter how many turn up."

"I am sure that they will then," said Denned, who had already double-checked the hidden audio system.

The three of them walked through the crowd towards the top of the mount. Parts of the crowd moved out of the way to create a small corridor for them to walk through. A few knelt on the ground, beseeching Jesus to touch them, which he did as he walked by. As soon as he reached the top of the mount, he climbed on a small platform made from stones and began talking.

"Today, on this mount, I am going to deliver a sermon that I think will change the way you think about life from hereon in. I want to explain the eight core principles that you need to follow to receive the grace of God. They are the eight Beatitudes."

****

After he had finished preaching, Jesus came down the hillside with Denned and Hennegy. The other disciples were providing a screen against many angry Pharisees. A leper, who was very badly disfigured, was sitting on the side of the road begging for mercy. Dr Nowlett had spotted him earlier and tapped Jestoo on the shoulder.

"This is an opportunity for a miracle," said Dr Nowlett.

"I thought we had agreed that there would be no more spur-of-the-moment miracles," said Yiler.

Nowlett put her hand on his arm. *"This one is easy. Denned, are you carrying the salve I gave you?"*

"You mean the one you told me to keep with me at all times?"

"Yes, that is the one. Do you have it?"

Denned was grinning. *"Of course, you told me to."*

"You could have just said yes. Jestoo, ask Jesus to ask Denned to mix up some mud and water. Denned, add a quarter of the tube of salve to the mix." Jestoo, Denned and Jesus did as instructed, with Denned now holding the mixture in his hands. *"Now, tell Jesus to walk towards the leper."*

"By your command," said Hennegy.

When the leper saw Jesus, he fell with his face to the ground and begged him to help. "Lord, if you are willing, you can make me clean."

Jesus reached out his hand and touched the man. "I will do this with the help of my father. Andrew, please get me some mud and water." Denned brought the mixture over and gave it to Jesus. He rubbed it over the infected areas on the leper. "With the grace of God, my father, be clean." The leprosy began to improve immediately.

Jesus helped the man stand. "Go and show yourself to the high priest and offer sacrifices for your cleansing as a testimony to them of what I have done for you." The Pharisees watched in silence as Jesus walked away.

****

Yiler and Nowlett were lying in bed having just finished reading. "The experiment is going really well, isn't it," said Nowlett.

"Far better than I had expected. The religion will be the unifying force that Earth so badly needs. My main worry is keeping the Pharisees sufficiently annoyed, so they keep up their verbal attacks, but not agitated to the point that they use physical violence against Jesus.

"It is a fine line. Ordering Jesus to tone it down has kept him on the right side of it though."

They lay down and were quiet for a short time. Nowlett broke the silence.

"I wonder if the military situation has improved at home."

"It must have done. The Santu have had it their own way so far. That can't last."

Part IV

Cessation of Creation

Chapter 11

Santu Flagship – *Santu Brightstar*

Admiral Tenru looked up from his computer screen. "Are we ready to recommence?" His patience had worn thin. The Santu were renowned for being impatient, and Admiral Tenru was a prime example.

"Damage was more extensive than anticipated due to the incorrect intelligence on the performance of the Deusi missiles," said Ship Commander Kendru.

"Excuses do not interest me."

"I offered an explanation, not an excuse." Kendru looked down at her screen as an alert appeared. "All ships are operating at over eighty percent efficiency levels. We are ready."

"Then give the order to launch the second wave."

Ship Commander Kendru pressed the fleet communication icon on her touch screen. "Attention, ship commanders. Launch second wave missiles." The ship vibrated slightly as her own ship obeyed the order.

"No going back now," said Kendru quietly.

The admiral returned his attention back to his computer screen. "Indeed," was his short reply.

Deusi Flagship – *Greenstar*

Admiral Ydarb stood in the real-time 3D holographic display on the bridge. It was his favourite piece of tech from the refit and upgrade programme. The Deusi and Santu fleets swirled around his head as he moved through the display. To his right were the icons representing the ships of the Deusi fleet, minus the fighters. He had disabled fighter display because the icons around his head had felt like a swarm of insects.

The icons were white, still for operational, flashing for out of action. Thankfully, there were only a few flashing white, and no red icons showing destroyed ships.

To his left were the blue icons of the Santu fleet. There were a lot of flashing blue icons for damaged Santu ships, confirming the superiority of the new Deusi missiles; the scientist's optimism had not been misplaced after all.

Captain Glanreen stared down at his display. "Admiral, the Santu ships have launched another wave. The computer estimate is that over five thousand missiles are headed our way."

The admiral had been surprised by the poor performance of the Santu missiles compared to his. "I don't expect that they will be more successful than the last batch," said the admiral confidently. "A lot of them may even be destroyed by the debris from the first salvo."

Admiral Ydarb had been part of a committee of officers that had orchestrated a radical change in tactics. Deusi ships traditionally had their own missile defence systems, in addition to their primary offensive function. The committee had proposed a radical redesign whereby ships would have one purpose only. The theory behind the redesign was that if a ship was optimised for one task, then the result would be a much more effective ship.

The fleet now contained four capital ships for every missile defence ship or MDS. Each MDS had capacity to cover eight adjacent ships, so the coverage overlapped in case an MDS was disabled or destroyed. This allowed the capital ships to forego their own missile defence systems, increasing their capital missile capacity by twenty to thirty percent.

The strategic withdrawal over a thirty-year period by the Deusi fleet was designed to allow time to refit and embed the new tactics. Newer units were withdrawn from the front line to be refitted with the older units fighting as a rear-guard action to cover the retreat to the Deusi home systems. Extracted units exaggerated the effects of superficial damage to convince the Santu that their missiles were a lot better than they were. The rear-guard units had two objectives, to draw the Santu into the Deusi trap, and to take out more Santu units than the rear-guard lost. They had succeeded on both counts.

Before the withdrawal, Deusi ships had been disbursed widely to protect colonies. Those ships retreated as if they were being forced down a funnel, with the narrow end of the funnel being the Deusi home worlds. By forcing the Santu forces to concentrate their forces at the Deusi home system, the furthest system from Santu, their supply lines, would be compromised. The hope was that this would present an opportunity to inflict enough damage on the Santu to allow negotiations to start on an equal basis between the combatants.

The admiral had been concerned that the plan would not work. However, now he had admitted to himself that he was wrong. The Santu had obviously been unaware of most, if not all, of the Deusi advancements due to their limited intelligence-gathering capability in Deusi territory.

Not a single Deusi ship had been destroyed because the MDS's had intercepted virtually all incoming Santu missile. Shields and armour had coped with what had made it through. In addition, five percent of the drives of the Santu missiles had failed before the missiles had moved into range of the MDS ships, which led the admiral to the conclusion that the missiles were a new class that had not been tested properly by the Santu. This surprised him because the Santu were normally very cautious about using new technology, unlike the Deusi, who were inclined to try new technology while in action.

Captain Glanreen walked over to the admiral. "Standard dispersal, they are making the mistake of spreading the missiles too widely and not focusing on specific targets."

"Why are the Santu doing that?" said the admiral, echoing the surprised tone of the captain. He watched the Santu missiles approach on the 3D display. "Are we ready to launch?"

"We are, sir."

"Order all ships to fire after the Santu's second wave has been dealt with," said the admiral trying to keep his voice calm as it dawned on him that this battle, that had been planned so carefully, might produce the result they had hoped for. He walked around the bridge projecting confidence to the crew.

Santu Forward Observation Platform No. 1

Lieutenant Legatod was calmly waiting for his systems to come online, so he could take control of the incoming missiles. He was the senior officer, so passing on the target coordinates to the other platforms was his responsibility. He knew that the Deusi would detect his signals, so there was very little chance of him making it back alive. He had been resigned to that for a long time. His family name and connections had guaranteed that he was going to be in command of the mission.

Legatod had used his active scanners to determine the targets for the next wave. The scanners were in hulls of 'failed' missiles. Safe use of the active scanners was possible while the Deusi fleet had been dealing with the first wave of Santu missiles. Any use outside that would guarantee that a Deusi missile would be heading his way. He had been very surprised that the data indicated that counter missiles had been launched and laser defences had been engaged on certain ships. He had extrapolated from the data that these ships were a new Deusi missile defence class, and that the other ships were carrying capital missiles only.

The platform's systems went live as the second wave of missiles came into range, and he sent the targeting coordinates to the other observers. He had estimated that it would be ten seconds before he received his first query. It only took five.

"Sir, are you sure about these targeting coordinates?" asked Chief Depu. "We are targeting a small number of medium-sized ships. The plan was to take out the larger units."

"My orders are to confirm targets, yours are to accept them." His control panel told him that all the observers were listening.

"I am entitled to raise queries since I am second in command, so please answer my question."

"If you insist. I have decided that those ships are missile defence ships, defending the larger units. If we destroy enough of them, we remove the ability of the Deusi fleet to defend itself. This is not a discussion, so implement my orders. I will bear sole responsibility for this decision, and I will send a signal back to the Admiral to that effect."

"That's not much of a comfort since I expect we will all be dead soon. Let's hope that your guess is correct."

Deusi Flagship – *Greenstar*

"Santu missiles are five minutes from impact," said the tactical officer.

"Admiral, I am picking up a signal from an unknown source," said the communications officer.

The admiral turned to her. "Can you be more specific?"

"Sorry, sir. I am trying to isolate the signal. I think that I have it, but… it is just not possible. The signal seems to be coming from an area where there is no ship." She was oblivious to the fact that everyone on the bridge had focused their attention on her. "I think… yes… I've got it." She sat in silence with a puzzled expression.

"Well, where are the signals coming from?" said Ydarb patiently.

"The signals are coming from some of the failed Santu missiles."

Admiral Ydarb strode out of the hologram to his command chair. "Are you sure?"

"I am one hundred percent certain that the signals I detected are from those failed missiles. I'm also sure that the signals are being directed to the incoming missiles."

"Scan those failed missiles for life signs," said the admiral.

The observation officer directed the active scanners at the coordinates isolated by the communications officer. "Sir, at least five of those missiles contain life signs. The rest of the missiles are too far out to confirm either way."

The admiral slammed his fist on his console. "The Santu have people inside them giving targeting coordinates to the incoming missiles. Get fighters to destroy any failed Santu missiles from the first wave. Damn it, those forward controllers must know the location of the Missile Defence Ships. Warn the captains."

"Admiral," said the tactical officer. "There is more bad news. The missile types are different from the first salvo. They were twinned and have just separated. The drives of the dormant missiles have ignited, and they are manoeuvring to line up on targets. The acceleration of the separated missiles is superior to anything we have."

"And I presume all converging on the missile defence ships?" said the admiral in a tone of resignation.

"It appears that way," was the whispered reply from the tactical officer. That was the reply the admiral had expected but did not want. The admiral began pacing around the bridge, still attempting to display an aura of confidence that he no longer felt. The admiral watched the crew getting anxious as they worked on a defensive solution to the Santu missiles. He knew that an answer was impossible in the short time available. His fleet was about to suffer catastrophic damage.

Santu Flagship – *Santu Brightstar*

A despondent Admiral Tenru turned his chair and addressed the officers gathered on his bridge. The expression on his face shocked them because losing control of his emotions was rare for him. "What possessed that lunatic Legatod to do that? For thirty years, we have pretended to take the bait and crawled towards Deusi Prime. We developed technology and weapons that would destroy the Deusi fleet. We had their capital ships at our mercy, and then Legatod changed the targeting parameters."

"His remit was too great," said Ship Commander Kendru, which was brave on her part because the admiral had drafted those orders. "He was given the authority to change the final targeting instructions. The orders should have set narrower parameters. Be that as it may, we should not waste time agonising over this. We have run simulations based on the information we received from Legatod before his platform was destroyed. All the ships he targeted were either destroyed or badly damaged. If Legatod was correct in his selection of ships to attack, the battle is over. We have won."

"Let's hope so," said Tenru. He paused for a moment. Even he was overcome by how momentous his next order would be for all Santu. "Commander, send the signal to our ships to cease fire." He paused again for a longer period. "When you have done that, send a message to the Deusi admiral demanding the unconditional surrender of his ships. Advise him that we have ceased fire to avoid unnecessary loss of life. Order him to come here on a disarmed destroyer to be given the surrender terms. The reply will tell us if Lieutenant Legatod is a future hero... or villain."

Deusi Flagship – *Greenstar*

Admiral Ydarb stood in the conference room surrounded by his key officers. Some of the officers were physically present. However, because of the large area of space that the fleet occupied and the matter of repairing their ships, some were present by hologram only. There was very little conversation.

Admiral Ydarb coughed for attention. "We have lost sixty percent of our Missile Defence Ship's with a further twenty percent badly damaged and out of action. There are a further ten percent just about serviceable, but one more hit will take them out. The Santu capital missiles are superior to ours. These two factors combined ensure that, if any more of them are fired at us, we cannot defend ourselves. We have run simulations, and no simulation has resulted in anything except complete destruction of the fleet. The only difference between the simulations is the speed of our destruction. I have no alternative other than to surrender to the Santu."

There was a stunned silence. No one had ever contemplated this outcome. They had thought the new tactics and technology had finally made them superior to the Santu forces. They were now coming to the terms with the fact that that their confidence had been badly misplaced.

"Anyone disagree with this course of action?" said Ydarb

There were a few shakes of heads. Before the admiral could say anything else, his communications officer interrupted. "Sir, I have a message from the Santu flagship. They have demanded our immediate and unconditional surrender and advise that they have ceased firing until they receive a reply. They have ordered you to take one disarmed destroyer over to their flagship to receive the surrender terms. You can take two officers with you."

Ydarb stared down at his feet disconsolately. "Signal them that we agree with their terms." Admiral Ydarb checked to see what destroyer was closest and noted that it was the *Steadfast*.

"Advise the Santu that I will depart in the destroyer *Steadfast* in ten minutes for rendezvous with their flagship. Please make sure you clearly identify the ship I will be taking, so there are no unfortunate accidents."

Santu Flagship – *Santu Brightstar*

"Admiral Tenru," said the communications officer. "The unconditional surrender and ceasefire signal from the Deusi admiral have been received. The Deusi destroyer *Steadfast* will be departing in ten minutes, with the Admiral on board."

"Acknowledged," replied Admiral Tenru. "Send the identifier code of that destroyer to all our ships. I don't want it hit with a stray missile from an overzealous captain. Also, advise all ships to keep missile defence online, just in case."

Deusi Flagship – *Greenstar*

Admiral Ydarb, with his key staff gathered around him, left the bridge and headed for the shuttle bay. The Deusi had seen themselves as the defenders of the independent star systems from

Santu expansionism. Now, they were viewed as the aggressors by most, if not all, of those independent star systems as one after another had sided with the Santu.

Ydarb's opinion was that those systems had been given very little choice. It was hard to decline when the prospect of joining the Santu dominated Federation had been dangled in front of them.

As Admiral Ydarb boarded the shuttle with two staff officers, he had come to terms with the fact that it was all over. As he strapped himself into his seat, he wondered if the purported high ideals of the Santu and its fledging Federation would extend to clemency for the Deusi. He doubted it.

Santu Flagship – *Santu Brightstar*

Admiral Tenru watched as the shuttle from the *Steadfast* docked. He admired the lines of the Deusi shuttle; its sleek arrow-like shape was much more appealing than the box-shaped shuttle the Santu used. He had mixed emotions when watching the Deusi admiral disembark. He knew he had to ensure that the surrender was handled with dignity, so his professional persona took over, despite his personal feelings. He walked towards the Deusi admiral. "Welcome to my ship, Admiral Ydarb. Please follow me to the conference room."

"Thank you for your courtesy," said Admiral Ydarb in a civil tone that seemed a bit of a struggle for him to maintain.

"Courtesy has to be offered even in the most trying of times," said Admiral Tenru, who couldn't have sounded more condescending if he tried. "I should advise you that I have a senior Santu diplomat on board who has the surrender terms for you."

"You were obviously confident of winning if you already had a diplomat on board and the terms drafted."

Admiral Tenru moved from condescension to outright arrogance. "With all due respect, the outcome, following your decision to engage us in open conflict, was never in doubt. The only question was how long the conflict would last until we won. Our new technology which you saw today for the first time, assisted by the error of creating Missile Defence Ships that were easily targeted, guaranteed the destruction of your fleet." He held open the door of the conference room. "Please enter."

Admiral Tenru stood as the Deusi sat down in the conference room. "Avatar Celet, Admiral Ydarb," said Admiral Tenru curtly. The Deusi admiral and Santu Avatar exchanged short introductions, and a Santu crewman placed refreshments on the conference table. The Santu helped themselves. The Deusi declined.

"Admiral Ydarb, I will read out the main surrender terms, and then I will present you with a detailed copy to take away for further consideration by your government," said Avatar Celet. "The fleet will stay in its current position until a reply is received. Please do not attempt to debate the terms with me. It is a waste of time. I expect a reply within ten days at the absolute latest."

"Understood," said Ydarb.

Avatar Celet opened a file and started to read the terms which he demonstrated by counting on his hands. "The summary terms for your unconditional surrender are:

- Cessation of all military activities.
- Elections must be held within six months to replace the current government.
- All warships and fixed installations will be boarded and taken under Federation control.
- All civilian dockyards will be taken under Federation control.
- All colonies, designated D3 to D15, will be evacuated. The colonists must return to the two Deusi home planets within three months. Federation ships will be made available to assist.
- These former colonies will be assigned to Federation members as needs dictate.

- No Deusi colonies will be permitted without the approval of the Federation Council.
- A limited Deusi presence will be permitted on all Federation planets and installations to encourage trade and the beginning of normal relations.
- Deusi merchant fleet and passenger vessels will be permitted limited access to all Federation space.
- Adoption of the Federation civic economic model is compulsory on Deusi Prime and D2.

These terms are non-negotiable, and compliance will be enforced with military action if required."

Admiral Ydarb was visibly shocked. "You appreciate that I cannot comment on those terms on behalf of my government. All I can do is forward them."

Avatar Celet stood up from the table. "Then please do so. Here is a disk containing the summary terms with appendices containing more information. Admiral Tenru, please escort the Deusi representatives to their shuttle."

After a polite, but stilted goodbye, Admiral Ydarb and his two staff members walked back to the shuttle. They did so in complete silence and did not speak until the shuttle had cleared the docking bay of the Santu Brightstar.

"Those terms will be impossible to comply with," said one of the staff officers. "How are we supposed to clear all of our colonies and rehouse everyone on Deusi Prime and D2? It will be a social and economic disaster for us. We have to renegotiate those terms."

"If only that were possible," replied the admiral.

Deusi Parliament Chamber

"You all have a copy of the unconditional surrender terms sent to us by Admiral Ydarb," said President Flanstid in a subdued tone. "The terms are short and to the point. We have a simple decision to make. Accept the terms or refuse to sign. I now open the floor to contributions. Please make sure that your comments are brief. We don't have time for lengthy speeches because of the ten-day response deadline."

The Deusi parliament chamber was an oval-shaped room with the president and her governing ministers at the apex of the oval, with the elected representatives gathered on two sides. The other end of the oval held the public areas where the media were gathered. The noise in the chamber was incessant, with multiple debates taking place, until the leader of the opposition stood up and the noise slowly dissipated.

"While I would like to engage with the Santu on the surrender terms, it is clear from the text given to Admiral Ydarb and the brief discussion that ensued, that no debate is possible. It is a take it or leave it situation. If we refuse the terms, the Santu will restart hostilities. With the grievous losses inflicted on our fleet, we are defenceless. Our fixed planetary defences and orbital platforms would easily be overcome by Santu forces. Therefore, we will have to accept the terms. No further comment."

There was an immediate outcry from the representatives from the colony planets. "How can we be expected to evacuate all the colonies within three months?" shouted one representative.

"That is an easy statement for you to make. You are not going to lose your homes and way of life," roared another.

"This is a betrayal of the colonies by the president," said a third.

The president tried to instil some order in the chamber. "Rather than emotional outbursts, could we please have a reasoned response from one of the representatives of the colonial planets?"

The head colonial representative started speaking. "My comments are for the benefit of all Deusi, not just my colony. I know that the combined 300 million population of the D5 to D15 colonies is small when compared with the Deusi Prime, D2, D3 and D4 populations. Even so, moving that many refugees will have a dramatic and lasting impact on our society and economy. I think we should stand up the Santu. They will not attack our colonies if we do not evacuate them."

"That's very easy for you to say," shouted one of the colonial presidents. "You do not live on one of the planets in the firing line, since you and your family spend most of your time on Deusi Prime. Maybe you should move your family onto my planet as a gesture of solidarity if you are that confident that the Santu will not attack."

"How *dare you* address me like that?"

President Flanstid held up her hand for silence. "Shouting at each other will not advance this debate. I know that the settlement terms are harsh. I can see that they will impact upon us severely for decades if not centuries. However, if we refuse to sign, you must take collective responsibility for the gamble that the Santu will not act on their threats. Any further comments?"

The debate carried on for a couple of days. The initial contributions were reasoned and balanced. As the debate wore on, they deteriorated with no one listening to any of the alternative views put forward. President Flanstid called for a vote when she had enough of the undignified shouting matches. The screen located behind the president showed the result a few moments later. Sixty four percent of the votes were in favour of accepting the proposals put forward by the Santu.

"The settlement terms have been accepted," said the president to a chorus of boos. "I propose that we set up a refugee committee which will work out how best to deal with the transfer of the D3 to D15 populations. It will be up to the committee to devise the repatriation plan. I suggest you that you include Federation ships in the effort. We can take a small amount of comfort from that disruption to the Federation. This session is adjourned. Oh, one more thing, I resign."

The president stood and walked towards the chamber door, flanked by two aides. General Lateel exited the private section of the public gallery and met her as she left. General Lateel opened her mouth to say something but stopped when Flanstid held up her hand and shook her head. They walked out of the parliament building in silence, and only when they were outside, they spoke.

"So, what about Earth?" said Flanstid as they walked through the garden path to the presidential private residence.

"I'll let them know what happened and give them forty days to finish," said Lateel. "They won't be happy, but we can't have them missing the Santu deadline for all Deusi ships to return to Deusi Prime."

"And then?"

"We just leave Earth to its own devices and return when it is safe to do so. Who knows when that will be."

Flanstid turned to look at Lateel. "You will tell the new president all of this, won't you?"

"Of course," said Lateel without a moment's hesitation.

Flanstid didn't believe her for a second.

Chapter 12

Yiler was alone in the kitchen of his cabin on the *Tesfa*. Nowlett had bailed out with a flimsy excuse of having to go to the lab, and so Yiler was left cleaning up after dinner when his computer chimed with an incoming message. He asked the computer to play it, but it was a read-only message. He walked over to his computer to access it. It was from General Lateel, marked urgent, and had come from an unscheduled message drone. This hadn't happened before. As he read it, he held his hand to his mouth. The message contained details of the disastrous military loss and the draconian surrender terms imposed by the Santu.

Lateel also told him that this would be the end of the Deity Creation experiment and other experiments on Earth for the foreseeable future. The team would have to come home within a maximum of three months and earlier if possible. Whatever they needed to do to finish the experiment would have to be done in that timeframe. There was no possibility of an extension. The route home would require numerous short FTL jumps to make sure that the *Tesfa* would come from the right direction into Deusi space. If boarded by the Santu, which was very likely, the ship's database would have to show that the *Tesfa* was merely an exploration ship. Every record and piece of evidence pertaining to the Deity Creation experiment and Earth needed to be eradicated from the database and ship.

He sat down and began to think about options. It was two hours later when he messaged Dr Nowlett to come back from the lab. She arrived a few minutes later. "This better be important. I was in the middle of an experiment."

Yiler gestured at his screen. "Trust me, it is. Have a read of this."

Dr Nowlett read the note and gasped. "I can't believe it. I fell for the propaganda that we could never lose the war." Dr Nowlett sat down on the bed.

"We should know by now never to trust politicians." Yiler sat beside her and held her hand. "The message from Lateel arrived two hours ago. I have been thinking about what we should do since it arrived."

"Why didn't you call me straight away?"

"It occurred to me that some difficult decisions might have to be made, and you tend to cloud my judgement with your alternative viewpoints. I have a plan formulated, and I am not sure that you are going to like it. When we thought we had twenty more years to expand the influence of Jesus, going slowly was the correct strategy. It avoided undue attention being focused on him. Now, we need a big bang, something that will attract widespread attention. I believe that there is only one way to do this."

Nowlett looked at Yiler suspiciously. "What do you have in mind?"

"We need to make a martyr out of Jesus at the hands of the Pharisee and Romans. He has to die for what he believes in and…"

"You want them to execute Jesus?" interrupted Nowlett.

"I don't want to. We have to."

"You want them to kill the man we have protected since he was a baby. The brother of our son. Jesus is a wonderful person. He is kind and caring. He sees the good in everyone. He has followed our orders unfailingly, albeit he thought that they were from his father. His message is one of love, hope and forgiveness, and you want to kill him. There must be a better way than this. Jestoo will not stand for it."

"You didn't let me finish. There is an 'and' to my plan."

"Yiler, it better be a good 'and' …"

"I want you to bring Jesus back to life after he is killed. I need his followers to believe that he died and was saved by God. That will be the ultimate miracle."

"Has reading Lateel's message caused a form of temporary insanity? I know that we had always intended for Jesus to die and be raised from the dead, but that was supposed to be when he died naturally aged sixty, after ten years of preaching. That would be easy to achieve because we would be in full control."

"Maybe I have gone insane but hear me out. Jesus must be the first person proven worthy to be admitted to heaven. Shortly after he is brought back to life, we will still stage a final event whereby he ascends into heaven to be with his father. The disciples will then proclaim that heaven is open to anyone who accepts the grace of God."

"Why can't we just leave Earth and let the experiment run its course with Jesus alive?"

"How do we explain to Jesus that God has stopped talking to him? He could live for another twenty to thirty years with absolute silence from his father. He will plead and beg for forgiveness for whatever he has done that has caused him to lose the favour of his father. It just will not work. It will eventually drive him mad."

"That is a reasonable point, but it isn't a justification for killing him. I am astonished that you don't seem to have the same emotional bond that I have with Jesus. I helped in the conception and birth. I inserted his implant when he was twelve. I have cured all his aches and pains, including five operations to cure the damage caused by his adolescent foolhardiness. He is like a second son to me, and you want me to assist in having him executed. You must know that Romans execute by crucifixion."

"You keep forgetting about him returning from the dead."

"Yiler, seriously. You know that is impossible. When you are crucified you die, end of story."

"Then, you must find a way to make it appear that Jesus is dead without actually being dead. Some form of suspended animation."

"Really, suspended animation after crucifixion. Is that all you want? It is impossible. You cannot create a convincing illusion of death in these circumstances."

"A medically induced coma then. Nowlett, the people you must convince have no way of checking whether he is dead or not."

"Even a child can check for someone breathing and a heartbeat. His followers are not that stupid."

"Nowlett, I don't want to argue, but I want to make one thing clear. The key part of my revised plan is him dying by execution.

Returning from the dead is ancillary. If you can do it, then great. If you can't, we work with the martyr angle only. Heaven will open to the masses but not exactly in accordance with Moses' plan. Despite what you said, I do have a strong bond with Jesus and Jestoo. Unlike you, I am apparently able to put that to one side to finish what we started."

"If that is your final word on the matter, I will tell Jestoo. He might take it better from me that you are planning to kill his brother."

"Nowlett, with all due respect, you seem to have lost sight of the fact that Jesus is the experiment. Please use something other than "Your father is planning to kill your brother" when you talk to him."

Nowlett stood up. She opened her mouth to say something and then closed it. She just turned around and left the room. Yiler took a few deep breaths to compose himself before getting into contact with Denned and Hennegy. They confirmed that they were alone before he turned on the speaker and started talking. He updated them on the military situation and on his plans including his proposed martyrdom of Jesus. When he got an initial silence from Denned and Hennegy, he began to fear the worst.

"Jesus is like a son to us," said Denned. "Has that ever occurred to you?"

"We have been minding him since he was a baby," said Hennegy. "Now, we are Peter and Andrew, his key disciples. Did you not even consider that this would create an emotional bond with him?"

"Not you as well. I just had an earful from Dr Nowlett on that point. You must treat this as an experiment that has to be completed. You can't get emotional."

"Maybe you would have had a different view if you bothered to come down to Earth," said Denned. "You have never met Jesus in person. You can't appreciate what he is really like until you do."

"Yiler, you are a callous fool," said Hennegy. "There is only one reason why I am not heading up to the ship in a drop pod to give you what you deserve."

"I take it that deference to your superior is not it."

"You take it correctly. The reason is that you have asked Dr Nowlett to come up with a way of achieving what you want without killing him. If anyone can do this, she can."

"Yiler, the answer to your next question will determine if I come up and kick your ass," said Denned. "Please tell me that you are not expecting us to participate in the execution."

"That is not part of my plan, I promise you."

"Who will then?"

"The Pharisees will do it with the help of the Romans. The persuasive arguments of Jesus about how they have lost sight of their true purpose have already caught the attention of the leaders of the Pharisees. By reversing our policy and getting Jesus to attack them vociferously, I think that this will quickly provoke them to make a move against him."

"They are cowardly bastards. I wouldn't be so sure."

"Have you told Jestoo yet?" said Denned.

"No yet. His mother was going to tell him." Yiler jumped as a loud hammering started on his door. "That could be him now."

****

Denned and Hennegy were standing beside Jesus in the main meeting square in Jerusalem. "I still don't understand why my father has changed his position on attacking the Pharisees in public. Suddenly, the prospect of them moving to stop me doesn't seem to concern him."

"The Pharisees are cowards," said Denned.

"Even cowards have limits that they can be pushed beyond. We'll see, won't we." Jesus walked onto a raised stone platform in the middle of the square, and the crowd started to clap and roar their approval. As usual, there was a small group of Pharisees gathered in front of the podium, and for the first time, the head Pharisee himself was present. Jesus waited until the crowd quietened down.

"Today, I want to talk to you about the scribes and Pharisees. I have restrained myself until now, but I can't any longer. I do not respect the scribes and Pharisees. Their position of authority is the only thing that gives them power. You should never ever strive to emulate them for they do not practice what they preach. They put burdens on other people's shoulders, but they themselves are not willing to lift a finger. Everything they do is done for people to see. It is superficial belief.

The Pharisees have deliberately made so many cumbersome and onerous changes to Jewish law that it is impossible for anyone else to comprehend. I want you to focus on the true intent of Jewish law, the substance over the form. The scribes and Pharisees have emphasized the form, and this must stop.

The Pharisees are hypocrites, who shut the door of the kingdom of heaven in people's faces. Their religion is hollow, and it prevents others from following me. The Pharisees win converts who end up worse than they are. The Pharisees neglect the most important matters of justice, mercy and faithfulness.

I pity the Pharisees because they will face God's wrath. God wants all his people to come for forgiveness, so it is not too late for the Pharisees if they change their ways. If the Pharisees do not change, then all of you have a much better chance of seeing the glory of my father than they do." Jesus stepped down from the podium to rapturous applause.

The Pharisees watched as Jesus walked away. The head Pharisee was shaking with anger. "I warned the high priest in Jerusalem a few weeks ago about Jesus. He was non-committal about doing something. After I explain what has happened today, he will have to take a firm stance. Jesus has to be stopped, one way or another."

****

Yiler had had a very quiet week on the ship. The rest of the Deity Creation Group was not talking to him unless they had to, and when they did, it was "yes" and "no" or staccato sentences. His breaking of the news of the Santu victory and his subsequent plan to Hyet, Sidion, Uhet, Cannet, Fawter and Konacht had gone as badly as

211

when he told Denned and Hennegy. The crew had taken their lead from Jestoo who was furious with him, so they were ignoring him too. The result was that he had spent all meal and leisure time on his own in his cabin. He had just finished his breakfast when the computer announced that Dr Nowlett has requested entry. He sighed as he pressed the entry button and she walked in. She had unilaterally revoked her automatic entry into Yiler's cabin

"Yiler," she said coldly.

"Nowlett," he replied in a similar tone.

Contact between them since Yiler had announced what he had planned for Jesus had been non-existent. He knew that Nowlett had not left the science lab in a week. She had asked for her bed to be moved there which he had organised without comment. Yiler had been tempted to contact her to check on progress but had decided against it on the grounds of personal safety.

"Notwithstanding my stated reservations, I have been investigating the possibility of doing what you want. I have a theory as to how it can be done."

Yiler looked relieved. "Go on."

"When we have a medical emergency away from a treatment centre, we can create a state of temporary stasis in the patient. Stasis brings down the patient's body functions to a level that barely sustains life. It creates a window during which the patient can be transported to the treatment centre. For the casual observer, stasis could make it appear that the person is dead."

"For the casual observer."

"If you carried out an intimate examination, you would be able to see shallow and infrequent breathing. You would also notice that the body did not become ice cold and rigor mortis did not set in."

"That sounds like it might work, but it would require limiting access to the body so no one could check. That might be difficult."

"Agreed, but I think the risk can be managed. I will use a larger than normal injection of stasis fluid along with nanobots. Combined they should be able to create a level of stasis where it is not possible for anyone to notice that the person is not deceased. It would require medical equipment and expertise far beyond what is currently available on Earth to determine otherwise."

"Isn't that dangerous? Does creating stasis cause damage?"

"Stasis is safe for a maximum of two days. I think the nanobots could be programmed to repair any damage if that safe period is exceeded, but no more than twenty-four hours, so three days is the absolute limit."

"So, stasis can't be permanent?"

"Correct, eventually a full organ shut down would occur, which would be irreversible. Two or three days is all that is attainable."

"How confident are you that this can work?"

"I am not confident, so I must test my theory on someone else. There is no way that I am going to attempt this for the first time on Jesus."

Yiler lapsed into thought. "If you are going to do a trial run, then why not make the most of it. Jesus raising someone from the dead would be a brilliant miracle."

Nowlett nodded in agreement. "To use your parlance, the ultimate one. If Jesus can raise someone from the dead, then it stands to reason that God can raise Jesus from the dead. It links perfectly."

"But what happens if we don't succeed? It would be the first failed attempt at a miracle. It would undo a lot of what we have achieved so far."

"If I have access to the target in a controlled environment, my chances of success are very good. I am not as optimistic with Jesus because I will get restricted access to him. The Pharisees, if they do as you think, will make the killing of Jesus a very public spectacle. There is no way that my first attempt could be in such conditions. However, my second attempt could be, as I will learn a lot from the first one."

"Have you anyone in mind for the trial run?"

"Yes, I do. I was reading a report from Denned and Hennegy a few days ago. Denned spotted that both Mary Magdalene and Martha, her sister, were crying. He went over and discovered that they have a brother called Lazarus, who is very ill. The women are convinced that he has very little time left. I need to carry out some tests to see if his condition is curable. If it is, then I will use him as my test subject."

"So, if you discover that it is curable, then we need Jesus to find out about Mary and Martha's brother and decide to visit after he has died."

"The second part should be simple enough. On the first part, I want to borrow Fawter and Konacht to go to Lazarus' house, so I can talk them through some exploratory procedures. These will give me the answers I need."

"This is your operation, pardon the pun, so go ahead and get them to do what you want. How will you find the house?"

"I will ask Denned and Hennegy to find out from Mary and Martha where the house is. They might also get some more information on Lazarus' condition and how long he has been sick. It might help me decide if he is suitable."

They left Yiler's office and went to the communication centre. Jestoo, Hyet and Sidion set up a link to the six ground operatives and Dr Nowlett explained what she needed to be done.

****

Denned and Hennegy walked over to Mary and Martha. "Mary and Martha, sorry to disturb you," said Denned. "Any news on your brother Lazarus?"

"Thank you for asking, Andrew," said Mary. "Unfortunately, we just got news from a neighbour that was passing by that Lazarus is dying. He is a young man with a family which makes it very hard."

"Where is his house?" said Denned.

"His home is in Bethany," said Mary. "His wife is looking after him. She is finding it difficult though because they have two small children."

"Why don't one or both of you go to help her?" said Hennegy.

"Well, we might now since we are in Jerusalem," said Martha. "It is only a short walk to Bethany. We didn't go before because we wanted to spend all our time with Jesus."

"I know that you are devoted to Jesus," said Hennegy. "We can manage without you for a couple of days while you help your sister in law cope with this very difficult situation."

"I'll go then," said Martha.

"So will I," said Mary. "Are you sure Jesus would not mind?"

"Not at all," said Hennegy. "I will tell him. Do you want me to put a word in with Jesus about seeing if he can help Lazarus?"

"No," said Mary immediately. "We know that he cannot cure every ill, and we don't want a special favour for ourselves. That isn't the reason why we became his disciples." Martha nodded agreement.

"Okay, I won't ask him then," said Denned. "You are both truly selfless. A great example to all of us. I will organise for a couple of disciples to walk with you to Bethany to make sure you get there safely. A couple of tall scary looking men because it will be dark by the time you get there. Will you be ready to go in an hour?"

"Yes," said Martha. "We don't need much time to gather what we need for the journey. Will we meet you here, Andrew?"

"Yes," said Denned. "We will see you shortly." With that, Denned and Hennegy walked away.

That went well," said Denned.

"Better than I hoped," said Dr Nowlett. *"If it is a wasting disease, it might be cured easily enough."*

"I hope that you are right," said Denned. *"Fawter and Konacht, can you get over here in an hour? You will need to look like disciples."*

"I am sure that we can do that," said Fawter. *"What names do you want us to use."*

"Abraham and Isaac," said Hennegy.

"Good as anything," said Konacht.

"I'll walk you through the medical side while you are preparing," said Nowlett. "Are you ready to use your medical skills again?"

Konacht started laughing. "With all the courses and technical updates that you made us do, I think we are practically qualified doctors at this stage. We'll be fine."

****

An hour later, Denned introduced Martha and Mary Magdalene to Fawter and Konacht. Martha had been concerned about walking with two strange men, but Denned had vouched for them personally. Mary Magdalene had decided that her reputation was already very challenged and walking to Bethany with Isaac and Abraham was not going to make it any worse.

On the way to Bethany, both Mary Magdalene and Martha were surprised about how much Isaac and Abraham quizzed them about Lazarus, his family, and the location of his house. Both women didn't like to walk in silence and normally enjoyed talking to people. However, they became exasperated with Abraham and Isaac because every time either woman tried to change the topic, the two men always brought the conversation back to Lazarus. They were very glad when they reached the sick man's house. Mary Magdalene was sorely tempted just to thank them for walking with them and then send them on their way, but she did not want to seem rude. She stopped at the door of the house and shouted "hello" to Lazarus' wife, Dinah. A few seconds later a very tired woman appeared. When she saw Mary Magdalene and Martha, she smiled broadly.

"Mary and Martha, I'm so glad that you are here. I don't think that Lazarus will last much longer. He has been asking about you every time he wakes up."

"Is he conscious now?" said Martha.

"Yes, but he won't be for long. He is drifting in and out. I am so worried. He has stopped eating and is only drinking water." Dinah leaned to her left and looked at Fawter and Konacht. "Who are these two?"

"Isaac and Abraham," said Mary Magdalene. "Because it was dark, Andrew, one of our leaders, sent them to walk with us to make sure that we arrived safely."

"Thank you both," said Dinah. "I can't tell you how pleased I am that you have delivered my sisters-in-law to me safely."

"You are welcome," said Fawter.

"Would you come in for a glass of water and some fruit, or do you want to get moving before it gets any darker?" said Dinah.

"We can stay for a while," said Fawter. "Thank you very much for your offer. We might be able to help in some way." Dinah spotted Martha frowning and looked puzzled as she stood to one side and ushered them in. She made a questioning expression at Mary Magdalene, who just raised her eyebrows.

"Where are the children?" asked Mary Magdalene.

"Because Lazarus is so sick and needs constant attention, they have been spending nights in a neighbour's house. You can see them in the morning. Let's go and see Lazarus in case he goes back to sleep. Isaac and Abraham, please help yourselves to whatever you can find while we talk to Lazarus." The three women went into the bedroom, separated from the living area by a drape.

Fawter and Konacht could hear muffled conversation as they had a drink of water and ate some fruit. "We need to check if there is a window into that bedroom," said Fawter.

"I'll just go over to let them know that we are leaving," said Konacht. He walked to the drape and pulled it back slightly. With his other hand, he placed a camouflaged eavesdropper on the wall. "Dinah, thank you for your hospitality. We have had some water and fruit and are heading back now. Mary and Martha, hopefully we will see you soon back with the disciples." He was pleased when he saw a large shuttered window.

"Thank you again for walking with us," said Mary. "I expect that we will see you in a few days."

Fawter and Konacht walked a short distance and then cut left to circle around to the back of the house. There was a small hillock with dense foliage about twenty metres from the house where they could remain unobserved. Fawter took out a thermal imaging scanner, so they could watch the occupants as well as listen. The three women stayed in Lazarus' room for twenty minutes until Lazarus went back to sleep, at which point they went into the living area. When Fawter and Konacht were satisfied that the women were engrossed in conversation in the living area, Fawter picked up the medical supplies and walked towards the house. He opened the window and climbed through silently. He placed a vial that released anaesthetic into Lazarus' nose and mouth. Lazarus was already in a deep sleep, so he didn't react. When Fawter was satisfied that Lazarus was properly sedated, he injected Lazarus with the nanobots and scanned his body. When he completed the scan, he climbed back out the window. As he walked back to Konacht, information from the nanobots and the body scan were uploaded to Dr Nowlett. Fawter and Konacht waited in silence for Dr Nowlett to let them know if Lazarus was a suitable candidate for resurrection.

****

Dr Nowlett sat in front of her computer in her laboratory, analysing the results of the body scan with Yiler seated beside her. Lazarus, as she suspected, did have a wasting disease. The body scan showed degeneration of the basal ganglia of the brain and a deficiency of the neurotransmitter dopamine. She modelled a few treatments on the computer until she came up with a solution that she was happy with. Firstly, she had to programme nanobots to repair the basal ganglia, then she would have to make artificial dopamine. She couldn't come up with any way to give enough dopamine to Lazarus before he was placed into his tomb, so she opted for a slow release patch that could be placed under the skin that would last at least ten years.

All in all, she reckoned that it would take three days to repair the brain damage and get the dopamine levels stabilised, so she was within, what she hoped, was the safe limit. She then calculated the amount of stasis fluid required. It was a fine balance between the amount required to induce a coma and the amount that could kill him. When she was happy with the calculation of the stasis fluid and dopamine levels, she started preparation. It took four hours to get the required doses into vials and the skin patch prepared, stored in a medicine case and transported to Earth in a drop pod. Fawter used a small drone to bring the medical case over to Lazarus' house. While all that was being done, Nowlett sent the instructions to Fawter and Konacht, so they could programme the nanobots.

"Fawter, you can go back into the house and inject the stasis fluid. Then insert the patch under the skin," said Nowlett after the drone had arrived safely. Two minutes later, Fawter had unpacked the medicine case and was setting up in Lazarus' bedroom.

"Isn't stasis fluid normally introduced by an intravenous drip?" asked Fawter.

"Yes, but we don't have the time for a drip. You will have to inject it in one go. It has been done before in emergencies where the state of the patient didn't leave any other option. It is not unprecedented. Any movement from the living area?"

"All fine," said Konacht. *"The three women are asleep in the living area. However, every time one of them wakes up, they look in on Lazarus. I should be able to give Fawter enough warning to get out in time if that happens."*

Dr Nowlett monitored Fawter as he emptied the syringes with the nanobots and dopamine in Lazarus and inserted the patch beneath the skin on his hip. The final step was the injection of the stasis fluid. Although Dr Nowlett didn't show it, she was relieved when she observed that Lazarus' heart rate and metabolism had stabilised at the sufficient rate to preserve life.

"It looks like it has gone to plan," said Fawter. *"Lazarus appears to be dead. Dr Nowlett, how is it looking from your end?"*

"Exactly what I expected, so I am satisfied with your work," said Dr Nowlett. *"There is nothing more that I need from you, so you can go back to the disciples as soon as you are ready."* Fawter climbed through the window and walked back to Konacht.

Yiler let out a deep breath. "Nowlett, I knew that the outcome was never in doubt." Nowlett glared at him, but a hint of a smile developed despite herself.

"We won't go yet," said Konacht. *"We have to see how Martha, Mary Magdalene and Dinah react when they check on Lazarus. It is getting light, so they should wake up shortly."*

Fawter and Konacht found a hillock that had a copse of trees with tall weeds and desert grass providing excellent cover. They sat with their backs to a tree without talking. It didn't take too long for Dinah to stir and check on Lazarus. When she did, she just held his hand and began to cry. She shouted for Martha and Mary Magdalene to come in. "Lazarus is dead," she sobbed, and the three women just hugged and started crying.

****

Yiler, Sidion, Hyet and Dr Nowlett had gathered in the conference room to assess how Lazarus was responding to treatment. Jestoo was in the communications room listening into the conversation. He knew that he would need to contact Jesus, and he preferred to do it in the peace and quiet of the communications room.

"Well, Dr Nowlett," asked Yiler, "how are things progressing with Lazarus?"

"All within normal parameters," she said curtly. Notwithstanding that the progress of the trial bode well for Jesus, she still wasn't happy with what Yiler was doing and wanted him to know that. "The regeneration of the brain damage is eighty percent complete and dopamine levels are back to normal. I think that in twenty-four hours we can safely wake him up."

"What sort of state will he be in?" asked Sidion. "Will he be able to stand up and move around?"

"I think that he should be able to."

Yiler leaned forward. "I don't want to wait until he is fully cured. It might have a better impact if he emerges from the tomb a little worse for wear. You would expect that from someone returning from the dead."

Nowlett shook her head. "Yes, every time I've seen a reanimated corpse, they have always looked a bit rough." Yiler decided not to respond to that and waited for Nowlett to start talking again. "So, do you want to contact Jesus and get him to go to Bethany tomorrow?"

"That would be the plan," said Yiler.

"Jestoo, over to you then," said Nowlett.

Jestoo took a couple of deep breaths and prepared to use his God voice. *"Jesus, my son, I need to talk to you on an important matter."*

Jesus had been discussing the concept of forgiveness of sin with a small group of confused disciples. Some of them still didn't understand how this could work in practice, especially if the sin was a serious crime. They had argued that it seemed too easy, and there had to be a different treatment for major transgressions. He always talked to his father alone, so he made his excuses and walked away. *"Father, I am ready."*

"You may have noticed that Mary Magdalene and Martha have been away for a few days."

"Yes. Peter said they had gone to see their brother Lazarus who is dying."

"That is correct. Unfortunately, Lazarus died a few days ago."

"Oh, poor Mary and Martha. They must be devastated."

"They are."

"What can I do to help? Should I go to them? I could offer them the comfort that Lazarus is now with you. That would be a great relief to them."

"Yes, that would be a good idea, except that Lazarus is not with me."

"Why not? I thought that he was a good man. At least that's what Mary and Martha said. What did he do wrong?"

"He did nothing wrong. He is a good man. A very good man. I want to help him, and at the same time, give a message to those who still doubt us."

"What do you have in mind?"

"I want to return Lazarus from the dead to show that I have absolute power over life and death."

221

Jesus was silent as he considered what Jestoo had said. *"It is hard to believe that we can actually do that. Can I do this whenever I feel like it?"*

"No, Jesus. You can't raise anyone you feel like from the dead. It can be done only to demonstrate my absolute power. The natural order of life and death must be maintained. We can't create an unrealistic expectation among our followers." Jestoo was beginning to perspire a little.

"That would have been amazing, but I understand your logic. What do you want me to do?"

"Go to Lazarus' tomb in Bethany tomorrow. His wife Dinah, Mary and Martha are there with a small crowd mourning Lazarus. Lay your hands on him, and we will wake him up together. Bring a small amount of your key disciples, your future apostles, with you to witness this. Twelve will be enough."

"I will do as you command, father."

"Thank you, my son, you continue to please me."

"Jestoo, that was excellently handled," said Yiler.

"Yiler, just following your orders. Nothing more."

****

When the conversation with his father finished, Jesus walked over to Denned and Hennegy and told them that they needed to go to Bethany. He asked them to select ten of the disciples most likely to become his future apostles and leaders to bring with them. He left out the part about raising Lazarus from the dead. He wanted that to be a surprise. Denned and Hennegy rounded up James, son of Zebedee, John, Philip, Bartholomew, Thomas, Matthew, James, son of Alphaeus, Jude, Simon and Judas Iscariot. Within the hour, they were on their way to Bethany.

Lazarus had been dead in a tomb for three days before Jesus arrived. He and his entourage went straight to the town tombs which were on the side of town furthest from Jerusalem. As they walked there, they spotted a small crowd gathered at one of the tombs. As they got closer, Jesus recognised Mary and Martha. Jesus was deeply moved by how sad and upset Mary and Martha were. He laid his hands on their shoulders, and they both looked up and smiled.

"Jesus, we did not see you coming," said Martha. "You are very good to visit us. We know that you have very important work to do in Jerusalem." Lazarus' wife walked over. "This is my sister in law Dinah. Dinah, this is Jesus."

"Dinah, I am very sorry for your loss."

"Thank you for coming to pray with us," said Dinah.

"No thanks required. Mary and Martha are very important to me, and I had to pay my respects on the death of your husband and their brother."

The crowd began to make some observations. "This guy must be a politician," said one. "They always go to funerals. They think that it increases their popularity."

Jesus knelt beside the three women and they began to pray. While Jesus and the women prayed, the small crowd began to get restless.

"Isn't that the guy who healed a leper a few weeks ago?"

"That's him alright. My cousin was there and witnessed the whole thing."

"If Mary and Martha are that important to him, surely he could have done something to have prevented Lazarus from dying in the first place. What use is just coming here to pray?" The "observations" were becoming louder, and the apostles glared in the direction of the offender who held up his hands. "Just saying."

Jesus stood up and moved to stand directly in front of the tomb. The tomb was a cave with a large and heavy stone laid across the entrance. "Take away the stone," said Jesus loudly.

"Denned, the nanobots are now the only thing keeping Lazarus unconscious," said Dr Nowlett. *"The stasis fluid is now inactive. I will give the instructions to the nanobots to make Lazarus fully conscious."*

A couple of large burly men made their way from the crowd and positioned themselves around the stone and prepared to move it. Martha grabbed Jesus by the arm. "Lord, by this time, there will be a very bad odour. Lazarus has been in there for three full days, and it has been very hot."

"Martha, did I not tell you that if you believe in me totally and absolutely, you will see the glory of God?" said Jesus. "Take away the stone."

The two men pushed it away and Jesus walked to the entrance of the cave. He looked up to the sky and raised his hands.

"Father, I thank you that you have heard my prayers for Lazarus. I know that you always hear me, but I am saying this for the people standing here. I hope that those who do not believe, will now see that you have sent me."

Those in the crowd who already believed, knelt. Those who didn't backed away to avoid the expected unpleasant odour. When the smell didn't materialize, the crowd crept forward again. Jesus called in a loud voice, "Lazarus, come out!"

The crowd waited expectantly.

"This guy is insane," said someone in the crowd.

At first, nothing happened. Then, faint scratching noises could be heard in the tomb. "It's rats," shouted one man, who started laughing, but the rest of the crowd stayed silent.

They had spotted Lazarus.

He was stumbling and moaning with his hands and feet wrapped with strips of linen and a cloth around his face. The moaning continued as he started to rip off the cloth covering his body. Unsurprisingly, the crowd began to panic, as they weren't used to seeing a corpse moving. A few went into a dead faint; their bodies could be heard hitting the ground. Others turned and ran away screaming. Only a few of the braver ones stayed rooted to the spot, transfixed by what they were seeing. Mary Magdalene, Dinah and Martha were the first to move. They ran to Lazarus and helped him remove the cloth that he had been bound with. When the cloth was removed from his face, his moaning stopped, as he recognised Mary Magdalene, Dinah and Martha. He dropped to his knees, and the three women surrounded him and hugged. "Dinah, Mary and Martha. I was in a damned tomb! What happened to me?"

Jesus had hoped for something more profound from the first man to ever be brought back to life, but you couldn't have everything he supposed.

****

Yiler, Nowlett and Jestoo were having dinner together in Yiler's cabin. It had been a while since they had done that. Yiler had decided to use the success of raising Lazarus from the dead to suggest a family gathering. He did so with some trepidation, but both Jestoo and Nowlett had agreed.

"It's great that we are sitting down together again for a meal. It's been a while."

"And whose fault is that?" said Jestoo.

"Let's focus on the success of your mother and not go over old ground."

"Fine," said Jestoo. "Congratulations, Mother."

"Thank you, Jestoo."

"I am delighted that you succeeded with the Lazarus experiment, but it now raises another issue," said Yiler. "How are we going to explain to Jesus that we want him to aggressively confront the Pharisees and bin our previous policy? What do we explain about this new policy ending in his arrest and death?"

Nowlett rubbed her hands over her mouth as she thought. "We have to tell Jesus what is going to happen to him."

Yiler put down his glass. "Why do you say that?"

"Let's assume that this pans out as you think. Jesus will be arrested, tortured and executed. It wouldn't make sense for him not to know in advance. Would an all-powerful god just allow this to happen? Of course not."

Jestoo nodded in agreement. "We must tell him that it is part of the plan. It would have been difficult to convince him before the Lazarus experiment. Suffering for the greater good was not likely to have persuaded him. Now, I can tell him that, like Lazarus, I will raise him from the dead to be at God's side after he endures the crucifixion."

"Nowlett, what do you think?" said Yiler.

"I think that Jestoo is correct. If we wait until after the arrest and incarceration to advise him, he will be suspicious. It would be the first time that something has happened that he didn't know about."

"I am pleased that you are unanimous on this," said Yiler. "I had already concluded the same. Fawter and Konacht have been monitoring the Pharisees, so we already know that they are planning to make an arrest within ten to twenty days. We can tell him now, so he can prepare."

Chapter 13

President Mactins was sitting in his office waiting for General Lateel. He had been very busy since his election, with endless meetings with Santu representatives, seeking to fully implement the surrender terms. He didn't really have time to meet with anyone else, but the e-mail message from General Lateel had intrigued him. The e-mail had not requested a meeting, it had instead told him the time that General Lateel would be at his office. The e-mail had also deleted itself from his mailbox as soon as he had read it. When he had run a check on General Lateel, he found no reference apart from someone who worked in an obscure department in the Department of Labour.

He looked up as a tall, well-built female entered his office. "General Lateel, I presume."

"You are correct, President Mactins. Congratulations on your recent election."

"I am not sure if that is the right expression for the job I have been given. What do you want?"

"That depends upon the answer to the question that I am about to pose to you. You have two options. The first is that I make a full disclosure to you of several covert matters that are of significant interest to the Santu. The legality of these activities is dubious. The second is that I tell you nothing, in which case you have full deniability, and I would be the one exposed if the Santu uncovered these covert operations. In the latter case, I would continue to run them. President Flanstid was made fully aware, but that was before the Santu's military victory. The changed circumstances require me to offer you this choice. Which option do you prefer?"

President Mactins stared at Lateel, while he scratched his nose. "Do the Santu know anything about you and the organisation you lead?"

"I believe that Santu intelligence are unaware."

"Are your operations a breach of the surrender agreement?"

"Definitely."

"Will they put Deusi Prime in danger if discovered?"

"No, the risk lies elsewhere."

President Mactins sat back and folded his arms. "I can't conceive of a single reason why I should know more about this. I have enough to be dealing with."

General Lateel stood up. "Then that is the end of this meeting. I will contact you again when I need to advise you further."

"How can I contact you?" said the president.

"You can't," said Lateel as she walked out the door.

****

Jesus had just finished a long discussion with his father. Understandably, he was struggling to process being told that the policy of non-confrontation was being reversed, leading to his immediate arrest and shortly after that his death. Even more shocking was the news that his father was not going to prevent it, because he considered it necessary to secure the future of their religion. Finding out that his death would not be quick, that it would involve suffering at the hands of the Pharisees, scared Jesus to his core. The comfort that like Lazarus, he would be raised from the dead, did little to dispel his fears about what was to come. His father had told him that he must bear this suffering to demonstrate an innocent taking the burden of the sins of humanity thus opening heaven to all the adherents to their religion. Jesus had argued strongly that the spread of the religion could be achieved through an extended period of preaching and baptisms and his death was not required, but his father did not concur with him.

Adhering to the more aggressive approach, his father had suggested a grand entrance into Jerusalem seven days before the feast of the Passover, with the disciples arriving on horses with banners flying. Jesus felt it was not necessary to shed every facet of what they had done so far. An entrance like that was ostentatious and not fitting with the message they were promoting. There was nothing meek about it. He had suggested riding into Jerusalem on a donkey, like any ordinary person. He wanted no notice to be given of his arrival, no large gatherings or fanfare. Instead, he would speak at smaller, more intimate meetings and attack the Pharisees. He told his father that the Pharisees were getting more agitated with him, and that these smaller meetings would be enough to provoke the Pharisees to arrest him within the short period that his father wanted His father finally conceded on the grand entrance but nothing else.

****

When Jesus arrived on the donkey in Jerusalem on the day agreed with his father, he was very annoyed to observe huge numbers of people lined up to greet him at the city's main entry gate. It was obvious that someone had ordered that word be spread about his arrival contrary to his agreement with his father. The crowd had broken off palm branches and were throwing them on the road in front of him. He, the donkey and the apostles were walking on a soft sea of green foliage as they entered Jerusalem. The crowd continually and loudly proclaimed him as the Son of David and as the Son of God, which was sure to irritate the Pharisees. Jesus stopped the donkey and looked back. "Peter, you will have noted the thousands of people. This is exactly what I didn't want. It is going to push the Pharisees over the edge."

"After what you did with Lazarus, people wanted to see you in the flesh."

"How did they find out about Lazarus? There weren't that many people who witnessed it. The word of other miracles spread much more slowly."

"Raising someone from the dead is the ultimate miracle. You can't really compare it with the others."

"That's not an answer."

"Jesus, I don't know how they found out. I can only surmise that the apostles and disciples were vigorous about spreading the news that you raised Lazarus from the dead, and this caught the imagination of the people. Anyway, there is not much we can do about it now. Where do you want to go?"

"I want to go to the temple."

"Jesus, do you remember the last time you did that? You completely lost it with the moneylenders."

"I promise that I won't do that again."

"Even if the temple is back to what it was before your intervention?"

"If that's the case, I promise that I will only have a quiet word with them."

****

"If that is your idea of a quiet word, I'd hate to see you have a stern one," said Hennegy as he stood with Jesus and Denned outside the temple. "You did the exact same as last time."

"I know, I am sorry, but those people deserved it. The temple is not a livestock market or a bank. I had to confront the money changers and merchants in the temple."

"I get that, but did you then have to start arguing with the high priests?"

"Yes, I did. They had done nothing to improve the situation."

"They didn't like it when you told them that the temple would be destroyed by God."

"I meant destruction in a spiritual sense rather than a physical one."

"I don't think that they understood that. They will be expecting the temple to collapse into a pile of rubble. Anyway, no point worrying over what cannot be undone. Time to move onto the first meeting. I hope that the room is big enough."

"I very much doubt it if this crowd is anything to go by," said Jesus wryly.

****

The day after Jesus' second visit to the temple, the chief priests and elders of the Pharisees were starting a meeting with high priest Caiaphas. There was a lot of shouting.

"The people are declaring him to be the king of the Jews."

"And the son of God."

"And that he can cure blindness."

"And leprosy."

"And he can raise people from the dead."

"He is threatening all of us. The people love him and believe in him. The same cannot be said for us."

"He said that he was going to destroy the temple."

"We have to do something."

"He must be stopped."

The priests and Pharisees kept shouting for a few more minutes until Caiaphas held up his hand for silence. "I too am fearful about the growing public adulation for Jesus. However, are you prepared to accept the consequences of us taking action?" The room fell silent. "The Romans are not pleased by what is happening, but they are going to sit on their hands and do nothing. It will be down to us. You have asked for him to be stopped. There is only one way that this can be done. He will have to be arrested and sentenced to death." There were some audible gasps and shocked faces among the high priests and the Pharisees.

"Does this really surprise you? You are going to have to get your hands dirty to achieve what you want. We might be able to get the Romans to help us, but we must make the first move. Are you, the senior high priests and the elders of the Pharisees, willing to accept the consequences of your actions?"

There was no response. "Well, assuming silence means no dissent, then let us set the plans in motion to arrest Jesus."

"When will we do it?" asked the head Pharisee.

"The day of the Passover," said Caiaphas. "There is so much else going on that we might be able to arrest him without attracting attention. What is the name of the apostle that we have corrupted to our cause?"

"Judas Iscariot," answered the same Pharisee.

"We need to contact him and pay the agreed price for marking out Jesus for arrest," said Caiaphas.

Uhet and Cannet had been listening in from outside the meeting and contacted Yiler. *"Yiler, the arrest will be on the Passover,"* said Cannet. *"Direct from the mouth of Caiaphas, I still can't believe it, but Judas Iscariot is going to betray Jesus to the Pharisees."*

****

Jesus and the twelve apostles met for the Passover meal. He broke the news that the Pharisees were planning to arrest him and that, once arrested, he would not be released alive. The apostles were shocked and vowed to defend him, but Jesus ordered them not to. After the meal, Jesus, his apostles and a few disciples went to the Garden of Gethsemane to pray. The garden was located at the base of the Mount of Olives and was an oasis of peace and calm in the middle of the bustling Jerusalem. Jesus often went there to think. He walked alone to a secluded part of the garden and asked his father if this suffering and death might pass by him. He was not surprised when his father replied that no other course of action other than his death was possible. He went back to the apostles to get some comfort from their company and found them asleep. "Why are you sleeping? Please get up and pray with me." All the apostles woke up and apologised to him.

"Jesus, I'm sorry but the time has come," said Jestoo.

Within seconds, chief priests, soldiers of the temple guard and elders appeared. Judas Iscariot gave Jesus a kiss on the cheek to identify him and the soldiers moved in to arrest him.

"Judas, are you betraying the Son of God with a kiss?" said Jesus, who had his line prepared in advance thanks to his father's warning. Judas made no reply and looked at the ground.

When the apostles saw what was happening, they surrounded Jesus. "Lord, should we strike with our swords?" one of them asked.

Before Jesus could answer, the man struck one of the high priest's bodyguards, cutting off his right ear.

Jesus grabbed him arm. "No more violence, I beg you." He looked at those come to arrest him. "Do you think that I am leading a rebellion? Is that why you have come with swords."

The lead Pharisee stepped forward. "It is because you are dangerous. You are not the Son of God, but because these fools believe it, we need to protect the population from this radical nonsense."

Jesus stared at the Pharisee. "I could stop you, but I won't. Do what you will."

****

Yiler, Nowlett, Jestoo, Hyet and Sidion were looking anxious as they sat in the conference room. It was only a few minutes after the arrest of Jesus.

"I was talking to Fawter and Konacht earlier," said Hyet. "They are very apprehensive about them trying to put Jesus into stasis."

"No need for them to be," said Nowlett.

Sidion frowned at that comment. "Dr Nowlett, I understood that it would be significantly more challenging to carry out the procedure because of the lack of access to Jesus. Have you come up with an alternative plan?"

"No, the problem still exists."

"So, why shouldn't Fawter and Konacht be apprehensive then?" said Sidion.

Nowlett breathed deeply. "Because I am going to Earth."

Yiler was appalled by Nowlett's suggestion. "Under no circumstances am I…"

Nowlett held up her hand with the palm facing Yiler. "Please do not say another word. This is not a discussion because saving Jesus requires medical skills way beyond those of Fawter and Konacht. I cannot place this responsibility on them. I will have to do it."

"Yiler, she is correct," said Hyet. "Fawter and Konacht, who normally are not bothered by anything, are really nervous about having to do this."

"If ever there was a situation where Mum's skills are required, this is it," said Jestoo. "The next twenty-four hours will be chaos, and there is no better person than Mum to deal with that, but only if she is on Earth."

Yiler sensed that he was fighting a losing battle. "Nowlett, can I talk to you outside for a moment?"

When they were standing alone in the corridor, Yiler spoke again. "I admit I am being selfish. It's just that I don't want to risk losing you; it will be a very dangerous mission because we are for once not fully in control."

Nowlett took both of Yiler's hands in hers. "Don't be silly. You won't lose me. I will be very careful and won't take risks."

"You promise?"

"I promise."

Yiler laughed gently. "I was about to tell you to get everything packed, but you have already done that, haven't you? No doubt it's already in the drop pod."

Nowlett smiled at him. "I can't believe that I have finally become predictable. I've tried to avoid that all my life." She stood up. "I'll say my goodbyes now. I don't want you to walk me to the drop pod." Yiler hugged her, and she started to walk away.

****

The morning after being arrested, Jesus was taken to the temple by four guards to meet with the high priests. Jestoo was talking to him to keep his spirits up, which was proving challenging.

"My son, you are very brave, and you bear this burden well."

"I am terrified of what is to come."

"I know, and I promise I will do all I can to alleviate the worst of it."

"I fail to see how you can make a crucifixion any less painful. I am to be nailed to a cross and left to hang for hours until I die from exhaustion and asphyxiation."

"I promise you that it will be short."

"Even so," said Jesus, *"what about a beheading instead of crucifixion? It would be over in an instant."*

Jestoo knew that his mother enjoyed a challenge but repairing the damage from decapitation was beyond even her skills. *"Unfortunately, the Roman's preferred method of capital punishment is crucifixion. I cannot change that."* The two then lapsed into silence.

When they arrived at the temple, Jesus had his hands and feet bound in shackles. Caiaphas, the high priest, was standing at the altar and Jesus was forced to kneel in front of him.

"Jesus of Nazareth, we meet again."

"We do indeed, Caiaphas. Why have you arrested me? I have done nothing wrong."

"I beg to differ. You have proclaimed yourself to be the Son of God, what you preach is blasphemy and you are a false prophet." The high priest curled his lip as he looked down at Jesus. "However, I am known for being a reasonable man, so I am giving you the opportunity to confess to your crimes."

"I will not confess. I would be lying and disclaiming the truth if I did. I am the Son of God."

"You are a blasphemer or else possessed by the devil…"

"Caiaphas, hold on a second. I know that I am the Son of God. I also know that you don't believe me. Neither of us is ever going to change our minds, so why don't we move onto whatever you have planned for me next. I don't want to spend the morning in a pointless debate with you."

"As you wish." Caiaphas nodded to two very large men standing to the side. "Let's see if I can persuade you to change your mind."

The two men marched Jesus away from the altar and through the Court of the Gentiles into a small windowless room that contained no furniture. There were two iron chains attached to the wall. The two men attached them to shackles on his arms. They then mocked, beat and condemned him for claiming to be the Son of God. Their treatment of him grew more savage, the longer that Jesus refused to break.

Nowlett, Denned, Hennegy, Uhet, Cannet, Fawter and Konacht were standing outside the temple. *"Yiler, this has gone too far,"* said Denned. *"Let us go in and get this sorted. The cowardly scum are beating Jesus while he is shackled to a wall. We can have him out of there in a few seconds."*

"Dr Nowlett has assured me that the nanobots are dulling the pain," said Yiler.

"This is true to a point," said Nowlett. *"The nanobots are doing that. However, as the physical damage gets worse, their effectiveness will diminish, and it is coming close to that point, I believe."*

"If he is in pain, we must intervene," said Uhet.

"I am ordering you not to interfere," said Yiler. *"Is that clear?"*

Hennegy looked furious. *"Crystal."*

"Dr Nowlett, you must make sure that my order is adhered to," said Yiler.

"I know what my responsibilities are, thank you."

The group waited in silence for the torture to stop. It was another hour until Jesus, bruised and bloodied, was brought back in front of Caiaphas. "Well, do you confess now? If you confess, you will only suffer banishment from Judea. The alternative is execution."

"I am the Son of God," said Jesus quietly. "I have no fear of death."

Caiaphas shook his head. "You are very foolish." He then sighed loudly. "Unfortunately, I cannot personally authorise you to be executed for your crimes. I need to bring you to the Roman Governor of Judea, so he can hear your case and then authorise it."

****

Caiaphas, Jesus and a small group of men including some of the high priests and the two thugs who had beaten Jesus, proceeded to the Roman Governor's residence. He ordered the remaining high priests and Pharisees to gather as many people as possible in ten minutes and follow them. Caiaphas reckoned that a visual and aural reminder that the populace was in favour of an execution could be vital in persuading Pontius Pilate to do what they wanted.

They were given entry to the governor's residence as soon as they arrived and were brought straight to the audience room. A small group had followed them to the residence, including Nowlett, Denned, Hennegy, and some of the apostles. Judas Iscariot was unsurprisingly conspicuous by his absence. Shortly afterwards, Mary, Mary Magdalene and Martha arrived, having been collected by the rest of the apostles. Mary was inconsolable and had to be helped to stand by the other two women. Uhet and Cannet had stayed behind at the temple to plant explosive charges to ensure that what Jesus had foretold about the destruction of the temple would become true, notwithstanding that he had meant it in a spiritual sense. Their plan was to detonate the explosives the moment Jesus died.

As soon as Pontius Pilate arrived and sat down, Caiaphas made his accusations against Jesus. "This man has repeatedly claimed to be the Son of God, which is a direct violation of the Jewish law. He is also claiming to be the king of the Jews. For these two reasons, I ask that he be condemned to death for his heinous crimes."

Pontius Pilate leaned forward with his head resting on the closed fist of his right hand. "Caiaphas, heinous is a bit of an exaggeration. I have explained to you before that this is a religious matter, not something for a civil court. Therefore, it has nothing to do with me. I can find no fault with Jesus from a civil law perspective; he is not guilty of breaking any Roman law. Is it true to say that other than Jesus' claim to be the Son of God, Jesus has followed all other aspects of the Roman law?"

"Yes, but there have been numerous breaches of Jewish religious law."

"Well, that confirms that this a religious matter over which I have no jurisdiction."

Caiaphas had anticipated the initial reaction of Pontius Pilate. From his extensive dealings with the Roman Governor, he knew that Pontius Pilate tended to go for the option that required the least amount of effort from him, so Caiaphas had a backup argument prepared.

"With all due respect, Governor, anyone who claims to be a king speaks against Caesar and that must be a crime. Also, there is a substantial risk of civil unrest from the disciples who follow him. I am sure that you can hear the noise outside the window. I believe that a crowd has gathered to protest his actions and show you what the people think. Why don't you seek their views?"

"Let's see what the crowd think then," said Pontius Pilate, who was never one to upset the masses. "Bring Jesus to the window to stand beside me." The audience room had a balcony overlooking a square outside the residence which was used for public announcements. Pontius Pilate walked out onto the balcony with Jesus following. When the crowd saw Jesus, they began shouting and booing. This quickly evolved into a chant of, "Crucify him!" The Governor was unaware of the fact that the crowd was comprised of high priests, Pharisees and their close associates. The counter cheering of the supporters was drowned out by the booing.

Pontius Pilate raised his arms in the air to silence the crowd. "What would you have me do with Jesus, the king of the Jews?"

"Crucify him! Crucify him!" continued the crowd.

"I still do not see that this man has done anything wrong, so I am washing my hands of all responsibility in this matter. This crucifixion is being permitted solely in response to the demands of your high priest. Centurion take him way."

The centurion brought Jesus down into the dungeons under the governor's residence. "This is the King of the Jews whom the governor has ordered to be crucified," he told the guards. "Treat him like royalty while you get him ready." The centurion stared sternly at the soldiers and then burst out laughing. "Only joking, you can do what you want." Jesus was thrown in with two other prisoners and all of them were whipped and beaten by the soldiers. A crown of thorns was placed atop Jesus' head.

Along with a small guard, the three prisoners were forced to walk in a procession to Mount Calvary, the Roman crucifixion site, carrying their own crosses. The crowd, again directed by the high priests and the Pharisees, taunted and abused them. Jesus' supporters were part of the crowd on either side. The Roman soldiers did nothing to protect the prisoners and just talked to each other as the crowd began to get violent.

Nowlett was standing beside Denned, Hennegy, Fawter and Konacht. "Guys, I want you to stop every person from the crowd who gets physically abusive." Within a few minutes, there was a string of unconscious bodies stretching back down the road. The crowd received the message that abusing the prisoners was dangerous and backed off.

At one point, Jesus collapsed under the weight of the cross. The physical abuse had taken its toll and the cross was very heavy. Nowlett saw her chance and dashed forward to Jesus' side. The other four Deusi blocked the attempts by the Roman soldiers to intervene and see what was going on, by pushing and manoeuvring the crowd into their way.

Nowlett was shaking with excitement and tension because thirty years of planning now rested upon her actions over the next few minutes. She put her hand gently under Jesus's chin and raised it until he was looking into her eyes. "I have waited for this moment for a long time. I have heard so much about you. Jesus, please take a drink of this."

Jesus took a long drink. "Thank you, my daughter. Maybe it's because I am so thirsty, but this water is the nicest water I have ever tasted. Thank you so much." He gave the canteen back to her and Nowlett shook it.

"There is some water left. Please finish it."

"I don't want to leave you without water. It's very hot."

She proffered the canteen to him. "Don't worry, I can get some more." Jesus took the canteen back and emptied it.

Nowlett tried to keep her emotions in check, but a tear ran down her cheek. "Please, let me help you carry the cross. It would be my honour."

Jesus raised his hand to touch Nowlett's face and wipe away the tear. "You are very kind to offer, but this burden is mine alone. Please don't cry and stop worrying about me. I have faith in my father. You must too."

"You never said a truer word." Nowlett helped Jesus back to his feet and then assisted him in picking up the cross. As she did so, she placed a flesh coloured patch on his lower back, that would slowly release a powerful pain killing drug.

Jesus' eyes widened as he looked over her shoulder. "Look out, a Roman soldier has spotted you." Jesus moved to get in his way. "Please don't hurt her. She was only giving me water."

The Roman soldier had seen Nowlett helping Jesus but initially was unable to get near her due to the crowd. "Get away from him," he ordered angrily as he pushed Jesus out of the way and brought down his arm to give Nowlett a crack of his whip on her back. Nowlett's right arm shot back and caught the whip. She twisted her body as Konacht had instructed her and wrenched the whip from the startled soldier's grip.

"I am so tempted to shove this down your throat, you idiot." Luckily for her, in her rage she said it in Deusi, so the soldier just looked at her blankly. She took the whip in both hands, snapped it and threw it at the breastplate of the soldier. He pulled his arm back to strike her, but Fawter moved towards the soldier who cried out as his arm was dragged back. Konacht pushed a section of the crowd towards Fawter and Nowlett, who made their escape as the people milled around.

"That was brave of you," said Fawter. "Textbook disarmament."

"*Nowlett, please be careful,*" said Yiler. "*That Roman soldier could have killed you.*"

Nowlett barely acknowledged him. "*I got the first full dose of stasis fluid and nanobots into him. That is all that matters.*"

240

Deity Creation

****

Uhet and Cannet were sitting in the shade listening to what was happening on the way to Mount Calvary. They spotted Caiaphas and his entourage going back into the temple. The two thuggish looking men who had dished out the punishment to Jesus, didn't go in and instead went to a nearby tavern. They ordered a couple of drinks and sat down outside the tavern, laughing and joking. They shouted for the tavern owner to hurry up, and when he brought their order out, they refused to pay. "Charge it to Caiaphas," one of them shouted as he kicked the innkeeper in the posterior.

Uhet turned to Cannet. "Do we have time?"

Cannet smiled grimly. "Oh, we do. We must make use of the close combat training that Fawter and Konacht gave us. They would be offended otherwise."

The two of them walked over to the tavern and stood directly in front of the table where the two men were sitting, blocking the sun.

"What do you two assholes want?" asked one of the men.

"What the bloody hell are you staring at?" asked the other.

Uhet leaned forward and placed his hands on their table. "We are staring at two of the most worthless pieces of shit that have ever walked."

"And two of the ugliest," added Cannet. "We had to block the sun shining on you, just to fully appreciate your ugliness."

"Your parents must be very proud of you," added Uhet.

"Assuming you know who they are, of course," finished Cannet.

The two men stood up. "You boys have just earned yourself an ass-kicking."

Uhet looked them up and down. "I very much doubt it. Admittedly, you two are very good at dealing with one man in shackles tied to a wall, but two fit men with no physical handicaps, I don't think so."

Three minutes later, Cannet walked into the tavern to find the owner cowering in a corner. Cannet knelt on one knee beside him. "I sincerely apologise for the altercation and the ensuing mess." He dropped three gold coins into the owner's hand. "I hope that this compensates you fully for the damage."

"It's more than enough."

"Great. We will carry those two away and dump them by the fountain. We don't want them discouraging customers after you have cleaned up."

****

The rest of the team thoroughly enjoyed listening to Uhet and Cannet beat the two thugs within an inch of their lives, although Nowlett was sure that Jesus would not approve. When the procession arrived at Calvary, the prisoners put their crosses onto the ground. Nowlett rushed in to give Jesus more water laced with stasis fluid and nanobots, but this time was forced back roughly by the soldiers.

Nowlett walked back to Fawter and Konacht. "I have to get a second dose of stasis fluid and nanobots into him."

"I know," said Fawter. "We will just have to wait for an opportunity."

Jesus was tied to the cross and then his wrists were nailed to the horizontal wooden beam. Mary and Mary Magdalene fell to their knees and cried inconsolably. The rest of the group, including Denned and Hennegy, did the same. The charge against Jesus, 'King of the Jews' had been written on a wooden board and nailed above his head. The cross was then lifted and planted into the ground. This immediately restricted the airflow to his lungs causing him to gasp for breath loudly. There was a lot of shouting and noise because the two other prisoners were crucified at the same time, one at his left and the other at his right.

While Jesus's supporters were gathered at the feet of the cross praying, the rest of the crowd and the soldiers verbally abused them. The taunting continued for a short while, but then the crowd began to get bored and dissipate. Crucifixions took at least three hours from beginning to end, and most of the crowd had better things to do. Eventually, with the two thieves dead, only one very bored Roman soldier remained to keep Jesus' supporters away from the cross.

"We need to give Jesus the stasis fluid and extra dose of nanobots," said Nowlett. "The readings from his implant show that he doesn't have much time left."

Fawter had a large water bag around his shoulder which contained an extra supply of the stasis and nanobot mixture without the food additive, which he kept separately. "Nowlett, what does this taste before the additive is mixed in?"

"Vile, it's like vinegar."

"I have an idea," said Fawter. "Konacht, give me a sponge from the medical kit that you are carrying." Konacht found it and gave it to him. Fawter dipped the superabsorbent sponge in the water bag and stuck it to the top of a long stick that he had picked up from the ground. He then put the additive into the rest of the mixture.

He walked up to the base of the cross and began to raise the stick with the sponge on top dripping liquid. The Roman soldier spotted what he was doing and moved to block him. "No water," he ordered. "Look, I know you are trying to help him, but it will only prolong things for the poor bastard. He has already lasted longer than most."

"It's actually vinegar. It's a bit of a joke on him."

The soldier squirted some of the liquid into his mouth and immediately spat it out. "That is horrible stuff. This guy really must have pissed you people off. Here, I'll help if this is what your idea of fun is. My spear is longer."

"I'll get some more vinegar," said Fawter. He squeezed the sponge to empty it, dipped it back in the mixture that had now been treated with the additive and brought it back to the soldier. The soldier stuck his spear into the sponge and lifted it to Jesus's mouth. To his surprise, Jesus drank it all. They all either kneeled or stood in silence.

"My father, why have you forsaken me?" whispered Jesus. His head fell onto his chest and his whole body went limp.

"That's that, I think," said the soldier. "I'll just double-check." The soldier stuck a spear into Jesus' side which produced a clear liquid instead of blood, as the nanobots closed off the blood vessels allowing only a small amount of plasma to be released. "He is officially dead, so I'm off home then. You can do what you want with the body."

Chapter 14

Uhet and Cannet triggered the explosives placed on the main temple building immediately upon the death of Jesus. It was like a volcano had erupted. The explosives tore the temple's curtain from top to bottom. Uhet and Cannet watched in satisfaction as the high priests, including Caiaphas, ran outside screaming and shouting.

Uhet turned to Cannet. "I have to admit that using the literal interpretation of what Jesus meant when he referred to the destruction of the temple was one of Yiler's better ideas. I wonder if the high priests will realise that Jesus' prediction of the destruction of the temple has come to pass."

"Possibly," replied Cannet. "Let's go over and listen." They walked over to where a group of high priests had gathered.

"I was told that Jesus said something about the temple being destroyed," remarked one.

"I also heard that he warned it was going to happen," said another.

"So, on the day that we orchestrate his crucifixion by the Romans, the temple collapses. That cannot be a coincidence."

"Maybe this wasn't such a good idea."

"Bit late now for second thoughts."

****

The group carefully took down the crucifix and commenced pulling out the nails and untying the ropes. All of them were crying. Mary gently took the crown of thorns from Jesus' head and threw it to one side. Water and cloths were taken out, and the group began to use them to clean the body. Mary gently cleaned Jesus' face and then leaned over to kiss him. "My poor beautiful boy," she sobbed as her tears fell on his face. "You were so brave." Mary Magdalene was cleaning Jesus' feet and barely needed any water because of the tears streaming down her face. Nowlett concentrated on cleaning the area with the wound from the spear and the holes in the hands and feet. She was sealing off the blood vessels to allow the nanobots, who had originally done the task, to reassign themselves to repairing other damage

"Dr Nowlett, did it work?" said Yiler. *"Is he still alive? We are getting nothing from his implant."*

"He is badly injured, but still alive," said Dr Nowlett. *"Yiler, we did it, we bloody did it. Denned and Hennegy, we need more stasis fluid and nanobots, what we have are containing the damage but not repairing it. I will give you small, slow-release patches containing both to tie into the bindings when we wrap up the body."*

While most of the group carefully bound the body, Denned and Hennegy did as Nowlett had ordered and applied the patches without anyone seeing. When the body was fully bound, they picked it up and carried it carefully to a nearby tomb that had been already opened by Fawter and Konacht. The body was gently placed on a stone bed and they all left apart from Mary. She placed her hand gently on Jesus' head and bent over and kissed him for what she assumed was the last time. Denned, Hennegy, Fawter and Konacht placed large stones in front of the tomb while the others watched silently.

Satisfied that the stones were locked into place, Hennegy beckoned the group to close in around him. "We have some difficult decisions to make, but now is not the time. My primary concern is that we are all at risk from the high priests and the Pharisees. We have to be very careful, or we could suffer the same fate as Jesus."

"What are you proposing?" asked Mary Magdalene.

"I think that we should all keep a very low profile for a few days, maybe even a week. No public meetings of any sort. I plan to gather the apostles in a safe house and discuss our plans for the future."

"Peter, we can't let my son's death be in vain," said Mary. "We must carry on his work."

"I agree entirely. I am just suggesting that we should temporarily stop until less attention is focused on us. The last thing I want to happen is that we are locked up and there is no one to continue the work of Jesus. Mary and Mary Magdalene, I will allocate two men to bring you to a safe location. Salome, who I think you already know, as she has attended a lot of meetings, lives nearby and has offered her house. I will contact you when we are ready to start again."

"Who have you asked to do it?" asked Mary Magdalene suspiciously.

"It's not Isaac and Abraham. I heard that you didn't enjoy their company when they brought you to Lazarus."

"Great," said Mary Magdalene.

****

On the evening of the Sabbath, the day following the crucifixion, Uhet and Cannet were standing in the kitchen of Salome's house arguing with Mary, Mary Magdalene, Mary mother of James and Salome.

"It's too risky," said Uhet.

"It is against Peter's orders," added Cannet.

"I don't care what you say," said Mary. "Because we were so upset, we did not anoint the body with oil as is the required ritual, and that has to be rectified. We have been arguing about this for two days, two days in which we have seen nobody looking for us. No Roman soldiers. No high priests. Nothing."

"I went into Jerusalem and all is quiet," added Salome. "Well, apart from the repair work at the temple. I think you are being unnecessarily cautious."

"So, that is settled then," stated Mary, mother of James. "We are going to the tomb tomorrow morning."

"We are going to have no part in this madness," said Uhet. "On your own heads, be it. However, Mary has too high a profile and would be a prize asset for the Pharisees. I won't stop you three, but I will stop Mary."

"Fine," said Mary. "Stay here and cower like the two old crones that you are, and I will keep you company. The door is over there by the way if you need some fresh air," she added, helpfully pointing it out with her hand. Uhet and Cannet stood up and left together. As soon as they were out of sight, they contacted Dr Nowlett.

"Nowlett, we have a problem," said Uhet. *"Three women are going to the tomb tomorrow. We have tried to dissuade them but to no avail. We have to wake Jesus up before they get there or move him to another location."*

"I'll break the news to Yiler," said Nowlett.

Much to Yiler's consternation, Nowlett had refused to return to the ship in a drop pod on the basis that her work wasn't done. She sat quietly at her computer in a tent set up beside the apostles' safe house. Apparently, an unmarried female staying in the house was offensive to the delicate sensibilities of some of the men. On the plus side, it meant that she and the rest of the ground-based team had a place where they would not be disturbed. It was late in the evening on the Sabbath day, and she was very tired. It was the first day after the crucifixion, and the nanobots had repaired most of the physical damage. Yiler, Hyet and Sidion were on the ship reviewing the data and trying to make helpful suggestions as to what remaining trauma should be focused on. With the news that Mary Magdalene and her two friends were on their way to anoint the body, they were all waiting for Dr Nowlett to give her opinion on whether Jesus could be brought out of his coma and moved.

Dr Nowlett closed the lid on her computer. *"He has improved sufficiently, and in my judgement, can be woken up."* Everyone on the ship and in the tent started clapping and cheering.

"Dr Nowlett, you are a genius," said Yiler.

"Lucky for you, because I would never have forgiven you if he died," said Nowlett drily.

Yiler started giving orders. *"Fawter and Konacht, go to the tomb and open it. Uhet and Cannet, do not let those women leave the house until we are ready. Drug them if you have to."*

"Already on our way," said Fawter.

"Happy to," said Uhet.

When Fawter and Konacht arrived at the tomb, they moved the stones aside and went in. As they had expected, there was no foul odour in the cave, just stale air. They carefully removed the bindings from the body and left them on the floor of the cave. They set up a camera in the corner of the cave, so that they could observe him waking up. Jesus started moaning gently and moving his limbs.

"He is nearly conscious," said Nowlett. *"You better get out of there, now."* Fawter and Konacht did as they were ordered and retreated to a safe distance. Jesus continued to moan gently, and his limb movements became more energetic. He suddenly turned on to his side, vomited violently and pulled himself into a foetal position.

"Jestoo, will you start to engage with him?" asked Nowlett.

Normally, Jestoo went to the communications room when he had to talk to Jesus. On this occasion, he had decided to remain in his room. He was sitting on his bed with his knees pulled up to his chest and arms wrapped around them. He was as white as a sheet.

Jestoo mentally adjusted to his God persona. *"Jesus, you have died and have arisen as I said you would."* There was silence.

"Jesus, can you hear me?" Still silence. Jesus hauled himself into a sitting position with his arms wrapped around his knees and his head resting on his arms.

"Leave me alone," whispered Jesus.

"Jesus, we still have much work to do."

"I don't care. Leave me alone." Jesus was now rocking from side to side and mumbling.

"Please, Jesus, you have to talk to me."

"No!"

"What's wrong?" asked Yiler.

"I don't know," answered Nowlett. *"Everything looks fine physically. Try again, Jestoo."*

"Jesus, it is your father. Please talk to me."

"I told you to leave me alone."

"This didn't happen with Lazarus," said Yiler.

Nowlett supressed a snarl as she answered slowly. *"Yiler, the obvious difference in Lazarus' case was that there was no physical trauma to the patient."*

"So, what's your prognosis?" said Yiler.

"You will be familiar with post-traumatic stress syndrome or PTSS. Unfortunately, I believe he is suffering from PTSS."

"Can you do anything to help? What about your nanobots?"

"Yiler, nanobots are useless for PTSS. Weeks, maybe months, of counselling are required to deal with it."

"We don't have months," said Yiler loudly.

"I am aware of that. I need to get back to the Tesfa with Jesus to try to treat him, but I very much doubt that I can get him back within a couple of days. Mental trauma like this could takes weeks to treat, and we don't have weeks. You are going to have to revert to plan B, I'm afraid. Send down a medical pod to pick us up immediately."

Yiler thought for a moment and then sighed. *"Jestoo, can you join us, please?"*

"Give me a couple of minutes," said Jestoo.

****

Jestoo jumped up from his bed, ran to the bathroom and was violently ill. He stayed in the toilet for a couple of minutes dry retching. When he was sure that he was finished, he walked back to his bed and sat down. He had convinced himself that this moment would never arrive. He had, like the rest of the team, been certain Nowlett would have been able to ensure that Jesus was fit to carry on after being resurrected.

The last thirty days had been difficult for Jestoo. Going to Earth to replace Jesus had always been a remote possibility. That possibility becoming probable had left Jestoo feeling increasingly anxious. His trips to Earth had been banned because Yiler wouldn't risk Plan A and Plan B being on Earth at the same time. He had been moved out of his engineering role on the ship because Yiler had decided that Jestoo should do nothing else except talk to Jesus.

Initially, when the team had heard of the Santu's victory and the nearing end of the experiment, Jestoo had two reactions. The first was sympathy for what Jesus was facing. He felt uneasy as to what he would be forced to observe. They were brothers after all, and even if Jesus didn't know that he existed, he felt that personal bond strongly. The second reaction, which he wasn't proud of, was that he was worried that he would be a failure in taking on the role of Jesus.

He deeply admired the commitment and dedication of Jesus to the cause of spreading the word of his father. He marvelled at the fearlessness Jesus displayed in standing up to the high priests and the Pharisees. Every action taken and every word said by Jesus was influenced and underpinned by his belief in God. He was a superb orator, his skills honed by regular speeches and public addresses.

Because of all of this, Jestoo was sure that he could not succeed in impersonating Jesus. The crucial difference was that Jesus believed in God. Jestoo knew otherwise. How could Jestoo be convincing when he didn't believe a single word he would be saying?

Jestoo had found the arrest, abuse and crucifixion of Jesus a traumatic experience. He couldn't imagine what it had been like for Jesus. The audio had been bad enough, so he had never switched to a visual feed. During the crucifixion, Jesus had implored him to intercede on several occasions, and Jestoo found it difficult to justify to Jesus why he could not. He felt guilty and partly responsible for the suffering Jesus endured.

After Jesus had been entombed, he had felt relieved. He didn't admit that to anyone. This was the first time since he was twelve that he had no one else in his head. He had gone back to his FTL drive analysis to keep himself amused, but his heart was only half in it. He was distracted by what was in store for him if Jesus didn't survive. He had hoped that his worrying might be unnecessary, but it hadn't turned out that way. Jestoo took a deep breath, pressed the exit button and walked out into the corridor and into the engineering chief.

"Jestoo, are you alright?" she asked.

"I'm going down to Earth to take over. Jesus is too badly messed up to carry on."

"Isn't that what you always wanted?"

"I thought so, but now that the day has come, I am not so sure."

"Jestoo, just do your best. That's all anyone can expect from you. If it's worth anything to you, I have total confidence in your ability to pull this off."

"Thank you, I really appreciate that. Sorry to be rude, but I better get going and meet with Yiler." Jestoo walked slowly to Yiler's office. Hyet and Sidion were still there when he arrived, and he sat down on the only spare stool. "Okay, what happens now."

"What happens is that Hyet will accompany you to Earth in the medical pod when Nowlett returns to the *Tesfa* with Jesus. Fawter and Konacht will meet you and bring you to your first... task."

Sidion grinned broadly. "Lucky you. A trip in a medical pod. You better take Dr Nowlett's anti-nausea treatment."

Hyett didn't look happy. "Yiler, why me?"

"You are the last male left who can be an angel. The women would recognise everyone else."

Jestoo coughed. "My first task is where?"

"In a few days, you will need to meet with the apostles. However, we will need a few practice runs first. We don't want you to meet the apostles as your first attempt to persuade someone that you are Jesus."

"Okay, I will go back to my room and get changed."

"Not straight away," said Sidion. "Unfortunately, there was physical damage to Jesus that I need to recreate on you. The wounds on the feet and wrists from the nails and the spear wound to the side. It won't hurt too much, I promise. Nowlett has given me specific instructions. Let's go to her lab. You too, Hyet, because you also need some work done to assist in blending in with the humans."

"Wonderful start," said Jestoo.

"Bloody surgery!" said Hyet.

Yiler opened his arms apologetically. "Sorry, Jestoo and Hyet, this has to be convincing. Sidion, be as quick as you can. We have twelve hours to get Jestoo into place and get prepared for him rising from the dead tomorrow morning. Nowlett will be back on the *Tesfa* shortly with Jesus."

"Can I meet him?" said Jestoo.

Yiler shook his head. "No, I don't want you distracted."

****

Mary Magdalene, Mary the mother of James and Salome started their walk to the burial tomb soon after sunrise the following morning. They bought some sweet-smelling spices to put on Jesus' body for the cleansing ritual.

"A thought just occurred to me," said Salome. "Who will roll away the stone that covers the entrance of the tomb?"

"We can ask someone passing by," said Mary Magdalene.

"At this time of the morning, we might be waiting a while," said Mary, mother of James. They walked in silence until the tomb came into view.

"Problem solved," said Salome. "Look." The other women looked and saw that the stone had already been rolled away.

"Do you think that Isaac and Abraham did that?" asked Mary Magdalene.

"It must have been," said Salome. "If it wasn't, then I hope that no one has interfered with the body. I wouldn't put anything past the Pharisees."

"Hyet, the women are just about to come into the tomb," said Fawter.

"Thanks, Fawter," replied Hyet. *"I have the full angel regalia on me. Jestoo, are you ready as well?"*

"Yes, I'll come out of my hiding place when the women leave," said Jestoo.

The women entered the tomb and saw a young man wearing a white robe. He was sitting on the right side on the stone table were the body had been lying. They were terrified and began to edge out of the tomb.

"Don't be afraid," said Hyet gently. "You are looking for Jesus of Nazareth, who has been crucified. He is risen from the dead; he is not here. Look, behold the place that they laid him which is now empty. Now go and tell his followers that Jesus is going into Galilee ahead of you, and you will see him there, as he told you before.'"

The women were confused and momentarily unable to speak. "Who the hell are you?" asked Salome.

"I bet you he is a Pharisee," said Mary Magdalene. "They want us to spread this news so that they can ridicule us when they produce the body."

"Tell the Pharisee leaders that we are not that stupid," said Mary, mother of James.

"Hold on a second," said Hyet. "I am speaking the truth."

"Well, you can speak the truth to the men who we are going to send here after we get back to my house," said Salome. "They won't be best pleased that you have taken the body, so if I were you, I would make myself scarce."

The women then left the tomb and ran back to Salome's house straight past Jestoo's hiding place. He hadn't any hope of stopping them. When they arrived at the house, they did not tell anyone else about what happened because they knew that it could not be true. They decided that it they didn't take the bait, then the body might be returned.

****

Jestoo was sitting with Hyet, Fawter and Konacht in a tent near the base of Mount Calvary. "Well, that wasn't a very auspicious start. Even when I do meet someone as Jesus, there is still the nagging doubt that my resemblance as a fraternal twin will be a problem. It would have been easier being identical."

"Mary having twins wasn't possible because it wasn't in the Old Testament," said Hyet. "Moses only made reference to one child."

"It was unfortunate that you didn't get a chance to talk to them," said Fawter, changing the subject. "They were supposed to meet you and go straight to Denned and Hennegy, who would then announce the news to the apostles."

"It's not a catastrophe yet," said Jestoo. "We just need to convince one person that I am Jesus, and we can easily set someone up."

"Who do you have in mind?" said Hyet.

"Mary Magdalene is the logical choice. She has absolute faith in Jesus. If anyone's faith is strong enough to mask the minor detail that I am not Jesus, it will be hers. She is very charismatic, and if she believes it, then she will carry people with her. How are we going to get Mary Magdalene out on her own?"

"A period of intense questioning from Mary Magdalene's new best friends, Uhet and Cannet, should do the trick," said Fawter.

"Maybe they should suggest that she should go back to the tomb to double-check if the body is still missing," said Konacht.

"Good idea," said Jestoo. "That should work."

****

Uhet and Cannet did as instructed, and about half an hour after they started, a very angry-looking Mary Magdalene left Salome's house muttering under her breath, walking towards the tomb. On the way, she thought about the events of the last few days, and she started to sob quietly. Jestoo, Hyet, Fawter and Konacht had run back to the tomb to get ready. Jestoo, Fawter and Konacht hid a short distance away while Hyet went inside and put on his shimmering white angel clothing. When Mary Magdalene came to the tomb, she wasn't overly surprised to see an angel sitting where the body of Jesus had been.

"Do not be fearful, for I know you are looking for Jesus who was crucified," said Hyet. "He is not here, for he is risen, just as he said he would. Come closer to see the place where he was." Cautiously, Mary Magdalene obeyed and moved forward.

"Why are you weeping?" said Hyet. "Jesus is risen from the dead."

"You have taken my Lord away, and I do not know where you have laid him. Please, will you tell me?"

"I told you that he is risen."

"I have had enough of this," said Mary Magdalene. "If you don't tell me then I am leaving."

"Over to you," said Hyet to Jestoo, who left his hiding place and moved to the entrance of the tomb. Mary wasn't paying a lot of attention to where she was going, so she turned and bumped straight into Jestoo.

"I recognise you," said Mary Magdalene, and Jestoo smiled broadly. "Aren't you the gardener, who minds the area around the tombs?"

Jestoo stopped smiling. "Woman, why do you think I am a gardener? I don't look like a gardener."

"Please, sir, if you have participated in this disgraceful act of carrying him off, I beg you to tell me where you have laid him. I want to rub the ritual oils on him and then entomb him in secret, where you can't touch him. You are so cruel."

Jestoo spoke her name sharply in his best impression of Jesus. "Mary Magdalene!"

The penny finally dropped as she began to smile. "Jesus!" said Mary quietly as she reached out to touch him. "You are not dead."

Jestoo was ecstatic. "No, I have not yet ascended to heaven. It is I, Mary, so do not be afraid. I am risen from the dead, and you are the first person I have decided to show myself to."

"Oh Jesus, oh Jesus," said Mary as she collapsed on her knees. "It can't be."

"It is me. Truly me, Mary. Here, hold my hands." Mary grabbed Jestoo's hands and looked up at him.

"Jesus, you sound the same, but you look different," she said.

"Hardly surprising since I was crucified, was dead for over two days and then rose again," laughed Jestoo nervously thinking if only I was a clone. "Maybe that's why you didn't recognise me. Mary, you must go to Peter and Andrew and tell them what you have seen."

"Why not go yourself?" she asked.

"Based on your reaction, I am worried that the apostles won't believe me. Better for you to prepare them in advance for meeting with me."

"That doesn't make a lot of sense, but if that is what you want, I will do it." Mary stood up, still holding Jestoo's hands. "I can't properly express what it means to have you back."

"I'm pleased to be back too because there is much work to be done. Go now." Mary released Jestoo's hands, turned around and then ran as fast as she could to the apostles' safe house. She burst through the door and shouted at the top of her voice. "I have seen the Lord."

She didn't get the reaction that she expected. Only Peter and Andrew jumped up with excitement about what she said. The rest remained seated and looked at her blankly. Mary told them again that Jesus was alive, so there was no longer anything to be sad about. The responses from the apostles remained less than encouraging.

"You're imaging it!"

"Impossible."

"Haven't we been through enough?"

"How do you think this is helping?"

"Have you been chewing coffee beans again?"

"Your close relationship with Jesus has clouded your judgement."

"It was an impostor, probably a Pharisee, out to make trouble."

Mary Magdalene was aghast. "Jesus brought Lazarus back to life. Why is it impossible to believe that God brought his son back to life?"

Peter and Andrew tried to support her, but the others just would not listen. She told them that she had seen him and touched him, but the apostles could not comprehend what she was saying. Despite Peter and Andrew's protests, they asked her to stop her foolishness and leave the safe house. Mary Magdalene went away, crestfallen. On the way to Salome's house she began to doubt herself, and she concluded that she should not tell the other women or else she would be ridiculed. When she got to Salome's house, she acted as if nothing had happened.

****

"Another disaster," said Jestoo as he lay on his sleeping mat in the tent with Hyet, Fawter, Konacht, Uhet and Cannet sprawled on theirs. "She thought I was the bloody gardener."

"Seriously, that's the part that you are worried about?" said Konacht.

"Look, you managed to convince Mary Magdalene," said Fawter. "That was an achievement in itself."

"I managed to convince her, but she has now changed her mind again. The apostles managed to get her to doubt herself despite what she saw and felt."

"The apostles are terrified of being caught by the Pharisees and crucified," said Uhet. "This has coloured their thinking. You can understand where they are coming from."

"I do, but these are the people being groomed to spread the word of God. Jesus rising from the dead was to be the catalyst for them starting. If they don't believe that he is risen from the dead, then the whole plan will fail."

"Yiler and Nowlett, any suggestions as to what we can do?" said Hyet.

"We just have to try again," said Yiler who was in his cabin on the Tesfa with Dr. Nowlett. *"Jestoo, you must show yourself to some more people until enough of them go to the apostles with the same story. Then, when you arrive, it will be easier to convince them."*

"We have to select carefully," said Nowlett. *"You can't just appear to random people. It has to be someone known to the apostles for this to work."*

"We will look for a suitable opportunity then," advised Fawter.

Everyone apart from Hyet, who Yiler wanted to use for any unexpected angel work, left the tent and picked hiding places close to the paths around Mount Calvary. They used binoculars to scan the passers-by for some familiar faces. After about an hour, Uhet spotted Cleopas and Bartholomew, two disciples who had been with Jesus since the wedding in Cana. They were walking from Jerusalem on the path to the town of Emmaus. Jestoo headed down to the pathway that went around the base of Mount Calvary to intercept them.

Fawter and Konacht hung back while Jestoo caught up with Cleopas and Bartholomew. As Jestoo approached from behind, he heard them conversing with each other about all the things that had happened over the last few days. Jestoo joined and began walking with them, but they didn't recognize him.

"Anything exciting happen recently?" said Jestoo. They both stopped dead on the road and Cleopas frowned at him. "Don't you know what occurred in the last few days?"

"No," said Jestoo.

Cleopas looked puzzled. "You must have heard of Jesus of Nazareth and know how he became a prophet for God and all his people?"

"And how our high priests and Pharisees handed him over to the Romans, who sentenced him to death and crucified him?" said Bartholomew.

"We were hoping he was the one destined to save Israel, and now he is dead," said Cleopas.

"Yes, I am familiar with that story," said Jestoo. They started walking again and all three reverted to small talk. When they neared the town of Emmaus, Jestoo made his goodbyes, saying that he wanted to journey on further. Jestoo couldn't believe that they still hadn't recognised him as Jesus. It was another waste of time.

"Stay with us in my cousin's house, because it is toward evening and it might be dangerous to go on," said Bartholomew. "We can walk on together tomorrow."

Jestoo was doubtful that he could use them to convince the apostles that he was Jesus, so it was with great reluctance that he went inside the house. Despite his reservations, he decided to try again. When they sat down to eat, Jestoo saw an opportunity. He took the loaf of bread, blessed it, broke it and began to hand it to them just as Jesus had done at the last supper. "Cleopas, Bartholomew, I am pleased to hand you bread."

"Sorry, who are you?" asked Cleopas. "Who are you to bless the bread?"

"I am Jesus, risen from the dead."

Bartholomew grabbed Jesus' clothes and pulled him towards him. "You might think that you're funny, but trust me, you are not."

"I am not trying to be funny. I am Jesus, and you have been my disciples since I met you in Galilee at the wedding." Cleopas and Bartholomew didn't respond, so Jestoo carried on. "You were there when I broke the bread at the last supper and entered into communion with you. You came with me to the Garden of Gethsemane and saw Judas Iscariot betray me with a kiss."

"You do not look exactly like Jesus," said Cleopas doubtfully.

"Cleopas, I have been crucified and dead for three days since we last met. Of course, I look different."

"Jesus, it is you," said Bartholomew. "Cleopas, he has proven it beyond doubt." The two men kneeled, gazing up at Jestoo.

Jestoo breathed a huge sigh of relief. "At last you recognise me. I would have expected a little more faith from you two. I have revealed myself to you because I want you to do something very important for me."

"Anything, Jesus," said Cleopas.

"I want you to visit the apostles in their safe house and tell them what you have seen and heard today."

"Why don't you go yourself and tell them?" asked Bartholomew.

Jestoo was getting exasperated with being asked the same questions. "It's too dangerous. I must be careful because the Romans still have spies looking for me." Cleopas and Bartholomew looked unconvinced.

"Fawter, I presume that you are armed to the teeth as usual," said Jestoo.

"We are fully equipped. Why do you ask?"

"Do you have flash grenades?"

"Yes, one each."

"How quickly can you get here?"

"We are thirty seconds away."

"Okay, set the grenades on low power and drop them in as soon as I say, 'I must leave you now'."

"Fawter, are the flash grenades the blue or red ones?" said Konacht.

"Very messy if you make a mistake," said Fawter.

"Ha bloody ha," said Jestoo.

"Remember to keep your eyes closed," said Konacht.

"I know how a flash grenade works, thank you."

Jestoo spoke to Cleopas and Bartholomew again. "It is vital that you do as I ask. Have faith in me. I must leave you now." Jestoo closed his eyes, and the flash grenades detonated. He jumped up and ran out of the door while Cleopas and Bartholomew were writhing and moaning in pain on the floor with their hands over their eyes. When they were able to see again, Jestoo was gone, so they ran outside to find him. Fawter, Konacht and Jestoo had found cover and could not be seen.

Jestoo's disappearance fully convinced Cleopas and Bartholomew that Jesus was risen from the dead and they did as Jestoo had asked. They went to the apostles and told them what had happened. Again, despite support from Peter and Andrew, the apostles did not believe them that Jesus was risen from the dead.

****

"Argh, for goodness sake," said Jestoo as he sat cross-legged on his sleeping mat. "What is wrong with these people? How, and why, would Cleopas, Bartholomew and Mary Magdalene come up with the same story? Did this not occur to the apostles?" Jestoo and the rest of the team on Earth had been asked by Nowlett and Yiler to link in with them.

"It is frustrating," said Yiler. *"I am afraid that there is no other option left other than you visiting the safe house."*

"Isn't that risky?" asked Fawter. "It might be under observation."

"I am prepared to accept the risk," said Jestoo. "There is one condition though. Unlike Jesus, who was unaware of the true situation, I am not prepared to be martyred. If I am arrested, I want your personal assurance that maximum force will be used to rescue me before I am killed. Is that understood and agreed?"

"Understood and agreed," confirmed Yiler.

Jestoo thought for a moment. He was getting a little concerned that Yiler was unhealthily fixated on completing the experiment. *"I would like Mum's assurance also."*

"Jestoo, I confirm that as well," said Nowlett. *"We will rescue you without fail, even if an attempt is made to give countermanding orders."*

Yiler looked devastated as he cut the link. "I can't believe that Jestoo even asked that."

Nowlett shrugged her shoulders. "Well, maybe you need to reflect on why he did."

****

Denned and Hennegy were trying to energise the apostles over their evening meal. The doors were locked because the apostles were still afraid that they might be arrested and crucified.

"We can't stay here forever," said Denned. "We have to carry on the work of Jesus."

"I agree," said Hennegy.

"Look, Peter, we are all getting tired of this argument," said James, son of Zebedee. "You and Andrew just cannot accept the truth. You are using that ridiculous story from Mary Magdalene, Cleopas and Bartholomew to justify carrying on. Jesus is dead. There is no point in carrying on without him."

"Have you forgotten Lazarus?" said Denned in an angry tone. "He was brought back from the dead. Why not the same for Jesus? Why would God not save his only son?"

"I don't think Lazarus was dead at all," said John.

"I think that it is time for my grand entrance," said Jestoo as he stood outside the safe house. *"Denned and Hennegy look fit to kill."*

"Flash grenades on the way," said Fawter. Fawter and Konacht were on either side of the house. They pushed opened two windows and threw in two flash grenades each. Fawter ducked down below the window beside Jestoo. Denned and Hennegy closed their eyes. The flash grenades went off and all the apostles were blinded and started shouting in panic. Fawter and Konacht hoisted Jestoo through the window, and he walked into the main room in the house, while the apostles were still stumbling around. When their vision cleared, they saw that Jestoo was standing in their midst.

"May you have peace," said Jestoo as he spread his arms with the palms of his hands facing the apostles. The apostles were terrified to see Jestoo standing in front of them.

"He's a ghost," shouted John. The apostles cowered back until they stood with their backs to the wall.

"Why are you so troubled with doubts in your hearts?" said Jestoo calmly. "Come see his wrists and his feet, and you will know that it is me. You must feel me and see me, because a spirit does not have flesh and bones."

Jestoo showed them his hands and his feet. Denned and Hennegy came over to Jestoo and touched the wounds. "Jesus," they exclaimed in unison, falling to their knees.

"Why are the rest of you still standing there, mouths hanging open? Is it because you have no faith in me? You have been stubborn in refusing to believe those who have seen me after I was risen from the dead. You have forced me to come here to prove myself. This is your last chance."

The apostles walked over and knelt beside Denned and Hennegy. Jestoo stretched out his arms, and the eight other apostles in the house touched them and examined the wounds. To Jestoo's great relief, all of them were finally convinced and started rejoicing loudly.

"Remember the words I spoke to you, that all the things written about me in the law of Moses will be fulfilled. My death was the last of those events. It was foretold that the Messiah would suffer and rise from the dead on the third day, and that is exactly what has happened. It was also foretold that my rising from the dead would be the catalyst for repentance and forgiveness of sins being preached in all nations. You must leave Jerusalem and spread the word. I can tell you now that if you forgive the sins of anyone, they stand forgiven by my father. Anyone who believes and is baptised will be saved, but anyone who does not believe, will be punished. It is time for me to leave you, but I will be back soon." With that, Fawter and Konacht threw in more flash grenades, and Jestoo made his exit through the same window.

The mood in the house changed, and the apostles decided that the doors and remaining windows could be unlocked. For the first time since Jesus was crucified, the house was filled with light and fresh air. The mood was dampened again when Thomas, the apostle who was not with them when Jesus came, returned to the house. Denned went over to him. "We have seen the Lord. He is risen from the dead."

Thomas shook his head doubtfully. "Andrew, unless I see the marks in his wrists and stick my hand into the hole that the spear made, I will not believe."

"Aw, for the love of God," said Jestoo.

****

The next day Jestoo was walking to the safe house with Fawter and Konacht. "I can't believe that I am doing this again. Surely, one person can't make that much of a difference."

"Well, Denned and Hennegy think that Thomas is a disaster waiting to happen, so yes, we do have to do this again, so he can witness it," said Fawter. "His lack of faith is already beginning to corrupt the others."

"To be fair to Thomas, he is right, Jestoo is not Jesus," said Konacht.

"That's beside the point," said Fawter.

"Do we have to use the flash grenades again?" asked Jestoo. "Could I not just walk in?"

"I think that you are right," said Konacht. "Anyway, we are running out of them."

A few moments later, the disciples were overjoyed when Jestoo walked into the house. "May you have peace," said Jestoo. "Thomas, is my arrival enough, or do you need more for you to believe I am risen from the dead?"

"I need definitive proof," said Thomas.

"Thomas, I can't do this for everyone who does not have faith. Why can't you just believe me?"

"If you are who you say you are, then you should have a spear wound from when that Roman soldier was testing to see if you were dead. I want to see it and put my hand in it."

"Fine, if that is what it takes." Jestoo opened his robe to expose the wound in his side. "Go on then, Thomas. Put your finger here in my wrists and take your hand and place it into my side." Thomas placed his finger and hands in the wounds and immediately fell to his knees.

"My Lord and my God!"

"Because you have seen me have you believed?" said Jestoo. "Happy are those who do not see and yet believe. Now, will you go and make disciples of people of all the nations, baptising them in the name of the Father, teaching them to observe all the things I have commanded you?"

Thomas rose and stretched his arms. "I will."

****

General Lateel sat in her office in the Department of Labour, reading the update report from Yiler. Thus far, the Santu had shown no interest in the Subdepartment of Administrative Affairs and Lateel hoped that it would stay that way. She could not stop herself smiling as she read about Jestoo's numerous attempts to convince people that he was Jesus. The important thing was that it was working and that the *Tesfa* would make it back on schedule.

She checked star charts to calculate a safe return route for the *Tesfa*. She had to make sure that it came from a direction that would not arise any suspicion when the *Tesfa* registered her return with the Santu. She also had to pick an uninhabited solar system where she could intercept the *Tesfa* and inspect it. All evidence of Earth had to be eradicated from the ship and she needed to double-check that it had been done. When she had finished her calculations, she put a message together and organised for it to be uploaded to a stealth drone, one of the few that she had left. The drone was safely dispatched with Lateel's last message to Earth.

Chapter 15

Dr Nowlett sat at the end of Jesus' bed in the medical room on the *Tesfa* with Yiler standing beside her with his arms folded. Nowlett had just injected a stimulant into Jesus' system that would bring him out of the induced coma that he had been in since he was moved to the ship. After she had examined Jesus, she had decided to keep him in a coma for three more days while she repaired the rest of the extensive physical damage. It also allowed her time to study some texts on post-traumatic stress syndrome, all of which referred to keeping stress to a minimum as the key to a successful treatment. She was justifiably worried because his stress levels were about to rise, as she explained to him where he was and why.

"Are you sure this is the best approach?" said Yiler.

"I can't see any other way other than telling him the truth, all in one go. His implant has been switched on continuously since he was entombed. I am pinning my hopes on the implant improving his cognitive function, even when he is unconscious. This increase in intelligence may allow him to process what I will tell him without a harmful level of stress."

Yiler looked worried. "That is a lot of ifs and maybes."

Jesus opened his eyes, saw Yiler and Nowlett, looked around him and focused back on them. To their surprise, he didn't seem to be terrified. He looked quite relaxed.

"How are you feeling?" asked Yiler.

"Father, is that you?"

"Biologically, he is your father," said Nowlett to Jesus, who looked confused.

"It's complicated," said Yiler, glaring at Nowlett.

Nowlett scowled back. "We agreed to tell the truth."

"Am I in heaven?" said Jesus.

"You are in a place where you can look down on the Earth from the sky," said Nowlett. Jesus looked even more confused.

"That's also complicated," said Yiler. "Jesus, please try to get up."

Dr Nowlett and Yiler stood on either side of Jesus and helped him stand. They walked him over to the closed view screen.

Jesus stopped and looked at Nowlett. "I recognise you. You were the kind woman who gave me water on the way to Mount Calvary."

"Yes, that was me."

"Did the Roman soldiers kill you too after you helped me?"

"No, I am not dead."

"Then why are you in heaven?"

Yiler decided to step in before Nowlett answered. "Jesus, I am going to open a… window. What you will see might be overwhelming, so we will keep a firm grip on you." Yiler pressed the button on the side of the viewscreen, and the screen opened. Jesus didn't stagger back, but only because he could not comprehend what the blue, green and white object in front of him was.

"Father, what is that?" he asked.

"That is the planet where you are from," answered Yiler. "We call it Earth."

"So, we are in the sky."

"Yes."

"Everyone thinks the world is flat, but it's a ball. Why don't we fall off it?"

Yiler was getting hopeful of a good result. "There is a force called gravity that… I'll explain another day."

"It's a beautiful world," said Jesus. "Can you point to my home?"

"I can do better than that. I can zoom in on Nazareth, and we will be able to see your house if there is no cloud cover." Yiler ordered the camera on the satellite to zoom in. Jesus watched transfixed as the blue and green ball got bigger and bigger and one area began to fill the whole screen. The area was yellow and brown, with a dark blue patch which Jesus assumed was the desert beside the Sea of Galilee. His mouth opened involuntarily as his home came into view.

"I am in heaven, so you have fulfilled your promise of me being at your side."

"If by that you mean that he allowed you to be crucified and appear dead and subsequently woke you from a stasis sleep and brought you up here, then yes," said Nowlett, who was steadfastly sticking to the truth.

"Why are you speaking in riddles?" said Jesus. "I don't understand what you mean."

Yiler elbowed Nowlett gently in the ribs, placed his hand on Jesus' arm and guided him over to some chairs. "Jesus, there is something we need to tell you. You should sit down."

Jesus sat down on one chair with Nowlett and Yiler facing him. As gently as they could, they proceeded to tell Jesus the true story of his birth, resurrection and ascension into heaven. Nowlett held his hands the whole way through. When they finished, there was silence for a few minutes.

Jesus removed his hands from Nowlett's grasp and placed them on his cheeks, rubbing them up and down slowly. He sat there quietly, with Nowlett and Yiler exchanging nervous glances. Finally, he spoke. "I do not want to believe you. However, my own preaching is that you cannot ignore the truth when it is staring you in the face, so I better practice what I preach. You probably think that I am angry."

"That was what I predicted as your first reaction," said Yiler.

"Well, I'm not going to be angry even though you deserve it. You fooled me into preaching a made-up religion, and then you almost killed me by the cruellest torture imaginable. However, I will forgive you for what you have done to me, as that is what I have been taught to do."

"I'm pleased that you can be so magnanimous," said Nowlett.

"It is easy to be so. The religion that I preached on your behalf is a beautiful religion. You did a really good job there, Yiler. It encourages love and peace and abhors violence. It encourages forgiveness when you are wronged. It gives hope to the poor and downtrodden. I've been wronged by your duplicity, but I absolve you from your sins. When you make the decision to push a rock down a hill, there are consequences. It cannot be stopped, and you don't know in what direction it will go. We have pushed the rock of religion down the hill of faith, it is gaining momentum steadily, and it will never be stopped. The fact that the religion is based on something you concocted makes no difference. Our religion will soon supplant the gods of the Romans and Greeks, who are cruel and evil. It will cause people to embrace love and peace and move away from brutality and violence. When that happens, I will have accomplished all that I could ever have hoped to have done. I just hope that my brother can finish what I started and get the apostles and my disciples out on the road preaching. How is he doing so far?"

"Patchy," said Yiler. "Very patchy. It is not going as well as I expected because of him having to put so much effort into convincing the apostles that he is risen from the dead."

"That was always a risk," said Nowlett. "Jestoo is not Jesus after all. He is not an identical twin; he is a fraternal twin. He has observed Jesus' life, but he hasn't lived it. He is doing his best, but he is simply not able to adequately portray the Son of God. Jesus, you have charisma and charm. You are a born leader."

"Thank you," said Jesus.

"You're welcome," said Nowlett. "Jestoo on the other hand is a lieutenant in engineering. How many people do you know who work in mechanical and electrical engineering who have the charm and charisma to lead as Jesus has?"

"I don't have an opinion because I don't know what mechanical and electrical engineering is," said Jesus.

"I think that question was directed towards me," said Yiler. "Not many, I assure you."

Jesus leant forward. "May I add something to the discussion?"

"Feel free," said Yiler.

"You can't allow Jestoo to attend large-scale public events because it seems that he is not a good orator. I suggest that you break the apostles into small groups, applying the divide and conquer principle. I am sure that you can come up with a few ruses to do that. Let Jestoo concentrate on convincing those small groups."

"Very sensible idea," said Nowlett. "Jesus, would you be able to work with us and come up with some ideas?"

"Maybe you could go back down yourself to help him," said Yiler.

Jesus went pale and started shaking, and Dr Nowlett grabbed his hands again and kicked Yiler in the ankle. "Jesus, ignore Yiler, you do not ever have to go back down there. Maybe we will let you recuperate for a little longer before you start helping us."

****

A few days after Jestoo had managed to convince the doubtful Thomas, the apostles were sitting in their house talking after eating their supper. Their confidence had been restored, and they were beginning to make plans to spread the word of God. Denned and Hennegy were trying to force the disciples to pick up the pace but with limited success.

"I need to get out of this house for a while," said Hennegy. "I am going fishing. Anyone want to come?"

"Isn't it a bit late for fishing?" asked James, who wasn't a fisherman. "I had thought it was a daytime activity only."

"Not at all," said Hennegy. "Night-time can often be the best time to land a large catch of fish."

There were some dubious looks, but Thomas, Philip, James, son of Alphaeus, and John agreed to go fishing with him. They gathered their gear together and went down to the Sea of Tiberias. They all boarded Hennegy's boat and went out into the sea, twenty metres from shore. To their surprise, following Hennegy's assurances on fishing in the dark, they caught nothing. It was dawn when they decided to call a halt to proceedings and go back to shore. Jestoo was standing on the beach where the boat was coming in. The apostles could not discern that it was him because it was a misty morning.

"My friends, you do not appear to have caught anything, do you?" shouted Jestoo.

"No," shouted back Hennegy.

"Cast the net on the right side of the boat," ordered Jestoo.

"Do you mean your right or my right?" said Hennegy

"Your right!" shouted back Jesus.

"Just checking," said Hennegy.

Jestoo triggered a small concussion charge that had been hidden by Fawter and Konacht. The men threw the net over the right side of the boat. The concussion charge stunned hundreds of fish that drifted gently into the nets. The men were unable to pull the net safely into the boat because it was weighed down with so many fish.

"It must be another miracle of the Lord," exclaimed Hennegy. The men brought the boat in, dragging the net full of fish behind it. When they finally managed to get the fish onto the shore, they saw that Jestoo had lit a charcoal fire and was warming bread.

"Bring over some of the fish you just caught," said Jestoo. Hennegy brought some fish over, while the other men secured the boat, and laid them carefully around the fire. "Come, take your breakfast with me."

When the other men came over, they recognised Jestoo as Jesus, and they started laughing and clapping. Jestoo broke the bread and gave it to them along with the fish.

****

Less than a week later, Jestoo arrived at the apostle's safe house. He spoke to Hennegy, James, son of Zebedee, and John, and asked them to come with him to a high mountain called Mount Tabor, where they could pray alone. Hennegy thought that this was a great idea and both he and Jestoo cajoled James and John to go along. They travelled in companionable silence as Jestoo was meditating as they walked.

When they got to the top of the mountain, they made a fire, gathered around it, and began to pray. Hennegy gave John and James some food from a bag. Shortly afterwards, Hennegy began to yawn and stretch out his arms. James and John began to do the same.

"Jesus, I'm sorry," said John. "I'm falling asleep. The heat from the fire and a full belly are a bad combination."

"Lie down, if you like," said Jestoo. "I can pray alone for a while." The three others lay down and within moments were sound asleep."

"Hennegy, are you actually asleep?" asked Jestoo.

"Of course not, I'm just acting."

"It's just that the snoring was very convincing." He heard a scrabbling sound behind him and saw Hyet and Sidion labouring up the hill. Jestoo started laughing. "Love the robes, guys."

Hyet, who was wearing robes in a style dating back to the time of Moses, was not looking too pleased. "You know what you can do. I had to walk up this pox ridden mountain in these robes, and I am sweating like a pig. I don't know how Moses was able to do anything wearing this crap."

"They are horrendous clothes," said Sidion, who was dressed like the prophet Elijah. "The hair implants and the fake beards are even worse. It feels like there are insects crawling all over my face." Sidion had made the mistake to complain to Yiler that she had nothing to do, which ended in Yiler deciding that she should be involved on Earth for the last few days. Dr Nowlett had performed the usual procedure to ensure that Sidion blended in like the rest of the team.

"I wish I had kept my mouth shut about being bored," said Sidion.

It took them about an hour to get the lighting and pyrotechnic effects ready. When they were satisfied, Hyet and Sidion hid behind some rocks and Jestoo steeled himself for another performance. Hennegy sat down beside James and John and woke them up. "Look at Jesus," he cried. "Something is happening."

James and John were jolted from a deep sleep and saw Jestoo's face beginning to shine like the sun while his entire body glowed with a white light. Then, with a blinding flash of light, two old men appeared, and Jestoo started talking to them.

"Who the hell are those two?" said James

"They must be the prophets Elijah and Moses judging by their clothes," said Hennegy.

"Peter, how do you know that?" said John.

"I am remembering descriptions from the Old Testament of the type of clothes they wore back then," said Hennegy, adlibbing speedily.

"Fair dues to your memory," said James. "I don't remember anything like that. Why are they here?"

"I believe that Moses and Elijah represent the two principal components of the Old Testament, the law and the prophets. Moses is the giver of the law, and Elijah is considered the greatest of the prophets. Shh... let's listen."

"Jesus, it is now time for you to depart to the kingdom of heaven," said Hyet.

"This must be done at Jerusalem in accordance with the scripture," advised Sidion in a deep voice.

"This is unbelievable," said John. Wisps of cloud slowly emerged and gradually surrounded the three men until they were barely visible to the naked eye.

"This is my beloved son, with whom I am well pleased," said a booming voice that came from the cloud.

James and John were clinging to each other in terror. "Who said that?" said James.

"It must be God," said Hennegy.

"You must listen to him," carried on the voice. There was a blinding flash of light, courtesy of another flash grenade dropped by Hennegy, and when James and John's vision had cleared, the cloud has dissipated and Jestoo was standing there alone.

"Peter, James and John, you have witnessed a special event," stated Jestoo. "God chose you for a special spiritual experience to strengthen your faith for the challenges that you will endure. Do not expect these events to continue indefinitely, and don't be afraid or resentful when they cease. I want you to tell the other apostles what you have seen."

"We will do it," said John.

"Go now and leave me here with Peter."

"Yes, Lord," said James.

Jestoo stood with Hennegy as James and John left them and walked back down Mount Tabor. He turned around as they heard Hyet and Sidion approaching. Both had already taken off their robes.

"I can't tell you how pleased I am to ditch that outfit," said Hyet. "The damn beard has to stay until we get back to the ship. Dr Nowlett sent down special surgical glue to hold it in place."

Sidion put her arms around Hennegy and Jestoo. "Well done, Jestoo. If that doesn't convince James and John, we might as well give it up. Only a few more of these and then we have the grand finale."

****

Yiler and Dr Nowlett remained with Jesus on the *Tesfa* while the rest of the team were on Earth preparing for Jestoo's ascension into heaven.

"Ready?" said Nowlett.

"Yes," replied Yiler as he linked all the implants. *"It is hard to believe, but we have reached the end of the experiment and will be going home in the next couple of days. We have achieved all our goals. We have had a God descend to Earth through his son as a human. We have had that son die for the sins of humanity. He was an innocent bearing the penalty of the guilty thus opening heaven to all who believe."*

"Still sorry about that, Jesus," said Nowlett.

"I've moved on," said Jesus.

Yiler glowered at them for interrupting his well-practised speech. *"The third great event was the resurrection. Jesus was raised from the dead by us. Now we come to the fourth part, the return of Jesus to heaven. With your dedication and professionalism, the ascension will be the most remarkable event yet. I am sure of it."*

"I also want to thank you all for your commitment to the experiment of creating a single deity," said Dr Nowlett. *"It has truly been a pleasure working with you. We face a somewhat uncertain future when we get back home, thanks*

to the Santu. No matter what happens though, we can pride ourselves on a job well done."

"*Even if we can't tell anyone,*" said Yiler. "*Let's make sure that this last event is the best one.*"

****

Forty days after Jesus had been taken from the tomb, Jestoo led the eleven apostles to the top of Mount of Olives in the east city district of Jerusalem. Denned and Hennegy walked beside Jestoo with the other nine following. None of the nine had the slightest inkling that they were about to witness the return of Jestoo to heaven, and that this was to be their final moments with him. However, by the time the apostles got to the top of the Mount of Olives, they had a feeling something was up. Even they picked up on the nervous tension of Jestoo, Denned and Hennegy.

"Lord, has the time come for you to free Israel and restore our kingdom?" said James, son of Zebedee. "Is that why we are here?"

"My father alone has that authority. I cannot tell you when, for I do not know," said Jestoo. "But I can tell you that you will shortly be empowered when you receive the Holy Spirit. From that moment on, you will be my witnesses, telling people about me everywhere - in Jerusalem, throughout Judea, in Samaria and to the ends of the earth. My friends, I promise that I am with you always, even unto the end of the world."

The group crossed the summit of the mount. The view was stunning, so Jestoo stopped to gaze at it and the apostles gathered about him. "Isn't the view amazing?"

Fawter and Konacht were in a hideaway about one hundred metres away. "*He is in place,*" said Fawter.

"*Uhet and Cannet, you can bring down the drop pod,*" said Konacht. Uhet and Cannet had been holding the drop pod at a height of three thousand metres above the mount in some low clouds. They turned off the manual control and engaged the autopilot to begin a slow descent.

"Let's start the lighting effects," said Fawter as he pressed his control panel. Beams of soft white light began to radiate from the ground around Jestoo. The disciples all moved back in awe. A loud bang from the sky startled the apostles, and they looked up. The drop pod, partly covered in a white cloud of exhaust fumes, was descending towards them. A few of the apostles got up to run, but Jestoo told them that there was nothing to worry about and to stay where they were. When the drop pod landed, the engines stayed idling to ensure a swift lift-off, resulting in a cloud of exhaust fumes that covered the top of the summit. The drop pod opened and Uhet and Cannet emerged, partly obscured by the cloud of steam and dust from the engines. Both were dressed as angels in shimmering white suits.

Jestoo coolly walked into the cloud while all the apostles watched, and when out of their vision, he stepped onto the entrance plate of the drop pod. He secured himself with a safety line that had been left there by Uhet and Cannet. With hands outstretched in blessing, he slowly ascended from among the watching group. As he gained height, the stunned apostles strained their eyes for the last glimpse of their Lord ascending into heaven.

"Time for the music," said Konacht as he switched on the music system in the drop pod. He was playing the best choral music ever recorded by the Deusi Philharmonic, at least that was what Yiler had told him; music wasn't Konacht's thing.

"This is the sweetest and most joyous music I have ever heard," said Denned.

"It must be from a choir of angels," said Hennegy.

While the apostles were still gazing upward, they heard voices from behind them. Hennegy turned first to see what it was and then pointed towards Hyet and Sidion. "Look over here!"

Hyet stepped forward. "We are angels who have come to escort Jesus to his heavenly home and his father. We have stayed behind to assure you that this separation from Jesus will not be forever. You will all see him again in heaven. Now, we must return him to his father." When Hyet and Sidion gave them a signal, Denned and

Hennegy dropped a couple of flash grenades. When the apostles had recovered, the angels were gone, leaving only eleven people on the mount.

"Everything has been proven beyond doubt," said James, son of Alphaeus.

"I agree," said Thomas. "I know that I had my doubts, but no more. Let us go to Jerusalem and begin spreading the word."

"Peter and I will stay for a while to pray," said Denned. "We will be with you shortly." The nine apostles started off down the mountain. When they were out of sight, the team walked over to Denned and Hennegy.

"Well done everyone," said Konacht.

"If I hadn't known that it was all staged, I might have believed it myself," said Uhet. "Let's get the gear packed up. The other drop pods will be here in thirty minutes to collect us."

Denned looked at Hennegy who nodded to him as a sign to continue. "Could I have your attention please? Hennegy and I aren't coming with you."

"Are you taking a later drop pod?" said Uhet.

"No, I meant that we aren't coming back to Deusi Prime with you," said Denned.

"Ever," added Hennegy.

Yiler was stunned. He'd had no inkling that Denned and Hennegy were thinking this way. *"Sorry, but I cannot allow that to happen. The whole team must return together."*

"Yiler, we weren't asking you for permission," said Denned. *"We were just informing you of our decision. Please don't start threatening us. There is no way that you can physically force us to return to the ship. The team won't assist you."*

"Damn right," said Fawter.

Yiler thought for a few moments. *"Why do you want to stay?"*

"There is a myriad of reasons," said Denned. *"We have spent just over thirty years on this planet. It is as much a home to us as Deusi Prime. We have a wide circle of friends here but very few left on Deusi Prime."*

"The main reason is that we want to finish out this experiment," said Hennegy. *"We had to cut it short because of the Santu. The apostles are not ready to be left alone. The apostles and disciples respect us and will follow us. We can spend the rest of our lives finishing what this group started. We both agree with what Jesus said after Yiler and Nowlett explained he was part of an experiment. We agree that Christianity could be a unifying force for humans with a positive impact. The principles of the religion will encourage humans to treat each other with respect and kindness. The barbaric nature in which they deal with each other must change. It doesn't matter if God exists or doesn't exist. All we have to do is get them to believe, and if we do that, Christianity will succeed."*

Yiler thought a bit more. *"You know that you will get no further support. I have no idea if, or when, a Deusi ship will return here. I will have to take back all the equipment. Your implants will remain functioning, but you will be the only two with them. You will, to all intents and purposes, just be humans."*

"We know," said Denned.

"Your decision is irrevocable."

"We know," said Hennegy.

"You will never see your sisters again."

"That was the most difficult part of my decision," said Denned. *"Yiler, can you meet with them when you get back and let them know that our assignment will not allow us to return to Deusi."*

Yiler sighed. *"I will respect your decision, and I promise I will contact them as soon as I can."*

Nowlett coughed to clear her throat. *"Denned and Hennegy, you have proven your loyalty so often during this mission, but this is the most loyal act so far. I think the chance of the success of the experiment has increased exponentially because of your decision to remain. It's very sad to say goodbye, but look at it this way, you will be the only members of the team, who will ever know if the experiment has worked. In that respect, I am jealous."*

"Thanks, Nowlett, it has been an honour working with you and the rest of the team," said Denned.

"Even Yiler?" said Jestoo who was sitting in his drop pod on the way back to the ship.

Denned and Hennegy started laughing. *"Even Yiler. We better catch up with the apostles to make sure they are behaving themselves."* They said their goodbyes to the rest of the team and walked away down the hill towards Jerusalem.

****

When the apostles returned to Jerusalem that evening, Peter and Andrew insisted they did so publicly without any attempt to disguise their identities. Peter and Andrew selected a district of Jerusalem for each apostle, and a public gathering was organised in each of the meeting squares. The people at the meetings listened to the apostles with a mixture of surprise and admiration. After the trial and crucifixion of Jesus, the followers of Jesus were not expected to be seen again, and if they were, they would be pale shadows of their former selves. The Pharisees had expected sorrowful and defeated apostles, ashamed of what had transpired. Instead of this, the people and the Pharisees saw happiness and triumph in the faces of each of them.

They spoke with strong voices, confident in every word they uttered. They did not mourn over Jesus but thanked God for allowing Jesus to walk among them. Each apostle told the story of Christ's resurrection and his ascension to heaven with certainty and conviction. The power and intensity of their testimony swayed most, if not all, of those present at the meetings and the conversions began.

One thing was abundantly clear, the apostles, encouraged by Peter and Andrew, no longer had any fear of the future or what might happen to them. Christianity had begun exactly as Yiler hoped it would.

Chapter 16

Jesus was sitting with Dr Nowlett and Yiler in the medical room on the *Tesfa*, waiting for Jestoo to be extracted from the drop pod. He was very nervous about meeting his brother for the first time. Dr Nowlett placed her hand on his shoulder, and he put his hand over hers. "He won't be much longer, Jesus. He is having a shower and changing into ship clothes."

"My stomach is in knots."

"Understandable," said Yiler, coming to stand beside his son. "I am sure that he is feeling the same. Speaking of which…"

Yiler nodded towards his other son as Jestoo walked into the medical room. He walked over to Jesus and stuck his hand out. "Jesus, I am so pleased to finally meet you," began Jestoo. "I'm sorry about everything. It has been very hard on you."

Jesus gripped Jestoo's hand and shook it firmly. "It was a shock to find out that my whole life was fabricated. Even harder to find out that the person that I had been talking to was not my father but my brother. Be that as it may, I am pleased to meet you, my brother. Mary would be so excited to know that I am no longer an only child. It always troubled her."

"I only spent a short time in her company when I was on Earth. From that brief time, it was clear that she is a formidable lady."

"You better believe it. I'm very sad about not being able to say a proper goodbye to her."

"Well, I did that for you yesterday. I sat down with her for a few hours and explained about the ascension. I think that she took great comfort from that. I also sat down with Joseph on my own for a while, but he didn't really know me. His dementia is severe."

"It's not the same as me saying goodbye personally. She would have given me one of her long hugs. I hope that Joseph slips away soon. He deserves a dignified death, and I would hate to see him reduced to being looked after by Mary like an infant. I would have been happier if I knew he was going to heaven as promised to him, but that was you lying to us. At least he believes that heaven awaits him."

"There is still a camera at the house at Nazareth. Maybe we can have one last look later before Denned and Hennegy retrieve it."

"Nowlett, can we have that one last look at Mary and Joseph now?"

"Of course," said Nowlett.

****

Mary awoke with a start from her mid-afternoon sleep. She put her hand out to touch Joseph, but he wasn't there. "Don't tell me that he has started wandering again." She slid out of bed and walked swiftly into the living area. She found Joseph sitting in the kitchen eating some fruit that he had chopped up.

"Good afternoon, Mary," said Joseph. "Would you like some food?" He offered her a slice of fig. "Why are you standing there gaping at me? Come on over and sit down." Mary sat down beside him.

Joseph looked around. "Where is Jesus?"

****

Jesus turned to look at Nowlett with a broad smile on his face. "Nanobots?"

Nowlett laughed. "Jestoo used the last of them after I programmed them to reverse the dementia."

Jesus walked over to her and put his arms around her. "Thank you, Nowlett. This will help my mother so much."

"Thank you, Jesus. It's my pleasure."

"I will miss them so much," said Jesus. "I suppose that next I should offer congratulations to Jestoo on completing the mission. Your ascension was spectacular."

"Yes, it clinched the deal with the apostles. Denned and Hennegy, or Peter and Andrew as they are now called, are confident that the ascension galvanised the disciples to start the work of spreading the word of God. I would have liked to have contributed more in my forty days, but it was very difficult when I couldn't attend large meetings. You are very difficult to impersonate."

"I think that the difference was that I believed what I was saying, while you didn't. Very difficult to portray absolute conviction when you know what you are saying is false. It is curious that all of us are happy with the successful conclusion but for different reasons. You are happy because you have completed the experiment and can go home. I am happy because my life's work will not be wasted. A religion of peace and love will be spread far and wide especially since Denned and Hennegy have agreed to stay behind."

They lapsed into silence as Yiler thought about what Jesus had said. "We have successfully started a religion on Earth with endless possibilities as to how it develops. I agree that with Denned and Hennegy deciding to stay on Earth to carry on the work, there is a much higher possibility that it will have a positive impact on Earth in the future."

Jestoo shook his head. "I think that nurturing this religion will be too much of a burden for humankind to bear and that, eventually, they will end up corrupting it."

Yiler shrugged his shoulders. "Time will tell, but I have more faith in the humans that you do."

"Clearly since you are also relying on the fact that they will accept that there will never by any physical intercessions by their god. Natural disasters will not be stopped. Accidents will happen. Immoral leaders, like the infamous King Herod, will be allowed to proceed uninhibited."

Yiler was beginning to get a little angry. "The first will be explained on the basis that humans shouldn't need to see God in order to be believe. The second by informing them that God has given them the gift of free will on Earth and it is up to them what they do with it. If a person or persons decide to use that free will for malevolent purposes, then that is their decision and they will only be held to account by God when they die."

Jestoo opened his mouth to reply, but Nowlett decided to change the subject before a row started. She put her arms around

Jestoo and Jesus and drew them in close to her. "Our amazing twin sons. Come on, Yiler."

Yiler did the same and for a moment, the family was locked together in a tight embrace.

Jestoo pushed Nowlett back and looked into her eyes. "I need to talk to you about something and you are not going to like it. We can't come back to Deusi Prime with you."

Yiler looked shocked. "Why not?"

"Dad and Mum, you are both geniuses in many ways but naïve in others," said Jestoo. "Before you ask, I have discussed this with Jesus already and he agrees."

Jesus nodded in agreement. "This implant to implant communication is very useful. Jestoo and I had a lot of conversations over the last few days. I am fully up to date."

Jestoo looked at his father. "Mum and Dad, this is the first time in the Deity Creation experiment that you have allowed your emotions cloud your judgement. You must know what will happen when we approach Deusi territory?"

"General Lateel will meet us on an SOE ship," said Yiler.

"Why?"

"She wants to make sure that all evidence of Earth and the Deity Experiment has been eradicated from the ship," said Yiler.

"So, what do you think will happen when she sees myself and Jestoo?"

Nowlett gasped. "She wouldn't."

"I think she would, to protect Earth. Two deaths to save millions of humans."

"We will go straight to Deusi Prime then and bypass her," said Nowlett.

"Assuming that we could do that at no risk to the crew, what would happen then? Again, you must know."

"We would be boarded by the Santu, as it would be the first time our ship ID registered with them," said Yiler.

"So, what will happen when Santu security sees us?" said Jesus.

Nowlett sat down on one of the beds as her thought process caught up. "We would be held in quarantine while you two are analysed and interrogated. They will discover that your DNA is different."

Yiler sat down too and put his arm around Nowlett. "They won't rest until they found out why. That means the whole crew will be interrogated."

Nowlett shook her head. "All it takes is for one person to crack under interrogation, and the Santu will be at Earth forty days after that. Under the treaty, they can eliminate any undisclosed Deusi colony. Yiler, would they do that?"

Yiler frowned. "I wouldn't put it past them."

"Now you see why we can't come home with you," said Jestoo. "We would be putting the lives of millions at risk."

"I wish I could disagree, but you are right," said Yiler glumly. "Neither of you can return on the *Tesfa.*"

"It's ironic that by choosing to stay here, I will be saving humanity," said Jesus. "Just not in the way that people might believe in the future."

"I can't comprehend why I was so stupid," said Nowlett. "I didn't see this coming."

"Mum, don't blame yourself," said Jestoo. "If the Santu fleet hadn't won, everything would have been fine."

"What are you planning to do then?" asked Nowlett.

"We will return to Earth but not anywhere within the Roman Empire," said Jestoo. "That will make sure that we don't meet any of the apostles during our lifetime."

"Have you a location in mind?" asked Yiler.

"The country furthest from Rome that has some semblance of a civilisation where we could blend in and establish ourselves is Hibernia, which is an island west of Britannia," said Jestoo. "The weather is horrendous there, which is probably why the Romans never occupied it. Let me show you on the map."

"Could I ask for one thing?" said Jestoo after a short period of silence.

Yiler smiled bleakly. "So long as it doesn't involve the FTL drive."

Jestoo laughed at the weak joke. "Nothing to do with the FTL drive, I promise. Could we get Denned and Hennegy up to the ship and have one hell of a going away party?"

"I can't think of a better way to end the experiment than a party with all of us together for one last time."

"We don't have much on board that could be used for a party."

Nowlett smiled. "Once we have enough of my universal taste improver, it doesn't matter!"

****

Jestoo and Jesus both wished that Dr Nowlett had invented a universal hangover cure as they walked gingerly to the shuttle bay the morning after the party. When they walked in, they saw that the Deity Creation team and the ship's crew had arranged themselves in a guard of honour from the door to the drop pod. They walked down the line, shaking hands and hugging everyone. Jestoo paused at the engineering chief as they shook hands.

"It has been an honour serving with you, ma'am."

"Lieutenant Jestoo, the honour has been equally mine. The boys and I wanted to give you a present. We spent all morning designing machinery not yet invented that you could make from the raw materials currently available. You could start a career as an engineer on Earth."

Jestoo felt a lump in his throat and saw that the chief's lip was quivering, so he just moved in to hug her. They separated and saluted each other. The two of them moved down the line until they reached the end where Yiler and Nowlett were standing. Both were red eyed from crying. Nowlett tried to speak but her voice cracked, and she just threw her arms around Jestoo. Jestoo could feel his neck getting wet from her tears. He put his nose into her hair and breathed deeply just to get one last smell of her. He was simply unable to speak.

"Jesus, look after Jestoo for me," said Yiler as he shook hands with Jesus.

"I will try to keep him out of trouble," said Jesus.

Yiler moved over to Nowlett and Jestoo. "Nowlett, come on, you have to let him go." He peeled her arms from around Jestoo and Nowlett wrapped them around Yiler instead and buried her head in his chest.

"Goodbye, son," said Yiler. "No male could be prouder of a son than I am of you." Yiler's upper lip began to quiver, and tears began to roll down his cheeks. Jestoo opened his mouth, but the lump in his throat prevented him from speaking. He stood behind Nowlett and hugged both of his parents as tightly as he could. It was Jesus who had to unpeel the arms this time.

Nowlett looked up from Yiler's chest. "Goodbye, Jesus. I am so sorry that we didn't have time to get to know each other properly."

"As am I, Dr Nowlett. I am lucky to have had two incredible women in my life. I would be truly blessed if I find a third one in Hibernia. Come on, Jestoo." He placed his arm around Jestoo's shoulder and slowly walked him over to the drop pod. Jestoo held onto his mother's hand until their fingertips parted. The two brothers walked into the drop pod, and the door closed silently behind them.

****

The *Tesfa* dropped out of FTL space at the coordinates provided by General Lateel, exactly forty days after leaving Earth. They were in an uninhabited system, but there was another Deusi ship waiting for them which immediately launched a shuttle. The crew of the *Tesfa* barely had time to gather in the shuttle bay before it arrived. The shuttle door opened and an SOE security team fanned out at the bottom of the exit ramp. General Lateel stood at the top of the steps.

"Congratulations everyone on a job well done. I am dying to find out what happened in the short period made available to you to finish the experiment."

Yiler and Nowlett stepped forward from the crew who were gathered in a group in front of the ramp. "General Lateel, welcome to the *Tesfa*," they said in unison.

Lateel looked around. "I don't see Jesus or Jestoo. Are they in their cabins?"

"I regret to inform you that both are dead. We decided to attempt a resurrection and ascension into heaven, but Jesus didn't make it despite Nowlett's best efforts. We substituted Jestoo, who convinced the apostles that Jesus had been resurrected. Unfortunately, Jestoo was captured by the Romans and put to death."

General Lateel stared at him and Nowlett. "Nowlett, is that true?"

Nowlett glanced around the shuttle bay. "You can't see them, can you?"

General Lateel brought herself to attention. "I think that you forget that I am a general, and you are not."

Nowlett engaged a very false smile. "I know that you are a general. I just forgot that you are an arsehole... ma'am."

"Don't push your luck, Nowlett. I don't see Denned or Hennegy either. Where are they?"

"A drop pod accident on the last day," said Yiler. He glanced over to an empty drop pod alcove.

Lateel stared at Yiler. "Drop pod accidents are very rare."

"Yes, we were shocked when it happened," said Nowlett.

Lateel stared at Nowlett. "Losing four of your group is somewhat careless."

Yiler grabbed Nowlett's arm before she said anything. "I would say unfortunate more so than careless."

Lateel pursed her lips. "My team will have to check your computer records to verify what happened."

"Unfortunately, we don't have any computer records," said Yiler.

"What do you mean, no records?" said Lateel angrily.

Yiler shrugged his shoulders. "You ordered us to eradicate all evidence of Earth and the experiment from the ship, so that is exactly what we did."

General Lateel looked incredulous. "That is what we are here to do."

"With all due respect, your orders were not clear on that point," said Yiler.

"Very careless of you," added Nowlett with a smile.

Lateel took a few deep breaths and smiled equally as falsely as Nowlett had a few moments ago. "No harm done. I'll just get the security team to do a sweep of the ship, just in case you have missed anything that the Santu might find suspicious."

"We haven't," said Nowlett through gritted teeth. "You won't find any trace of Jesus or Jestoo."

"Or anything else," said Yiler.

"Let's see, shall we. Start the sweep of the ship." The crew parted like the Red Sea did for Moses, and the security team walked through them and started to search. Yiler and Nowlett were right; the security team didn't find anything.

Epilogue

Yiler was standing at the cooker making dinner when he heard the apartment door swish open. "Hi, Nowlett," he shouted.

"Hi, Yiler. That is a wonderful smell. Why are you home early from the university?" Nowlett closed the door and hung up her coat.

"One of my students had a thesis review booked with me, but he cancelled at the last minute because he had been arrested by the Santu. I thought I would surprise you with a cooked meal for your last day at work."

Nowlett walked into the kitchen and sat down with her legs splayed in front of her. "I prefer to call it a temporary absence from work."

Yiler walked over and sat beside her. He put his hand on her very large baby bump. "And how is Jestree today?"

Nowlett slapped his hand away playfully. "Both of us are fine, thanks." She moaned loudly. "My back is killing me. Why didn't I use the bloody uterine replicator?"

Yiler smiled as he backed away slowly. "That decision had nothing to do with me. I presume that we will use the uterine replicator the next times."

Nowlett's eyes opened wide. "What next times?"

Yiler started laughing. "I think that we should have two more children, a boy and a girl, otherwise the Yiler and Nowlett names would end with us, which would be a shame. I foresee a bright future for both. After all, my first two male progeny managed to create a religion on Earth. Imagine what will be achieved when your genetic material is thrown into the mix."

Nowlett laughed loudly. "I can assure you that I will help you enthusiastically on that one."

The End.

Acknowledgements

I would like to thank my test readers, my wife Sheena, sister in law Clodagh Byrne, colleague Liz Buckley and friend Pat Keane, for all their comments and observations. Thank you to my nephew Oisín, who was the first to edit the manuscript.

Finally, I would like to thank Marguerite Tonery and Claudia Bauch of Tribes Press for improving and polishing the manuscript to produce this finished book.

References

Pearce, E., Stringer, C., and Dunbar, RIM. (2013). New insights into differences in brain organization between Neanderthals and anatomically modern humans. Source: The Royal Society Publishing (https://doi.org/10.1098/rspb.2013.0168).

Norris M., Siegfried, D.R. (2012); Anatomy Essentials for Dummies, 1st Ed.; John Wiley and Sons Inc.

Your Guide to Understanding Genetic Conditions. Source: U.S. National Library of Medicine (https://ghr.nlm.nih.gov/). Multiple Contributors.

Note: Although, I have taken my basis from research literature, I have adapted the scientific outcomes and modalities to science fiction.